Polly Williams is the author of three previous novels, *The Rise and Fall of a Yummy Mummy*, *A Bad Bride's Tale* and *A Good Girl Comes Undone*. She lives in London with three children and a very understanding husband. Visit Polly's website at www.pollywilliams.com.

Praise for Polly Williams:

'Witty, moving, beautifully written' Wendy Holden

'Smart and funny' *Heat*

'A sharply written novel about the trials of playing hip happy families' *Tatler*

'Funny and honest, this is a refreshingly thoughtful take on the hushed-up trials of making the transition to parenthood' *You* Magazine

'Like *Sex and the City*, but set in London with a believable flesh and blood heroine ****' *Red* magazine

'The sort of book you'll devour' *Glamour*

'Fun, laughter and tears blend with love, lust and a tangle of misunderstandings in this splendid romp' *She*

'Another sparkling read from the fantastic Polly Williams' *Star* magazine

'A brutally honest book. I laughed out loud, cried and couldn't put it down for three days' Pearl Lowe

'Impossible to put down' *Company*

'A page-turning read that brings home the dark truths of young motherhood' Camilla Rutherford

'A cracking read' *Sunday Express*

'Stylishly written' *Telegraph*

By Polly Williams

The Rise and Fall of a Yummy Mummy
A Bad Bride's Tale
A Good Girl Comes Undone
How to be Married

POLLY WILLIAMS

How to be Married

headline
review

First published in 2010
by HEADLINE REVIEW
An imprint of HEADLINE PUBLISHING GROUP

1

ISBN 978 0 7553 5935 6

Typeset in Sabon by Avon DataSet Ltd,
Bidford-on-Avon, Warwickshire

Printed in the UK by CPI Mackays, Chatham, ME5 8TD

Headline's policy is to use papers that are natural, renewable and
recyclable products and made from wood grown in sustainable forests.
The logging and manufacturing processes are expected to conform to
the environmental regulations of the country of origin.

HEADLINE PUBLISHING GROUP
An Hachette UK Company
338 Euston Road
London NW1 3BH

www.headline.co.uk
www.hachette.co.uk

For Ben

Acknowledgements

Special thanks to Jane Morpeth, Lizzy Kremer, Jo Dickinson, Kate Byrne and everyone who has worked on this book at Headline. Many thanks also to Alison for the flowery bits, and, of course, the husband, Ben, for the married bits.

One

I wake up with a jolt. The day I've been anxiously antici-
pating for the last month has finally arrived. Yes, it's
Friday, 25 May, 7.33 a.m., and in just over five hours I
will be sitting down to my first lunch as a corporate
wife. I will meet Tom's new colleagues and their spouses,
the gorgeous Anderson & Co wives, for the first time. I
will be expected to say the right thing at the right
moment, smile brightly, not spill wine down my dress,
or, God forbid, drink so much that I forget not to be
myself. This is Tom's break after all, a big job, the
reason we moved back from Canada. He gets a pulse in
his temple when he talks about it. And things have been
so bad between us recently – he says I don't support him
properly, I say he's a workaholic – that this meet-the-
spouse lunch needs to go well for other reasons too. It
really does. I'm not going to screw up.

To pre-empt my natural leaning towards chaos and
lateness I've organised ahead. I even chose my dress
yesterday afternoon to avoid the usual nothing-to-wear

last-minute frantic wardrobe rifling. The dress is hanging on the back of the door, a blue floral print tea dress, fitted, not too booby a neckline, small fabric-covered buttons. I sit up on the pillows and stare at it, not entirely convinced. Could it be a bit Mary Archer? Too fragrant wife? A bit religious cult prairie dress even? The longer I stare the more certain I am that its prudishness demands the agony of the silver strappy sandals that I bought for my cousin's wedding last summer. (I managed the church service then went barefoot.) Yes, with the heels the outfit may be just about me enough, whatever me is these days, while still looking appropriately wifely. One thing's for sure, I'll have damn good hair. I've booked a blow-dry, confirmed the appointment three times. Whenever I attempt a blow-dry myself I end up resembling a member of a Christian rock group, or someone with access to a hairdryer without one of those funnel attachments. I'm not good with whirring bits of domestic kit, especially things with attachments. Hoovers, hairdryers, food blenders, they just weren't designed for the likes of me; someone, my husband says, 'about as practical as a daffodil'. That's him being nice by the way. He's said far, far worse things.

I swing my legs over the side of the bed on to the warm, bare floorboards, and run through my tight but foolproof drill: drop Danny off at nursery; bomb to client's house; back home to shower and change into Mary Archer dress and killing killer heels; blow-dry and chance to read deliciously rubbish magazines; wow husband's colleagues with beauty and wit at The Ivy. Simple. I check my reflection in the dressing-room mirror and yawn. A thirty-four-year-old hedge-haired brunette with her mother's teal-blue eyes yawns back at me. She is not unattractive, especially if she stops yawning and lifts her chin to add a bit of jaw definition. But she has both crow's feet and a light scattering of T-zone acne, the two least attractive symptoms of youth and middle-age closing in a cruel pincer movement. Still. She doesn't look hung over, which is a miracle. Yes, I almost blew my carefully laid plans last night. Tom was working late and my old mate Chloe popped over and . . .

Well, it wasn't grown up and it wasn't dignified. But it *was* fun. The most fun I've had in ages. A bit of background. Chloe and I go way back, all the way back to sharing clothes and boyfriends in our early twenties – in both cases I usually got the hand-me-downs – and a colourful six-month interval sharing a tiny cockroachy studio apartment and pull-down bed in Chelsea when we were both horribly skint and trying to establish ourselves as a make-up artist (her) and florist (me). We used to joke that we were like a married couple then. That was before either of us knew what real married couples were like, of course. Anyhow, forward wind many years – two husbands, one divorce (Chloe's), a few wrinkles, and some extra poundage around the old hips (mine) – and we're the same but different. I've recently

3

returned from a two-year stint in Toronto, and a particularly bad *annus crapus*. Chloe has been in London, finding herself again after her divorce from a photographer whom she married in Las Vegas two years ago. (The wedding was sweetly ironic. The divorce wasn't.) We're still catching up.

By 9 p.m. we were high as kites, Chloe trying to wax my armpit, telling me how much better it was than shaving and that all the make-up artists did it. Me with my arm in the air, shaking with laughter – the first time I'd properly laughed in months, the laughter coming out in gulps like bubbles under water. The air was thick with the smoke of Chloe's psychotropic weed – how can anyone smoke that stuff and remain sane? – and the fumes of red wine. Chloe wielded her wax strips and drunkenly squealed, 'I'm going to get you.' I shouted, 'Shush! Danny's sleeping! Ow! You enjoy my pain, sicko!' and flicked at her with a manky tea towel crusted with dried scrambled egg. Then, of course, Tom walked in, all stern and husband-like, in a suit, after a long day at work. Chloe tried to swallow her giggles, which was worse because she started gagging, went puce and her cheeks puffed up like whoopee cushions. I started to giggle too. But Tom didn't. His sense of humour totally malfunctioned when he discovered that we'd consumed two of his most coveted, expensive bottles of wine and that there was nothing in the house to eat apart from fish fingers and out of date Petits Filous. I kissed him and said jokingly, 'Darling, you know, I'm not a natural!

I know how to look after hyacinths, not husbands!' He didn't laugh then either. His last words to me before he rolled over and went to sleep were 'Don't be late tomorrow'. I kissed him on the lips. 'Stop fussing. I won't.' Said with tipsy confidence. 'Trust me.'

I empty the basket of laundry on to our bed, releasing a baffling tsunami of clothes. Tom's odd socks. Danny's odd socks. My jeans. Danny's jeans. Looking at the higgledy pile I realise that actually my clothes are not entirely dissimilar to Danny's: jeans, stripy T-shirts, hoodies. Yes, I'm walking round in a cheaper, scruffier, outsize version of mini-Boden. It makes me wonder. Maybe when the wedding ring is slipped on the finger, or when the baby arrives, a primal part of the female brain whispers: 'You're married now. Why wear heels? Nasty uncomfortable things. Now, what about a soft rubber sole? A comfy elasticated waist? Re-laaaax.' Or maybe I'm making excuses. Maybe my wardrobe is a symptom of wider marital negligence.

I pick out my work clothes from the pile: faded jeans, roomy grey knickers, and, because nothing else is clean, an ancient T-shirt with an open Rolling Stones mouth and the words Lick Me scrawled above it in peeling red letters. (Chloe brought it back from Las Vegas.) Which I cover with an old pink cotton cardigan. There's no point dressing up when you're a florist and rushing between appointments, especially when you know the client won't be there. The clothes get splashed with water, or dusted with pollen, and you need to be comfortable. I walk through to Danny's bedroom. A slice of sunlight breaks through the gap in the black-out curtains and stripes across his perfect, dewy infant skin.

'Danny, sweetie, time to wake up.' I gently pull back his *Thomas the Tank Engine* duvet.

He rubs his eyes with clenched fists, so adorable at this time in the morning, docile with sleepiness, more baby than boy. I kiss him on his cheek, which is creased by the pillow. 'I had a Daddy dream,' he says, looking puzzled, as if unsure if he's still in the dream. 'Where's Daddy?'

'At a meeting. He had to leave early this morning, sweetie.' I resist adding, 'Again.'

After a rushed bowl of Cheerios, I carefully pack my boxes of flowers into the boot of the car and drive Danny to nursery, a tall, red-brick Victorian building, five minutes from our house. The nursery is quiet and empty. Normally Danny is the last child to arrive in the morning. Today he is the first. The only person here is Scary Hanna, Danny's key worker who looks like a character from a Grimms' fairy tale, all straight black centre-parted hair and too many teeth. She grips Danny's hand so he can't run after me. I kiss him hurriedly and jump back into my ancient silver Audi before he can pluck the heart strings too hard. 'Love you!' I shout, tooting the horn as I drive off. The moment I am out of sight of the nursery, I switch modes. I am not a mother. I am a florist and I will do my best to forget about Danny until I see him again later. Today I need to focus.

The traffic is surprisingly light. I sail through three green lights, which is unprecedented. I've recently been wondering if my car number plate carries a secret code to make lights go red, or for road works to suddenly appear at critical junctions. To my astonishment there is also a metered parking space directly opposite Dr Prenwood's apartment in Belsize Park. This never happens either. I usually have to park streets away. Someone is smiling on me today.

I ring the bell and listen to the housekeeper – Aysha, a Muslim lady who always wears a leopard-print head scarf and a wide smile – fiddle with the numerous security locks behind Dr Prenwood's front door. Eventually the door opens. Aysha is holding a Dyson with one hand, her jaw with the other. She is not smiling. 'Morning, Miss Sadie,' she says, speaking through clenched teeth.

'Morning, Aysha. Oh dear. Are you OK?'

'Not so good, not so good.' She shakes her head.

'Oh no, what's the matter?'

'Terrible toothache. Terrible infection.'

'You poor thing. Agony?'

'Agony. I'm waiting for my blasted, lazy-bones dentist to call back with an appointment. Have you ever tried to get an emergency dentist appointment in London? It'd be quicker to fly to Pakistan.' She shakes her head. 'Come in.'

I slip my trainers off in the hall and pad across the thick, white carpets in socked feet, carrying my cardboard 'coffin' boxes from yesterday's Covent Garden Market. This is the only flaw in my plan. Normally I'd never give a client yesterday's flowers but I just couldn't figure how I'd fit in the market this morning too. And something had to give.

Dr Prenwood – aka 'Syringer to the Stars' – is a buoyant, waxy-skinned sixtysomething who has made enough money filling the frowns of London's glitterati to afford a weekly £200 flower budget, which gets him two big vases of flowers that should last a week. His apartment is everything my house is not: immaculate, tidy and childfree. It is wrapped in gold silk wallpaper, like a posh present, the walls studded with framed press cuttings about himself. There are puffy white sofas with gold claw feet that are covered in dust sheeting when he goes on holiday, which is frequently. There are gleaming gold taps. Polished loo-roll holders. Unsurprisingly, Dr Prenwood has a thing for showy displays, the floristry equivalent of big coiffed hair. He doesn't go for my signature simple seasonal arrangements: bunches of hyacinths or sweet peas wound with raffia and a trail of pussy willow. Oh no. He likes wire trickery, rose-studded spheres, twisted dogwood, thick fists of peonies, the whole shebang. (Haven't yet worked out his sexual persuasion but am thinking, on basis of flower displays, possibly not heterosexual.) This is a nice little number, one of the better jobs I've managed to secure since returning to London and building up my client base.

I open my khaki canvas sundry bag on the kitchen table, take out all my bits – secateurs, florist wire, florist foam, other bits and pieces – and get to work, stripping leaves, slicing the stems at an angle, carefully prodding the tight pink roses into the foam sphere. I hum along to myself as I do this, as I always do, losing myself in the methodical twist and push of flower, the slight crunch of the foam, like a small bone being crushed, imagining myself as a kind of plastic surgeon, cutting off unsightly lumps, improving proportions, distracting the eye with huge, youthful blooms.

Somewhere in the apartment I hear a phone ring. The vacuum cleaner noise stops. The kitchen door opens.

It is Aysha, smiling at last. 'I've got the appointment! It's either in ten minutes or in two weeks, can you believe it? I'm going to have to run!'

'Brilliant! Run!'

'Bye, Sadie!' She grabs her handbag and clatters out of the apartment, the front door shutting behind her with a clunk.

I push the last pink rose into the foam, plant the giant rose-impaled ball on the top of a black vase so it looks like strawberry ice cream on a cone and stand back to admire my work. One vase done. As I finish the second I'm aware of a dull hum behind my eyebrows. A hangover hum. Damn. So I didn't get away with last night. I pour myself a glass of water and clean up, not leaving even so much as a droplet of water on the marble floor; like fairies, florists should leave only magic behind. I slip on my old white Converse trainers, throw my sundry bag over my shoulder, tuck the empty cardboard boxes under my arm, and pull the front door.

I pull again. The door doesn't budge. I pull harder. No movement, not a click, not a millimetre of give. There are six locks. I turn each one and tug, trying to find the blasted one that is locking the damn door. I drop the boxes and tug harder. Nothing's budging. I dump my sundry bag and try to turn all the locks simultaneously. Nothing's budging. I realise with a shudder that I've never actually let myself out of the apartment. Aysha has always been here when I've left. And I don't have a key. Why didn't I think? Shit. I pull and pull again. I open the letter box and shout into the corridor. 'Hellooo! Is anyone there? I need a hand.'

My voice echoes around the empty hallway.

In frustration I throw myself at the door. My shoulder now aches. My mouth feels dry. My headache tightens like a belt.

Calm. Think, Sadie. Think. Who can I call? How long do emergency dentist appointments take? Will Aysha even come back? I check my phone, scrolling furiously through the phonebook. Yes! Dr Prenwood's number. Thank God. I dial. There is a pause, then a ringing tone. The phone on a console table a few feet behind me is ringing too. It rings three times and snaps to answer machine, my phone and Dr Prenwood's phone in sync. Oh no. I've got his bloody home number! I feel a bead of sweat drip down my nose.

10

Fucking up is not an option. It's so not an option. I phone through to directory enquiries and get the number of Prenwood's clinic, slide down the wall and crouch on the white hall carpet.

'Dr Prenwood's Skin Clinic,' says a breezy voice on the other end.

'Hi there! I need to speak to Dr Prenwood, please.'

'I'm afraid that won't be possible. May I ask who's calling?'

'I'm his florist. I need to speak to him, please.'

'Sorry, madam, he is engaged in treatments. No one is allowed to disturb him in treatment.'

'I understand that but this is an emergency. I'm locked in his flat. I'm meant to be at this lunch . . . Sorry, please, can you make an exception? I'd be so grateful. I'm desperate.'

The woman coughs. 'Excuse me, madam. If you'd like to leave your name and number I'll pass your message to Dr Prenwood.'

'When do you think he'll get the message?' I try to remain polite but I want to scream at her cool faux efficiency.

There is a pause. 'I cannot speak for Dr Prenwood, madam.'

'I'm not asking you to speak for him. I'm asking you when you think he'll get the message.'

'As soon as he is available, madam. Now if you'd like to leave your details. I have people waiting in reception.'

I leave my details, hang up and pace about the

apartment, foraging for spare keys. I open cupboard doors, I rifle through drawers. I come across diaries and syringes and medical journals, even a gold condom. But no keys. My breathing comes faster. There is now a waterfall of sweat sliding down my nose. What the hell am I going to do?

My phone rings. I dive towards it. 'Hello? Dr Prenwood?'

'Sorry, no. It's the Steven Hart Salon here. You were scheduled for a blow-dry . . .'

'Yes, I know but the thing is—'

'We do like more warning of a cancellation, Ms Drew,' says the receptionist wearily. 'Josh is very busy.'

'I'm not cancelling! I'm—'

'So you are going to attend your appointment? How late do you think you'll be?'

My eyes start to water in frustration. 'I don't know! I'm locked in an apartment. I don't know when I'm going to be freed. Soon, I hope. I'll come straight over as quickly as I can.'

There is a pause. 'Well,' says the lady eventually. 'I will let Josh know. In future . . .'

I hang up. What's wrong with these people? Hell, what's wrong with me? Of all the blimming days. Suddenly overcome by thirst, I pour myself a glass of cranberry juice from the fridge and gulp it back, clumsily splattering my cardigan and T-shirt with pink juice. Damn. I strip off my cardigan and run cold water over the stain, which makes it bleed further, then sit down at the kitchen table and put my head in my hands. I should phone Tom and warn him but I can't face it. No, I've got to get out of here. I walk to the long Georgian windows, pull back the crunchy yellow silk curtains, and peer out. As I thought, three floors up. I shout through the letter box again. I make another call to the clinic. Then I sit on the sofa and cry, big, fat, pitiful tears of frustration. It is now a quarter to one. I'm not going to make it. I imagine the wives in their designer frocks filing into the restaurant, all the 'Lovely to meet yous', the 'This is my wife . . .'. Oh God. Tom is going to kill me. This is going to turn into the mother of all rows.

With trembling fingers I admit defeat and call him. It goes straight to voicemail. Then there is a sound. The hair on my scalp tingles. Is that the key in the lock? I jump up and run to the front door, just as it swings open.

'Aysha!' I shout, wrapping her in a bear hug. 'You came back!'

'What are you still doing here?'

'You locked me in.'

Aysha puts her hand to her swollen left cheek. 'Oh, no. Oh, I didn't! Oh, I am *so* sorry.'

I grab my sundry bag and leap out of the door, like an animal released from its cage. 'It doesn't matter. I've got to go.'

Can I make it? Yes! I think so. I pelt down the stairs, across the street to my car. Oh no . . . Oh sweet Jesus.

'No!' I kick the wheel clamp. Not today. Not me. I run towards the main road, arm waggling in the air. 'Taxi!'

The traffic is now terrible. The taxi crawls through the streets towards central London, the meter bouncing up a pound every minute, the air rushing in through the window, hot, fumy and close, like there's a big thunderstorm brewing. I keep looking at my watch, as if I can will time to go backwards. Will Tom check his phone? Why hasn't he called?

Eventually we pull up outside The Ivy. A group of paparazzi, lurking around the entrance, snigger. 'Easy,' one of them says gruffly as I push past.

The doorman stops me, politely obstructing my way. 'Can I help you?'

'I'm late. For lunch. In the function room.'

The doorman glances at my enormous sundry bag, my trainers, jeans, and – oh God – my Lick Me T-shirt. I forgot the pink cardigan.

'It's the Anderson and Co lunch. I've been locked in. I'm horribly late,' I blurt.

'Upstairs,' says the doorman, seemingly taking pity. Then he hesitates. 'I'll get someone to escort you up.' He turns and mouths something to one of the cloakroom girls and I'm accompanied by a pretty brunette in a pencil skirt and high heels.

With every stair my heart pounds harder. I catch a glimpse of myself in a mirror. I look a fright, pale with raw pink patches on my cheeks and frizzy Christian rock group hair. I stop, three steps from the top, unsure if I can go further.

The cloakroom girl looks at me suspiciously. 'You OK?'

'Fine, fine,' I say, terrified of being booted out. In my fluster I stumble on the stair, falling forward and dropping my sundry bag, which I evidently haven't closed properly, because it explodes like a homemade bomb, spurting bits of wire and foam over the stairs. 'Shit. Sorry.' I scrabble to pick everything up at once, then climb the last few steps to the landing and try to collect myself. I can hear a hubbub of chat and laughter coming from the other side of the dark wood door.

'You've missed these,' says the cloakroom girl warily, handing me the secateurs.

At this moment a waiter edges past with a tray, leaving the door to the function room wide open. I am frozen to the spot, staring into a room with stained-glass windows and an arrangement of long tables filled with men in suits and glossy women eating and chatting. The hubbub of chat stops as my presence registers. There is a bemused silence, a sprinkle of laughter. People stare, mostly at my Lick Me T-shirt. I grip the secateurs. The moment goes on for years. I look around desperately for Tom. I see a couple of faces I recognise, a young agent type in his late twenties, and Perfect Pam, the wife of one of Tom's business colleagues who lives not far from us and has a son at Danny's nursery. Her mouth has dropped open in disbelief, displaying half-chewed asparagus.

'I think you're in the wrong place, love,' says a man with a red puffy face sitting near the door. 'We've got a function going on here.'

Someone laughs. The others continue to stare, some look puzzled, others irritated.

'I know.' I smile helplessly, wishing I was still locked in the flat. 'I'm Sadie Drew, Tom Harrison's wife. I'm, er, here for the lunch.'

Two

'Look, I'm sorry about yesterday. How many times do I have to say it? You know what happened. I practically killed myself trying to get there on time.'

Tom shakes out *The Times*. 'You knew how important it was.'

'I'll make amends next time I see your colleagues and corporate clients. I'll be on my bestest behaviour. I'll curtsey if you like.'

'Well, you'll have to wait until the Anderson summer party at the end of August. Which perhaps you'd like to turn up to in September?'

'Oh fuck you, Tom! If you're never going to get over it.' I drop my coffee cup into the filthy, crowded sink. Neither of us has loaded the dishwasher. 'If you're going to bang on about it all bloody weekend, well, there's no point in me being here.'

'Go on then, leave,' he says quietly, anger hissing out of his ears like steam from a coffee pot. 'Then maybe we can all relax.'

'Right, that's it.' I pick up my handbag from the top of the microwave. 'I've had it.'

'What?'

'I'm going.'

'What? Where?' Tom puts the newspaper down, more attentive now.

'Somewhere where I don't feel like the worst wife in the world. Somewhere where my worth as a human being is not dependent on whether a cleaner with a rotten molar locks me in an apartment. Or whether or not there's a hairball in the shower plughole . . .'

'Sadie, it is practically fucking breeding. It's the kind of thing that Channel Five makes documentaries about.'

'It is *your* hairball, not mine. Have you checked your hairline recently?' This is mean and childish and I know it. It doesn't stop me. 'You're the one who's losing hair right now, Tom, not me.'

'I wonder why,' he snorts. Now he looks really, *really* pissed off. Mentioning his receding hairline is like him mentioning my love handles. I've crossed the line.

But still I don't feel remorseful. Just defiant. I sling my handbag over my shoulder. 'Right. Danny needs to be picked up from Finn's house in twenty minutes. He's got a swimming lesson at three.'

'Can't do the swimming lesson. Busy,' he says in a deliberately breezy voice intoned to irritate.

'You'll have to.'

Tom rubs his jaw, more anxious now he realises I might be serious. 'But the football's on.'

'Good.'

'You're enjoying this.'

Actually I am, in a pent-up horribly dysfunctional way. 'And don't forget his antibiotic eye drops at four. He'll protest. A lot. Bar holding him down in a headlock I suggest you bribe him with a biscuit. Ginger biscuits in the big packed lunch stuff tin, second shelf, oh, never mind, you'll have to just find them. And your mother is—'

Tom puts his hands over his ears like a child. 'Jesus, Sadie. You sound like you're about to take off! Please, disconnect your tongue for a minute. You know the kind of week I've had. I'm still jet-lagged from New York. And I really need a tiny bit of peace and quiet, just to unwind for a few bloody minutes without jumping in the car and blazing around London like a taxi driver on steroids—'

'You *told* me to leave!' I interrupt, clinging on to the words that trapped him even though I know he probably didn't mean them. 'So I am.'

'Don't be such a drama queen. You want to martyr yourself, Sadie Drew? Point taken. Now sit down and finish your coffee, for God's sake, and let's try and rescue what's left of this Saturday morning.'

'No,' I say, surprised at my own commitment to this domestic rebellion. 'I'm going out.'

'You can't! What about Danny's stuff? I've got things to do. The football's—'

'Just watch me.'

I stomp out of the house and slam the front door feeling liberated. I've never done this before. Threatened it. But I've never actually left the house, left the day's arrangements to just hang. Yes, this will show him. I'll . . . I'll . . . what exactly? I stop on the pavement. Where the hell am I actually going to go? Shopping? An exhibition? These are things I always say I want to do, if I had more time, but now, presented with this glorious seized opportunity, they lose their allure. I'm still too fired up to look quietly at paintings and think remotely intelligent things about them, or to shop for that matter. I'll end up buying an unflattering yellow dress with horizontal stripes. Or yet another navy Gap T-shirt. I glance behind me to check that Tom is not smugly witnessing my hesitation from an upstairs window. He's not, thank goodness. The blinds are down. For want of a better idea I start striding quickly, hot and flustered, towards the Tube, still not sure where I am going.

Because I don't want to go all the way into town – crowds, noise, precarious consumer decisions – I emerge from Regent's Park Tube station on the Marylebone Road. Traffic thunders past. It seems louder and fiercer than normal, everything does. Only Regent's Park itself looks calm, a place of blossomy refuge amongst the speeding cars, rushing people and rabid low-flying pigeons. Next to the gate there is a small flower stall. Roses. Sunflowers. Tulips. I feel the flowers exert a pull over me, as they always do. I try to ignore them but, in the same way that it's impossible for teenage boys to ignore topless beauties on the beach, find I cannot. I steal a glance. I hover. I hesitate. And then I break and buy myself a bunch of glossy lipstick-pink tulips, petals like tongues, even though I could buy them for a quarter of the price at New Covent Garden Flower Market and do not need any more flowers in my life. But what the hell. In the park I find a suitable spot, away from other people, beneath a cloud of scented cherry blossom. I sit down, try to get comfortable. This is difficult. Other women look pastoral and pretty sitting in the park. I don't. I start to itch. My lower back aches. I rub my arms. Now that I'm immobile I realise that there's a bite to the air. Even though it's sunny, clouds, densely bunched like lilac-grey hydrangea, are starting to fill the sky to the west. It could be rain. I should definitely have dug my sweater out of the dirty linen basket before I stormed out.

I try to overcome my fury at Tom – I can't seem to do anything right – and talk myself into enjoying this wild stab at freedom. This is the first time I've been in any park on my own in years, since we had Danny probably. There's no child badgering me for a Mini-Milk. No husband checking emails on his crackberry as we walk. The horror of yesterday's lunch begins to fade and I'm filled with an odd sense of anticipation. Yes, I am alone. Anything could happen! Anything happens to pissed off young(ish) wives on their own in London parks. I've seen the scene on primetime TV a hundred times. Right on cue, an attractive blond twentysomething lollops past, his jeans hanging off his waist, bulldog on a thick metal chain lead. My mind starts to race. His dog could run up to me and I could get entangled in the lead and we'd have to get stuck in a conversation and then . . . He walks right past without a second glance. Well of course he bloody well does.

The gloom returns: the lunch, the row, everything. I am unable to stop running over it all in my head – rewind, pause, rewind – trying to make sense of where things started to go tits-up. It was way before Aysha's rotten molar that's for sure. But it's hard to know the exact moment a marriage tips from great to rather less great to kind of crap actually. Or the exact point that the path you were both travelling along together suddenly forks. All I know is that we were mostly happy in Toronto. Perhaps living in a foreign country suspended us from reality for a little while. Tom had a nice, safe, if rather unchallenging, media marketing job with nice hours and a nice boss. We rented a modern serviced apartment in a nice safe block. It had two bedrooms, a bright and spacious lounge with hardly any furniture. Even I found it difficult to make it messy. And if I did, Tom didn't care, not like he cares now anyway. He was far more relaxed then. And I was a new mom, an émigrée. I wasn't trying to work as well. Life there was comparatively easy. In Toronto, most days, we'd eat out or get takeout. Hell, we'd have picnics by Niagara Falls. We'd ski at Blue Mountain, hang out on hot July weekends on Wasaga beach. The air was fresh. The roads were wide. There were no in-laws to complicate things. Still, being Brits, we got homesick for our expensive, overcrowded island. And when Tom was offered the job in London – he applied for it without telling me, with a word in the boss's ear from an old friend – there was a hunger in his eyes I'd never seen before. He said it was his big break. He liked Toronto but it was provincial compared to London. He missed the cut and thrust. No, I didn't put up much of a fight. I'd begun to have a niggle, a feeling that I should get back to my career before it was too late. Yes, the babymoon was over. We were going home. Back to real life.

It became real a bit too fast.

I imagined returning to London would be like starting anew in my old life, picking up from where we left off last time we lived here, in those happy, loved-up early days. No matter that we didn't have children then. That shit hadn't happened. And I have to admit that I held tightly to rather a lot of assumptions. One of my assumptions, the main howler, was that Tom had the same assumptions as me. I'd decided how life would unfold. Like this. We'd stay in London for a couple of years I supposed, then we'd move to the countryside, maybe Sussex or Oxfordshire, with our growing brood of poetically beautiful children. I'd only go into London when I needed to for work, and the rest of the time I'd throw long lazy lunches on a trestle table covered in striped French linen in our vast walled garden while the children climbed apple trees and we got drunk on posh wine with our envious visiting London friends.

It hasn't happened like that, obviously. Firstly, Tom's changed. He's stressed. He's tired but fidgety, obsessed with proving himself as if his sperm count depended on it. He's getting a business lunch tummy. London's also changed. It feels faster, more aggressive, and more expensive than I remember it. And it's harder to enjoy with a small child than I imagined. The yellow crime placards – 'Serious Assault. 5 p.m., Monday . . .' – dotted around the neighbourhood like perverse inversions of those brown tourist heritage ones have kind of lost their edgy allure. Plus many of my old London friends have moved out in search of good schools and more space. Which seems sensible enough to me. But when I wondered aloud to Tom when (not if) we would do the same thing he shuddered and looked at me as if I'd suggested relocating to Outer Mongolia and living naked in a yurt. No, he said, no way. He's got to be within a thirty-minute commute of Soho. The English countryside will age him overnight: Spar shops, manure and mud, the 4x4 Sloaney mafia, no he couldn't bear it. After three years in Canada he needs to be at the heart of things. In other words, Tom has things to prove. He feels that he spent his twenties ambling from job to job and underachieving and that this is his big opportunity, Willy Wonka's golden ticket. Maybe it is. All I know is that the job that lured us back from Toronto – a senior role in a large, successful corporate speakers and entertainment agency, Anderson & Co, with a path to a directorship – has changed his priorities, and not in a particularly family-friendly way. He is working longer and longer hours. He is paranoid about losing his job – works harder still. He checks his emails before breakfast, before we go to bed, after sex, not that there's a lot of that right now. Last week he said how relieved he was now that Danny is almost three and we're 'finally getting our life back', as if it were a good DVD he'd lent to a friend.

But I want the sequel, volumes two, and three. And Tom's no longer sure he wants another child at all. This breaks my heart into a million, trillion shards. Because I do want one, with every screaming cell of my body. And there's the goddamn rub.

I stretch my bulb-white legs out on the grass, lean back and gaze up at the umbrella of pink blossoms. A wind stirs them and some shower down, so perfect and pink they look like those sugar ones you get on posh cupcakes, or the confetti at our wedding three years ago. Another lifetime. I close my eyes. But Regent's Park begins to intrude. Loudly.

'So I said to him, nah, I'm not going down no manky old clinic on my own . . .' shouts a voice.

I open my eyes. To my left is the culprit. She is slim and young enough to still want to sunbathe and wearing a pretty floral skirt hitched up her thighs and a black lace bra, the tanned flesh of her slim torso unfurled across the grass like a flag. Men saunter past very slowly, staring. Tom would too if he was here. He wouldn't be able to stop himself. The woman glares back at the men as if mildly affronted by their leering but doesn't cover up. Although I am only thirty-four it's already hard to remember having such brazen self-confidence. But I did. I actually remember looking out for glimpses of my body reflected in shop windows, in car wing mirrors. Now, of course, I generally avoid it. Or I get a glimpse of myself and assume it's someone else. It takes a few seconds to register.

To the left of the Shouting Young Person is an old woman sitting neatly against an old oak tree, arms clasped around her knees. She is smiling as if mildly amused at the vulgarity of her youthful neighbour. Slim and elegant in a tailored pale grey dress and matching jacket, her silver hair is elegantly coiffed around a handsome face that is slung between two prominent cheekbones. Vivid scarlet lipstick. She reminds me a little of Nan, my late maternal grandmother – same hair, same ballerina straight back – which indirectly reminds me of my mother, who I met in this very park on a visit back home last year. She stood on her tippy toes and plucked a blossom off the tree in full view of a tut-tutting park warden. She didn't care. She didn't give a stuff about things like that after her diagnosis. No, she stuck the blossom under my nose, the petals pushing into my nostrils. 'Sniff, Sadie, sniff! I bet you don't get blossoms like this in Toronto.' She was always trying to get us to return to London, her campaign unashamedly stepping up after Danny was born: 'Do you really want Danny to grow up saying cookie?' Mum stuck the enormous twig of blossom in the lapel of her red wool jacket – it made her look so frail and tiny, bless her – and we carried on walking towards the café for coffee and carrot cake. Now she's gone, of course, pushing up the daisies. I got home too late.

I glance at my watch. Almost time for Danny's swimming lesson. Will Tom remember? Will he remember to pack Danny's goggles? Will he realise that Danny needs a sweet pick-me-up and a juice straight after swimming or he's liable to melt-down? It does rankle that I'm the one who has to remember all this stuff, that Tom doesn't think it's anything to do with him, or it just isn't important compared to his shiny new career. The only thing that is important is that I turn up to a lunch I didn't want to go to looking like a clone of all the other wives. That I play a part I never auditioned for.

Suddenly a cool wind stirs the park, rippling across the grass, making the sunbather reach for her sweater. The sunlight seems to just switch off, as if the afternoon has been dunked like a biscuit into a cup of over-stewed tea. English weather! I quickly stand up, brush down my jeans, grab my tulips. The wind is acting up, more like a gale now. The blossoms start to spin off the cherry tree, swirling around me in confusing clouds. *The louder you scream, the faster* . . . Then rain, the drops falling like a shower of pins. The sunbather is running towards the park gate. I'm hit by a rising anxiety, a weight on my chest like an elephant's foot on my breastbone. Something *is* happening. And I don't like it. Feeling vulnerable, I glance over at the oak tree to check that the old lady in the grey dress is OK. But she's nowhere to be seen. There is a terrible noise, an atomic clap. Shit! What the hell *is* that? God throwing toys out of his pram? Then – blimey! – there's a dark cloud rolling over the park towards me. The cloud looms closer. For a moment I'm mesmerised: this strange storm is like watching the feelings inside me take physical form. I scrabble towards the big oak tree for shelter. Then there's a dull thump and it all goes black.

There is an old face looking down at me, a face that I don't recognise, a strange, coppery taste in my mouth and a feeling of unspecific wetness, like I'm standing in the shower or Danny's pouring a beaker of water on my head. Or . . . Oh Lord. Have I wet myself?

'Should I call an ambulance, darling?' says the old face.

'No. No thanks.' I look around. To my immense relief I haven't wet myself. I am sitting on soaking wet grass against the oak tree, which provides some shelter against the torrential rain that is hissing through the sky all around us. A rivulet of water drips down my neck. The face is smiling now. Her lips are old person thin but still cupid bowed and painted red, geranium red. Of course. It is the old lady in the grey dress who was sitting beneath the tree earlier.

'I wouldn't want the fuss either. It's only a bit of blood.' She points to her forehead.

Blood? Shit. I press my fingers to my forehead. It hurts.

She clicks open her handbag, a glossy crocodile handbag as sturdy as something dangled off an old royal arm. She pulls out a tissue. 'According to Persian legend the first tulips sprang up from the drops of blood shed by a lover, you know.'

'Really? Thank you.' What on earth is she talking about? I dab the tissue against my forehead.

'A branch, a little one,' says the lady, pointing upwards. 'Just missed your eye. You're lucky. Your lovely flowers less so.'

The tulips are scattered over the ground, like those painted wooden ones you get in Camden Market. The grass itself is covered in a pilled blanket of pale blossom, twigs, small branches and litter which appears to have been sucked from the park bins. The lady picks up some tulips, bending from the hips with a kind of creaky grace, and hands them to me.

'Thank you so much. What on earth happened?'

The lady shrugs. Her shoulders are very narrow, childlike in their petiteness. 'A butterfly beating its wings in Colombo or something.' She laughs. 'I'm really not too sure. But I must say it was rather fun. It's certainly blown the cobwebs away, hasn't it?'

I smile, grateful for her humour and non-hysteria. (Exactly the opposite to how I'll be at her age I suspect.) The torrential rain is stopping, but the day is still dark. And the air feels strange, too close, as if the sky is screwed on like a tight jam jar lid. A slow, pernicious anxiety begins to grip me. I need to get home. 'I've got to go.'

'I'd give it a minute. You'll get soaked to the skin. Look, I've missed one.' She picks up the last pink tulip off the wet grass and holds it up reverently. 'Delightful.'

'I'm a florist,' I say and it sounds like I'm saying 'flodist'. I am not sure why she needs to know or why I feel the need to explain myself.

An amazed smile spreads slowly across the lady's face. 'Then, my dear, we were meant to meet.' She holds out a dainty liver-spotted hand. Her hands look older than her face. There is a diamond the size of a bulb on her finger, locked on by a large knuckle. 'Enid. Enid Fisher.'

'Sadie.' I smile, shaking her hand, which feels as delicate as a chicken wing. Sweet old thing. The kindness of strangers in London always comes as a bit of a surprise. I've increasingly come to expect to be mugged, not hugged.

We stand for a few moments and, like two easy old friends, silently watch the rain together, clattering down like dropped beads. Loud and hypnotic, it drums my hangover away, and much of my anger. Eventually the rain subsides a bit. 'I think I might brave it. Will you be OK here?'

'Of course. I'm not the one who got bumped on the head.' The lady glances at my left hand. My wedding ring is a woven gold band, with trenches of potting compost stuck in the weave. 'Ah, you're married. That's good. Your husband will look after you.'

'I doubt it,' I say, thinking of the last time I was ill –

flu last month – when Tom's nursing amounted to one cup of tea and a request not to breathe in his direction as he had an important meeting the next day.

'Then you'll have to retrain your husband.'

I laugh. 'You know, you're absolutely right. But first I'm going to make a mad dash for the Tube. Here, you have the tulips. I insist. You've been very kind.' I put them in her arms.

'Oh thank you! What a treat. One minute.' She clicks open her queenly handbag again and slides out a white card. 'Please take this. I've just lost my florist. And I particularly need someone who understands tulips. It's absolutely imperative. Do call me, won't you?'

'Thanks.' I smile politely, knowing I won't call her. I only go on personal recommendations. Besides, Tom complains that I'm stretching myself too thinly as it is. He says I don't have to work now. He doesn't understand that irrespective of finances, I absolutely do have to work, otherwise I'm at risk of losing myself completely.

She looks at me intently with beady blue eyes, still bright even at her age, not milky or pink. 'I know quite a bit about husbands, too.'

O-K. Mad granny alert. 'I came to the park to escape mine,' I laugh, stuffing the card into my jeans pocket. 'Thanks for all your help. Bye bye.'

Three

I slam the front door and step intrepidly into what Tom
calls The Corridor of Chaos, otherwise known as the
hallway. There's an overflowing recycling box containing an embarrassing number of empty wine bottles that
we forgot to put out again, *Thomas the Tank Engine*
wellies – unwearable on account of the smear of dog
poo on the left boot that hasn't yet been scraped off –
Danny's lunch box, old leaky anoraks and four broken
umbrellas. A room might stay tidy for a few hours, well,
until I walk into it, but the hall is never tidy. The
Corridor of Chaos can always be relied upon as a source
of petty arguments when other issues are thin on the
ground. Of course Tom would never actually consider
tidying it up himself. He works too hard. Whereas I
work part-time. Plus, I am a woman. I am a mother –
but *not* a new mother and therefore one who should
have got this domestic thing down by now – and
cognitively attuned to such matters, unlike him whose
mind is best saved for more important issues, like

pension provision, or mortgage rates, or the latest episode of *The Wire*.

The yap of a small dog. My soul yaps back. Oh no. I reluctantly push open the kitchen door. And there he is. Teddy, the world's most spoiled, unlovable dog, a yappy, snappy Jack Russell in a pale blue crystal-encrusted collar, and Rona, my mother-in-law, looking pristine and pressed amongst the mess of the kitchen, the human equivalent of a white Basildon Bond envelope on a pile of old torn newspapers. Rona is the yardstick of domestic efficiency, the kind of woman who keeps a tidy hallway, house, life. Tidying is encoded in her DNA, as is crumble-making, hand-washing cashmere, sending 247 Christmas cards every year and, before he retired, throwing endless dinner parties for her husband Ted's dreary business associates. Rona doesn't believe in immigration, or state handouts, or women having careers. She believes in kitchen roll.

Sitting gingerly at the kitchen table, careful not to rest her arms on its sticky surface, she crosses her slim legs in camel-coloured slacks – she loves camel slacks, preferably by Country Casuals – and clasps her manicured hands (tasteful colourless varnish always) in her lap. With her neat, clean sixtysomething profile, skin lightly tanned from tennis, ash-blond hair always immaculately blow-dried, she looks like she's stepped out of an advert for menopausal vitamins or an expensive muesli brand. While she gets more vivid every year, Tom's father, Ted, in contrast, is fading. He now spends most of his time playing golf in Hampshire, feigning forgetfulness and senility to get out of the demands and duties of marital life. Rona prefers the Kensington *pied-à-terre* she bought with Ted's pension funds. She also spends increasing amounts of time here, now that she can drop in unannounced – 'I can see you'd appreciate a bit of help, Sadie' – and generously dispense nuggets of sage wifely advice. Without the protective shield of the Atlantic it's got up close and personal quickly, far too quickly. And she does not hide her disappointment.

I started at a disadvantage of course. When I met Tom he was dating a girl from his home village in Hampshire after bumping into her again at a dinner party in west London. Her name was Lucinda Lawn. From a good Hampshire family – old friends of the Harrisons of course – baby blonde, demure, slim, with wide brown eyes like Bambi, she had a suitably non-threatening junior job at a London auction house and an ill-disguised desire to wed the man she'd fancied ardently at school, give up her job at the earliest opportunity and bear his children. Rona adored her. Lucinda Lawn was everything she wanted from a potential daughter-in-law. Then I interrupted her son's destiny.

The lovely Lucinda has apparently never got over it. Nor has Rona. OK, it didn't help that I got pregnant a few months into the relationship. It didn't help that we moved to Toronto. And it doesn't help that I am a woman who has never, in living memory, cleaned behind a fridge and has absolutely no intention of doing so.

'I let myself in, hope you don't mind, Sadie.'

Teddy leaps up at me, trying to hungrily sniff my crotch. I fight the urge to give him a gentle whack. This would send Rona apoplectic. She believes in smacking unruly children but not psychopathic dogs.

'Down, Teddy! I wanted to pick up the shopping I left here a couple of days ago, the Harrods bags . . .' She stops, stares at me, puts a hand to her mouth. 'Good God, what have you done to your face?'

I touch my forehead. It stings. 'Oh it's nothing, really. A wind-tossed branch, I think. I got caught in a storm. Wrong place wrong time.'

'That's how you got it?' Rona narrows her eyes and looks at me suspiciously, as if I might have got it by putting traffic cones on my head and staggering down the street drunk on Special Brew. 'Well, it's unfortunate that it's actually on your face. Not hidden in the hair-line. But I'm a little confused, dear. Aren't you meant to be taking Danny swimming? I'm sure Tom mentioned something about swimming on the phone.'

'He's taken him today. I went for a walk in the park.'

'Alone?'

'I wanted a bit of space.'

'Space? From your family?' The corners of her mouth twitch. 'I see.'

I flick on the kettle. Ignore her. Ignore her and she might decide to go away. 'Tea?'

'If you have fresh milk.' She coughs. 'Is that Trish woman still looking after Danny too?'

35

Trish is a lovely West Indian woman in her fifties – her two children have left home – who lives locally and helps out if the nursery hours don't tally with mine and Tom's. 'Yes, occasionally.'

'It's a lot of different childcare for such a young child, isn't it?'

'Not compared to many children,' I answer stiffly, refusing to be drawn into her stocks to be pelted with maternal guilt. 'I only work part-time, Rona.'

'Yes, you're right. It's just that things have changed since my day.'

'My day' is the yardstick by which everything, especially anything to do with women and their long-suffering families, falls short.

'I'd never have dreamed of putting Tom in nursery so young. One didn't then.' She sits straighter on her chair, pulling at the silk geometric print scarf around her neck. She likes to wear scarves. They hide her neck, which is the part of the anatomy that reveals her age. That little cough again. 'I heard about the catastrophic lunch. I must say it all sounds very peculiar. Tom tells me you got locked in an apartment.'

'Dr Prenwood's apartment, yes.' I throw Earl Grey tea bags into the pot.

'Dr Prenwood?' A faint flush rises on Rona's collarbone. In an ideal world, she'd pretend she didn't know him at all and put down the waxy immobility of her face to something vaguely natural, like Vitamin C facials, but as she asked me for his number when she discovered what he did, lying is not an option. We both know hers is a late blooming, artificially forced, like a hothouse gerbera. She brushes some invisible dust off her left knee and pauses. 'I'm pleased you're here actually, Sadie darling. There's something I wanted to talk to you about.'

'Oh yes?' I smell trouble.

Teddy leaps on to her lap. Rona lifts him up and lets his smelly, doggy tongue lick her face. 'I apologise in advance if you think I'm interfering, because I really don't mean to. But . . .'

Uh oh. I offer her a Duchy oaten biscuit. She loves a Duchy. It's the royal connection that gets her.

'. . . reluctantly, I feel that I have no option but to step in at this point in time. Ah, Duchy. Your favourite, my little Teddy.' She sniffs her tea, checking for a whiff of sour milk, and dunks her biscuit. 'Goodness, I read a terrible story in the *Daily Mail* about a five-year-old girl who died choking on a Hobnob. You should always supervise Danny when he eats biscuits, you know.'

'Right.'

Rona loves alarmist stories involving domestic accidents. They fuel her belief that we're all potentially seconds from disaster. 'I'll get to the point.' Rona pauses, pulls at her scarf. 'Since you got back from Toronto I've had time to get to know you a bit better, which has been wonderful, and to see how you work as a family, which has been . . .' She clears her throat and pulls at her scarf. '. . . interesting. But a few little things are making me a bit concerned.'

I feel the heat rise on my cheeks. 'I'm not with you.'

She dabs at the biscuit crumbs collected in the corners of her lipsticked mouth. 'Excuse me, this biscuit's a bit stale.' She feeds the remainder of the biscuit to Teddy, who slobbers noisily all over her fingers. 'To be blunt – I know that you appreciate my honesty – your marriage, well, it seems a bit turbulent right now, if I may speak so boldly. And I'm worried, terribly worried actually – I've had terrible sleepless nights recently, playing havoc with my complexion – about the kind of environment you're bringing Danny into.'

'Danny? Danny is fine,' I bristle, crossing my arms across my chest. I feel a surge of anger towards Tom, even though she's not his fault, not exactly. But I know he'll make excuses for her. His loyalty towards Rona is always undiminished by the harder facts such as her character disorder. And he always reminds me that I agreed to a peacekeeping truce when it comes to his mother and the violent personality clash that became apparent the very first time we ever met. Her first words to me: 'Goodness, a brunette! Tom normally has a thing for blondes, Sandra. It is Sandra, isn't it?'

'I am not criticising you, Sadie. Don't be defensive. Look, I know I've been blessed with a wonderful marriage but that does not mean I sure as hell didn't have to work at it too. Marriage can be tough, especially when you've got young children.'

'With respect, Rona, I'm not sure this is any of your business.'

'Don't think I haven't struggled with this, Sadie,' she sighs. 'I'd much rather pretend everything was rosy for the sake of familial relations. But that would be the coward's way out, wouldn't it? Because it is my business when it's my son and my grandchild involved, very much so. These flowers you fiddle around with . . .'

'I'm a florist!'

'They can't be a substitute for . . .' She stops and looks at me cryptically. 'You know what.'

'Listen, Rona.' I put on my soft talk-to-mother-in-law voice. It's meant to get my point home as quickly and painlessly as possible without further debate. Rona is like a chronic condition – eczema, or a bad back – and cannot be cured, only managed. 'I appreciate your concern . . .' Like hell I do. '. . . but Tom and I are fine, really. We've had a difficult few months, as you know. He's working very hard. We're settling back into London. It's a bit of a culture shock after Toronto. And yes, we're chasing our tails half the time. We're busy, too busy. But that's life. We're fine.' I suddenly don't feel that we're very fine at all. But she's the last person I'm going to confide in. However much I tell myself that Rona is just a difficult character to be borne, I cannot make her words not hurt. I cannot brush her off. She retains this terrible power over me, made worse by the knowledge that we are bonded – by Tom, by Danny, by our linked helixes of DNA – for life.

'I'm not going to pussyfoot around like everyone else, and say, oh it's hunky dory when it's not,' she says, rubbing the dog's ears. 'And I know you wouldn't want me to.'

'Rona . . .'

'So I'll speak plainly. Yes, you've had a rough year, but that doesn't explain why you seem so unwilling to really throw yourself into being a supportive wife.'

'Excuse me!'

Teddy opens one eye and looks at me malevolently. 'Sadie, please. You know that Teddy can't tolerate abrupt noises.' She digs in her handbag for a pot of scented lip salve and applies it casually with her little finger. 'Look at what Ted and I have achieved, darling. We're celebrating our thirty-fifth wedding anniversary soon. But let me tell you, it takes work. You can't just muddle through.' She rubs her lips together. 'Life is not a bowl of roses.'

What? A bowl of . . . I think of my own mum, my sweet, kind mum, who so loved roses, especially the antique pink ones in her favourite fishbowl vase with its sprinkle of pale blue crystals at the bottom like an ocean floor. I can see it now, pride of place on her white tablecloth, the cakes on the doilies. Mum liked to bake. She baked endearingly badly. The cakes she made always tasted of something else – the chocolate always tasted of coffee, the coffee cake tasted of molasses – but once you accepted the differential between expectation of taste and the actual mouthful, they could be quite delicious. I miss her horribly.

Rona narrows her eyes again and her make-up creases into one long feathery taupe line along her eye socket. 'This is Tom's moment. He wasted away much of his twenties, Sadie, I can't tell you how terribly, terribly painful that was to watch, as a mother.'

'He was hardly on the streets.' If anything the pressure to succeed was the one thing that filled him with self-doubt and a vaguely slacker-like defiance. 'I think you're too hard on him, Rona.'

'You don't understand, Sadie. Ted and I . . .' she sighed. 'Lord knows how much we spent on his education. We did everything, everything, we could to help him get along in the City, or some other place worthy of his indisputable talents. And he ended up in a media marketing job in . . .' She winces. '. . . Toronto, of all places.'

Despite all my best efforts not to, I smile. To her Canada might as well be a suburb of Slough.

'It's no laughing matter! At this critical point in his career Tom needs a wife who is prepared to put her needs aside for his. It's *his* big break, and as head of the family, you should see it as yours too.' She pauses, weighing me up. 'Feminism never got a woman anywhere but the divorce courts, Sadie. I'm sure you know that in your heart of hearts.' She stands up, pulling her olive Smythson Nancy bag over one shoulder. 'And, sorry, I hope you don't mind me saying this, but you do look a bit unkempt, darling.' She smiles coldly. 'You're not in the Canadian mountains now.'

41

Rona thinks that beneath the Canadians' thin veneer of sophistication they are all really just rednecks in bearskins.

'You look like you've been scything flowers in the field, not arranging them. What happened to that girl, that lovely girl there!' Rona points to a photograph on the wall. It is one of my favourite photographs, me and Tom in Positano, Italy, on our honeymoon. Tom, tanned and tousled, happy and post-coital, has a protective arm around my waist. I'm beaming like an idiot, wearing a lovely silver and leaf-green dress, smocked at the top, showing off my neat pregnant bump, a full swishy skirt. I felt good in that dress. I certainly didn't feel like Mary Archer in that dress. Three years ago in September. It already feels like a different space–time continuum.

'And the house? You've got this lovely little house. But it looks like your idea of cleaning is sweeping crumbs off the table on to the floor.'

How does she know?

'Teddy could do a better job quite frankly, darling. Don't you have a cleaner? Can't you increase her hours?'

'She left last month.' The rather embarrassing truth is that she resigned, citing 'impossible working conditions'. I refused to do that mad British thing of tidying before she came. And I refuse to become my mother. Mum used to do everything for Dad – cooking, buying his underpants, reminding him of his mother's birthday – and resented it. She'd half-jokingly call herself 'the feminist who realised too late'. And she'd tell me, her hazel eyes sparkling, 'Sadie, the more you do for your husband the less he'll do himself. Look at your father, he's domestically disabled. He's damaged goods.' And we'd stare at Dad idly trimming his nostril hair in front of the hall mirror and shake our heads. 'If I didn't love him I'd have divorced him years ago,' she'd sigh. Her advice was always to get a career and forget about 'dreary domestics'. Don't 'end up like me'. So I didn't.

Rona shakes her head. 'Listen, I know you're creative, Sadie. Tom loves that about you, your quirkiness. But do you have to be quite so untidy?'

I look around. OK. Well, it's not perfect. There may be piles of old newspapers on the table, baby wipes on the toaster, food on the floor. But, well, there's flowers on the table, a bunch of yolk-yellow freesias that smell of summer. That's the most important thing.

'Is it really so difficult, darling?'

It is actually! I want to shout back. Running my life – trying to get back on top of my career – and running the family's life shouldn't be so damn difficult but it is. I bite a strip of dry skin off my bottom lip and taste blood.

'You need to move on. You're not the first woman in the world to lose . . .' she stops, hesitates. She lets me fill in the gaps.

'Just leave, Rona.' I am so furious now I can barely speak. I know that the peacekeeping truce is in danger of being violently broken.

'I'm only saying all this because I care about you.

Now where are those shopping bags? Excellent. Well, I've enjoyed our little girlie chat. No hard feelings I hope. You know I mean well. Come on, Teddy.' Teddy leaps off her lap and immediately starts sniffing at my crotch again. Rona scoops him up, tucks him under her arm, and picks her way through the mess in the hallway. Just as she steps out of the front door, she whips around to launch her deadliest, lowest-flying missile. 'It's just that I fear that if you're not careful, you could lose everything, Sadie. And I wouldn't be able to live with myself if I hadn't been the one to step in and warn you in time.' She touches my arm lightly. Teddy snarls. 'Call me if you need anything, anything at all that might help you get back on your feet.'

Four

I quickly wipe my tears away. The post-row adrenaline-fuelled anger and exhilaration has gone. Now I just feel tired and vulnerable, Rona's words buzzing frenziedly around my head like trapped bluebottles. The front door slams.

'Mama!' shouts Danny as he thunders down the hall wearing a red and black stripy pirate jumper and his swimming goggles. I kiss him. He smells of rain and sugary E numbers. He presses a sticky wet finger to my forehead. 'Mama has an ow.'

'A very little one. It doesn't hurt. How was swimming?'

'Water up nose,' he sniffs.

Tom appears looking dishevelled and grumpy. His T-shirt is splattered with a large Ribena stain. He looks like a man who's been battling with an energetic toddler and lost. 'Shit. What happened to your head?'

'I got caught in . . .' I hesitate, unsure of what's happened, of everything suddenly. It all seems rather unreal, like it never happened at all, the wind, the rain, the elegant old lady who helped me, Rona's visit. 'A funny, ferocious little storm.' For some reason I don't elaborate. I don't want to say that I was knocked out. I don't want him to think I'm a liability.

'Oh right, yeah. Heard the weather warnings on the radio.' Moved by the sight of my bruise perhaps, or maybe out of habit, Tom kisses me on the top of my head.

I lean my head against his chest and let it rest there for a moment. It's somehow easier like this with the mythic backdrop of storms and bleeding head wounds; we can play the primal role of husband and wife – him Tarzan, me Jane – without both of us getting pissed off with the other for not doing enough around the house and claiming to be the more tired party, or the fact that I'd rather read *Grazia* than talk about his work because I'm tired and *Grazia* is escapism and he's becoming symbolic of the things I want to escape from. Like trying and failing to be a corporate wife. Like the furry hairball in the shower plughole. Or the fact that if Rona's right I may be about to lose everything. 'I'll fix Danny supper.'

'Already fed and watered,' Tom says proudly, like he's conquered a small continent rather than just done the thing I do every day without comment. 'I took him out.'

'Great,' I say, although a little part of me thinks, 'damn'. In the unspoken credit rating system of our marriage Tom is now in the black. Having thus proved himself as not entirely useless he'll use this as leverage for doing nothing else for the rest of the evening. Whereas I'll be in debt for a tedious job, for example loading the dishwasher, unloading the washing machine, or worse – the job that's hung over me all year – tidying the utility cupboard, or the 'futility cupboard', as Tom calls it, an unfathomable box room housing sticky lids of old washing liquids, might-come-in-useful bent paper party plates, and tins of flageolet beans that are likely to remain unopened in situ until they naturally decompose. Even discounting my gaffe at the Anderson lunch, Tom now starts the week with a huge tactical advantage. 'Where did you go?'

Tom shoots Danny a sharp don't-tell look.

Danny grins. 'McDonald's.'

'Tom!'

'Well, it was easy . . .'

'Got a free car!' squeals Danny.

If I took Danny to McDonald's Rona would probably report me to social services. No, I have to take the less popular option: fruit and vegetables, foul-smelling fish oil capsules squeezed into organic yoghurts. 'You've just missed your mum. She popped round to collect her shopping that she left here the other day,' I say briskly, knowing I can't go into Rona's outburst here in front of Danny, not wanting to go into it at all. Tom flinches slightly. I wonder if he knows what she said.

'On the subject of the old folks, your pa phoned,' he

says, shaking rain out of his dark wavy hair. He looks better with his hair ruffled and boyish, as he always used to wear it, rather than slicked down and corporate. 'Said he had some important news that he'd like to deliver in person.' He raises an eyebrow. 'Must say he sounded very bouncy.'

'Well, he would, wouldn't he, dating a forty-four year old months after Mum's death?' I feel my blood pressure shoot up. I cannot think about Dad and Loretta without feeling that he's betrayed Mum, all those years of marriage. And by betraying her – dead or not – he's betrayed me. 'Where are the lovebirds now? Miami? Marbella? Mars?'

'In some swanky hotel near Cancún apparently.'

'Perhaps they'd like to stay there.'

'Is Grandpa and Loretta coming to tea?' asks Danny excitedly. He adores Dad's new girlfriend.

'Not today, honey,' I say. 'Grandpa's on holiday again.'

'Oh.' With a shriek, Danny throws himself against my legs, hugging my jeans, putting each of his little feet on top of my trainers. 'You can be monster then. Like Grandpa. Let's go for a hike, Mummy monster!' he squeals.

I start to walk, lifting his feet on mine, relieved to be retreating from Tom, from the possibility of confrontation.

'Mummy monster. Mummy monster,' Danny giggles. 'Hiking.' We stomp up to his bedroom for a cuddle and the thousandth read of *Slinky Malinki*. I turn the light out and stay there with him for a while, perched on the side of his white toddler bed, lacing my fingers through his glorious chocolate curls, smoothing the duck-down at the edge of his hairline. I can no longer remember loving Tom as fiercely as I love Danny. It occurs to me that I might have fallen out of love with my husband and in love with my son. Is this normal? After a while Danny's eyes grow vacant and round, like planets. The lids close slowly, as he fights and loses to sleep. When he's snoring lightly, I kiss him and close the door quietly behind me and pad back downstairs to my husband.

'Danny would be better off learning to fall asleep alone, sweetheart,' Tom mutters. (Rona's words.) He is sprawled on our new low-backed lime green sofa, head craned back. I sit next to him. He moves away from me very slightly. We're like two territorial animals in a too-small cage.

Something hard jabs me in the lower back. It is a toy fire engine, wedged behind a cushion. There is also a stray blue sock in the wedge. A sweet wrapper. Yes, a mess in other words. Tom doesn't feel he has to clear it up because he's been looking after Danny. I resent clearing it up because it's Not My Sofa. When we came back from Toronto, I was looking forward to being reunited with my ancient George Smith from my single girl flat. It is upholstered in floral linen, shredded in places by the claws of long dead family tabby cats: it was once owned by my mother. And it was a sofa that I could have let Danny go wild on without worry. But Tom wanted something better, now that we – i.e., he – can almost afford it. So we have to sit on this hard, modern green thing and my lovely old George Smith is festering away in storage. Recently I've been wondering if there are parts of me in storage too.

'You know what the books say. Bad habits and all that.' Tom rotates his socked foot. It is a blue striped M&S sock. Just the sight of it infuriates me. It's as if the blue striped M&S sock represents everything that's wrong with our relationship, a pilled cotton-mix unsexy symbol of the great differential between courtship and marriage. God, I hate this sock. I hate it so much I think it hates me back.

'Your mother . . .' I stop. I want to tell him what Rona said but the words stick in my throat like a sharp fishbone.

He looks guilty. I'm now certain he knows what she said. 'Yeah?'

'She was on vitriolic form. She said I was—'

Tom winces. 'Shit. Sweetheart, we both know what she's like. Don't let her get to you. She means well, although maybe it doesn't look like it sometimes.' He moves up to me on the sofa and shrugs an arm around my shoulders. It is a husband's habitual gesture, reassuring, not passionate, and a way of quieting me. I go along with it, not wanting to dig it all up either, not having the energy to get angry again. I curl my body into his familiar, barrel-shaped chest with its deep underground sounds that vibrate in his ribcage like echoes in a cave. I always used to say to him if he were a building he'd be a Victorian rail-station, all girders and sweeping arches. He says I'd be a conservatory: brittle, sharp but full of light and flowers.

I've always loved the chunky solidity of Tom's body. That and his smell, of course. I've dumped perfectly lovely men because they didn't smell quite right; you know, that horrid whiff of bad breath or scalp, like the tang of cow parsley. Not even the most expensive aftershave can hide a man's true smell. Sure I had doubts about Tom when we first met – he seemed too cocksure, too good looking for me with his pale blue eyes and endearingly scruffy tufty hair – but I was swayed by the smell of his skin: surprising, organic, woody almost. I decided that the smell was a clue to the kind and funny soul beneath the Paul Smith suit. It made me think that although we were really different in so many ways, where it really matters, where our roots were tangled, we connected. Plus I loved the way his eyes twinkled with filthy thoughts. I fancied the pants off him.

Tom says he knew in one split second at Lara's wedding that I was The One. Earlier in the evening he was sitting next to his demure date, the lovely Lucinda Lawn, watching me on the dance floor, apparently whirling around in abandon, arms in the air, hair tousled, feet bare (shoes were killing me) and laughing loudly (too much bubbly). He said he knew we'd get married at that moment. It was like a strobe light flashing in his brain. He dumped the lovely Lucinda the next morning and besieged me with phone calls, begging me for lunch. I was too hung over to say anything but yes.

But I was convinced it wouldn't last. When it came to women Tom was too successful. It unnerved me. Yes, he was a catch. But he had History. Whilst I'd had two imperfect but serious relationships bridged by expanses of very single singledom, Tom had had so many dates and dalliances that I soon realised that if we went to a party together and the host was one of his mates then chances were he'd have been entangled at one time or another with most of the women in the room. Lord knows how the lovely Lucinda coped with this. Charming, good looking and energetically boyish, women loved him despite themselves. I couldn't understand why he was with me. 'It's true. You're not my type at all, Sadie,' he'd say in those sex-soaked early days, pulling up my sweater and kissing a path from nipple to belly button. 'I used to go for willowy blondes. What's happened to me? You're a bonkers brunette. But I love you truly, madly, deeply. I want you barefoot and pregnant. I want you to be mine for ever.' I giggled, unable to hold back the fizz of happiness that I was so wary of, and told him my earnest little theory about our connecting roots. He laughed and slapped my bare bottom and pulled me back on top of him, calling me his 'naughty little flower girl'. He hasn't done that for a while.

I wouldn't blame him for dropping the 'naughty' – my naughtiness disappeared when I had Danny and embarked on an ongoing mission to fill up my sleep tank, with its Danny-shaped leak. As for the 'little'? Fair dos, I'm two dresses heavier these days. But he hasn't called me his 'flower girl' for a long time either. I know I'm thirty-four now but I cannot help but wonder. Have I changed or has Tom? Or have we both changed each other, marriage itself being a kind of heated form of containment that makes a relationship lose its original shape like a favourite silk top in a tumble dryer.

Yes, I fell unexpectedly pregnant – dodgy condom moment in a yellow Mini in a New Forest car park, it happens you know – nine months into our relationship. We married soon after that. Since then life has hurtled forward – relocation, baby, no sleep – with barely enough time to catch a breath, certainly not to properly think or spend quality time together, not in the way that couples who date for two or three years before marrying do. Not in the way that I'm sure Tom and the lovely Lucinda would have done, had they stayed together and had she managed to drag him up the aisle.

I stroke Tom's belly, feeling an overwhelming urge to prove Rona wrong, to claw back those feelings we had when we first met. My fingers walk the familiar route beneath Tom's shirt, one step, two steps, between the buttonholes. I know I should be more adventurous. But there's usually such a small window to have sex without interruption these days that it's best just to stick to the time-tested routes rather than get lost on the long way round. (The days of urgent sex in New Forest car parks are, sadly, over.) But also, more curiously, I find that the longer Tom and I are married the more inhibited we both get, as if our mutual familiarity has created a weird new kind of self-consciousness born of expectation. Maybe one day I will indeed plunge a finger where the sun don't shine or wear a black rubber gimp mask but right now I'm going to stick with what I know. So I stroke my fingers into the thick fuzz of coarse hair on his belly that arrows towards the willy I once named, in happier times, the leaning tower of Pisa, on account of its impressive size and its predilection to lean left. 'Danny's asleep. It's been a horrible couple of days. Let's make up.'

Tom stiffens. Not like that. He tenses. He coughs. 'Not now, Sadie.'

This rejection makes me even keener to have sex, partly to mend the day and fix the row but also, in all honesty, because I'm mid-cycle and I could be ovulating. There are only three or four nights every month that I initiate sex and these nights are usually the very same three or four nights that Tom, curiously enough, doesn't want to touch me, which just goes to disprove every sexpert's theory about men behaving like lascivious goats whenever any woman within a one hundred yard radius is in her fertile period. 'Shussh.'

'Sweetheart, I'm fried. Work . . .'

My hand goes floppy. I pull it out from under his

shirt. 'Is this because of the Anderson lunch disaster or is it something else?'

Tom turns towards me, his heavily lashed blue eyes look a little desperate. 'Let's not over-analyse. I'm just tired.'

'I think we should talk about it.'

'Sorry, Sadie. Not now. I'm so knackered I can barely think straight and I've still got to prepare for this nightmare meeting first thing on Monday.'

It feels like I'm stuck in one of those anxiety dreams: I am running late for an incredibly important appointment but the faster I run the further I have to go. Danny's sibling isn't even a twinkle in the eye yet, more a glower. The gap between them is growing bigger and bigger. As is the distance between me and Tom. 'But—'

'Please, don't make it worse.' He presses the bridge of his nose with his fingers and looks away. 'Look, Sadie, we need to concentrate on getting our marriage back on track before we make any other commitments. I'm not trying for another child now. It would be irresponsible.'

'Who mentioned children? What about sex?'

He looks sad all of a sudden. 'Come on, Sadie. I'm not stupid.'

'Why? Why don't you want another one?'

'Not just yet. Not until . . .' he pauses. '. . . we're in a better place.'

I inch away from him and fold into myself, pulling my legs towards my chest. Inside a silent scream rises up through my belly and fills the room with white noise.

'For God's sake, why not now?' I try to make my voice sound normal but it comes out all annoying and squeaky, half woman, half gerbil.

'Because . . .' Tom strokes the back of my neck. He smiles a deflated, apologetic smile. It reminds me of the kind of smile a couple of ex-boyfriends delivered before they dumped me from a great height with the words, 'I love you, but I'm not in love with you.'

'We're not ready.'

'We are!' I've had enough of compromise. All that democratic marriage baloney. I want to be a dictator, just for a while. It would be for the greater good. We can work out our marriage later.

'Your mum's died. You're grieving. You need to heal.'

'Why do you keep coming out with all this psychological claptrap? You're not a therapist.' My voice isn't squeaky now. Oh no. I stand up and look at him like he is the most risible human being on the planet and I don't even want to be in the same universe as him, let alone the same room, and like his willy is less leaning tower of Pisa, more peanut.

'Well, maybe it wouldn't be the worst thing in the world for you to see a therapist. One minute you're stoned off your head like a teenager . . .'

'It's called having fun?' Tom used to love the fact that I liked to have fun, that I wasn't one of those women obsessed by their weight, or looks, or money. Now that's being turned against me.

'In your state of mind I'd call it drug abuse.'

'Since when did you start channelling the morals of the fucking Bible belt? You've changed, Tom. You're so uptight. You've turned into a suit!'

Tom buttons up his shirt. 'Oh, please. If you have an issue with it then you shouldn't have married me.'

'Perhaps I shouldn't,' I say and immediately regret it because I don't actually mean it and there is a flash of hurt in Tom's eyes. He looks down to hide it. He hates showing his hurt. (In all the time I've known him I've never seen him cry.) Now I'm trapped by what I've said, a bloody-minded part of me digs deeper. 'And if you wanted a Stepford wifelet you shouldn't have married me. You should have married Lucinda Lawn! I'd rather hang myself on my own florist wire than become your plus one.'

'For fuck's sake.' His cheeks have gone red, making his stubble follicles white. This only happens when he's explosively pissed off.

I suddenly realise that we're not arguing about the baby, not even the lunch, or Stepford wifelets. We're arguing about a hundred things – some of them yet to identify themselves – and they're all funnelling down into the aperture of this conversation like grains of hot sand.

He puts his head in his hands. 'You seem so angry with me, Sadie. About my job. I honestly don't under-stand why you're so resentful of playing a supportive role.'

'You sound like your mother. Anyway, be precise, you mean a wifely role.'

He hesitates. 'Well, yes, I suppose.'

'Funny. I wasn't aware I'd signed up for a full-time unpaid post. I thought I'd fallen in love and got married in the twenty-first century.'

He looks genuinely bewildered. 'What's embarrassing or compromising about being there for your husband?'

'Like the other Anderson wives, you mean?'

'Why are you so dismissive of them? I don't get it. It's as if you think they are stupid, that they're beneath you.'

I snort. I actually find the slick, groomed Anderson wives, such as Perfect Pam, terrifying, completely terrifying and intimidating. I feel like I fall short. But I'm too proud to say this so I don't correct him.

'You say you want another baby, Sadie, that you'd like a brood of babies, and to live on a hill in Wales or something ridiculous but we're not coping very well with just one, are we? You don't think it through. You live in some abstract universe. You don't think about the boring details, little things like bills or mortgages or . . .' He closes his eyes and presses his fingertips into the lids. 'We've been teetering on the brink of chaos since we came to London.'

'You choose to work these ridiculous hours!'

'Choose? Are you totally mad? Have you any idea how cut-throat things are? We're not in Toronto now. This is London. It's a bear pit filled with scared, testosterone-pumped fighting bears. And that's just the women.'

'Oh, come on. You sound like David Brent. It's a bloody international corporate speakers' agency not MI5.'

'I don't care what you think . . .'

'I know that.'

'I want this directorship, Sadie. I *really* want it. It's the first chance I've had to really make something of myself in my career and actually secure things for the family.' He shakes his head. 'Anyway, you're the one who insists on still working, even though you don't have to now. It doesn't make you happy. You're not coping. I mean, look at the place.' He pauses. 'Look at you.'

'Me?' A hush drops over the room like a bell jar. I glance at my reflection in the deco mirror above the fireplace. That's me. Sadie Hannah Drew, mother of one, wife of Tom Charles Harrison of Kensal Rise, daughter of Margot Drew, recently deceased, and John Drew, recently shacked up with Loretta Tracy Norris and currently diving off Mexico. OK, I look a bit worn around the edges. Jeans. Muddy trainers. A holey cashmere jumper with a bit of melted Jaffa Cake on the cuff. Is that so bad? Do Tom's friends secretly think, 'Thank fuck I didn't marry that Sadie Drew. Nice girl. But what a handful, and what a hicky scruff. Poor old Tom.'

Sniffing back tears I retreat into the kitchen. I've blown it again. The more I raise the issue of the baby, the deeper he digs in, and the more of an issue it becomes. And of course the more of an issue it becomes the more explosive it becomes and the more reason Tom has to think we're not ready. A horrible catch 22. God, I hate his rationalisations, his lack of impulsive emotional response. Who cares if everything isn't perfect? Life isn't perfect! And how on earth can I be the happy wife when the one thing I really want – another baby – is being denied me? No, I can't see the way out. Digging my hands into my pockets I slump miserably against the wall. My fingernail catches on the corner of something stiff inside my left pocket. What's this? I pull it out. A creamy white card. Enid Fisher, it reads, followed by a smart St John's Wood address. Funny old bird. I walk to the bin, press my foot on the pedal. The lid lifts up. I stand there for a few moments, holding the card over the bin. But something stops me. I don't throw it away.

Five

My bruise is like a little yellow cloud. I touch it lightly
with the fingers of my left hand as I drive to New
Covent Garden Market, the dawn skies pink above the
streets of Vauxhall. I choose my flowers for the day, big
bunches of lilies, tulips and ranunculus, and stock up on
foliage and foam from my sundry man, nod at Wayne,
Dom and Nick, all the cockney flower boys who make
the market a sunny place even at the darkest ungodly
hour, always there with a funny aside and a discount.
Real men. I grin. This is my world, my secret London
world, like one of those snow globes encased in plastic,
little citadels, of the city but independent of it, with
its own rules, hours and smells. Whereas at home I
struggle to remember how long a ready-meal has been in
the microwave and forget to buy milk or bread, here
I am punctual, organised. It's not a struggle. By 9 a.m. I
am driving west.

Beep! A man slams his horn and pokes a bald head
out of his car. 'The lights. Move it, lady!'

I step on the accelerator, turn the corner into the heart of St John's Wood. I check the house number again. Yes, this one. Blimey. I thought Enid Fisher's address might be a mansion flat, perhaps a mews. But this is a house, a really rather grand house, Regency, painted pale grey, a little faded but a proper multi-million-pound pad, the kind that might get snapped up by a rich Russian, gutted and redeveloped with swimming pools and screening rooms. There is a black wrought iron gate, its ironwork intricate – garlands of flowers – and an eight foot fence swagged in dark, glossy ivy. As I approach, the heavy black gates swing open, jerkily, stopping a couple of times, before finally yawning wide to reveal a gravel drive; beyond this, a path contained within a tunnel of high, dark hedges, leading towards a large hyacinth-blue door. I wonder who has buzzed me in. I step out of the car and look around. The smell of lavender hangs heavily in the air. I hear a squelchy sound – the sound of digging? – coming from somewhere beyond the high hedge. 'Hello?'

The gates shut behind me. A man-shape shadow moves behind the hedge. I feel uneasy, tighten my grip on the car keys.

The man appears carrying a spade. He is tall, weatherbeaten so hard to age, but possibly in his late thirties with a head of wild corkscrew curls, greying above the ears. 'You the florist?' he asks sullenly. His mouth looks slightly too large for his face.

'Yes.' I notice his eyes are a startling ivy-green against his tan. 'Sadie, Sadie Drew.'

'Eddie,' he says, looking at me warily. 'Your car full of tricks?'

'Flowers. Is Mrs Fisher at home?'

He nods, walks up to the front door and pushes it open with thick, muddy fingers. Unlocked, it opens a few inches. He cranes his head round the door. 'Angie, the new florist's here.'

I hear small, light footsteps. A Filipino lady in her fifties. She has dark, silver-streaked hair pulled into a neat ponytail, black dancing eyes. 'Please come in, madam.'

I step into the hallway, a large square space, the polished oak floorboards dappled by the red and green light that drops through the stained glass windows. The walls are covered in photographs, old black and white photographs of ladies in 1930s silk dresses, flowers in their hair, cocktails in their hands, handsome men with their arms looped around their hand-span waists. There are African masks on the wall too, big faces with googly eyes and teeth like tools, an umbrella stand, a pale grey coat hanging from an ivory peg, an enormous fan made from peacock feathers hanging on the wall, a wastepaper bin that appears to have been made from an elephant's foot. Not your average St John's Wood house. From the hall, a large wide staircase covered in a thick lilac-coloured carpet sweeps upwards. It is down this staircase that Mrs Fisher walks slowly, haughtily, bejewelled liver-spotted hand on the banister. She's wearing a cream tailored dress, with gossamer thin blue and green scarves around her neck, and a matching silk turban whipped around her head like piped icing. She looks like an improbable cross between something from a vintage *Vogue* illustration and *Dynasty*. 'Sadie?' she smiles. 'I'm so very pleased you've come.'

'Thanks,' I say, a little lost for words at Mrs Fisher's unexpected glamour.

She smiles at her housekeeper. 'I'll deal with the florist, Angie. Now, Sadie, do you have my precious black tulips?'

'Queen of the Night, as you requested on the phone. I'll fetch them from the car.'

Mrs Fisher nods. I bring in two cardboard boxes of purple-black tulips, my sundry bag and a white and pink stripy apron which I tie around my waist. 'You said you have your own containers?' I pluck one tulip out of the box and follow her into the kitchen. It's a large, sunny room painted pale pink with a long wooden table in the middle, polished to a high shine like an enormous lump of dark chocolate. The table is flanked by six beautiful wooden chairs, the kind of chairs that look like they've been sat on for generations, shiny with the friction of backs and bottoms. Above the marble work-tops, copper kitchenware dangles from the hooks like polished suns, reflecting light around the room. It makes my cluttered Ikea kitchen look like a dingy caravan kitchenette.

'Ah,' she says, brushing the petals of the tulip against her chin. 'Gorgeous. The colour of a Sri Lankan foot.'

I laugh. 'That's a new one.'

'My husband's favourite flower.' She holds the tulip up to the light and turns it slowly like someone checking a wine glass for smears.

'He's got excellent taste, Mrs Fisher.'

'*Had*, darling, had. He died three years ago. I've had tulips on my kitchen table ever since, black whenever I can get them.'

'Oh, I'm sorry.'

'No matter. He's still with me,' she says breezily, blue eyes sparkling in the powdered creases of her face. 'We were married for fifty-eight years. You kind of become each other after that amount of time. And as long as I'm still here to read and dance and gaze at tulips, so is he.'

Ah, I see. Mad as a hat stand. 'Shall I work in the kitchen or would you rather I use another room?' Perhaps I'll get sent to a servant's quarters or something. Hell, there's room in this house.

'Here is perfect. But do sit, darling. Must be a devil on one's back.'

I sit carefully on one of the wooden chairs, unpack my grubby looking mechanics from their beaten leather bag, feeling a little awkward as she watches. Most clients don't hang around. They leave me to get on with it. I am staff after all and quite happy with my below stairs role, in fact I prefer it. But Mrs Fisher doesn't look like she's going anywhere. She's watching me intently, smiling gently, as if something about me amuses her. 'Glass of water?' she asks eventually.

'That would be lovely, thank you. I hope you got home from the park that day without getting too wet, Mrs Fisher.'

'Oh I got soaked, soaked to the skin!' Her eyes light up. 'But I loved it, didn't you? All that wind and blossom! Such drama. And I love Regent's Park. I get so terribly bored of the heath, one does after seventy-odd years.' Mrs Fisher opens a few kitchen doors before she locates her glasses. She fills one with water then reaches for a packet of menthol cigarettes on a shelf, offers me the glass, then a cigarette. I notice her fingernails are perfectly square and buffed.

'No, thank you. I don't smoke.' Florists, like nannies, aren't meant to smoke. It damages the flowers. Clients normally don't like the idea of smoking florists either. It ruins their image of us as pastoral, fresh, organic creatures.

'Nobody does these days. Such a shame. I adore smoking.' She inserts a cigarette into a long black holder, lights it with a match. 'Don't you just hate all these laws, all these bloody doctors pretending that we can all be immortal if only we didn't do this, didn't do that?'

I think of my mum – she'd agree absolutely – and laugh.

'Quackery, sheer quackery. Death comes knocking no matter what you do. Better to be smoking and smiling when the grim reaper arrives than grimacing on a treadmill, don't you think? What's that silly old Wilde quote again? "One can survive everything nowadays, except death . . ." Or some such.' She imperiously blows out cigarette smoke, which scarves up and collects inside a hanging copper pot like a ghost. 'Life doesn't speed up as you get older, Sadie.' She sits down neatly on a chair, her legs gracefully locked together, falling to one side, the finishing school position. 'All rubbish. Everyone here is intent on dooming me to endless leisure-time, which would be fine if Albert was around of course. But a little less fun on your own.' She smiles. 'There's actually a limit to the number of books you can read in a day, especially with my eyesight, and I refuse to go the way of audio books. It would be like resigning to a wheelchair.'

'I quite agree, Mrs Fisher,' I laugh, relaxing a little. 'Have to say, love your turban.'

She smooths it with her hand. 'Thank you. I do sometimes worry that it makes me look a little mad, you know in that particularly tragic way that English women do go mad, the ones who never have children? We become caricatures of ourselves because we have too much time on our hands, always have done. A lifetime of vanity with only ourselves and our husbands and our lovely houses to think about,' she adds wryly. 'The word tulip was originally derived from the Persian word for turban, you know.'

'I didn't know. How fascinating. May I ask where you keep the vases, Mrs Fisher?'

'Pantry. If you can find them. It's rather a mess. Angie, my housekeeper, dear Angie, she keeps forgetting about the pantry. She forgets whole parts of the house sometimes.' She laughs. 'We both do. It's too big for just the two of us. We're like silly old dolls rattling around a doll's house.' She points to a small door. The air is cool and undisturbed in here. Amongst the tins of food, coffee and biscuits, there are a selection of crystal vases and two big earthenware urns of a classical design. I pick up an urn and take it back to the table. 'May I use this, Mrs Fisher, or would you rather use the crystal?'

'My last florist, Paula, only ever used the crystal. She was a bit like that. Couldn't see the beauty in a bit of humble clay. You know the type.'

I do know the type. And I wonder about Paula and why she is no longer here. But it would be impertinent to ask. Florists don't ask personal questions.

'From the hills of Sri Lanka, outside Kandy.' She runs her fingers around the urn's rim wistfully. 'Albert and I lived there for about ten years. He was a diplomat. As you can see when we came back to London we imported half of the country.' She smiles, a wide smile, exposing even, ivory teeth. She must have been a bit of a stunner in her youth. 'Right!' she says, clapping her hands together. 'I will leave you in peace, Sadie. Or would you like some music? What a silly question. Of course you would like music.' She switches on a stereo, turns up the volume and Frank Sinatra's voice begins to build like a wall. Then she turns on her heel and swishes out of the room trailing a cloud of chiffon scarves. Of course, as soon as she has gone I have a bit of a nose. One of the perks of the job. I note the expensive Fortnum and Mason teas, the Indian silver tea set, the tortoiseshell hairbrush on the shelf, the spotlessness of the Aga which looks like it's never been used. I walk over to the window and look out at the garden. I'm hit by a wave of longing. It is a beautiful, large, colourful garden, walled, the kind you might get in the country, neatly tended with ornamental bushes, clumps of lavender and honeysuckle that hang off weather-worn trellising. There is also a trellis arch, covered in what look like grapevines, and white wrought iron garden furniture. Beneath an apple tree at the back of the garden is a swinging bench. Hidden in the borders are small statues, their stone faces green and mossy, staring back like wide-eyed children.

Someone coughs behind me. I turn around, guiltily. It is the moody gardener, his ivy-green eyes flashing. 'What's the fee?'

'Excuse me?'

'How much are you charging my aunt?'

Aunt? 'A hundred and fifty.'

Eddie looks at me sternly. 'Listen, don't take her for a ride. I'm sick of people thinking they can charge her whatever they like because she's old and lives at a good address.'

'Mrs Fisher asked me to come here,' I interrupt, incensed that he could even think such a thing. 'I wouldn't ever—'

'OK,' he says more softly now. 'Sorry.' Then without another word he leaves the room.

Well, I won't come back here again! The rudeness! I get down to work, slicing the ends of the tulips at an angle, bunching them into harmonious clumps, so that there is a rhythm in their sizing, the smaller buds playing off the larger, more mature ones. I arrange them in the earthenware urns, in time to Sinatra. There are so many tulips. And soon I am lost in my task, as I always am, the bend of the stems, the feel of the firm stalk skin between my fingers. My foot taps on the marble floor. Sinatra sings 'Love and Marriage' – something about love, horses and carriages. As my fingers work, Rona's mouth comes into view, her plumped-up Prenwooded mouth – 'You need to support your husband' – and my fingers work faster. Suddenly Sinatra booms into 'Too Marvellous for Words'. I stop still. Our song. The first dance at our wedding. And I feel as if it were yesterday, not three years ago. Tom's arms around my thickening waist. I really was beginning to show then. Me laughing as I catch a bit of white tulle wedding dress on the heel of my gold sandal. The lovely feeling of the freesias on my head that I'd twisted into a garland crown. Feeling more beautiful than I'd ever felt, despite my small pregnant bump, looking forward to a future, a family. But these images are swiftly, brutally, replaced by others, like a garish, loud ad break interrupting a soft romantic drama: the disastrous lunch at The Ivy, Rona's mouth moving, Teddy yapping, Tom flinching away from me on the sofa. Then the song stops with a jaunty ba-boom! To my horror I realise that there are tears trickling down my cheeks. And, worse, far worse, Mrs Fisher is leaning against the kitchen door silently watching me, her red painted mouth twitching from side to side but otherwise expressionless. Mortified, I wipe the tears away with my sleeve.

'Frank has that effect I'm afraid,' she says with such kindness that I fear I'm going to start blubbing all over again. She doesn't look embarrassed or make excuses to leave but continues to stand there watching me, as if waiting for something.

'Oh, just a terrible cold!'

'Of course.' She walks over to the urn of black tulips and touches a flower lightly. 'Lovely.'

I smile, trying not to make ugly snotty noises as I sniff. The tulips do look rather beautiful, surprisingly so considering the uniformity of their darkness. I was worried they'd be too gloomy.

Mrs Fisher's eyes flick from my fingers to my face and a smile flickers at the corner of her mouth, as if she's struggling to hide her pleasure in finding me thus undone. 'Marriage problems?'

I pick up the last tulip and place it in the vase, run my fingers through their stems so that they fall outwards prettily like the rays of the sun. 'I may as well walk around with "marriage problems" tattooed across my forehead.'

'Oh, don't worry. No one else would know.' She taps her forehead with her nails, her diamond rings flashing.

'A sixth sense, darling. I knew the moment I met you in the park.'

'Oh.' I smile and wonder why I don't feel more embarrassed that I have been caught blubbering to Frank Sinatra.

'Is that why you came here today?' Her hands excitedly twist her scarves, as if she cannot bear the suspense. 'It is, isn't it?'

'I came here to do your flowers, Mrs Fisher.' Although something about the way she's looking at me – amused, unconvinced – makes me doubt myself. OK, I suppose I was just a *teeny* bit intrigued by her line about knowing a lot about husbands, however bonkers it sounded. It seemed serendipitous that I met her and not long after Rona declared my marriage to be in a state of emergency. And, a bit spookily, I just couldn't throw her card away. Something odd and powerful prevented my fingers from releasing that stiff white card into the rancid cavern of our kitchen bin. 'Where would you like me to put the vases, Mrs Fisher? Would you like a vase in each sitting room?' I ask briskly, trying to uphold some kind of professionalism.

A new expression I haven't seen before flickers across her face, a fleeting contraction of lines, then it's gone. 'The sitting room to the left of the stairs only.' She nods towards a large, grand moulded door with a cut glass door knob. 'That room is off limits. You can peek into any room, cupboard or jewellery box in the house, but that room is my private little kingdom.'

'Understood,' I say, thinking of the room in my own house that is shut, sacred and private.

'The other vase can stay and cheer me up in the kitchen. Now, a cup of tea?'

'You're too kind, Mrs Fisher, but I really must go.'

'I will certainly take grave offence if you decline my cup of tea. And you know that one must not offend old ladies, especially ones in turbans.' She puts a feather-light hand on my arm and smiles kindly. 'Besides, tea is an excellent antidote for every spectrum of human colds.'

Resignedly I sit back down on one of the wooden chairs, sensing that she's not going to give up easily. She calls Angie who makes tea in a patterned gold and turquoise teapot. Then Mrs Fisher sits down, hands clasped in her lap. She doesn't speak at first. Just as the silence stretches to the point of awkwardness she says, 'I was happily married for fifty-eight years, Sadie. There is *nothing* I don't know about marriage. Here, look at this photo. Albert. Me and my Albert.' She picks up a framed black and white photograph off a shelf: a handsome man in his thirties with a chisel jaw and a beautiful woman with dark curls and a cinematic face, all light, shadow and cheekbones.

'Very handsome couple.'

'Weren't we? When I was younger, I . . .' She stops and looks up dreamily, eyes roaming the garden out of the back window, pupils shrinking as she focuses on something far away. 'Gosh, it all seems so long ago. But before all my friends died – I'm the last one standing, not dancing, standing – I used to be the one they came to. I used to say that I was far cheaper than a greedy divorce lawyer. A diplomat's wife knows everything there is to know about wifedom, I used to tell them.' She laughs, a loose rattle like the sound of a shaken dry seed pod. 'Me and the girls, did we have a hoot!'

I smile politely. Right. I've got her number. Some clients pay you to do their flowers but are actually paying for a bit of company. I've often thought it something magical about the flowers themselves, these little blasts of hope and colour, that opens people up in unexpected ways.

'Iris, Ruby, Maud . . . Oh, Maud. She died, two years and seven months ago. I miss her, I really do. We'd meet up in Claridge's when I was in town to dissect our marriages, discuss sex in deliberately loud voices to amuse ourselves, all that sort of thing. Quite a stir we made. Gosh, I enjoyed making a stir, don't you?'

I nod but actually I can't remember the last time I created a stir, other than one of embarrassment.

'We'd order the champagne cocktails – no, sorry, Maud liked a Martini – and we'd be deliciously indiscreet. Iris . . .' Mrs Fisher laughs at some ancient private joke. Actually it's more of a schoolgirl giggle and strangely incongruous in someone her age. 'Ah, I apologise for rattling on, Sadie. Old age. Not enough distraction. The mind flips back so easily. It's like turning the pages of a book.'

'No, it's fascinating.' Right one here.

'I don't know about that. But we certainly thought *we* were fascinating,' she laughs. 'We all thought we were the most marvellous wives too of course. Without much justification.' She smiles kindly. 'Now I am sure you really *are* a marvellous wife, Sadie.'

'Actually I fear I am quite the world's worst wife,' I say, taking a sip of Earl Grey tea from a small bone china cup.

Mrs Fisher throws back her head and laughs, really laughs, from the belly so that the jewelled brooch on her lapel shakes. Her age seems to fall away and I think, for a moment, I can see her in her youth, laugh like champagne, dark curls clustered around her face. Yes, there's *something* about Mrs Fisher. Strangely, I feel an odd, most unlikely and totally unexplainable affinity with her. It was there in the park. It is here now. 'Oh, I'm sorry, my darling. But that's quite the funniest thing.' She pats my hand. 'I am sure that you are *not* the world's worst wife although, gosh, I wish you were. That would make my decade.'

'I am.' I have caught her giggles now and for a moment I quite forget about the extreme oddness of the situation, the fact that we're strangers, that she's my client. 'Honestly.'

'Goodness, you remind me so much of . . .' She stops. 'Go on, tell me why you're so bad. Humour me.'

'Let me think. There are a wealth of examples to choose from. Well, I refuse to take his suits to the dry cleaners,' I say, wanting to entertain her. 'On principle.'

She shakes her head. 'Oh dear. Principles are dreadfully dull things, darling.'

'My brain kind of shuts down when it comes to all that domestic stuff. I hate the idea that he expects *me* to do it because I earn less than he does and I am a woman. He didn't expect me to do it when I was his girlfriend. No, then he valued me for my independence and unwifely indifference to fuss and food and domestics. He wanted someone unlike his mother.'

Mrs Fisher laughs. 'He said that?'

'He did. He said most men did marry their mothers, subconsciously at least, but he was the exception to the rule.'

She shakes her head. 'Men have a wonderful capacity to deceive themselves.'

'They do! I tell you, Mrs Fisher, the moment we got married and had a child, it's like a switch flicked in his brain and he started to see me as A Wife. And it's got far, far worse since we got back to London from Toronto – we'd been there over two years – and he's taken on this big job. He's trying to prove . . . something.'

'Ah. I see,' says Mrs Fisher, more thoughtful now. 'Still, I don't think you qualify as a bad wife. Is that all?'

'God, no. Last week I shrank all his precious new John Smedley cashmere in the wash.' I cough, feeling a little ashamed. It was the fourth night in a row he'd worked until 10 p.m. and I was pissed off. 'On purpose.'

She raises one sharply plucked eyebrow and her

forehead crinkles. It strikes me that actually there's nothing too horrible about old age, not if you present yourself nicely. I like the way her life is etched on her face. I much prefer it to Rona's embalmed look. 'Go on.'

'I am two dress sizes bigger than when we first met. I think he has to accept me the way I am but—'

'My darling, it's the little things that destroy a marriage, not the big issues. The big issues one can fight a good, honest, bloody battle over. The small things just eat away silently from inside, like termites demolishing a house.'

'Oh.' Is my weight a big or small issue? I suck my belly in and pursue the matter no further.

'More please.' She drums her fingers on the table.

'Er . . .' I smile, trying to pick out one of my thousands of daily cock-ups. 'Well, I nag him. Rather he says I nag him, which I don't. About working late. About not helping out enough with Danny.'

She shakes her head, growing more serious. 'This is not good. Not good at all. Men don't hear things in repetition. The more often you say something the better they get at blocking it out completely. Their brains are quite extraordinary like that. They can slam them shut like a door.'

'OK. But he doesn't help, not in the way I want him to. When he does help, it's an event. He gets this smug look on his face. But he doesn't do the day-to-day stuff, the non-event stuff. It's like he wants a medal for taking

Danny to nursery when I do it ninety-nine per cent of the time and he never even notices.'

'You do sound cross.' She takes a sip of tea, holding the handle daintily between her fingers in a way that people under forty never do, and puts the cup back on the saucer. 'Now, my dear, regular fellatio?'

Oh. My. God. *Fellatio?* I am so stunned that for a moment I can't speak at all.

'I didn't think so.'

'Birthdays,' I say in a tiny voice, staring at my muddy fingernails, disarmed by her candidness. 'Birthdays, anniversaries, that kind of thing.'

There is a deafening pause. 'I think I've heard enough.'

Oh. I was on a roll there. I was about to come clean about the fact I broke wind in bed this morning. And the time I threw my mobile phone at his head and it gave him a black eye the night before an important meeting. Or the time I made him sleep on the sofa on Valentine's night because he bought me a hand-blender instead of flowers, saying that he thought I'd had enough of flowers. A hand-blender? I almost went at him with it whirring.

Angie pokes her head into the kitchen. 'Ready for your elevenses, Mrs Fisher?'

Mrs Fisher stares at her for a few moments. 'No. No thank you, Angie. Not today. I'm far too busy.'

Angie looks puzzled. 'No elevenses, madam?'

'I think not,' she says thoughtfully, twisting her chiffon scarves. 'I'll skip them today.'

I jump up. 'Oh, please, don't let me interrupt anything. I must be getting . . .'

She looks at Angie. 'That will be all for now, thank you, Angie.' Angie leaves. Mrs Fisher has a quiet authority.

'Mrs Fisher, it's been a real, unexpected pleasure,' I say, suddenly a bit weirded out by the turn in conversation. 'But I must pick up my son from nursery.'

She pats my arm. 'Call me Enid, please. Now if you do want any tips, any tips at all, I'd love to give them. I never grow bored of the sound of my own voice. The pleasure would be absolutely all mine.'

'That's very sweet of you, Mrs . . . Sorry, Enid. But . . .'

'It's not sweet of me at all. I find other people's marriages hugely intriguing, far more compelling than any book, always have done. You'd be indulging me, not the other way round.' She claps her hands. 'I tell you what. You bring me tulips, I'll help you bloom into the perfect wife. Now doesn't that sound irresistible?'

Six

Ten minutes late for nursery today. I'm gradually getting faster, shaving seconds off my time every morning, like an unfit runner getting fitter. Thing is, I'm reluctant to improve too much. Being late has certain advantages. Firstly, you avoid the awkwardness of having to make polite chit-chat with Scary Hanna, Danny's disapproving key worker. Secondly, if you're the last to arrive all Danny's little friends are already there so there's more distraction and less reason – not that he needs a reason, of course – to cling on to my legs and wail, which breaks my heart to smithereens and makes me want to scoop him up, carry him home in my arms and feed him peeled grapes and Smarties. (Possibly his intention.) Thirdly, I don't have to interact quite so convincingly with the other mothers if I'm late. I don't have to coo over their new babies or enquire politely into their endless, blooming pregnancies. I swear I live in London's most fecund postcode, a sort of battery farm for raising children with absurd showbiz names.

'Bye, Danny!' I wave. 'Love you.' The nursery door slams behind me. I walk down the concrete path, trying to digest the rather surreal events at Enid Fisher's house yesterday. My digestion is interrupted by an unavoidable social situation on the horizon: Perfect Pam, fellow Anderson & Co wife and therefore witness to my recent humiliation at The Ivy, Queen of Pregnant, owner of the most splendid breasts in London and master of cupcakery, is, most uncharacteristically, late too. She is actually the reason I am here, scuttling down West Kids nursery's concrete path. When Tom joined Anderson it was on her recommendation, via her husband Seth, that we sent Danny here. Obviously I should be grateful. But actually I just feel unwillingly indebted.

Shit, she's seen me. She's waiting in ambush at the nursery gate, where the path meets the liberation of the pavement. She rests one hand on her neat round bump – the proportions of a mixing bowl – the other is holding one of those slightly irritating 'I'm Not A Plastic Bag' canvas bags, out of which pops the head of a nutty brown loaf. (I'm swinging a lurid planet-killer plastic bag filled with a pair of 'accident' pants soiled by Danny at nursery yesterday. Class.)

'Hi, Sadie. Goodness. That's some bruise.' She puts her hand across her mouth and looks at my forehead in horror, as if part of it were actually missing.

'Oh that.' I'd quite forgotten. 'War wound. It's nothing. I got caught out in that freaky storm last weekend. Got walloped by a flying branch in Regent's Park. Yes, as you do.'

Perfect Pam looks a little unsure. 'Are you OK?'

'Looks worse than it is.' I still find it unimaginable that Pam was once a girl about town – Chloe's circle, for God's sake – who held down a senior PR job and used to dance on podiums in nightclubs well beyond dawn. She had pop star boyfriends and even did a stint in A&E having her stomach pumped after taking one too many narcotics in Glastonbury's Green Field. But Pam now is, well, she's Perfect Pam, wholesome, sweet, as if she exists strictly on the milk of freshly suckled Devon cows and organic superfoods. Unlined by London, or work, or life itself it seems, let alone the improbable past excesses that Chloe tells me about, Pam is the kind of woman I imagine most men would love to marry: efficient, always smiling, huge knockers – tantalisingly glimpsed today in an unbuttoned Persil-white shirt – mumsy enough not to be threatening, glamorous enough for them to want to show her off. Even though we are of similar age she makes me feel like a hapless sulky, bulky teenager.

'You're amazing, Sadie. If it were me I'd take to bed for at least a week and use the excuse to delegate my entire family to the nanny. You do battle on, don't you?'

'Muddle on more like it.'

She laughs, as if I am actually joking. 'And I just wanted to say that I really admired your spirit turning up at the Anderson lunch wearing that fantastic T-shirt!'

'I suppose it was too much to hope that people wouldn't notice.'

She laughs and her vast pregnancy breasts swing. 'I think it was brilliant!' Everything in Perfect Pam's world is Brilliant! Fantastic! and comes with exclamation marks. 'You made the rest of us Anderson wives look so stuffy and overdone in our silly summer dresses!'

'I would have paid thousands for a silly summer dress at that point but thank you all the same,' I add gratefully. To be fair, Pam was one of the few wives at the lunch to go out of her way to talk to me, rather than look at me like I had stumbled in from the street armed with stolen gardening instruments. I edge past her bump, out of the gate.

'Wednesday night then.' She pushes her bump forward slightly, trapping me between her flesh and the gatepost.

'Wednesday?' I stare at her blankly. Her bump feels hard and full of baby.

'Didn't Tom mention it?' Pam leans back, freeing me, and swings her bag over her shoulder. 'Just a very low-key dinner at mine, totally relaxed . . .'

You always know when someone says a dinner is going to be 'totally relaxed', it'll be anything but.

'I thought it would give us all a better chance to get to know one another.' She sighs. 'It's so easy for us wives to get on because we have so much in common . . .'

We do?

'. . . but the hubbies need a bit of extra help when it

comes to after-hours play, don't you think? It's like you have to arrange play-dates for them.'

Yikes. I feel like she is talking a different language, a happy wife language from a world where wives throw networky dinner parties for their husbands. The only thing I throw at Tom is his unwashed socks, perhaps the odd dinner plate. Standing there on the path, feet twitching towards the gate, I have a quick inner struggle not to find Pam irritating. I tell myself she means well, that I should be thankful to be invited out for dinner. I tell myself that I am a judgemental misery bucket. I consider the possibility that I secretly resent Pam for being pregnant, as if there is a finite number of opportunities for pregnancy in the world and she has taken mine. Yes, Tom was quite right when he said that this irrational Pam irritation, like so many things in life, is My Problem. He also joked that I'm jealous, which isn't as funny as he thinks, implying as it does that I might be justified in being jealous and am therefore further down the wife food chain.

'Give you an excuse to pamper yourself beforehand? I'm sure you're missing all those North American blow-dries, manis and pedis.' She leans back against the gate. 'We've got to that stage in our lives when we have to start making more of an effort, haven't we? God, isn't it a bore? It must be even harder with a husband like Tom.' She rubs her pregnant belly in a circular fashion, round and round like she's polishing a table.

'Sorry?'

'Doesn't he mix with all those glamorous media-types? The speakers and the like? I'd hate it! At least I know Seth is tucked away safely in the finance department with the dull old suits.'

Seth and Pam have always struck me as unmatched in the attraction stakes. It's not just his squashy, strangely foetal face or the fact that he has more hair in his nostrils than on his head. It's more his mannerisms, the way he throws punches at the air when he jogs in his all-in-one Lycra jogging gear around the streets of Kensal Rise. When he's not jogging he walks with his hands clasped behind his back like Prince Charles. He is a man not at home in his own body. Nor a man who looks like he'd be good in bed. He is certainly a man eclipsed by the sensuous milk-top beauty of his wife.

'But I think it's brilliant that you feel that you don't have to compete right now,' perseveres Pam breezily. 'That your marriage is strong enough for you not to have to, you know, play the game.'

'I've always trusted him,' I say weakly. In fact I'd always assumed that if Tom wanted a Botoxed motivational speaker he'd be with one, rather than someone with green florist foam beneath her fingernails. I feel a cold trickle of paranoia run down my spine. What if I'm wrong? Does she know something I don't? A few days ago I didn't realise that my marriage was in such a bad state that I might 'lose everything'.

'Of course. And why *should* you make an effort, Sadie?' Pam pauses, searching for the right words, and speaks in a whispery, collusive voice. 'I know about everything that happened in the last year.' She taps her nose. 'I won't tell anyone, promise. But I just want to say that if anyone's got an excuse, it's you, Sadie, so don't load any more pressure on yourself, honey.'

Seven

Do I really have an excuse? And if I do, how come Perfect Pam, of all bloody people, knows about it? There's only one explanation: Tom must have told her, or maybe he told Seth. Damn Tom. He's so less guarded than me. Whereas it takes me a long time to trust anyone, Tom makes life-long friends in the time it takes to down a pint. Perhaps it's no surprise that he's settled back into London and I haven't.

'You OK, Danny?' I shout downstairs, leaning over the banisters, checking just in case Danny has had a Rona-style accident, electrocuted himself on the remote control or drowned himself in his beaker of orange juice.

'Yeah,' chirps Danny above the sound of cars whizzing around a track on the telly.

I fish out Danny's clean mini-me clothes from the laundry basket and stagger forward with the enormous pile of washing that I've avoided for the last week or two, hence its size, dropping socks and pants as I go. Danny's bedroom smells deliciously of Danny. I love the smell of

Danny. Even the yucky things. I used to sniff his wee-sodden nappies when he was little for that asparagusy tang of baby, my baby. His room is a typical boy's room, filled with books, plastic tools, toy cars and rubber dinosaurs and, oh dear, a mouldy bottle of forgotten half drunk milk rolling beneath his bed. I shove his clothes into the chest of drawers and close his bedroom door. Then I take a deep breath and walk to the far end of the corridor to the room that haunts my dreams. The room of the house that contains my excuse, as Pam puts it. Even though we've only been back a few months I know this door so well, each gloss white panel, the stiffness of its door knob, then its sudden sharp release at about sixty degrees. The door, of course, is shut. It is always shut. I make sure of it. I think of Enid's shut living room door and wonder about the parallels. Maybe we both have rooms that are shut off inside ourselves. Do not trespass! Explosive emotional material inside!

I stand outside for a few moments, steeling myself, then gently push the door open and step on to the coir carpet. It's the smallest bedroom in the house, a teeny rectangular room painted honeysuckle yellow. It's quiet here, still, clean and, unlike the rest of the house, immaculately tidy. It backs on to our small garden, which seems right somehow. Danny's old cot is in the corner. There is a small, empty white chest of drawers along one wall, its drawers lined with scented flowery paper. On the other wall is a tall airing cupboard. Between the two bits of furniture is a chimney breast.

On its mantelpiece is a little jam jar vase containing a solitary flower – a hyacinth at the moment. I will change the water later this evening, every evening, swap the hyacinth for an Alexis rose perhaps. I don't let the flower in this room ever wilt. I always want something to be growing here.

I step towards the airing cupboard, guiltily, greedily, like a binge eater approaching a fridge. The doors swing open easily. On the deep slatted wood shelves is a small stack of neatly folded baby clothes, mostly white, although a few are pink. I was quite certain that she was a girl from the moment I found out I was pregnant. With Danny I craved Marmite and meat, with this one I craved jelly tots, strawberries and ice cream, the sweeter the better. I pull one of the Babygros out of the pile. It is impossibly tiny – 'newborn' it says on the label – shaped like a flattened chicken, crisp, unused, still smelling slightly of shop and heated by the boiler to a warm body temperature. I crush it to my mouth and stay like that for a few moments inhaling it, my eyes filling with tears. She never stood a chance, jettisoned out of my treacherous body far too early. It happened the week after we moved back to London. She is tragic. But she is not an excuse. She is a million dreams and hopes all smashed, like a chandelier dropped to a concrete floor.

I give myself a few moments. Then I fold the Babygro neatly, taking care to keep it pressed and symmetrical, shut the airing cupboard door with a click and resume my normal chaotic self.

Eight

Tom is working late again. Just as well. Supper consists of two liquefying leeks in the fridge and a bowl of pistachios. Chloe and I are drinking Tom's favourite wine because neither of us can be bothered to go to the off-licence. I know that if Tom could see us now he'd be pissed off and the muscle in his jaw would twitch. He doesn't wholly approve of Chloe. I suspect it jars that while we're starring in our own domestic soap opera – 'Asleep on the sofa, part two. Rowing on the sofa, part three' – Chloe, freed from her unfaithful husband and unfettered by children, is living out her very own young divorcee's version of *Sex and the City*. So yes, we're different. She cannot fathom the torrent of emotion, the intensity and neediness of children, how they turn your relationship upside down, turn lovers into domestic taskforces, fill you with such physical yearning. Perhaps I cannot fathom how divorce tests a belief in love. It worries me that Chloe, who was the world's biggest romantic in her twenties, has become so flippant, so

90

ready to dismiss her own potential for falling in love again. Perhaps time has damaged us both a bit, which is worrying since we're only in our thirties and may have another sixty years of damage to go.

'Oh, I don't want any of that silly love bug business,' she says in her throaty London accent, leaning back in the kitchen chair, her body all long and bendy from so much yoga, her beach-blond hair tumbling over her shoulders. 'I'm quite happy with no-strings sex right now. Honestly. Don't look at me like that, Sadie Drew! I am. Not all women . . .'

'Just because your marriage didn't work out doesn't mean nothing will work out.'

'Sadie, my love, while I understand that you're a hippy at heart and would like nothing more than to marry me off to a hirsute young man on a Stonehenge slab and beget a brood of children, you do need to realise that I can imagine nothing, absolutely nothing, worse.'

I laugh and spit out a pistachio shell. 'OK. Point taken. And who am I to advise you anyway? I'm hardly an advert for marriage right now.'

Chloe grins and leans forward on the table. Her earrings – long, dangly silver things – tinkle. 'Sounds like you could be. Now tell me more about this mad old dame in St John's Wood who wants to turn you into the perfect wife. You met in a tornado-like storm? I'm loving it. It's like *The Wizard of Oz*!'

'Yes, and I'm not sure I fancy being Dorothy, thank

you very much. She probably kills florists and buries them in the Provençal lavender borders like an upmarket Rose West.'

'Top up, please.' Chloe taps her empty wine glass. 'There was a time when Sadie Drew would have thought this a wonderful adventure and signed up right away.'

'And then bedded the rude, muscular gardener!' I say, suddenly remembering a different version of myself circa the mid 1990s.

'Muscular. Is he indeed?'

'But a bit of a prick. Otherwise I'd send him in your direction.'

'I'm not sure about gardeners. All that faux peasantry and organic nonsense. I get more than enough of all that at work. Not my cup of tea.' Chloe resists any attempts by her friends to match-make. Sometimes I wonder if she's scared of something actually working out. 'But, funnily enough, I kind of like the idea of this Enid character.'

'You do? I thought you of all people could be relied upon to tell me not to be so ridiculous and sensibly point out that trying to turn oneself into the perfect wife is tantamount to turning oneself in for a voluntary lobotomy, or swapping one's personality for a hostess trolley.'

Chloe laughs. 'It depends on the spirit in which it's done, no? If you've got a clear objective in mind, and it's a choice – I mean, no one's saying bake or die, are they? – and it's under the tutelage of a mad old glamazon in a turban, well, that's different. Any woman who wears a turban *and* mentions fellatio to her florist on the first visit deserves a second hearing if you ask me.'

'What's a turban got to do with it?'

'I don't know. It kind of makes it OK. I mean, you couldn't accept marriage advice from an over-qualified marriage counsellor frump in an acrylic mix skirt suit in some hideous council office, could you? No. That would be wrong. Whereas this is kind of random and bonkers and a bit glamorous so, well, it's kind of right. Am I making sense?'

'No.' I smile. 'Not really.'

'I fucked up my marriage, Sadie,' she says in a much quieter voice, her flippancy suddenly gone.

'It wasn't your fault!'

'Well, whatever. Is it about fault in the end? I don't know. The marriage failed. And it was horrible. Really horrible.' She slowly stirs the pile of empty pistachio shells on the table with the tip of her finger. 'And we didn't even have children. I can't imagine what it would be like if . . .' her voice trails off. 'I didn't do anything about my marriage. I just let it drift, thought everything would work out. And if it didn't work out, hell, it wasn't major.' She looks up and smiles sadly. 'But, well, it was quite major. It hurt quite a lot.'

'Yes, I know.' I am a little shocked. She's not someone who confesses easily to vulnerability. I'm grateful that she can put aside her usual cynicism in the hope of helping me. Although if Chloe thinks my marriage is in serious trouble things must be bad. We sit in silence for a few moments, mulling it all over. There is just the ticking of the big wall clock, the grumble of the bathroom water pipes above us. I pour more wine.

'And also,' she says suddenly, taking a large slurp of wine and brightening up. 'The place is a mess! You might learn how to run a house.'

'The treachery!' I flick her with a tea towel.

'Don't come at me with your domestic weapons of mass destruction!' Chloe yanks the tea towel out of my hand. 'You know what? I'd love to meet Enid. Take me with you next time, please, I beg you. Swap you two Chanel lipsticks. No, make that three. And I'll bung in a free nail varnish.'

'I'm not going back. She's completely mad. And I'd rather die than turn into the perfect wife. Besides, if you really love me you'll let me have the nail varnish anyway. You could write it off as a charitable donation.'

'No. I like you undone, darling.' Chloe clinks her wine glass against mine. 'Very nineties grunge.' She stands up, walks to the sink and pours herself a glass of water.

I notice that she's lost weight and feel a twitch of restlessness. Yes, I really should make more of an effort not to eat my body weight in Hobnobs. 'Shame I'm in the wrong century and twenty years too old to pull off the look.'

'Don't be ridiculous. You're a natural beauty. Although, to be brutally honest, the bruise isn't really helping. It looks like it's been expertly whipped up by a make-up artist on a film set. Do you want me to cover it up?'

I touch it lightly. Today it barely hurts at all but there is still a ridge around it, like I've got a two pence piece beneath my skin. 'You're saying I look like I'm auditioning for *Shaun of the Dead*?'

Chloe smiles one of her big smiles and screws her face up. There's a collision of sandy freckles and eyelashes. It seems impossible that she is single. I find it hard to believe any man wouldn't adore her and feel blessed calling her his girlfriend, or wife. 'I've just finished a job so I've got all my gubbins with me. You know I can't resist a challenge.'

'I'll take that as a yes.' I pull up a kitchen chair.

'Relax. I'll make it vanish faster than my husband did.' She fills my glass then starts pulling out essential bits of make-up kit, presumably the industrial stuff not designed for flawlessly skinned supermodels.

'Tom says I shouldn't drink,' I say, taking a sip of wine. 'Tom says drink is a depressive.'

'Tell him it's better than psychotropic weed.'

'Don't! He'll pack me off to an NA group.'

Chloe rummages in her handbag. 'Which reminds me, before I forget. Here's the number of that motivational guru chick I did the make-up for last week. She wrote some famous book about spring cleaning your life or some such nonsense. She's desperate for a florist. Annette . . . Western, I think. Did her face last week.' Chloe pushes one of her cards towards me with 'Annette' and a number scrawled on it. 'Weirdly, I think she might even be with Anderson but I wasn't sure. Anyhow I didn't say you were Tom's wife – wasn't sure if you'd want me to – just that I knew someone who was a bloody genius with flowers.'

'Thank you.' I stare at the card. Annette. 'Funnily enough her name does ring a bell. Can't quite place it though.' I push it into my purse. 'But I'm not sure I should take on any more clients. Tom says I'm . . .' I quote with my fingers, '. . . overstretching myself.'

Chloe rolls her eyes. 'No offence but you're hardly Nicola Horlick, darling. Anyhow she'd be an excellent client, high profile, loads of dough.'

I take another sip of wine, very nice wine actually, it's slipping down a treat. 'Maybe she can hypnotise me or do whatever she does and make me into the perfect wife. I'd prefer a shortcut.'

'Right, tilt your head back a bit, let's have a look at you,' says Chloe, dipping her squishy make-up sponge into some thick beige foundation. She starts to dab at my bruise. A comfortable silence falls for a few moments. 'Squeal if it hurts.'

'Ow!'

'A bit of pain is good. Talking of perfect wives. How about my old mucker, Pam, have you seen much of her?'

'Perfect Pam? Yes, I bump into her at Danny's nursery, her son Ludo goes there too. And, of course, being an Anderson wife, she was at The Ivy lunch. But I'm trying not to think about that.'

Chloe starts to giggle and does something feathery on my forehead with a big fat powder brush that makes me sneeze.

'I always forget that you and Pam know each other.'

'We go way back. Before she became non-ironic retro wife, obviously.' She arranges a selection of make-up on the kitchen table. 'Funnily enough she used to be a lot more fun.'

'Perfect Pam makes pancakes now, you know!'

'Pam-cakes.'

'She has gingham bunting in her garden! She carries an "I'm Not A Plastic Bag" bag!'

'Don't. I fear that now you're back in town our paths are going to inevitably cross.'

'What a good idea! Next weekend. I'll invite you both to tea!'

She laughs and shakes her head. 'Otherwise engaged, darling. I'll be washing my hair or shoe shopping for my gay wedding in Ibiza.'

Chloe is the kind of woman who is always being invited to weddings in Ibiza. She's got more glamour in her small toenail than I have in my whole body.

'Of course. I forgot about that. Now have you found your dress, *The* Dress?'

'This afternoon. In Matches.' Chloe dabs at my nostrils now. 'Gold no less. Plus serious make-up. I'm thinking glitter and colour and eyelashes that look like

97

they're about to take off. I don't care if I'm thirty-four . . .'

'Hardly old.'

'Exactly! Thirty-four and divorced. Some achievement,' she adds drily, picking up her red handbag, which is the size of a small fridge. She pulls out something gold and shiny like a toffee wrapper. 'I refuse to go quietly. I hate all this dreary let's-be-chic-now-we're-in-our-thirties rubbish. Look, I'll show you. Check this out.' She shakes out the dress. It is a shiver of gold sequins, cut so high it must be difficult to sit down without flashing her knickers.

'If Icarus was a woman.' I stare at the dress, fascinated. I have never owned or worn such a dress. 'Why not practise your Las Vegas make-up on me, as I am a wee bit drunk . . .'

'A wee bit?' she laughs. 'You're slurring, Sadie dear.'

'Good! I'm taking a night off from the demands of my cordon bleu cooking schedule, as well as my sparkling marital social life. And as Tom will probably roll in at ten and fall into bed without even noticing that I am here at all there is no reason for you not to use me as a guinea pig.' I sit up in my seat and shut my eyes. 'Go on. I'm channelling Kate Moss at her most decadent. Show-time!'

'Oh, you won't regret it.' Chloe starts to giggle. I start to giggle. We put Primal Scream on too loud to get us in the mood. Then she starts to work. And the fun stuff starts. The boring heavy duty foundations and powders are pushed to one side and she pulls out a girls' world fantasy of make-up: sparkly ivy greens, poppy reds and eyelashes with glitter-dipped ends. We finish off the bottle of wine and open another. Finally, she steps back and laughs. 'You look fucking cool!' she shouts. 'Right, put my dress on now. I want to see the whole monty.'

I look at the tiny gold dress doubtfully. 'Beyond the call of duty.'

'Put on the goddamn dress,' she says. 'I want to see how the thing hangs together. Don't wuss out on me.'

'It'll never fit.'

'It will.' Protesting, she pulls off my navy sweater and I shake my legs out of my jeans. Thankfully, the dress is forgivingly stretchy, which means I can actually fit into it, despite the fact that Chloe is a perfect ten and I most certainly am not. I tug it down over my hips. But it barely covers my bottom. My legs poke out from beneath, pale and lumpy and not entirely hairless. 'Oh my God, Chloe. It's a fucking sequin handkerchief. You're a shameless exhibitionist.'

'I am just single. Now go check yourself out in the mirror.' She shoves me towards the full length mirror in the hall.

Who the hell is that? Half showgirl, half trannie. 'Oh. My. God,' I yell.

There is a screech from the top of the stairs. 'Mama!'

I look up. Danny, bewildered and bleary eyed in his pyjamas, is standing at the top of the stairs. 'Mama? Where's Mama?' he whimpers.

'Baby, it's me!' I squeal. 'Did we wake you? Sorry, sweetie.'

As I lurch drunkenly towards him, he steps back, horrified, and the whimpers become wails.

The front door opens. I swivel around. Tom! Tom hasn't yet seen me. He's looking behind him, chatting to somebody. Oh God. Two other people. Visitors. Men. In Suits. I'm frozen to the spot. Then it happens, as if in slow motion. Tom turns, his jaw drops open. The men in suits open their mouths, no sound comes out.

Primal Scream howl about how they want to get loaded and have a good time.

'Tom,' I slur. 'Hi.'

There is a hideous pause. Tom stares at me in disbelief. Then looks back at his colleagues. 'Er. This is my wife, Sadie. Sadie, these are two directors from Anderson and Co, Sebastian and Roman. You met them at the lunch.'

Oh shit.

'Hi, I'm Chloe.' Chloe steps forward, in an attempt to rescue the situation. 'We were just . . .'

Tom shoots daggers at Chloe. Danny starts to whimper again.

I tug down the gold sequin dress. 'Sorry, I wasn't expecting . . .'

Sebastian and Roman grin, lopsided, embarrassed schoolboy grins, and stare at the floor. The air is chewy with tension.

Tom clears his throat. 'I left a message on your mobile.'

Obviously I didn't hear my mobile because Primal Scream was on too loud. And, actually, is still on too loud, loud enough to wake my poor helpless young child, who starts to run as if his life depended upon it, into Tom's arms.

'It's OK. Daddy's here,' Tom says, hugging Danny close and looking up at me despairingly.

Nine

'Your tulips,' I say, spreading the flowers out on Enid's kitchen table a little nervously, anxious that she like them. My eyes are still stinging from crying this morning – Tom and I had a big showdown again last night; no, he didn't see the funny side of the gold dress – and I avoid looking at her directly in case they're still pink and puffy. 'Black. As requested.'

Enid blows cigarette smoke out of the open back door. A breeze blows it back at her and it curls above her head. Today she is dressed in a startling pale blue kimono-like housecoat embroidered with cockatoos. Her silver hair is pulled off her face by a large red silk scarf, fixed with a jewelled beetle brooch. 'I never get bored of them.'

'I've also brought some glass vases with me, Enid. The crystal vases can look a bit heavy. But it's nice to be able to see their stems in the water, don't you think?'

'Like peeking at ladies' legs in a swimming pool.' Enid leans out of the kitchen door and grinds her cigarette on the outside wall, leaving a grey smudge on the honey-coloured brick. 'I'm pleased you came back, Sadie. I feared I might have scared you off.'

I still can't quite believe I'm here either. But something kind of strange happened. When I woke up this morning I had this strong, powerful sense, a sense as visceral as a smell, or a sharp, citrus taste, that Mum wanted me to come. It was overpowering and unambiguous. I kept hearing Mum's voice, that soft, gentle voice, clear as a bell inside my head as I brushed my teeth: 'What have you got to lose, Sadie?' I quickly fill four square vases with the tulips, then nudge in a spray of grass to add extra texture. 'Do you like the bear grass?'

'I've had tulips on my table every week since he died. I've grown conservative in my old age, Sadie. But I do think I can manage a bit of grass. Hell, why not?'

There is a flicker of movement in the garden. I glance out of the kitchen window. Is it Eddie? It is Eddie. He is standing, silhouetted against the buttery morning sun, one muddy-booted foot on a spade, his whole body leaning on to it. I cannot help but notice that it is a very good body, a bit like the body Tom used to have before the expensed lunches, stress and board meetings started taking their toll. Enid smiles knowingly to herself, as if she's watching me watching him. I quickly look away and tuck more stalks of bear grass into the corners of the vase.

'Sugar rush?' she asks, prising the lid off a round silver cake tin with her curled diamond-encrusted fingers. She puts two brownies on chintzy side plates. 'Let's adjourn to the sitting room.'

I get a strange déjà vu. My nan loved to use that word, 'adjourn'. Her house wasn't grand like this, of course. It was a modest Victorian cottage by the canal in west Oxford. But it was a palace to her, who'd grown up in a tiny cottage in a small village in Devon, the local flame-haired beauty. After escaping the village and marrying my grandfather – a history teacher at Magdalen College School – she'd insisted on 'civilised living', as she'd called it: napkins in napkin holders, doilies on a polished silver cake stand, and never, ever such improprieties as elbows on the table, all of which had driven Mum mad and made her desperate to flee the nest at the earliest opportunity in the sixties.

'This way, darling.'

Nervousness flutters in my chest like a bird. I follow her across the grand hall to the sitting room to the left of the grand staircase, not the intriguing one on the right. Inside the room there are two enormous dark red sofas scattered with pink and green silk cushions. On the wall hangs a large tapestry, a pattern of water lilies and lotus flowers, and many photographs in gilt frames. When I look up at the ceiling I start at the sight of one of the biggest chandeliers I've ever seen, like a million clustered teardrops. It is just like the one Nan used to have in her house in Oxford, albeit far bigger. She'd spent ages saving up for it, her pride and joy. As a child I remember going to stay and whiling away endless hours between tea and walks, staring up at it, mesmerised. I got to know every drop and shimmer, the exact slant of the dust on the largest upper drops, the route of the wires that ran between the candle bulbs and up into the ceiling rose. It seemed impossibly glamorous. I adored it. My mother always thought it imposing and ghastly and sold it when Nan died, which we rowed about at the time.

'Heavens! Music! I've forgotten the music.' Enid reaches for a remote control, its red-flashing modernity at odds with the age of her hand and the elegance of her silk sleeve. 'Don't worry. Not Frank,' she says with a wink. A deep, French voice booms out of her music system. 'Let's not tire our tongues with dull chit-chat. Shall we dive in?'

I swallow hard, embarrassed and nervous in equal measure. I pick up a pink cushion and turn it anxiously on my lap, pulling at its silk fringing.

'Don't be shy. I'm perfectly unshockable I promise you. Now, background, please.' She addresses me more sternly. 'Don't wallpaper the cracks, Sadie.'

'OK. Well . . .' I don't know where to start. 'There's something I want but he doesn't want . . .' It sounds so stupid. I hesitate. 'God, sorry. It feels so odd telling you this. We hardly know each other.'

She waves her jewelled hand dismissively. 'Who gives a hoot?'

I squirm on the sofa. What on earth am I doing here? 'I'm sorry, Enid. This is a little strange. To be honest I feel a bit embarrassed and kind of uncomfortable about the whole notion of being a good wife. It feels, er, kind of retrograde.' I put the cushion back on the sofa and pick up my handbag. No, I can't do this.

'Retrograde?' she repeats, looking puzzled. 'Retrograde? Tell me what is wrong with trying to be a good wife? You try and be a good florist, don't you? What's more important? You modern women – gosh, I sound about seven thousand years old saying that – seem to spend hours reading magazines about where to buy this or that, how to perfect your figures and careers, and yet when it comes to the single most important role in your life, you find it belittling to even consider improving it,' she says indignantly.

I put my handbag back down.

'You don't grasp control of your marriages, just let yourself get buffeted about on half truths, hormones and unexamined feelings. I'm all for women taking control. This idea that marriage, romance, is purely about chemistry or fate is just another way of making women passive onlookers to their own lives. Be proactive! Be a good wife! Make a good marriage! A good marriage means a good life. And there is nothing, absolutely *nothing* wrong or shameful, in trying for a good life.' She stops, pauses for breath. 'Now, put aside your misplaced foggy feminist agenda and tell me why you're here.'

Gosh. Well. That told me. I start again. 'I guess I need to take my marriage a bit more seriously.'

'My darling, marriage is far too important to be taken seriously!' she laughs, her face crinkling up like one of those pampered hairless pugs. 'Carry on.'

'Oh.' I'm unsure how to respond. 'Well, it's just that he – my husband, Tom – he's not happy. He told me. My mother-in-law told me. I feel like the whole world's telling me. It seems we're not just in a rough patch, as I thought, we're in dire straits.' A bit of brownie sticks in my throat. 'Which is bad enough. But it's complicated by the fact that I want another baby . . .' My voice breaks. I look down, embarrassed again.

Enid leans forward on her elbows, her face tight with concentration, as if trying to work out a perplexing equation.

'Yes, I have a little boy, Danny. But I lost one. A few months ago, when we came back from Toronto, shortly after my mother died.'

'Your mother died too?'

'Cancer.'

She leans back and sighs. There is a new softness in her eyes. 'OK. I think I understand now.'

'Tom doesn't. He didn't even cry about the baby,' I say quickly, surprised at how easy it is to confide in her. 'He doesn't ever talk about it. And he doesn't want to try again. He says we have to sort out our marriage first.'

Enid takes a sip of tea. 'He's right, isn't he?'

This question throws me. Rightness isn't the point. I feel a bristle of irritation that she doesn't immediately take my side. She obviously doesn't understand. No one understands. 'But another baby would fix things.'

Enid laughs. 'I'm not sure they ever do that, darling.'

'I worry that he's using this "marriage isn't working" line as an excuse to stall, to avoid committing to a bigger family, that maybe he doesn't want to commit to a bigger family because he doesn't want to commit to me.' I'm not sure I've actually articulated this to anyone else. Not even Chloe. Just saying it out loud makes me feel as if something tight inside has loosened a little bit. Or perhaps Enid's spiked my tea with some dozy talking drug and I will end up buried under a lavender bush after all.

She cocks her head slightly to one side like a bird. 'Go on.'

'That all this stuff about me being messy, or not supportive enough, or late, or whatever else makes me such a shit wife, well, it's all just self-justifying deflection.' The words rattle out of me like a hail of bullets. I squeeze my nails into my palms, leaving little red half moons on my skin. 'Maybe part of him actually *wants* me to be a crap wife because it gives him a reason to hold back from me, to not fully commit. Other times I panic that if it wasn't for Mum dying and losing the baby he might have left by now. Maybe he's only with me because he feels sorry for me.' I pause for breath. The upholstered hush is broken by the sound of a carriage clock ticking, a bee throwing itself against the window pane, and Enid's fingers lightly drumming on the arm of the sofa.

'Do you love him?' she asks eventually.

'Yes,' I say with a certainty that confuses me – I spend a lot of my time hating him too.

'You're compatible?'

'I think so,' I say with less certainty. 'Well, we used to be. We were madly in love.'

'To be in love is easy, no? It's staying in love that's hard. But if you do love him despite everything, well, then, darling, your task is not so difficult.' She gives me a stern, headmistressy look. 'But it will still require effort, work, and an open mind. It's a project, you have to see it as a project. Now, darling, are you in or out?'

I feel slightly disorientated, like the day is separating and reassembling itself in a new unexpected way. My mother's words spin around my head again. What have I got to lose? I swallow hard. 'In.'

Enid claps her hands together. 'Marvellous! Shall we give ourselves a deadline? I always find deadlines to be most helpful.'

I think about this for a moment. Then I know the answer. By September. I want my marriage fixed by our wedding anniversary. 'September, third of September.'

She frowns. 'September? Well that's tight. But we'll give it our best shot. Right, the first thing I used to tell all of my girls—'

There is a knock on the sitting room door. It is Eddie. He looks at me, slightly puzzled. I feel the heat rise on my cheeks. 'Hi, Sadie,' he says. 'I'm off now, Aunty E.'

'Bye bye, my darling boy.' She blows him a kiss and

he closes the door quietly behind him. 'Marvellous, isn't he? Now where were we? From looking at you, the way you present yourself.' She sweeps her eyes over me, lingering disapprovingly on my shoes (white-gone-grey Converse), then upwards (skinny jeans, cheap navy Topshop T-shirt). 'I think I can read your mood.'

I laugh: the image of me in that gold dress with hairy white legs sticking out and Tom's colleagues staring in horrified disbelief flashes up with hideous clarity. If only Enid knew the half of it.

'Is your house in similar shape?'

Worse, far worse. I grin sheepishly. 'Kind of.'

'Employ help, darling. Get things in order. Messy houses make men moody. There's a primal part of them that expects the woman to organise the feathers in the nest, which is a dreadful bore and the reason God invented housekeepers. And make sure he's always well fed. Husbands are terrible on an empty stomach. But never forget that husbands will, of course, ultimately forgive their wives for neglecting them, or the house, even if it does cause tension. But they will *never* forgive their wives for neglecting themselves.' She stares at my shoes. I curl my feet beneath the sofa. I get the message.

'It is also very important not to be needy. You are the happy, golden girl with a million friends, remember?'

'I am?'

'You need wifely comrades. Now, have you got a good network? Have you got your own Iris, Maud and—'

Hmmm. The truth is that since we came back from Toronto I haven't made a great effort. A lot of my old friends who used to live here have moved to new neighbourhoods. And I've not been feeling very social. Apart from with Chloe, very unmarried Chloe, of course, who compensates by being a one woman party in high heels. 'Not really.'

'I did wonder when I saw you alone in the park. I was never alone in a park at your age,' she adds disapprovingly. 'Now get yourself a decent network, darling. When marriage hits a rough patch it's not husbands that make it bearable, it's other wives. Surround yourself with them. Don't be complacent. Learn how they do things. Ask questions.'

I try not to laugh, imagining myself interviewing Perfect Pam on her wifely skills, falling asleep as she tells me.

'You may smirk.'

Smirk? I bristle. God, it's like being back at school. Why am I putting myself through this again?

'But modern life is very isolating.' Enid sighs and gazes out of the window. 'We were not designed to live our lives alone, or even with just our husbands. Gosh, Albert and I would have gone potty without company. Is that your notebook?' She points to the pad of paper falling out of my handbag. It is indeed my indispensable hot-pink spiral-bound notebook, part of it diary, part of it notes, what Tom calls 'the wife's scrapbook'. He usually smiles when he says this, as if the idea of me as

111

a wife is intrinsically amusing and that it is fitting that I own a twentieth-century paper item, not a BlackBerry or an iPhone. It bashes along in my cluttered brown leather handbag, amassing raisins and receipts between its pages. Still it works for me: it documents random notes on my clients, shopping lists, Danny's play dates, scrawled telephone numbers that I will never phone, details of miracle anti-ageing creams that I've read about in magazines and will never buy.

'Yes.'

'Pass it over. I want to jot something down.'

'Why write it down?'

Enid looks at me in surprise, as if I've said something unfathomable. 'To write something down is to understand it. What will you refer to in your weak moments if I do not write it down? A pen, please.'

I smile to myself at the unlikelihood of me rifling through my pink notebook for wifely inspiration. Hang on a minute, Tom, I've got to consult my notebook! He'd have me sectioned. I pass her a biro – leaky and green-inked of course – and lean forward to see what she's writing. Hers is a neat swirling well formed hand, quite the opposite of mine.

Don't neglect self, or house. Embrace wife friends. Feed husband. Pretend you're dating again. E x

Ten

Feed husband, I think, smiling to myself. That would tickle Tom. Except I can't tell him. This is my little secret. My bag of tricks. I open the front door. There is a strange scent in the hallway. It is a scent I vaguely recognise, strong, artificially floral, the kind of perfume that white-coated shop assistants assault you with when you walk into John Lewis's beauty department. Tom appears from the kitchen, tight jawed and strained. 'Your dad is here,' he hisses. 'I was trying to do a bit of work and—'

'He can't be. He's in Mexico for another week. Danny, don't drop your coat on the floor.'

'The Girl from Ipanema' booms from the living room. 'Is that my baby?'

Oh God. It's him. 'Grandpa!' Danny shrieks and runs off into the living room.

'Told you,' Tom mouths silently, looking at me as if it's my fault that Dad and Loretta have arrived and stopped him working. I don't think either of us realised that we'd also be marrying each other's parents when we exchanged vows. Mother and father-in-laws are for life, it seems, not just for the odd, awkward family Christmas.

Dad is lying across our new lime green sofa, feet on the arm. He is tanned, has lost a fair bit of weight and is wearing a pink floral shirt with khaki shorts, blue socks and cream leather German sandals. It's not a good look. 'How's my Sadie?' he booms, his dentures radioactively white against his tan as he leans forward to kiss me.

'Fine,' I say, choking on his aftershave. He is awash with it. He never used to wear it at all when Mum was alive. 'Where's Loretta?'

In answer comes the sound of high heels punching holes in our floorboards. 'Just having a pee pee!' shouts Loretta, toppling into the room. 'Ciao, my little smasher!' She pinches Danny's cheek. 'How are you, Sades?'

'Fine, thank you. Gosh, you look . . .' Words actually fail me. Loretta, never one to dress conservatively at the best of times, is wearing a fuchsia pink jumpsuit with matching heels. Her hair is bleached straw-yellow. Her forty-four-year-old skin has been suntanned to the colour and texture of a handbag. '. . . so well.'

'We feel it! It was bloody gorgeous!' she beams. 'Wasn't it, John?'

I hate the way they answer in the collective plural, as if this makes their union more acceptable somehow.

'When did you get back?' I stutter, still stunned at the ambush of tan and pink and holiday bonhomie. 'I wasn't expecting you.'

Dad punches my arm. 'Surprise!' He starts to laugh. 'Boy, you should have seen Tom's face at the front door. Get the pressies out, Loretta bunny!'

Bunny? Euw! I can't get my head around my father's personality transplant. He was happily married to my mother for thirty-odd years. They lived a quiet existence on the outskirts of Reading. He enjoyed gardening and reading and watching documentaries on World War II. She liked theatre and pottery. Theirs was, by most standards, a solid, harmonious marriage. Dad didn't love in a showy way – he wasn't a man of big romantic gestures – but with deep, unfaltering affection. His eyes became brighter if she was in the room. At a party he would stick close to her all night. Not once do I remember him even glancing at anyone else. After Mum died, Dad was, as she feared and predicted in her last weeks, distraught and lost, unable to cook for himself, unable to manage the house. Then he met Loretta.

Dad later sheepishly confessed that he resorted to advertising for 'friendship' in the local personal ads. Loretta Norris, a middle-aged divorcee from Milton Keynes – 'fun, sexy, curvy, GSOH, likes travel, eating out, good times!!!' – responded. Since dating Loretta, my father's gnarled feet have barely touched British soil. Having infected my father with her love of expensive holidays (he used to be happy with a B&B on the Isle of

Wight), they have clocked up thousands of air miles. 'Redistributing your inheritance on a global scale,' as Tom once put it.

No one is allowed to comment on their union except in the most glowing terms. I once dared to allude to the problematic nature of such an age gap. 'You little madam!' Dad boomed, purple-faced, vein in his neck throbbing. 'I count myself the luckiest man on the blasted planet! How many widowed men are lucky enough to find a Loretta in their twilight years? How can you *not* be happy for me? I won't hear a word said against her!' I hadn't, at that point, said a word against her, so I'd guessed that mine was not the only word of warning to fall on his ears. Not that he listened, obviously. As my mum used to say, he's always been a stubborn old goat.

Loretta empties a straw beach bag on to the rug. 'Get an eyeful of this!' she squeals. She always sounds like she's doing a low-cost supermarket voice-over, Midlands, regional, overenthusiastic, in italics. 'A car, my little smasher!' She holds up a painted tin car, which, of course, Danny loves. 'A bottle of duty free for you, Tom.' Loretta hands Tom a bottle of whiskey. Tom smiles politely and doesn't mention that he doesn't drink whiskey.

Hesitantly Loretta hands me a large straw hat festooned with plastic flowers, a cross between a cartoon Mexican hat and a plastic flower arrangement in a two star hotel. 'I hope you like it, Sadie.'

116

'She spent bloody ages choosing it,' says Dad, gazing at Loretta like a love-struck hound.

'I thought you'd appreciate the flowers,' says Loretta. 'Kind of cheap and cheerful. But—'

'It's lovely, Loretta, thanks.' I take the hat and swing it awkwardly in my left hand.

'Put it on, girl! Put it on!' thunders Dad. 'Let's get into the spirit of things.'

Tom starts to laugh. I glare at him. 'Go on, Sadie,' says Tom. He's enjoying my pain.

I put the hat on, feeling ridiculous. It sits too tight on my head and the brim droops in front of my eyes so I have to swivel it round in order to see. As I do so a yellow plastic flower of indeterminate species drops to the floor.

'Careful!' says Dad. 'You're shedding.'

Danny looks at me warily, as if scared I'm about to turn once again into the horrifying apparition that appeared in the gold dress and glitter-tipped eyelashes.

'We wanted something that'd put a smile on your face,' explains Dad, swinging his legs back up on to the sofa.

'Has anyone offered you tea?' I ask, trying to smile graciously and distract attention from the hideous hat.

'Would kill for something stronger, love,' says Dad. 'We've developed quite a taste for the high life, haven't we, Loretta?'

'Make mine a Sex on the Beach!' she giggles.

Tom and I exchange horrified glances. It's not even 4 p.m.

117

'Mama,' says Danny slowly, his little face scrunching up in puzzlement. I know it's coming. 'What's sex on the beach?'

'Nothing!' says Tom, scooping up Danny and tickling him. 'I'll fix those drinks. Would a glass of wine do instead, Loretta?'

'Smashing. We like our vino cold and white. Don't we, bunny?' says Loretta, looking at Dad.

Tom and I scuttle into the kitchen and shut the door.

'Oh my God,' I hiss, whipping the hat off my head. 'He is worse than ever. It's like having Del Boy in the house. It's all so . . . so . . . awful. I'd forgotten. Can't they retire to the Costas or something?'

Tom opens the fridge and pulls out a bottle of Sauvignon Blanc. 'You've got to laugh. You've got no choice.'

'Well,' I say, realising that actually I am angry, angrier than I should perhaps be at the sight of my father and the plastic flower hat. But every time I see Dad with Loretta it feels like a fresh betrayal of my mother, my adorable, wonderful mother who was so unlike Loretta in every way. 'It just feels too soon. Way too soon, Tom. It's not right.'

'What you doing in there, growing your own grapes?' bellows Dad from the living room. 'We need to shoot soon. I'm taking Lottie out west.'

'Oh, what are you going to see?' I ask, walking back into the room with the wine. My mother used to visit London regularly. She used to love the National Portrait

118

Gallery. My father didn't share her enthusiasm. 'Only go to keep the missus happy,' he'd explain cheerfully.

Dad winks. 'Well, as Loretta's only been into central London a handful of times . . .'

Loretta shakes her head. 'Five times in my whole life! I always say you can get everything you need in Milton Keynes. Plus you can park.'

Dad swigs back his wine. I notice his nose is red at the end. It doesn't look like sunburn. It looks like an old man's strawberry-textured booze nose. 'I'm going to take her on one of those bicycle taxis.'

Oh God, I can see them now, hooting with laughter in the back of a rickshaw taxi, Loretta's candyfloss hair whipping off her face, fuchsia jumpsuit flapping in the wind, my father leaning back in his chariot as if he were Spartacus.

'Then we're going to have a whip around Selfridges.'

'I've never been to Selfridges,' says Loretta, reapplying her pink lipstick and noisily smacking her lips together. 'I want to see all those luxury frillies. Choose myself something a bit special,' she adds with a coy smile. 'You know.'

'Then we'll partake of some posh nosh. Have a bit of bubbly,' says Dad with another ghastly wink. Loretta blushes and grins. She waggles her foot up and down. The heel of her shoe drops away and dangles, exposing cracked yellow soles. There is an awkward pause. 'We are celebrating.' Dad clears his throat. 'I'm happy to announce that Loretta has agreed to be my wife!'

'*Wife?*' I gasp, horrified. This can't be happening.

Loretta smiles at me apologetically but with mischief in her eyes, like a child who knows she's about to do a really bad thing but is going to do it anyway.

'Well, er, congratulations,' says Tom, shaking Dad's hand. 'Fantastic.'

Dad slaps Tom on the back. 'Thank you, my son.'

My mother has been dead barely a year. I'm appalled, horrified, unable to speak. Loretta refuses to meet my eye. Dad is staring at me, waiting for my blessing.

'Yes, congratulations,' I say eventually. 'Excuse me a sec.' I walk out of the room and into the kitchen to decompress. *Married?* Fuckety fuck fuck. I go through all the reasons I should be happy: he seems happy, he has someone to get old with. But . . . but . . . Oh it just makes my skin crawl. Does that make me a bad daughter? I mean, sure, Mum would want him to meet someone else. But not, so not, Loretta. And not months after her death. I try to calm down and not look like I'm hyperventilating when I walk back into the room.

'Well, we're not going to tie the knot until next year. Thought we'd combine it with Loretta's forty-fifth. But, in the meantime, we're going to throw a helluva engagement party,' Dad says, bouncing Danny up and down on his knee.

'Right,' I say, happy to leave it right there. I sit down on an armchair, so Loretta's cracked soles are no longer in view.

'You tell them, Loretta,' Dad says, with a nod. 'You're the boss.'

'Well,' says Loretta, fiddling with the gold locket and chain around her neck. (It seems preposterous that my father's mug shot is in that locket, but it is. She left it here once and I checked.) 'We're going to have a bit of a summery do. We're thinking a barn just outside Milton Keynes, a bit of razz and dazzle, a knees-up.'

'Lovely,' I say weakly.

'Invite all your mates, Sadie. Your family must come too, Tom. The more the merrier.' Dad stretches, his saggy man-boobs pressing against the floral shirt. 'Let's burn some cash, guys! It's time to party. You don't get engaged every day, do you?'

Eleven

'Pretend you're dating again, my arse,' I mutter under my breath as I rummage furiously through my underwear drawers trying to find something resembling the kind of knickers I might have worn when I was one and a half stone lighter and still cared about what I looked like in those two seconds between the underwear being revealed and being ripped off. The only pair I find are, rather embarrassingly, relics from that exact era, their pink lace preserved only through lack of use (the 'hand-wash only' label put me off). My bras are worse, too scaffolding to be sexy, partly because I always figured that it's better to support my boobs in something industrial than let them bounce about in flimsy lace and subject them to gravity. (There's also the matter of my pencil-stub nipples – since breastfeeding Danny you could hang hats off them. They need to be flattened and contained.) But now, looking at my strapped-up appendages in the mirror, I rather wish I had something lacy. My breasts look like two beige warheads.

'Get a move on, Sadie!' shouts Tom from downstairs. 'We're late.'

This is Tom shorthand for 'You're always late'. And maybe he's right. But is accidental lateness worse than deliberate working lateness? Plus, there are mitigating circumstances. Danny had a meltdown earlier when I said we were going out and Rona, who Tom asked to babysit, kept asking where everything was about a hundred times, 'just in case of emergencies'. Then she crushed her hand to her mouth as if reliving trauma. 'Sadie, I looked in the kitchen drawer to check I had the back door key in case there was a fire and we had to get out quickly and all I could find was a . . . a . . . Rizla packet – have you taken up smoking? – and about a thousand rusty old nails!' she gasped, as if I'd deliberately booby-trapped the house to offend her. I then spent twenty minutes foraging for the spare back door key, which turned out to be hiding in a cunning 'safe place', so safe no one would ever find it, inside a tube of spare loo roll in the downstairs loo nestled beside a dusty ball of hair and a broken Transformer limb.

'Give me five minutes!'

'Pam said seven-thirty,' Tom shouts. 'It's almost eight.'

'Coming!' I lie. It should get me another five minutes. I consider for a moment the leaf-green and silver smocked dress – the one from the honeymoon photograph. Dare I? I wrestle it on and get my answer.

The smocking cuts into the flesh under my arms. Shit, I have fat armpits. I never knew such a thing was possible. I reach for my standby Going Out outfit instead: skinny Gap jeans and a pale blue Jaeger silk blouse which shows off a bit of cleavage and looks pretty against my eyes. Then I slip on a favourite old pair of heels – fake crocodile skin, cool I hope, but who knows, and so uncomfortable it feels like the fake croc is alive and biting. Outfit sorted, I run to the bathroom to locate my make-up bag. I unearth it beneath Danny's flannel and a split carton of fuzzy cotton-buds. Yes! One of Chloe's foundations. Better, better . . . and mascara. Where the hell is my mascara?

'For God's sake, Sadie,' shouts Tom's exasperated voice. 'Come on!'

I clatter down the stairs in my heels. Rona and Tom are quiet when I walk into the sitting room. But the room is still full of floating words and unfinished sentences like they've been discussing me. Teddy leaps up, his sharp little claws scraping down my legs.

'Down, Teddy!' Rona stares at my feet in disbelief. 'A pair of heels?' she barks in the way Lady Bracknell might say, 'A handbag?'

'Thought I'd make a bit of an effort. Those Anderson wives are a rather glam bunch. I don't want to look like I've been working in a field or anything.'

Nothing in Rona's expression acknowledges the dig except a slight twitch at the corner of her mouth.

'Even though I'm sure no one will notice as they'll be

124

too busy talking about school league tables and property prices,' I add, glancing at Tom.

Tom rolls his eyes. He thinks I'm being difficult. Maybe I am. Old habits . . .

'Have you had those heels a long time, Sadie?'

'Forever.' I glare at her. Teddy starts to sniff them, tail wagging as if they are puffing out scent of bone.

'Lasted remarkably well for something high street, haven't they?'

I try to catch Tom's eye, but he's pre-empted me and has averted his eyes to duck out of the conversation and the responsibility to take sides. 'Right,' he says quickly. 'Let's go.'

I pick up a bunch of yellow freesias left over from a job at a photographic studio and run upstairs to give Danny his final kiss goodbye. I find him sitting bolt upright in his bed in his *Thomas the Tank Engine* PJs, not looking the least bit sleepy. I ruffle his lovely head of chocolate curls and kiss his cheek. 'Have a lovely time with Granny.'

'I'm not allowed to call her Granny,' he corrects.

Ah, yes. Rona has decided that 'Granny' is far too ageing a title and has made the ridiculous request that Danny call her Rona, which is terribly confusing for him and pisses me off. I want him to have a proper granny, a soft, nurturing person like my mother. 'Call her Granny if you want. I'm sure she won't mind, darling,' I say naughtily. 'I'll see you in the morning.'

'Sadie!' shouts Tom. 'We need to go!'

Rona waves us off from the door. 'Now you go and enjoy yourselves. Tom, you deserve some light relief. You're doing so well! So well. I'm so very, very proud. So is your father. And you absolutely must not worry about Danny. I'll call you if there are any problems. If in doubt I'll dial 999!'

'I really wish she wouldn't do the whole catastrophist thing, Tom,' I sigh, as we walk down the street. 'The most likely disaster waiting to happen is Teddy taking a bite out of Danny's leg.'

Tom squeezes my hand. 'I know, I know. It's just Mum. Ignore her. You know what she's like. Danny's in very good hands. Let's try to actually enjoy ourselves for once.' He smiles at me. 'You do look very pretty tonight, Sadie.'

'Thanks.' I walk with just a little bit more of a bounce. But as we approach Perfect Pam's front door – tasteful Farrow and Ball green, enormous silver knocker, one olive tree either side of the step – I begin to feel nervous. This is the first neighbourly evening social we've been invited to since arriving back in London, unfortunate that it is also an off-duty Anderson event too. Still this is what Enid was talking about, branching out, making a wifely network, I remind myself. The first step.

Pam opens the door, all smile, enormous knockers and perfect bump. 'Hi, guys!'

'Sorry we're late. My fault, obviously,' I say, handing her the flowers.

'Gorgeous!' Pam sniffs the flowers. 'Come in! Please excuse the terrible mess!'

I feel instantly relieved when I hear the words terrible mess but then I notice that there is no terrible mess: Pam and Seth's hallway is spotless. It has silvery floral wallpaper and waxed honey-colour wooden floorboards. There are no muddy dog poo wellies. No wet coats decomposing on the floor. No evidence of her two children at all apart from arty professional-looking black and white photographs of them on the mirrored console table, alongside a grand flourish of lilies and green roses, teased into a cylindrical vase studded with silver beads and broken bits of glass.

'Oh don't look at that miserable bunch of flowers!' laughs Pam, as if the flowers were a clump of weeds from the garden rather than a bunch that must have cost little short of £70. 'I'm sure they're quite the least fashionable clump you've ever seen.'

'Not at all,' I say. 'I love the vase too. Very unusual.'

'I made it,' smiles Pam. She has the kind of smile you see blown up poster-sized in dentist's surgeries.

'Made it? You are clever. I last made a vase in pottery class at school. It leaked.'

'Well, shamefully, I have to admit that I didn't actually throw the clay but I stuck all the glittery bits on it with little Tallulah.'

'Wow,' says Tom. But he is not looking at the vase. He is looking at Pam's dress. To be more precise, he is looking at the way Pam's dress shows off her cleavage to eye-popping effect. (It is the Grand Canyon of cleavages. Despite the efforts of my beige warhead bra, it makes mine look like a crack in the pavement.) Pam's dress is midnight blue, all soft, flattering draped jersey. It clings in all the right places. She's also wearing designer-looking cork platform heels. One sexy mama. Suddenly all my efforts seem totally pointless. I don't even feel pretty. I feel frumpy and very *not* fecund and pregnant.

'Follow me!' says Pam, wiggling down the hall. Tom stares at her behind. He cannot help himself. Old habits . . .

The moment we get into the dining room it hits me that yes, we are indeed late and what can only be called A Dinner Party – shit, didn't these things die out in the eighties? – is in full swing. Couples face each other over a large, long, refectory table covered in white linen. On the table are a bewildering number of tea lights in pink and green glass pots, curious little arrangements of glittery twigs and flowers floating in vintage rose china tea cups. There are even napkins rolled and tied with raw twine, a daisy carefully threaded through each one. The female guests are smiling hard and looking rather uncomfortable. I feel too immature to be here. Like I'm playing with the grown-ups.

'Guys, Tom and Sadie, our new neighbours and fellow Anderson people. Hot off the plane from Toronto!' Pam announces.

There is a collective 'Ah!' from The Dinner Party and we are ushered to our seats. I glance into the kitchen, noting the efficient blackboard – 'Judo, Mandarin class, PTA, green curry paste' – and the orderly stacks of glossy recipe books. There are no visible floating socks. No sticky finger marks. Just bountiful, organised matriarch-ruled family life.

'I'm not going to embarrass you all with a formal introduction,' continues Pam. 'This is so not a formal household,' she adds. 'So I'll be quick. This is Nick, head of Anderson's American division.'

Nick is overweight and has a gleaming bald head that strongly resembles the dangling pendant ball light that hangs above it. He looks even older than anyone else here. He raises a hand in silent salute.

'And this is Tara, his wife.' A skinny, cookie-cutter blonde in a sexy halter-neck black dress, who looks younger than the rest of us – late twenties? – smiles uncertainly.

She turns to the next couple. 'And this is Alex, a new Anderson recruit too, aren't you, Alex? Assisting . . .'

Alex looks down, as if embarrassed to be labelled an assistant.

'He is our hero,' sighs Pam. 'Alex was a proper househusband until recently, weren't you, Alex?'

Alex mutters something indecipherable under his breath.

'Oh, yes, sorry, he's also been working on a TV script, which I am sure will be massive once he sells it. It will be! Don't be modest, Alex! And this is Ruth, his wife. She has a proper job,' she adds. 'Lawyer. Lives just down the road, the avenue. Her twins Louis and Callum have just started at West Kids nursery.' She winks. 'Yes, I got her there too, Sadie. I tell you I'm turning it into an Anderson crèche! I should be on commission.'

Ruth? I stare harder. Now she *does* look familiar. I think I saw her last week rushing into the nursery in a suit and running out again even faster. This evening she is wearing a badly fitting silk blouse that droops over her shoulders, black trousers, the kind of thing that looks thrown on in a what-the-fuck-shall-I-wear moment. There is a bra strap poking out from under her blouse, thick and the colour of an Elastoplast, which I find reassuring and marks her out as a different subspecies of career wife from the scary power version she could be. I am pleased to see that there is a free seat next to her.

Pam sashays into the open-plan kitchen. It is, of course, Shaker style with open shelves displaying tastefully mismatching enamel kitchenware that might have been designed by Nigella and an oven as big as a bunker. She brings a plate of Parma ham wrapped around figs to the table, bends down and serves up an eyeful of cleavage. Everyone makes 'ooo' noises, the men, I suspect, for quite different reasons to the women. Seth sloshes ruby-coloured red wine into enormous green glass goblets. I make a pact with myself not to get drunk and embarrass Tom. I won't let him down. I am going to behave like a good wife, the kind of community-minded reliably socially accomplished wife that other Anderson wives want to invite to dinner. Yes, I am. I really am. But I'm also desperate for a drink, something to curb my shyness and nerves. So I lunge at my wine goblet. As I do I catch the sleeve of my blouse on one of the tea lights that is artfully camouflaged by a glitter-dipped twig arrangement. There is a smell of burning.

'Sadie! Your sleeve!' shouts Pam.

There's a flurry of activity as everyone flaps the air with their linen napkins, sending bits of raw twine and daisies flying across the table.

'Fuck!' I say, feeling the singe burn against my skin.

Tara throws a glass of water at my arm.

'Fuck!' I shout as the San Pellegrino hits. There is a sizzle. A stunned silence.

Eventually Seth speaks. His voice is adenoidal. 'Are you OK?'

'I'm fine!' I squeal too loudly, wishing that I could throw the French linen tablecloth over my head and run from the perfect house with the perfect twine-tied napkins. Tom shoots me a what-have-you-done-now look, although I think I also detect a more affectionate smile playing at the corners of his mouth too. 'Honestly, it's nothing. Just a little singe.' I push up my sleeve to hide the smouldering scorch mark.

Pam laughs. 'Is she always this accident prone, Tom? First she gets locked in that flat, does some amazing Houdini-like escape, and appears like something from *Lost*, making all of us lot look like over-primped poodles at a dog show. Next she narrowly escapes a falling tree in a freak storm . . .' She looks at me and laughs. 'You need to be wrapped in one of my knitted tea cosies.'

Everyone starts to laugh, high and loud, in a collective release of tension. Hilarious.

Only Ruth gives me an understanding smile. 'It's just the kind of thing I do all the time,' she whispers. And I like her immediately.

The dinner party grinds on. There is much admiration of Pam's evident homemaking skills. And a few things are established quickly by the loudest voices. Seth has just bought Pam a Prius. It is parked next to their Range Rover. Nick lays down proof of his solvency with a nonchalant mention that he and Tara are going to an eco-retreat in Argentina next month. (Alex, Ruth's assistant husband, is tight-lipped and noticeably silent.) We establish that Tara used to work 'in fashion', something to do with a small jeans label set up with friends, based in Notting Hill. She gave this 'career' up three years ago after meeting Nick and realising that her first marriage was a sham. 'It was terribly romantic,' she says without any obvious irony. 'We got married as soon as our divorces came through.' She is now a happy Anderson wife and stepmother to Noah, Nick's eight-year-old son from his first marriage. Her relief is palpable when she mentions that Noah has started boarding school. 'Now that he's gone, I feel I am at the stage when I can concentrate on a career again,' sighs Tara. 'Something new.'

'Oh, yes, like what?' asks Ruth politely, forking her way into wilted spinach.

Tara looks blank. 'I'm not sure yet.' She takes a sip of wine. 'But I want to do something. I want to make my mark. I need to do more than . . .' she stops.

'In London, the trophy wife thing is a bit over, Sadie,' Pam explains, as if I were a visiting Inuit. 'It's fashionable to at least look like you've got something going on. Not us, I'm afraid, Tara.'

I kick Tom's leg hard under the table. To my horror, I realise that I've got the wrong leg because Tom doesn't look up but Pam's husband Seth does. A slow sloppy grin starts to spread across his face. Jesus. He thinks I'm coming on to him. I look away quickly and stab at the monkfish.

God, what kind of woman dares cook tricksy monkfish at home?

'It's different in America, isn't it, Sadie?' asks Pam loudly, as if I were slightly deaf or under six. 'Here, more wine.'

'Well, I guess, in America – Canada is a bit different – there are both kinds. But those heiresses, you know the Lauders and the like, a lot of them have high profile careers these days.' I smile apologetically at Tara, not wanting her to think I'm trying to put her down. Seth is still staring at me, undressing me with his eyes. I cross my arms across my chest, self-conscious of the warheads.

Pam tosses hair off her face. 'You know what? That's

fine. But . . .' She breathes in and swells up her formidable chest. '. . . let's not run down the role of wife and mother here.'

Seth pats her hand uneasily, as if trying to field An Issue. 'No one's doing that, darling.'

Ignoring him, Pam bends forward. 'I can say hand on heart . . .' She slaps her left breast, making it shudder. Tom blinks. '. . . that *I* am proud to be a wife. I am proud to have taken his name, to run the home, to look after the next generation.' Then she looks at Alex and confusion flickers over her face. 'Oops, sorry. I do not mean to run down your role as househusband, Alex.'

'I wasn't exactly a househusband. I was working on . . .' starts Alex, looking a little irritated.

'The TV script. Yes, of course,' adds Pam, compounding Alex's embarrassment. 'I don't even do that.' She sighs. 'I know this makes me sound prehistoric but I am happy to have Seth as head of this household.'

Ruth and I exchange glances. I know we are on the verge of giggling and absolutely must not giggle so we look away quickly. Tom is gazing at Pam in drooling open-mouthed admiration. And I realise that the idea of being nurtured and nourished by Perfect Pam and her big knockers is possibly a more enticing prospect than coming home to a couple of liquefying leeks and a stoned wife having her armpits waxed by her divorced fashion friend.

Pam's husband Seth, however, is looking a little

weary. 'Oh, ignore the wife. She's exaggerating. She wears the trousers around here. Did I want a goddamn muesli-munching Prius, darling? Or did I not?'

'Feminine wiles.' Pam giggles and bats her eyelashes.

She's flirting with her husband! When was the last time I flirted with my husband? Yes, Pam is a woman behaving like a new date, not a wife! Just as Enid advised. Watch and learn, Sadie. Watch and learn.

'You can be at home with the children and work. Sounds like you've got the best of both worlds, Sadie,' sighs Tara.

'I think so,' I say, shooting Tom a look.

'Oh and I bet you meet some interesting people,' says Pam. 'What a great chance to snoop around their houses, eh? Have you got any juicy stories? Go on, spill the beans!'

'Well, client confidentiality and all that. Besides, it's not that exciting, really. But well, there's one lady, an old lady, who I met a couple of weeks ago who's pretty up there.'

Tom groans. 'Sadie's working for a rich old dear who lives in a grand old house in St John's Wood, called, er . . .' Every time I've mentioned Enid, something in him bristles, as if he feels that she's a threat in some way. Ironic considering.

'Enid,' I say.

'Sadie met this Enid during the Regent's Park storm,' says Tom with a knowing nod, as if this explains something. 'The day she got walloped by that branch.'

'And what about your other clients?' asks Ruth. 'How do you get them?'

'Some are old contacts, others are friends of friends.'

'I bet Chloe Mansfield knows tons of people,' says Pam. She turns to Ruth and Tara. 'I knew her years ago and turns out she's a good friend of Sadie's too. Fashion and flowers are pretty loyal bedfellows, aren't they?'

'They are indeed,' I say. 'And, yes, she's been amazing, recommended me to some really nice people. I don't know how I'd have got started again without her.'

'Ah, Chloe, poor thing,' sighs Pam musically, wiping crumbs off the table with the edge of her hand. 'It must be so bloody difficult being single at our age.'

Tara nods. Ruth looks unconvinced.

'I think it sounds rather a lot of fun,' guffaws Seth, winking at me. He stops laughing when Pam shoots him a rocket-propelled grenade of a look across the sautéed potatoes. She briskly clears the plates and brings out the *pièce de résistance*, a trifle. How did she know it's Tom's favourite pudding? Or are her wifely skills so finely tuned that they extend to husbands every-where?

'Woman after my own heart,' says Tom, salivating. 'God, I haven't had trifle for about four years.'

We've been together about four years.

Pam glows. To her credit, she does not practise false humility when it comes to her hostess skills. After the pudding come great rounds of creamy blue cheese, grapes dried on the vine and sliced pear, which even I am struggling to fit in. Dessert wine. I didn't even cook this grandly for Thanksgiving, let alone a supposedly 'low-key dinner'. The more domestic skills Pam lays out before us, the more a little part of me deflates. I should be big enough to enjoy her generosity. But I can see how much Tom enjoys it all – he's eating the food like a hostage who's been rationed on stale crust and water. When Tom said things were 'tough right now', was he also referring to my cooking?

As the evening draws to a close, the conversation inevitably turns to schools – I give Tom a told-you-so look – then property prices and then . . .

'So are you two going to have any more sprogs?' asks Seth suddenly, gazing at me with a drunk, sloppy grin.

I freeze.

Pam nudges Seth unsubtly. He doesn't appear to notice.

'Not yet,' says Tom quickly, staring at the tablecloth.

'You don't want to leave too big a gap,' chips in Ruth breezily.

An image of the Babygro, teeny, towelling and folded in the airing cupboard engulfs me. I look at Tom. He is still looking at the tablecloth. I really want him to smile or squeeze my hand or do something to indicate that we are in this together. But he doesn't. He just carries on staring at the tablecloth, only the Adam's apple rising and falling in his throat betraying any emotion at all. My eyes start to fill. Everyone stares at their food, sensing a non-dinner-party topic has intruded, that someone might be about to vent an embarrassing volume of emotion and ruin pudding.

Pam touches my hand lightly. 'You OK?' she whispers.

I nod, touched by her concern.

'It's great to have such an interesting new Anderson wife recruit, Sadie. In fact there is a reason I invited you here tonight.' Pam looks up and smiles. 'All of you.'

Aha. There's an agenda.

'I thought as we four all live so close to one another, and have husbands in the same company, we wives should maybe get together a bit more, do a bit of fundraising maybe. Anderson are very good when it comes to charity, sponsorship, things like that.'

'And tax breaks . . .' mutters Seth under his breath.

'What's with The Wives? Surely women work there too?' I ask, grateful to Pam for swerving the conversation away from babies.

There is a guffaw of laughter from Tom, Seth and Alex.

'A few. But most are there in a secretarial capacity as far as I can make out,' says Ruth. 'It's a very blokey company, and culture.'

'So are you interested, ladies?' asks Pam.

'I'd love to but I'm kind of frantic at work,' says Ruth quickly. 'I know that sounds terribly selfish but . . .'

'Well you do have a job and twins,' I say, putting forward her defence.

'Oh, don't worry, Ruth. I'd do all the organising,'

says Pam. 'It won't take up much of your time at all, I promise.'

Seth laughs. 'Don't worry, Ruth. You should have seen her when she did work full time. Bigger balls than Alan Sugar.'

'I can't just sit around this house getting fatter and fatter until the baby comes,' adds Pam. 'I need to focus my energies somewhere.'

'So do I,' says Tara. 'I'm in.'

'I'll count you in too, Ruth. OK? Marvellous. Sadie?' pushes Pam. I get a glimpse of the tenacious careerist she once was, or might have been had she not realigned her energies.

My sensible instinct is to say, no thanks, dreadful idea. But I remember Enid's advice: embrace wife friends. 'OK,' I say weakly.

Tom looks up and smiles. It is a smile of surprise, and, perhaps, relief.

'It's a deal then.' Pam raises her glass. 'Now will someone please finish off that irresistibly squidgy blue cheese before a pregnant lady succumbs?'

Twelve

It's 9 a.m. Sunlight is leaking through the-gap-that-never-closes in our pale grey velvet bedroom curtains. From downstairs comes the clang and clatter of Rona and Danny having breakfast, interspersed with Teddy yapping. Tom is lying next to me, his Roman nose coated with the sheen of night-time sweat, his mouth dry from all the wine we drank at Pam's last night, the leaning tower of Pisa nudging my thigh. If we were dating then I probably would do two things: go downstairs and make him a surprise breakfast and bring it up on a tray, then jump on him enthusiastically. However, as monster-in-law is already up, I can only jump on him enthusiastically. He won't be thinking of coffee and croissants then! Oh no. I edge closer to him, run my finger up his thigh, applauding myself for the foresight of wearing a plum silk negligee, rather than those comfy old favourites, the striped flannel pyjamas.

'Morning, Mummy!' shouts Danny suddenly from outside the bedroom door.

The door starts to open. And my seduction is aborted. Admittedly, part of me feels a teeny bit relieved. And if we were dating and I felt relieved then I'd probably assume I was in the wrong relationship. Danny charges in, jumps up on the bed. I hug him, then start back. Strange. Danny looks different. At first I can't work out why. Then I realise. Danny's hair! 'Danny, baby, what's happened to your hair?' I nudge Tom sharply in the ribs. 'Tom, look!'

Danny grins and runs his finger over his shorn head. 'Rona cut my hair. She said I looked like gypsy.'

I crush my hand to my mouth, horrified. The audacity! 'Granny *cut* your hair?' I say slowly, in disbelief.

'What's wrong, Mummy?' Danny looks anxious.

I force myself to smile, not wanting to upset him. 'Nothing, sweetie. It looks very smart.'

'Rona says it's good to look smart.' Danny grins now he's got my approval and snuggles into the duvet. 'Even if Mummy doesn't.'

Tom winces at me. 'Leave it,' he whispers. 'It's done now.'

I lie there trying to leave it, reminding myself of all the reasons that I really *should* leave it – marriage, sanity, blood pressure – then I leap out of bed.

'Sadie!' Tom calls after me. 'Don't.'

Rona is downstairs, in a spotless white towelling dressing gown and matching spa-style slippers, reading the *Daily Mail* with her Ralph Lauren tortoiseshell reading glasses perched primly at the end of her nose. Teddy is curled in her lap slobbering over a bone-shaped dog biscuit. 'Hi, Sadie,' she says, more cheerily than usual. 'You look like you enjoyed yourself last night. You must drink lots of water.' Rona plunges the cafetière down. 'Caffeine?'

'You cut Danny's hair!'

She doesn't flinch. 'Isn't it cute?'

'I loved his curls.'

'Oh.' She looks up, surprised. 'You mind? Sorry, Sadie, I was only trying to help.' She hands me a cup of coffee calmly. She is smiling. I think part of her enjoys the conflict and deliberately seeks it out. 'It was in his eyes. He was going to get a horrendous eye infection. Even little Teddy needs a trip to the grooming salon once in a while, darling. And a man in Tom's position can't have a son who looks like a gypsy. When was the last time Danny went to the barbers?'

'Barbers? Rona, Danny is not yet three! He's only got about a hundred hair follicles. He's had four hair cuts in his entire life, courtesy of my nail scissors.'

She sits back down at the table, sniffs haughtily. 'I won't try and help again then.'

I shake my head; the cheek of the woman. Should I explode? Or should I bite my tongue and obey my husband? Tom, I suppose, is right. It is too late. The curls have gone. The deed done. 'Let's forget it,' I say, walking out of the room, knowing that I will *never* forget it.

'Apology accepted,' she calls after me.

I pad back upstairs. From the hall I can see Danny and Tom cuddled up in bed, looking sweet together, identifiably father and son with their blue eyes and golden, easily-tanned skin. Danny is flying his model aeroplane into Tom's ear.

'Daddy,' says Danny, in his high butter-soft voice. 'Do spitfires spit fire at baddies? Or do they fire spit?'

I smile, lean against the banisters and luxuriate in the sweet family scene. It makes me feel instantly calmer. Rona hasn't got this. And she can't take this away from me.

Tom laughs, pulls Danny towards him in a big bear grip, then kisses the top of his head. 'Spit fire. Well, bullets. They have special kinds of guns beneath their wings.'

Danny nods gravely, holds up his model plane and studies it with new reverence, as if Tom had just unlocked its secrets. 'Cool.'

I lean back against the wall and imagine another child beside the bed, a small baby, wrapped in a pink blanket, holding up her fingers in front of her face and turning them slowly as if underwater.

'Daddy,' says Danny chirpily. 'Will that lady pop round again with biscuits?'

'What lady?'

'She came round when Trish was looking after me. Mummy working.'

'Oh right. Yes.' Tom lowers his voice to a whisper. 'Um. No. Probably not.'

'Was she one of Mummy's friends?'

'No . . .' Tom hesitates and clears his throat. I can sense his unease even from where I am standing. 'She was a lady from work, Danny. She was just passing.'

'Looked like princess.'

Something in me freezes.

Tom looks up, clearly agitated. He sees me in the hall then. We stare at each other, our gaze locked but not connecting. He looks away first.

Thirteen

There is an enormous billboard advertising lager beside the road. 'Do you know who your husband was with last night?' is the slogan. I accelerate too quickly and continue driving east. Drive, drive, drive. Don't think. Don't fall into the paranoia hole. But I can't help it. The thoughts start marching into my head like determined soldier ants. Chloe once told me that the reason she first suspected that Ian (skanky ex-hubby) was having an affair was because he no longer wanted to sleep with her. This, coupled with his uncharacteristic niceness got her wondering. Of course, a few weeks later, the knickers – not hers – down the back of the sofa confirmed things. As did the foot and hand model who turned up on her doorstep five months pregnant. So I haven't found the knickers and if another woman turned up pregnant on my doorstep I'd almost certainly end up splashed across the front page of the *Daily Mail*. But am I being stupid? *Am* I? Would an affair explain things? Would it explain why he doesn't want another baby? Although Tom's not exactly nice-bombing me, he's working later and later, leaving earlier and earlier and he doesn't want to sleep with me. And who the hell was that woman from work who came to the house the other day? Why was he so uneasy when Danny mentioned her? I look at Danny in the rear-view mirror. He is swinging his legs happily from his car seat, staring out of the window and excitedly noting every lorry, digger and industrial vehicle that passes. I consider pressing him for more information but decide against it on account of such probing being morally dubious and the information being unreliable. 'Looked like princess' tells me more than enough.

'Are we there yet?' he chirps.

'Five minutes.'

Thirty minutes later we arrive at Columbia Road market. My legs, unused to being exposed in a dress, feel goose-bumpy and vulnerable. Although Danny insists I am 'a very pretty Mummy' today I wish I'd just worn my jeans rather than take Enid's sartorial advice to such extremes before 9 a.m. We stand in front of a stall. 'Look, this is a hyacinth. Isn't it lovely?'

The florets of the Blue Jacket hyacinth are clustered like small, firm, unripe grapes around woody white stems. They will be perfect. Not for a client. For our house, the house I will no longer neglect. Hyacinths are Tom's favourite flower.

Danny pokes them with his finger. 'Smells of honey.'

'Three bunches, please,' I say. 'Also, one bunch of narcissus, some widow iris.'

'Good choice. Nice blooms these.' The stallholder, a bald man with a comforting face like a pie, pulls out the flowers, their wet stems dripping from their trug containers. I stand closer to Danny, resting a hand on his shoulder in case the crowd swells like a river and carries him away downstream.

Danny looks up at me and grins. He loves it, the people, the excitement, the mummy-time, the plants spilling from pavement to road, as if taking over the street, softening its bricks and hard surfaces, banishing the smell of exhaust with peaty jungle smells, brightening the east London grey-scape with paint-bright splashes of colour. The cut flowers themselves, although not as good quality as those at Covent Garden, are impressive in their numbers. I'm struck, as I am again and again at flower markets, by the beautiful melancholy of cut flowers, the way they are cut down in their prime, their bodies teased and wired and displayed, until, finally, sapped of their life-giving sugars and having selflessly given the very best of themselves, they die, each flower as perishable as love itself.

'I'll knock a couple of pounds off for those lovely legs of yours,' he says.

I blush and can't help but self-consciously cross one leg in front of the other.

'And this little fellow. Cute as a button, aren't you, lad?'

Danny looks up at me uncertainly, trying to recall my advice about strangers. He digs his hand in his pocket to find his toy car and holds it up to the stallholder. 'Want to race?'

The stallholder shakes his head. 'Would love to, son. Gotta work though.' He laughs. 'What you need is a brother, my lad.'

For a moment everything stops very still. Then I remember to breathe again.

The stallholder stoops down, hands on his apron-clad knees. 'Or a little sis? They can be good fun. I've got five little sisters, would you believe it?'

Danny shakes his head in disbelief. Five sisters is beyond unimaginable.

The stallholder winks at me. 'Better get on with it, love.'

'Obviously,' I say, smiling tightly. I don't know why I'm not better at this. It's happened enough times. 'Come on, Danny.'

Danny yawns. We have been up for two hours already and he's starting to flag.

'How about a croissant before we hit the road?'

He hesitates, reflecting on a way to optimise my suggestion. '*Pain au chocolat*! Pomegranate juice.'

'You west London child!' I laugh. 'I didn't eat pomegranate until I was in my teens. Come on.' I take his small warm hand in mine and feel a surge of love for him, for his pure concentrated boyishness and the happiness, unexpected happiness – I had no idea I could love someone so much before he was born – that he has brought me. Along with this comes the fear of loss though. That's the hardest thing. That's the thing that Tom says I need to get over. Not everyone you love is about to die, he says to me as I sigh into my pillow and stare at the neon digits of the alarm clock, unable to sleep.

In the café Danny swings his legs from the chair and peels back the layers of pastry to get to the sausage of soft chocolate in the centre. He sucks up the orange juice – unsurprisingly, they didn't have pomegranate – fascinated by its journey up the straw. I sip my tea and eat a cream cheese bagel and gaze out of the café's smudged sheet-glass window at the men dwarfed by the huge palms in their arms, the tourists, the east London hipsters with their thick dark fringes, their sunglasses hiding the excesses of the night before, the . . . the . . .

I sit up straighter and squint. It takes a few seconds before I realise who it is. The curly corkscrew hair. Those ivy-green eyes. Eddie! I stay very still, unsure whether I should wave or sit it out anonymously, not sure if he's seen me or not. Then he turns and glances at the menu which is pinned up on the café window. All it will take is a glance to the left and . . . He starts back from the window, then hovers uncertainly before coming in. He is taller than I remember, the hand that pushes open the café door is as big as a spade.

'Hi there. It's Sadie,' I say, wiping my mouth. I now

have unseemly streaks of cream cheese all over the back of my hand. 'Enid's florist.'

'I remember,' he smiles, a wide smile, much more relaxed than last time I saw him.

'This is my son Danny,' I say, pulling down the skirt of my dress which has risen up over my pale round thighs.

Eddie bends down. I notice his curls are slightly matted at the back where he's slept on them. 'Hi, Danny. That looks good.'

Danny gives Eddie a quick glance and returns to the more compelling task of peeling apart his *pain au chocolat*.

'Buying plants, I guess?' No, he's buying cushions. Duh.

'Just browsing. I live up the road. The bagels are very good.'

'Oh. I thought you might have lived . . .'

Eddie laughs. 'With Aunty E? God, no. But a lot of my landscaping work is in the posh bits of north London so doing stuff at hers works well for me.'

'You're there a lot,' I say, sounding oddly stalkerish.

'Ah, yes.' He rolls his eyes. 'A bit of a restyle, that's why. A project. She sure likes a project does dear Aunty E. But I'll be done by September, then she can employ someone to just maintain it all.'

'Join us if you like,' I say impetuously, surprising myself.

'Will do. First, coffee.' I watch him as he places his order at the counter. He is wearing worn-in jeans, a beaten-up leather man bag over one shoulder, old scuffed white trainers. He puts a steaming cup of black coffee on the table and drags up a chair. 'I need this,' he says, blowing the hot coffee. 'I guess you're used to the early starts.'

'Not that early for me, sadly. Danny woke up at six today, didn't you, Danny? I thought we may as well get up and do something.'

Danny is showered in crumbs. They're in his hair, ears, everywhere. He digs in his pocket and pulls out his red tin car, then a blue one. 'Race?'

'I'm sure Eddie . . .'

'I'd love to race you,' says Eddie. 'Blue or red?'

'Blue.' Danny grins. 'I'm always red. Red wins.'

'Ah, we'll see about that.' Eddie puts a teaspoon at one end of the table, his saucer at the other. 'Come on then, first one to get from teaspoon to saucer.' He pushes the car along the Formica table top.

Danny squeals when he gets to the saucer first. 'I win! Red wins!'

'Goddamn!' Eddie puts his head in his hands. 'I'm beat.'

I'm charmed. It's hard to square the man sitting here with the person who warned me against ripping off Enid. He's sweet, playful. And he does that really sexy thing of looking at my mouth when I talk.

'I'm sorry about what I said the other week,' he says. 'It was very rude of me questioning your fee. I didn't mean—'

'It's OK.' Oh, I forgive him instantly and completely.

'No, really. I spoke out of turn. It's just that Enid gets ripped off by everyone, plumbers, builders, gardeners ... The last gardener charged five hundred quid for planting a few spring bulbs. That's why I stepped in. I'm probably overprotective,' says Eddie, resting his chin in his hand, smiling at Danny as he pushes his red car up his arm.

I find myself wondering about his single status. Could he do for Chloe? No. Chalk and cheese. 'So she's your aunt?'

'Great-aunt. Late grandmother's sister. Outlived the rest.' He sips his coffee. 'You're coming back I hope. Don't let me put you off. Anyway, the duchess is very much looking forward to your visit. It's all she can talk about. She is a bit obsessed. She gets these obsessions, crushes on people, not very often – she's not generous with her approval – but if she likes you she *really* likes you, if you know what I mean. Sadie . . .' He hesitates and studies my face with such intensity I blush. 'Do you mind me asking exactly what went on that day in the park?'

'It was a storm. Lots of wind. Bucketing down.'

'A very stormy storm,' clarifies Danny, making wave motions with his hands. 'Very whooshey. Mummy cut her head on a whooshey branch.'

'Why do you ask?'

Eddie shrugs. 'Well, it's like she's been a bit of a changed woman since it happened. I wondered if there was something she wasn't telling me. Like she was the one who got the whack to the head.' He laughs. It's a warm laugh. It's kind of dirty too. 'I imagined her being swept over the treetops like something from bloody *Mary Poppins*.' He puts his hand over his mouth. 'Naughty word, sorry, Danny.'

Danny grins. 'I know that word already.'

'Eruditely put, Danny, thank you,' I say. 'No, I was the one who got bashed on the head. She helped me, offered me a tissue, that's how we met. She was very sweet actually.'

Eddie drains his coffee. 'Oh well. Who knows the mysteries of Enid Fisher's brain? Of any woman's brain come to think of it. Anyhow, I shouldn't complain. She is in a far better mood. That's the puzzling thing, you see. She was getting very . . .' He stops and looks sad. '. . . maudlin, and that's me being diplomatic. Cantankerous might be a better description. The last of her close friends died a couple of months ago. She gave up a bit after that.' He turns the coffee cup round and round on its saucer. I notice his thick, tanned fingers, the mud under the fingernails, just like mine. He stands up. 'But not any more it seems. Your flowers are working wonders, keep it up. Right, well, I won't intrude any longer. Danny, I'll win next time, mate.'

'Next time, mate,' parrots Danny, grinning.

Eddie strides out of the café door into the crowds of people and plants on the pavement. He waves and is quickly swallowed into the street. The day suddenly feels less colourful.

Danny grabs my arm. 'Mummy, there he is!' He points out of the café window.

'You mean Eddie? Where?' I scan the crowd of bobbing heads. 'No. He's gone, sweetie,' I say but actually I do have the sensation that I am being watched.

Fourteen

Idle conundrum thoughts blow in through the open window as I sit on the lime green sofa dunking milk chocolate digestives in my Earl Grey.

Idle thought one

If I can fancy Eddie just a *teeny* bit, it makes sense that Tom fancies other people too. Marriage doesn't stop you fancying other people. It's just supposed to stop you fucking them. But whereas I rarely work in proximity to men – Eddie being the rare exception – Tom works in close proximity with sirens: slim, urban, professional single women who have time to go to the gym and shop for fashionable clothes and wax their bits on a regular basis. Plus he's a man in a marriage officially 'needing work'. He's successful. Good looking with a twinkle in his eye. He's even funny, sometimes. Yes, I can see how if you weren't married to him he might appear rather attractive.

Idle thought two

Why did Tom smell of perfume when he came home last night? Not my perfume.

Idle thought three

Who was he talking to late last night on the telephone as I bathed in my new 'Seductive Spa experience'? How come *both* of us looked so flushed afterwards?

Idle thought four

Pam has left a message on my phone asking me to 'drop round or call when you have a moment to discuss an Anderson wife get-together'. I cling on to the 'when you have a moment' like an escape raft. This means that she is presuming that I may not have a moment, doesn't it? This means that I can procrastinate.

Idle thought five

Which cleaner shall I employ? Pat, a fat, moody fiftysomething with no references? Or Anna, the super-keen, twentysomething Bulgarian with great references and good legs?

The answer is suddenly very obvious. I call fat Pat: 'You've got the job.' Later she comes round and I sheepishly set her a vague list of tasks – 'loos, sticky bit behind the fridge, ring round the bath' – that I hate doing myself. She is polite but looks at me through narrowed eyes like she's seen my feckless, middle-class type many times before. Although she does the yucky bits, when she leaves the house still looks a little bit like I might live here. I realise I'd need to employ an army of industrial cleaners to eradicate all the evidence. Further action is clearly needed. Oh yes.

If I'm going to do this wife thing at all I need to do it properly.

So what do I do? I make myself a coffee so strong it feels like my head might blow off. I turn up fast, frenetic dance music really loud. I go on a sock hunt, looking under sofas, behind bedroom radiators, hunting down lost socks until they're all neatly matched up. This takes ages. The ironing takes far, far longer. I get confused by the dial on the iron – what do the symbols mean exactly? Why is it bellowing out steam when I'm not pressing the steam button? – and singe Tom's shirt with a dirty great iron mark. Then I make the mistake of ironing Danny's *Thomas the Tank Engine* pyjamas – beyond the call of duty but I've got into my stride now – and the Thomas transfer thingy comes off on the iron rendering it unusable, which brings further ironing to an abrupt halt. But I won't be beaten. I'm a woman on a mission. I air the duvet on the washing line. I remove all the strange, random bits – rusty nails, Rizla papers, old chapsticks – from the drawers they've inexplicably accumulated in. I plan what we're going to eat for supper: lamb chops;

broccoli; couscous; strawberries. Idiot-proof non-cooking surely. I even prepare the broccoli in advance, chopping it into neat florets and putting it – ready to go! – in a bowl which I cover smugly with cling film. I can't remember the last time I covered anything with cling film. Then I take a long look at my labours, pour myself a glass of wine so big Danny could drown in it and breathe a sigh of satisfaction. House in order. Food prepared. The stage is set. Nigella, move over.

Once Danny's in bed I set about un-neglecting myself. I put on fresh clothes: nice clean jeans, a white T-shirt, bare feet, which I tan up with some bronzing powder so they don't look like the feet of a cadaver. Yes, I am channelling the Jennifer Aniston off-duty look, homely but sexy. I finish it off with a quick squirt of the Jo Malone he gave me for Christmas.

At 7.30 p.m. the front door slams. Tom comes in, unknotting his tie, shaking summer rain out of his dark hair. 'Wow. Have the fairies been?' he asks, looking around in disbelief. 'The Corridor of Chaos is no longer. Don't tell me you've been cleaning.'

'I have.' I feel a brief shiver of shame in claiming fat Pat's work as my own but remind myself the lie is for the greater good. 'I have indeed been cleaning. You'll also find the duvet puffed and aired. Your socks matched. Your shirts ironed.'

'Are you feeling all right?'

'Never better. Tea, darling?' I wiggle my hips a little as I walk towards the kettle.

He hangs up his light khaki coat on the peg and looks at me warily. 'Something stronger.'

I pour him a glass of wine and bring him a bowl of roasted almonds and wonder if he's noticed my sexy off-duty Jen outfit. It seems not. Tom sits down at the kitchen table and spreads out the *Evening Standard*. I try to ignore the fact that even though I haven't seen him since seven-thirty this morning, he is so entranced by my company that he still prefers to read about politicians' holiday plans on returning home twelve hours later. Normally I'd comment on this; tonight I bite my tongue. Husband fed, happy, in a clean, comfortable home. He's got to be in a good mood. So he can't be angry with me for asking breezily: 'Tom, Danny said a lady came round. Someone from work. I was wondering who it was.'

Tom doesn't look up. 'Hmmm?'

'Last week, when I was finishing off the flowers at that Belsize Park gallery and Trish was looking after Danny. Danny said a woman came in—'

'Oh that must have been Annette,' he says quickly, his jaw tensing.

'Annette?' I feel like someone's thrown a bucket of cold water at my face. I don't feel like Jen now. 'Who is Annette?'

'Annette Eastern,' he says and adds rapidly, '. . . one of our clients.'

The woman Chloe mentioned. The one who wants a florist. But it's not Annette Western, it's Annette Eastern.

I knew she sounded familiar. Oh God. I remember now. She's the one . . . 'Otherwise known as "Psyche Viagra"?'

Tom winces. He coined this phrase. He was terribly pleased about it at the time. Bet he's less pleased about it now. 'Yeah. Annette Eastern.' He looks at me wearily. 'We were on the way from a meeting in west London to the City. She does a lot of stuff in the City. I had some papers to collect . . .' He pauses. 'Look, I'm tired. It's been a ball ache of a day. Why are you looking at me like that, Sadie?'

'You didn't mention it, that's all.' My voice is sharper now. I'm trying not to snap. I bet Jen doesn't snap, she'd just crumble prettily.

'Should I have done? Listen, next time, if you like, I'll make a point of writing every future move of mine in that pink notebook of yours. But right now I'm going to jump in the shower.' He gets up and releases a whiff of unwashed man, a cross between a restaurant kitchen and a locker room.

'And by the way, Sadie. You've got something stuck to your foot.'

I look down at my Jennifer Aniston bare feet. A long piece of loo paper is stuck to my heel, stained brown by the bronzing powder. Hell, I tried.

Fifteen

A beautiful day. I punch the security code into the gates, drive in, get out of the car and breathe in great lungfuls of fragrant summer air. Here at Enid's, I realise, is the closest I've come to that fantasy I had in Toronto about Returning Home To England. Here the grass is green and lush, the flowers firm and yellow. The honeysuckle exudes a sweet scent. Bees drone prettily. And life seems simpler, solvable, like a crossword puzzle. I smooth down my hair and adjust my new tasteful tortoiseshell hairslide, bought to replace the plasticky ones that come in cheap Tesco multi-packs and are one up from a scrunchie. I hope that Eddie won't be here. I hope that he will. The strangely enjoyable, pink-hued dream in which he took a starring role last night is still floating in my head. I'm worried that he'll look at me and know, in the same way that when I saw Tom blowing breath into his cupped hands and sniffing this morning I knew he wasn't checking his breath to kiss me.

I hear footsteps. Eddie opens the door. 'Hi, Sadie. Hey, you look well.'

I grin stupidly. Is this what Tom hungers for too? The affirming smile of sexual attraction from someone other than one's spouse? I have to admit it feels good, damn good. And, actually, the sliver of brown belly that peeks out from under Eddie's T-shirt rather suggests that it would feel good too.

'Come through. The duchess is in the garden.' I follow him, through the hall and into the kitchen, where the crystal vases are already laid out on the table, sunlight smashing into them and casting streaks of rainbow on the walls. I spot Enid through the window, sitting on a tartan picnic rug in the garden wearing her blue silk housecoat embroidered with cockatoos. On the rug is a wooden tray: a pot of tea, a jug of milk, a small chocolate cake. Angie stands behind her carefully combing her hair, teasing it into neat silver curls along her neckline. In the sunshine Enid looks older than she does in the soft reflected creams and pinks of the house interior.

'Albert's birthday today,' whispers Eddie. His breath smells pleasantly of warm toast.

'Am I intruding?'

'Not at all. She'll be better for having seen you.' He puts his hand on my back. I can feel his fleshy heat through my (ironed!) white shirt. It spreads a warm glow over my body. 'See you later,' he says, stomping off in his big gardener's boots. 'I'm working out front.

Then I've got to shoot to a landscaping job up the road.'

Enid's face lights up when she sees me. She turns to Angie. 'Thank you, Angie. That will be all.'

Angie shuffles past me with her hairbrush, dark eyes dancing, closing the patio door gently behind her.

'Black tulips,' I say cheerily, holding one stem up to her. 'The best I've seen all year.'

'What better way to celebrate Albert's birthday than with chocolate cake and dark tulips?' She is silent a few moments, watching my face intently. 'I hope you don't think I'm batty celebrating my dead husband's birthday.'

I shake my head too vigorously.

'I suspect it might look a bit Miss Havisham to a youth.'

'Oh no. It's sweet,' I laugh. Yes, Sadie the youth. I like it.

'He so loved his birthday.' She smiles a slow, secret smile. 'We'd go dancing, you know. We'd always go dancing. He was just the best dancer, quite the Fred Astaire.' Enid pats the blanket. 'Do sit down, darling. Pretty blouse.'

No longer do I even pretend this is a normal client and florist relationship. I sit down casually on the tartan rug and admire Eddie's borders, the seeding grasses and flowers, the soft whites and buttery yellows, his intelligent, subtle planting. 'Eddie has done a very lovely job with your garden, Enid.'

'Hasn't he just? He's very talented, my Eddie.

163

But . . .' Enid looks wistful. 'I do so wish there were more people here to enjoy his work. This is a garden that demands parties, don't you think? Parties that start in the afternoon and drift on into the night. When everyone drinks too much and flirts with each other's husbands.'

I feel a pang of pity. Where are her family? Her friends? I pick a daisy and twirl it in my fingers.

'Most of my friends are dead now, darling, in case you're wondering.'

I start a little. The way she appears to read my mind sometimes unnerves me.

'Don't feel sorry for me. We all end up six feet under. You included,' she adds wryly. 'Life throws a random set of cards. I had a big love. Not everyone has that.' She fans herself with her hand. 'Goodness. It is getting hot, isn't it? Thank heavens for global warming. Keep burning those fabulous fossil fuels that's what I say. I'm so jealous of all the lovely Mediterranean summers you'll enjoy. Part of the reason Albert took the foreign postings was because of the intolerable British climate. Now, Sadie. How are you getting on with our little project?'

I swipe a bee away from my leg. 'Well . . .'

Enid laughs, as if further problems will delight her. 'Oh dear, oh dear! I can see that we do have our work cut out, don't we?'

I smile weakly, my mind suddenly racing with thoughts about Tom, about infidelity. She'll think I'm paranoid, neurotic. Hell, of course I'm neurotic.

'What is it? What's bothering you? I can see troubled thoughts creasing in your brow. Have a piece of chocolate cake. Cake always helps. In moderation, of course. Fat thighs don't help at all.'

'Thank you. It looks delicious.'

She slices a particularly slim wedge of cake – a ladylike portion, not the trucker's portion I normally go for – and expertly transports it from one plate to another on the back of the silver knife, just like my nan used to do. 'Yes?' she says, fixing me with a shrewd stare. And I know that I won't be able to fudge her. 'Go on.'

'There's this woman, oh dear, it's just a hunch, Enid. She's a client of his. And she visited our house,' I gabble. 'Tom reacted strangely when I confronted him about it . . . Oh, it's a few things, things that don't quite add up. I know I sound silly.'

Enid puts up a hand to stop me. 'Darling, you do not sound silly, not at all. I believe we know things intuitively . . .' She slams a palm against her heart and her jewelled beetle brooch wobbles. '. . . before we can prove them. Ignore a hunch at your peril.'

'Oh dear, really?' I was rather hoping she'd tell me I am paranoid and silly.

'Don't worry. Easily investigated. You know Maud and I spent weeks investigating her husband's paramour, a little minx called Valerie.'

'Was Maud's hunch right?'

'It was.'

'Oh.'

'You need to sleuth around a bit. Imagine you're in a film. You're the heroine. Play the role. Life is so much easier if you imagine you're playing a role.'

'I don't know, Enid. I feel slightly duplicitous, even coming here. I feel like I'm plotting. We always promised one another no secrets. Total honesty.'

'Honesty in marriage is hugely overrated.' She takes a small, neat bite of chocolate cake and dabs at her mouth with a white linen napkin. 'Intimacy doesn't mean honesty. Intimacy thrives on mystery, darling. The girls and I, we never assumed our husbands were being wholly honest with us and we were certainly never wholly honest with them.'

I laugh. 'Isn't that a wee bit disrespectful?'

Enid giggles. 'Deliciously disrespectful. I promise you that the friends of mine who had the best marriages, and the longest, were the ones who held something back. Mystery makes passion, darling. A buttoned up blouse is sexier than a little black dress. Crossed legs are sexier than open ones, no?'

I laugh, shocked once again at Enid's unexpected vulgarity. 'I didn't mean . . .'

She drums her fingers on the side of the chair. 'What did old Nietzsche say again? "Women's modesty generally increases with their beauty." Something like that, if my memory serves me correctly. The inverse is true too. Only ugly women have to flaunt themselves.'

I nod dumbly. I've never read any Nietzsche. And I'm not entirely sure how she jumped from mystery to modesty either. But I guess she has time to reflect on such things. It strikes me that it must be very different to be rich and childless. All that time to improve oneself, to refine. Mum always said that too. The women who don't age are the ones without children. Then she'd smile and add, 'Lonely though.' She didn't have much time for overt sophistication, or tricksy philosophers. She liked simple things. Babies. Flowers. Food. We're similar like that. Except that she loved Joanna Trollope.

'Well, Sadie,' says Enid decisively. 'I think what you need to do is at least look like you have a mysterious, naughty little secret. Let *him* wonder. Maybe you have a lover,' she says in a French accent. 'Maybe you don't. And your cheeks should tell the same tale.'

'My cheeks?'

She laughs, pinches at the apple of her cheeks. The skin bunches up like crumpled crêpe paper. 'Colour, my darling. Bright of eye. Flush of cheek. Post-coital I think is the term I'm looking for.'

I blush.

'That's more like it. Right, pass that pink notebook of yours.' She writes something in it. 'There you go!'

I lean over her shoulder to see what she's written in her elegant looping hand: *Bloom! Hold a secret close to your heart. Never tell your husband! E x*

'Never tell Tom what?' I ask, slightly exasperated. Can't she just talk in modern English sentences?

167

'It doesn't matter, darling! You can be thinking about your dry cleaning for all I care. But you need to *look* like you're thinking of a lover, someone secret and rather delicious, especially if you suspect he may be playing off-piste. It's the best way to rein them in, I promise you. Look like you're holding something back. Men find it simply irresistible. It makes them feel that they might lose you and that they still have to chase you. Men are programmed to chase. It's in their blood. They're like fox hounds. Oh and one other thing, darling. I don't mean to speak out of turn but . . .' She studies my face for a moment. 'Have you ever considered red lipstick?'

'You're politely saying I need to wear make-up?' I laugh at her blithe impertinence. God, she is so like my nan. Are there a finite number of personalities in the world that get repeated randomly throughout history? Or is it that we are drawn to those who remind us of the familiar?

'A bit of glamour goes a long way. All the best actresses wear red lipstick.' She stands up, a little shakily. Then her face pales.

'Enid? Are you OK?'

She manages a smile. 'Oh, a funny turn. It's the heat.'

'You better sit down.' I help her sit back down and bring her a glass of water.

'Would you call Angie, my dear? I think I might need a little lie down.'

I get Angie and then, before leaving, search for Eddie

in the front garden. He is cutting back a lime tree with an electric saw. He whirrs it to a stop.

I struggle to hold the stack of flower boxes in my arms without dropping them. 'Eddie, would you mind checking on Enid in a while? Angie's with her. But she had a little funny turn.'

'Shit.' Eddie pushes back sweaty hair off his head and nimbly clambers down the lower branches of the tree. 'Thanks for telling me. I'll go check.'

As he passes me I drop a flower box. It falls softly into a lavender bush. Eddie leans over and picks it up for me. A woody sweaty smell. It's one of the sexiest smells, a smell of soil and sweat and leaves. He hands me the box and our fingers just touch. For a little longer than is perhaps strictly necessary.

Sixteen

Annette. Psyche Viagra. Enid has stoked my suspicions so that the small flame of doubt is now a raging bonfire. Annette is under my skin, coiled up in my thoughts, creeping into my dreams. I think about her as I drive up to Dr Prenwood's in Belsize Park. I imagine her naked. I imagine her face as she comes. In my head she is a glossy brunette, petite, big round tits turned up at the ends like noses – unlike mine that face the floor. Annette. Annette. Even her name reminds me of a really annoying girl at my school who all the boys adored and all the girls hated. She always wanted to be centre in netball and would laugh far harder at a boy's jokes than a girl's. One of those. Yes, *she* is my little secret.

At Dr Prenwood's apartment I'm jumpy and on edge. Every time Aysha the housekeeper opens the front door to put out a bag of rubbish and the door clunks I panic that I'll get locked in the apartment again, locked in forever while my husband runs into the sunset with a reassuring brunette with big tits. On the drive home I bite my fingernails. I call Chloe. 'It's me. Can I ask you something?'

'A bit tricky.' Her voice lowers to a whisper. 'I'm at a shoot. Actress has acne. In floods of tears, refusing a close up. A bit of a situation.'

'Sorry, it'll only take one minute . . . Annette Eastern. You said Western. But I think that's the same Annette you said wanted a florist? You gave me her number.'

'Yeah, yeah. That's her name! I knew it was something like that. I did her make-up for a *Marie Claire* article – London's hottest therapists or something, hon, that's right.'

'Quickly. What's she like?'

'Oh, I don't know. Can't really remember. Bit up herself. But take away her specs and she's a nose job away from looking like Gisele's twin sister. That's the only reason she got into the magazine, obviously.'

My stomach lurches unhappily. 'Oh.'

'Not that blusher!'

'Pardon?'

'Sorry. I'm talking to my assistant. Sadie, hon, I've got to go. Call me later if you like.'

'One last thing. Do you think I'd suit red lipstick?'

Chloe laughs. 'That's got to go down as one of your more eccentric questions, Sadie Drew.'

'Do you?'

'Why not?'

'Would you give me a make-up lesson?' If this is war, I need war paint.

'Happily. But I've got to—'

'Go. I know. Bye.' I click the phone shut, feeling queasy. She looks like *Gisele*? The luscious, legs up to her earlobes, Brazilian supermodel bombshell, Gisele? Damn. How can a puffed up duvet or a paired sock compete with bloody Gisele? I need to up my game. At the traffic lights I pick up my handbag and rummage through it. It must be here somewhere. I pick up my pink notebook, hold it upside down and shake it out on to the passenger seat. A squashed raisin drops out. A pen. I shake the notebook again. And then, fluttering down like a sycamore leaf, Annette's number, scribbled on the back of Chloe's card in a round, confident hand. Dare I?

Seventeen

For years my mother wore the same rose-pink lipstick. It came in a ribbed gold case with a small, hexagonal sticker on its lid. Mum would pout in the mirror when she applied it, then kiss a piece of loo roll. As a little girl I was thrilled when she let me play with it, twisting it up and down, fascinated by the angle of the lipstick tip, the way it always wore to a neat point. It smelled of Mum, in particular the Mum I especially liked, the Mum who dressed up for 'a do', i.e. social engagements that took place after 6 p.m. and generally involved a glass of dry white wine, perhaps a fancy cheese board. The lipstick would leave traces – smudgy kisses – on glasses and mugs and sometimes my cheek. It lived in the magical cavern of her handbag alongside other unfathomable things such as her conical yellow plastic Tampax holder and her collection of emergency hairpins held together by a thin, green rubber band. When I grow up I'm going to wear lipstick, I would tell her. Which would make her laugh and pat my cheek. But I grew up and despite owning lipsticks – many were Christmas stocking fillers from her – I never used them, opting instead for smear-it-on-in-the-dark lip gloss, and, more recently, chapstick. Lipstick has always felt too dry and too grown up.

But I'm sure I've still got one somewhere. Not in the bathroom cabinet. Not in my make-up bag – duh, that would be too obvious! No, I find an old red lipstick lurking at the bottom of the old shoe box where I keep cheap high street accessories: bangles, pendants, belts. Probably on account of its age the lipstick is hard to apply and drags along the lips. Its garish red makes my teeth look a little yellow. It feels strange, like I've been kissed on the mouth by an ageing aunt.

Smacking my lips together like Mum used to, I walk downstairs and start guiltily poking around Tom's work desk. It doesn't take long to find the book. In fact there are three copies of it, glossy and fat with a spine the same red as my lipstick. Not having time to study it now, I slide it under my arm, grab Danny, still munching Marmite toast, and bolt to the nursery. Scary Hanna gives me a cross *late again* look and stares at the piece of toast as if it were the devil's Pop Tart. As I'm leaving I spot Perfect Pam circling by the nursery gate, twirling a pink polka dot umbrella like someone from an old Hollywood musical, even though it's no longer raining. She's got her 'I'm Not A Plastic Bag' bag over her shoulder. And she's seen me. There's no back route. I'm trapped.

'Oo,' she says, giving me a sideways look, like I've

got something to hide, like an affair, or a cold sore. 'Nice lipstick.' She laughs and taps her front tooth. 'A little smudge.'

'Thanks.' I rub my tooth with my sleeve. 'Gone?'

'Gone. Did you get my message?'

'I did! God, I'm so sorry not to have returned your call. It's been mental.'

'Don't worry. I understand,' she says through a slightly forced smile. Her expression changes. She cocks her head to the side and stares at Annette's book tucked under my arm. 'What are you reading?'

I clamp it closer to my side. 'Oh just trashy stuff. Nothing interesting.' I stop and stare out at the passing traffic, trying to deflect her attention.

Pam peers closer. Recognition lights her face. 'Annette Eastern, isn't it? *Spring Clean Your Heart!* I LOVE that book! Amazing. You know what? It made me commit to Seth. Not joking.' Her eyes burn with the fire of the converted. 'Made me realise that I'd been cluttering my life with men who didn't commit and who weren't good enough because I didn't think *I* was good enough.'

'So you're a fan?'

'Totally! My ex, the pop star guy – Flash Pete, say no more – he refused to even discuss marriage.' Pam speaks in low conspiratorial tones. It is quite hard to hear her against the traffic. 'Normally I wouldn't have given a man like Seth a second glance but after reading this book, you know what I thought? I thought, actually, I do need to spring clean my life of clubs and Flash Petes and waking up in the morning and not knowing the surname of the man beside me.' She slaps her hand against her fleshy décolletage. 'I deserve it. That's what she tells you to do, stand in front of the mirror every morning and say, "I deserve a rewarding, supportive relationship. Yes, I deserve it."'

'Like the L'Oréal ads?'

Pam stares fiercely off into the mid-distance as if plugging into the experience all over again. 'It's all about getting rid of people that hold you back, drag you down.'

'Oh.' Something stabs into my left side like bad indigestion. Do I hold Tom back? If Tom had married someone else, like Perfect Pam for example, only blonde, would his life be much easier? He'd have meals cooked for him. The house would be ordered. And so there would be less arguments. More babies. And Tom could sail to career triumph on the smooth seas of domestic harmony. He'd have been made a director weeks ago.

'Yeah, you know,' whispers Pam breathily. 'The negative people, the moaners, the ones who are always . . .' She does quote signs with her fingers. '. . . glass half empty.'

Fuck, is that me? It *is* me. 'I better go, Pam. Or I'll be horribly late and lose all my clients in exemplary Sadie Drew fashion.'

'Don't put yourself down,' says Pam, swinging her

I'm Not A Plastic Bag over her shoulder. 'That's another thing that Annette Eastern said: if you put yourself down, who's going to want to pick you up? Hey, look, it's Ruth. Hi Ruth!'

Ruth, the nice one from Pam's dinner party, looks different today, her figure all angles in her trouser suit, her features wrought. 'Hi there. I can't stop . . .'

'You look formidably smart,' I say. 'If I wanted a lawyer, I'd want one who looked like you.'

Ruth runs her fingers through her hair. 'No, you wouldn't. I've got to run home first. Look.' She points at her feet. 'I left the house with . . .'

I glance down. It takes a second before I notice. Yes, same colour. But different shoes. 'Oops,' I laugh.

'Honestly, I despair of myself. I set out, towing the twins along, both screaming at me like I'm a sicko trying to abduct them, strangers glaring, you know the situation. Or maybe you don't.'

'I do,' I say.

'Well, my feet felt funny. The left foot in particular felt too tight. We were about fifty yards down the road when I realised.' She groans. 'God, I need my wife back!'

'I bet you do. I honestly don't know how households function with two parents working,' says Pam.

'I should roll my eyes,' groans Ruth. 'But I hate to say I almost agree with you, Pam. To think that I was the one who encouraged Alex back to the workplace. Talk about an own goal. I'm kicking myself, with my odd shoes, obviously.'

'Did you get my message?' asks Pam suddenly, with the look of someone racing through a mental checklist in her head.

'Um. I think so. I'm sorry, I've been frantic,' says Ruth.

'Are you both around on Saturday, four-ish? Well, check your diaries. Let's have a meeting about those fundraising ideas we were talking about at dinner. An Anderson wife powwow,' says Pam. 'I was thinking that maybe I'd invite some more Anderson wives, broaden it out a bit.' She digs in her handbag for her mobile phone. 'I'll call Linda now.'

'No!' I say too loudly, resisting the urge to wrestle the phone out of her hands. 'Let's keep it small.'

'Oh, maybe you're right. But I was going to invite Chloe too, now that our paths have happily crossed again through you.'

'She doesn't qualify though, does she?' I can't imagine that wild horses would drag her. 'She's not an Anderson wife. She's not even a wife.'

Pam taps her nose. 'Contacts, Sadie. I wanted to pick her brains. Plus, she's local. And I'm sure she gets bombarded with freebies, things that would be perfect for raffles or bric-a-brac stalls.'

Bric-a-brac. Oh God. How did I get involved in bric-a-brac stalls? Part of me recoils. I'll be making trifles and offering finger bowls at dinner next.

'Ruth, anything you could bring to the table?'

'Free divorces? Settlement advice?' says Ruth wryly.

'Four p.m.,' adds Pam, tapping her dotty umbrella on the pavement. 'Bring a cake or something.'

A cake. Lordy. I've only baked two cakes in my entire life, one for each of Danny's birthdays. They both sank in the middle like craters.

'Be careful what you ask for, Pam,' shouts Ruth as she runs off down the road in her odd shoes.

Back home, I scoff two Penguin bars intended for Danny's packed lunch in quick succession and Google Annette. Ah, here's her website. There is a photograph: shiny blond hair blow-dried into waves around a beautiful face, wide apart hazel eyes, one of those alienating fuck-you smiles of the super-successful. My stomach twists. I feel slightly sick. She is Tom's self-confessed type. A sexed up version of my predecessor, the lovely Lucinda Lawn. I read her blurb. 'Annette Eastern has had two bestsellers on both sides of the Atlantic. Through her books, telly appearances, workshops and speeches – see "upcoming events" for latest dates and book online – she's coached thousands, inspiring companies, couples and individuals – yes, you at the back! – to spring clean their hearts! Annette Eastern lives in London and LA. She regrets that she isn't able to respond personally to any emails to this site.' Jee-sus. I unwrap another Penguin bar, stuff it in my mouth, and flick through her book again. The book falls open on the title page. Written in a round, confident hand is a personal inscription.

To darling Tom, thanks for all your wonderful

support! What would I do without you? Love, hugs, etc. A x

Darling Tom! Love? Hugs? A wave of fury thunders through me. Fingers trembling, I pick up the phone and dial her number. It goes straight to answer machine. She has a booming, transatlantic voice. I leave my message. Of course, I make no mention that I am married to Tom.

Eighteen

Chloe's warehouse apartment is in the dodgier end of Kensal Rise where you can get a decent cappuccino but you can also get indecently mugged. Not unlike a gym or a yoga studio, all stripped wooden floors and enormous metal-paned windows, it's freezing cold in winter and heats up like a greenhouse in summer. But, like Chloe, it always looks great. Today sunlight spills across the floor, a warm breeze pours through the open window. I lean my head back on the arm of her candy pink sofa. 'I need to not look like I'm involved in a David Blaine style sleep deprivation experiment. In fact I want a post-coital bloom. Will you show me how?'

Chloe laughs. 'Post-coital bloom? Tell me, Sadie,' she adds sternly.

'Nothing.'

'Enid's advice, isn't it? Oh, I just love Enid. How about I do another mean-streets gold dress look? Do you think she'd approve?'

'Very funny.' I kick her gently with my foot. 'Something easy, natural, that I can wear every day. You know, something that won't totally embarrass Tom in front of his colleagues?' Or, more importantly, make Annette think that I'm a complete frump.

'You mean perfect sex-sozzled wife make-up? Get yourself over here, girl.'

I lean towards her on the sofa, offering her my face for inspection.

Chloe looks puzzled. 'My God, do I spot the residue of red lipstick? Has hell frozen over?' She leans closer. 'Or is it jam?'

'It is so not jam, Chloe Mansfield. It is lipstick. I kid you not. One of Enid's suggestions.'

'I like it, Sadie. I just can't believe you're taking this all so seriously. No, I don't mean it like that. I think it's great. Honestly. If you're going to do something, do it properly I say.'

'I haven't turned into a walking talking hostess trolley?'

'Nope!'

'Are you sure?'

'Sure. Oh. Lordy. Hang on a sec, your nails!'

I starfish my hands on the kitchen table and look at my jagged nails. Yes, they have green crescents. But I am a florist. 'They're bad?'

'Feral!' she laughs, holding my face in her cool hands and studying it for a moment. 'You can't wear red lipstick *and* have dirty nails. Too Eastern European hooker.' Chloe studies my face dispassionately. 'OK, I'm thinking sexy Gwyneth. Natural and pretty. Something that you can easily apply . . .'

'. . . with one hand while simultaneously brushing Danny's teeth and wiping his bottom? Sounds like the kind of thing I'm after.'

'Your skin is very good, you know,' says Chloe, dabbing foundation on my cheeks with her wedge shaped sponge.

'That's spending a couple of years in fresh Canadian air for you. But it's still the colour of rice pudding.'

'I love pale skin. Close your eyes.'

I close my eyes. 'The lids feel all flickery.'

'Stress, my love. Open the eyes. Look up.' She puts concealer under my eyes, then the thick pink paste of Touche Éclat. 'So you reckon you're on course for turning into Perfect Pam sometime soon?'

'Yes indeed,' I laugh. 'I've hired a cleaner, a secret cleaner, fat Pat. Tom thinks I've had a personality transplant.'

'You're not pretending you're doing it, are you? Sadie! You can't do that!'

'Why shatter the illusion? It's not such a bad deception in the great scheme of things.' I pause for a few moments. 'The fridge is better stocked than Nigella's. Honestly, you've seen nothing like it. I sank a small fortune in Tesco. I'm even considering asking Pam for recipes. Talking of Pam, you're coming on Saturday to this fundraising thingy, aren't you? She said she was going to invite you.'

'What, Kensal Rise's very own WI? Stupidly, yes, I said I'd go. The invitation took me by surprise. I've not seen her properly for years. I'm afraid I might have to flake out nearer the time though.'

'Flaking out is forbidden. You have to come.'

'Beyond the call of duty. You are an Anderson wife. I am not. I don't see why I have to go.'

'I will feel shy and alienated and socially retarded without your support.'

'Moral blackmail.' She smiles. 'Now sit still, Miss Fidget.'

It's nice to be in someone else's hands, relinquishing control as brushes and sponges massage my face. It's nice being sober while she does it too, unlike last time. I might be able to actually remember how to do it myself. I reflect on the contrast between the two sessions: one, deranged high wife in glitter-tipped lashes; two, sober blooming wife, with tasteful peach blusher.

'Come on, what's troubling you?' she asks suddenly. 'I can always tell, you know.'

'Psyche Viagra visited the house last week. You know, that bloody Annette Eastern woman, the one you said was a nose job away from being Gisele's twin sister? I found a copy of her book in Tom's home office with this hideous handwritten touchy feely dedication to Tom in it. He's late all the time. I occasionally get the whiff of another woman's perfume on him. There's something up, I know it. He's not himself.'

Chloe steps back and looks at me. She shakes her

head. 'You don't honestly think . . . God, you do, don't you! Of course Tom wouldn't.'

I shrug. 'I don't know any more, Chloe. I just don't know. Am I the mug? I have to ask myself that question. I'd like to think that I'm not. But, well, life appears to be contradicting me. Here's me trying to be this great self-improving wife while he's off being a perfectly crap husband. The irony isn't wasted.'

'Look down.' Chloe cocks her head on one side and applies something above my lids. 'I'm sure your fears about Annette are unfounded. He's just not like that.'

'He was.'

'When he was in his twenties!'

'He doesn't need Viagra yet.'

'You're being paranoid.'

'He looks at women in the street. He stares at Perfect Pam's tits.'

'All men stare at Perfect Pam's tits.' She brushes my face with a soft feathery powder brush. 'They're marvels of nature.'

'He doesn't want to sleep with me.'

Chloe's face furrows. I can see that she doesn't think this is a good sign either but is too tactful to say anything. 'Maybe he feels under pressure. Nothing like a bit of pressure to give men performance anxiety. But don't worry, he'll want to pluck your knickers off with his teeth when I've finished with you, promise. You already look a million dollars and I haven't even applied your mascara. Here, take a look.' Chloe steps back, admiring her handiwork. 'You'll end up with six children.' She winks. 'You won't thank me then.'

It is pretty. My eyes seem to have more light in them. There is a pinky glow to my cheeks. 'Looks like I've been shagging in a haystack. Thanks, Chloe.'

'Sit down, sit down. Let's not forget the lipstick.' Chloe paints on one of her lipsticks carefully with a small brush. Unlike my dry ancient lippy, this feels squidgy and smells nice. 'There you go. It's not a pure red, too hard for your face. It's called Hot Cherry Pie. Softer.' Chloe sits next to me on the sofa, crossing one skinny-jean-clad leg over the other. 'Take it. All the stuff I've used. It's easy to apply. Any fool could do it.'

'Thanks, Chloe. I'll repay you in freesias or something.' I purse at my reflection in the mirror, raise an eyebrow, turn to the side and admire my flushed post-coital cheek colour. 'Right, now I'm ready.'

Chloe looks puzzled. 'Ready for what?'

In answer my phone beeps. Voicemail. My heart starts to pound. I check the number. Annette. A bite! Yes!

Nineteen

'What do I do?' sighs Ruth, leaning back on Pam's sofa and hugging an embroidered cashmere cushion to her chest. 'He wants sex twice a day now. I think it must be something to do with being in a testosterone-soaked office. He was a twice a month man when he was looking after the kids.' She covers her face with the cushion. 'And I can barely be bothered to have it once a month. Our libidos are on totally different schedules.'

I splutter into my glass of wine. After reluctantly agreeing to Pam's idea for a clothes swap sale – no one dare not agree, she's on a roll – the subject of fundraising has been happily lost in a mist of gossip and wine while the children play upstairs. A pot of tea, currently stewing to treacly blackness beneath Pam's knitted tea cosy, remains untouched. Ditto the chocolate chip cookies, Pam-baked and the size of small plates, each one looking capable of adding a dress size.

No, I didn't attempt to bake but resorted to bringing pink peonies instead. Tara has brought some Italian biscotti wrapped in pink crinkly paper from a posh deli. Ruth apologised for not bringing anything – has been in the mitigating grip of formidable Proper Job sounding work crises. Chloe brought wine because she doesn't do cakes, ever. You can tell from the baffled, slightly pained expression on her face that she doesn't normally do wifely tea parties either. Sitting on the sofa in her skinny black jeans, star print shirt and pink neon heels, surrounded by crafty knitted cushions and sequin fringed cashmere throws in a fug of baking smells, I've never seen her look more out of place.

'All in the timing of bedtime, Ruth. Either go to bed really early and make sure your reading light is out before he comes to bed or wait until he's asleep and then creep into bed yourself,' Pam declares, sounding suspiciously well practised at the art of conjugal avoidance.

'Right, this definitely calls for more alcohol.' Chloe opens the second bottle of wine. 'Anyone for another glass?'

Every glass in the room rallies towards the bottle, apart from Pam's which is filled with elderflower cordial.

'But once a month is a bit harsh, even by my standards. Surely you can't get away with that? How long have you been together?' continues Pam.

'Ten years,' says Ruth.

'Ah,' nods Pam, as if this explains things. 'I'm only six years in.'

'Give it another four and you'll understand,' says Ruth drily. 'Throw in a set of twins and then you'll *really* understand.'

Chloe and I start to giggle. And I am surprised to register that I am actually having rather a nice time, considering I only came here under sufferance to fulfil Enid's ridiculous brief of making a wife network. The wine is nicely wearing away the week's rough edges. Everyone's noticed my new make-up, which makes up for the fact that Tom hasn't. And amongst such a distracting girlie group there is some respite from obsessing about Psyche Viagra. (Three days until I do her flowers. How on earth am I going to keep still for three days? Her author photograph – that blondeness, that fuck-I'm-clever smile – is imprinted on my retinas, the first thing I see when I wake up. Part of me longs to quiz the other wives about her but I know that I can't. I can't risk gossip heading back via husbands to Tom.)

'Did you have different libidos when you got married?' ponders Tara, who is sitting on a silver leather pouffe, arms wrapped around her bare tanned legs, looking increasingly concerned. I suspect that there are a lot of private conversations going on in the privacy of our own heads.

'When we first met, well . . .' Ruth smiles. '. . . you're on heat then, aren't you?'

Ruth is so open I'm beginning to feel rather repressed. Or just not drunk enough.

'Then I went and had twins. Certain things

expanded, as our romantic life shrank,' Ruth adds.

'You don't mean? Oh God!' says Chloe, crossing her legs. 'Sadie, promise to remind me never to have children.'

'No, I never did do my pelvic floors. Does anyone? And Alex is obviously in the throes of some kind of middle-aged sex surge,' sighs Ruth. 'Whereas, at the moment, quite frankly, I'd just like a good night's sleep, preferably without him snoring like a stun-gunned elephant seal beside me.'

'I think it's the thought of the sex which is so bad, Ruth. You're probably tired, no?' Pam smiles coyly. 'But it's often not that bad once you get down to business. And I do find that if you fake pleasure, just a little bit, it weirdly has the effect of creating it.'

'Argh!' groans Chloe. 'I can't believe I'm hearing this.'

Ruth shrugs. 'Well, I'm terrified of getting pregnant again. And I am rather hoping that Alex feels the same. I've put a large photograph of the twins as pink wailing newborns on the bedside table to remind him of the potential consequences of his actions.'

'Girls, girls, girls,' despairs Chloe. 'You can't speak like this! We're meant to be at our sexual peak! This is it, the top of the goddamned mountain. My ex-husband and I hated each other by the end of our disastrous union but we still had a great time in the sack.'

'You haven't got children,' condescends Pam, patting her belly to illustrate her point.

'I just wish it was socially acceptable – and legal, of course – to farm him out to a sex worker once in a while,' sighs Ruth, ruffling her short crop with her fingers. 'What am I saying? They probably all do that in that office anyway.'

'Lordy,' laughs Pam, hands shooting to her belly again as if to shelter the unborn baby's ears. 'Imagine if the hubbies could hear us now. They'd be mortified.'

'Good.' Ruth leans back and kicks off her heels, exposing little hose socklets. She looks at Tara and grins. 'Still, I guess it must be much harder work being a second wife,' she says. 'I bet he sees you as his dessert.'

Tara's mouth opens, then shuts, as if she is about to say something then thinks better of it.

'It's your second marriage too though, isn't it?' I ask, intrigued. 'Tell me. Does one get better at it second time round? Is marriage like tennis, or the piano? Practice makes perfect?'

Tara blushes, crosses one long, slim leg over the other. 'At first it's like being given another shot at it. All the passion that had dribbled away in the old relationship is there again which is wonderful.' She hesitates. 'But . . .'

Ruth puts her hands over her ears. 'Don't tell me there's a but. Please. Don't shatter my fantasy get out clause.'

'The truth is that the novelty wears off and you're almost back to where you were the first time round, if you know what I mean. We even argue about the same things that I argued about with my first husband,' says Tara quietly.

'I knew it,' says Chloe, nodding to herself. 'Just the old patterns repeating themselves, right?'

Tara winces. 'Kind of.'

'Well, at least you're still in the wild throes of passion,' sighs Ruth. 'At least you might get another couple of years of preferring sex to sleep.'

'Actually, I could handle a lot more sex, if you know what I mean,' giggles Tara, her neck flushing pink. 'I feel like we've been married for decades already, not three years. His libido has equalised to its normal level. Mine has too but . . .' she giggles. '. . . at a somewhat higher level.'

'A woman after my own heart!' laughs Chloe, raising her glass. 'Go Tara!'

Ruth nudges Tara and laughs. 'Hey, let's do a swap.' There is a boozy outbreak of laughter and more wine is poured. Pam swoops forward in a jingle jangle of bracelets and waves her plate of chocolate chip cookies just below our noses. 'It's an act of female disloyalty not to eat a biscuit if all the women around you are eating biscuits,' she says. 'It's guilt inducing and unsisterly.'

'There goes the sisterhood then,' says Chloe, waving the plate away. 'Not for me, thanks. Besides I never thought you were the guilty type, Pam.' She laughs, tipping her wine glass towards Pam. 'I knew this lady before she became a wife. Let me tell you, girls, she was quite a different creature.'

'Oh, rubbish,' smiles Pam tightly.

'She danced on tables and had lots of delicious boyfriends with interesting piercings. And she felt about as guilty as Las Vegas.'

'Not Pam! Pam is the perfect wife,' sighs Ruth. 'And I don't mean that facetiously, Pam. I mean it with gasps of genuine admiration.'

Pam smiles, trying hard not to look pleased. 'Oh of course I'm not. One just has to try and be the best wife one can be that's all.'

Chloe starts to laugh. 'Oh come on, Pam, this isn't the fucking 1950s!'

'It might as well be,' says Tara quickly, biting into one of Pam's biscuits. 'I tell you, something shifts in them the moment you become a missus. That little sexist monster that's been buried under layers of metrosexuality? Well, it digs its way out. Even in second marriages. They think they'll be different. They won't be. No, I tell you, the moment they slip that ring on your finger they expect you to do for them what their mother did for their father, and, of course, what their first wife did for them too. Their brains are still hard-wired like cavemen. They want sex, food and sock pairing, probably in that order.'

'Maybe that's where I went wrong,' laughs Chloe. 'Mine only ever got the sex. Takeout if he was lucky.'

'Mine gets the food and the shelter,' says Ruth. 'And should count himself lucky for that, quite frankly.'

'And what about Alex, Ruth? What kind of wife was he when he was househusband?' asks Pam.

Ruth laughs. 'Oh the same old-fashioned rules apply.' She takes a large gulp of wine. 'Ever seen those hilarious Good Wife Guides from magazines like *Good Housekeeping* in the fifties? You know the kind of thing, "Don't complain if he's late home. Have dinner ready and the children washed and prepared and quiet." That sort of thing?'

We all nod.

'Well, a modern househusband isn't far off it. But with different rules of course.'

'Like what?' giggles Tara.

'Oh you know. One!' declares Ruth, wagging a finger in the air. 'Prepare the children. Wash their grubby hands thoroughly before your wife arrives home in smart work gear. Two! Remove your emasculating apron. It is important your wife still sees you as a man, especially if you're doing traditional woman's work. Three! Don't mention that all the other mothers were at the nativity play. Four! Very important this. Don't *ever* say that she looks tired.'

We all laugh and the room is warm and drunken and female feeling.

'Sadie . . .' Pam nudges me with her elbow. 'You're very quiet. What kind of wife are you?'

'Yeah, go on,' says Tara. 'What's your deal?'

'Well . . .' I hesitate. Oh to hell with it. 'I am the opposite of the good 1950s wife. In fact, I'm probably the world's worst wife, as Chloe can vouch.'

Chloe shakes her head. 'You're just Sadie first, wife second. As it should be.'

'My Good Wife Guide would go something like this. One! Always make sure there is nothing edible or within its sell by date in the fridge.'

Pam splutters into her glass of elderflower juice.

'Two! Sex should be sporadic, unimaginative and conducted in old crusty bed linen preferably while wearing flannel pyjamas.'

'Hear! Hear!' shouts Ruth, raising her glass in the air.

'Three! Insist on embarrassing your husband in front of his colleagues at every opportunity. Remember he works hard just to moan about it.'

The laughter quietens. And I'm aware of getting slightly bemused looks. Have I gone too far? 'But what I can say . . .' I continue, breaking the hush and raising my glass to the air, exhilarated by my group confession, '. . . is that I'm working on it. I'm working on becoming a better wife.'

'She's taking the advice of some ancient marriage guru in Hampstead,' says Chloe, raising one eyebrow. 'Seriously, not joking.'

I wish Chloe hadn't told them that. I feel extremely silly and exposed all of a sudden. I put my glass back down on the table, sobering up quickly.

'Not marriage guidance?' says Ruth. 'Wouldn't rate it personally.'

'No, no. Nothing like that. She's a client, an old lady,

rather grand. We kind of got talking. She's very sweet, eccentric, well into her seventies. I think she's lonely. Well, I know she's lonely. Her husband died a few years ago. She's been offering me advice on . . . well, I guess, on being a wife.'

'Marvellous!' hoots Ruth, putting her hand behind her ear. 'Hark! I hear the sound of quacking. How much does she charge?'

'Charge? Oh, no. She pays *me*. To do her flowers, I mean. Although I've now started just charging her cost. And we chat. It's nice. She's nice. I like her. It's totally informal.'

'Hey, why don't you bring this lady to one of our powwows?' asks Pam. 'I'd love to meet her.'

'She won't. I've been trying to meet her,' says Chloe. 'Sadie keeps her hidden away like a naughty little secret.'

'Hmm, very suspicious.' Tara giggles. 'Perhaps the bloom in your cheeks is not blusher. You're not actually having an affair, are you, Sadie?'

I smile and think of Eddie, the way he smelled of sweat and soil. 'I wish.'

Twenty

A red light. I sit in the traffic, fighting the urge to pick my nose and wondering were I to marry again would I marry someone like Tom? Would the fact that I loved the twinkle in his eyes or his bad jokes or the way the hairs grew up the back of his neck like fur really compensate for his shortcomings? Or would I think, no, this time I want someone who doesn't work late every night because he needs to prove something to his mother, who isn't impressed that their sofa cost five thousand pounds, someone who actually notices that there is a fresh flower in clean water in the nursery every day? Or even someone who notices that I am wearing Hot Cherry Pie lipstick. That would be a start. It really would. This morning I would have had to streak across the kitchen naked with wet Weetabix stuck to my nipples for him to even look up from his BlackBerry.

Trying to imagine oneself married to another person is a pretty damn big What If. It's like imagining yourself with long, thin legs or Kylie's bottom. Besides, there is love between me and Tom. Really. It beats during mundane moments. When he kisses Danny goodnight. Or when he reaches out to me in his sleep, his thick hairy arms like boa constrictors pulling me towards him, tightening their embrace to the point where it's almost not comfortable, almost angry, as if he's trying to squeeze us back to where we were when we first met. And I sometimes glimpse a heartbreaking tenderness behind the weariness of his eyes. Just not very often.

Is that enough? Is that all one can expect from marriage after a few years? A kind of loving, resigned acceptance. Mum certainly accepted a lot, Dad's grumpy moods, his inability to wash up or cook, his terrible DIY. He once replaced all the plastic light switches in the house with brass ones but put up every single one upside down. Mum just smiled stoically and said she'd get used to it. She always said acceptance was the way to happiness – she'd read it in one of those pocket-sized meditation books – and that we make life harder by fighting everything. And she didn't believe in teasing oneself with What Ifs.

The traffic lights turn amber, then green. I lift my foot off the brake, rub my nose with my sleeve, nearly run over a cyclist.

A few minutes later I'm on Enid's road driving past the posh houses, high-tech burglar alarms, nicely maintained trees. I start to feel a little nervous now. When I went to the market this morning I was perhaps over-enthused by the attention my lipstick and tight jeans were getting from a not-so-ugly barrow boy so I decided to go off message with her flowers. I hear the squelch of a spade in wet soil. 'Hi Eddie,' I call out over the high hedge.

Feet move through grass. The sound of a spade being dragged. Then he is in front of me, all springy curly hair and green eyes. 'All right,' he says. He pauses, staring at me for a little while. 'You look different.'

'Do I?' I blush furiously.

'Exceptionally well.'

I grin despite myself. I can feel the grin getting wider and wider, slinging from earlobe to earlobe. And I can't help but wonder if I've put on the scarlet lippy less for Tom, or Enid, and more on the off-chance of spotting Eddie. 'Is Enid at home?'

'Do you really think she'd miss one of your visits?'

'I aim to please.' God, why did I say that? Pure Alan Partridge.

Eddie puts his booted foot on the spade and leans into it. I notice the defined musculature beneath his T-shirt. There's something very sexy about seeing a man using his physical strength in the nurturing organic environment of the garden: it's that gentle strong man thing. It's certainly sexier than a man in a suit getting fatter and fatter on business lunches. 'How's little Danny boy?'

'Very cute. Lovely.' I am flattered that he remembers my son's name.

'Bring him up here to race his cars sometime,' says

Eddie, effortlessly flinging his spade over his shoulder and walking back to the flower beds. 'Tell him I want the red car this time. I'm wise to his tricks.'

Enid is sitting neatly on the edge of her white sofa, clutching a large, dog-eared copy of the complete works of Shakespeare. She is wearing a navy and white suit, back straight, hair pinned up in an elegant up-do. On her tiny feet are shiny red patent pumps. She slams the book down on her lap and looks at me waspishly. 'Well, well. Don't you scrub up well?'

'Thank you, Enid.' I bask in her praise like a schoolgirl. 'My friend Chloe – she's a make-up artist – she gave me a much-needed lesson.'

'Really? Oh send her my way, would you? I'd so love a make-up artist. Does she do hair too? Marvellous. Will you get her to call me?'

I nod, trying to imagine Chloe taking on Enid as a client. She's about sixty years too old.

She pats the sofa. 'Do sit down.'

I hesitate. 'The flowers . . .'

'The flowers can wait, my dear. Sit. Could you put this old tome on the shelf for me? Thanks. The print is making my eyes go funny. Now, are things improving on the domestic front?' she asks, picking up a delicate china tea cup. 'Tell all.'

'Well . . .' I hesitate. How to spin this?

'Ah.' Enid gives me a sidelong glance.

'I suspect I'm not *yet* a paragon of perfect wifehood,' I laugh. 'But the fridge is stocked with food, my lippy is

200

on and the house is clean. I'm not entirely sure he's noticed though, or cares.'

Enid raises an eyebrow. 'Oh I think we'll have to pull out all the stops then. I think we'll have to get you baking.'

'I don't bake.'

'Don't say don't. Get a recipe or two off a friend. Wow him with a home cooked meal.'

'Right,' I say smiling, wishing that life was indeed that simple. Was it once? Were husbands so like dogs? If so, modern women have got a raw deal. Men are far trickier beasts these days.

'Don't worry. These things take time. Resistance is always most intense in the early days. Husbands do not like change. They like routine, even if that routine is not ideal. It takes a bit of time for them to embrace new ways. In the meantime hand me that notebook, darling.'

I rummage in my handbag, pull out my notebook.

She holds the notebook away from me so I cannot see what she is writing. I hear the pen swirl its way across the page in her neat hand. Then she shuts it. 'Read it later. Now are those Anderson wives turning out to be your own Maud and Iris and Ruby? Do tell.'

'Maybe.'

'Now show me your hands.'

'My hands?'

'Yes, your hands, darling.'

I hold out my right hand. Is she going to read my palm or something?

Enid holds my hand in hers and straightens my fingers. She looks at my nails, stroking along the edge of each one, as if checking for smoothness. 'As I thought. An improvement. Keep it up. Is your Chloe friend responsible for this too?'

I nod.

'Excellent. Any man will struggle to be happily married to a woman with dirty fingernails,' she says. 'Right, the flowers.'

'I'll go and get them.' I stand up, walk to the door and stop. 'Enid, there is something I haven't told you.' I hesitate. 'The tulips . . .'

'Did you hear that, Albert dear?' She speaks to the photograph and taps the glass in the frame with her finger. 'Your tulips are here.'

'Well . . .' I shift from one foot to the other. 'They are not the purpley-black today, Enid. I thought . . .'

Enid's eyes round. 'Not black? Whatever do you mean, not black? Did they not have Albert's black tulips at the market this morning?'

I take a deep breath. 'They did, Enid. But I thought that perhaps you'd want to consider another colour. Summer is here. And I remember how you admired my pink tulips that day we met in the park.'

Enid mutters to herself. 'Pink tulips? Pink tulips?' as if I've suggested filling the vases with chopsticks. 'I don't do pink tulips. No,' she says, shaking her head. 'Pink tulips won't do at all.'

This is the response I dreaded. I have overstepped the

mark, forgotten that I am the florist, she the client. Who am I to get this old lady to change the habit of years? 'I'm so sorry, Enid. I thought you might appreciate a change.'

'I've had black tulips in my vases every week since he died,' she says slowly, looking close to tears.

I glance at my watch. There's nothing I can do. I can't go back to the market now. And I've wasted all these tulips. Damn. 'I can either come tomorrow morning with new tulips. Or I can return next week.'

Enid stands up, holding on to the sofa arm for support. 'Next week.' She looks so disappointed. 'I'll get Angie to call you to confirm.'

Feeling like I've failed in some vitally important test, I walk out of the room, dejected. The dynamic has changed. Angie opens the front door for me. 'Goodbye, madam,' she says with some finality.

I walk down the front path, through the tunnel of hedges, and sling myself into the car, heavy as a bag of soil. In the boot are boxes stacked up with the offending pink tulips. Oh, well. Enid, this house, everything, it always was too bonkers to last. I put the key in the ignition. Suddenly there is a commotion at the front door. Enid and Angie are talking animatedly. Then Enid totters down the path in her shiny red pumps. 'Wait, Sadie!'

I hang my head out the window. 'Yes?'

'The tulips,' she says. 'I've changed my mind. I will indeed take the pink tulips.' She looks over her shoulder, where Eddie has emerged from the undergrowth. 'Eddie, my darling, will you help Sadie back in with the boxes? She has brought jolly pink tulips for me.'

Angie looks puzzled. 'Are you sure, madam?'

Enid stands up straight and slaps one hand on the flank of the car. 'If Sadie can wear lipstick, I can embrace a pink tulip.' She stares ahead into the mid distance. 'Yes, I do believe that the time might be right for a pink tulip.'

At home later I stir my coffee with spirit, elated at my triumph with the tulips. I may not be putting a smile on Tom's face but I have put one on Enid's and that feels really good. I lean back in the kitchen chair, open my notebook, carefully flicking through to the last page.

If you're not happy pretend you are, darling. Fake it until it becomes real. E xx

I smile. Crafty old thing. Perfect Pam would approve.

Twenty-one

Today is *the* day. It is the day I venture into the lair of my blonde nemesis. It should be raining. Or thundering or doing something operatic. But it is sunny and the sky is high, benign and blue. Psyche Viagra's flat is not as far from mine as I'd hoped, only eighteen minutes and thirty-two seconds by car (not at rush hour). Easy adultery distance? I think so. It's a white stuccoed apartment block in Belsize Park. The communal hallway has a marble floor and paintings of seascapes on the wall. The porter checks my name off a list hidden from view and directs me to the lift, a brass and mirrored cube that smells of air sprays. When I get to the third floor I see that the door of the apartment is being held open by the foot of a housekeeper or cleaner, a middle-aged lady in a navy overall. 'Hi, love,' she says. 'You the new florist?'

'I . . . I am,' I say falteringly over the mound of flower boxes in my hands. Annette's budget was a generous one. 'Hi.'

'I'm Louise. Come in.'

I walk in, heart in my mouth. The apartment is enormous, with a vast square hallway that leads to an open plan show home living room. The dark wood floors are polished up to a high gleam. There are two beige L-shaped sofas, a large rectangular glass coffee table on which large art books are neatly piled, a vast flat-screen telly embedded in the wall like a window. On her artfully arranged bookshelves, prominently displayed, are a selection of awards. I squint at one. Yes, inscribed on a pyramid of Perspex: 'People's Choice Award: *Spring Clean Your Heart!*' Something tightens inside.

'The kitchen.' Louise pulls back a white sliding door to reveal a generic posh apartment block kitchen: enormous American fridge, granite worktop, emerald-coloured glass splashback, numerous gleaming stainless steel utensils. It doesn't look like the kitchen of someone who cooks, or makes any kind of mess ever. Well, I suppose it would be worse if Psyche Viagra excelled at bestsellers *and* cupcakes.

Effecting an air of brisk professionalism I get to work at the kitchen table, spreading out an ostentatious mix of pale roses, eucharis, jasmine and hebe. Louise brings over three large square glass vases and I cut the flowers and arrange them, knotting the bunches tightly with twine, bending flexigrass over the flowers like girders. It takes longer than it should because my mind is on other things. Like the fact that on one wall of the kitchen is an enormous photo montage display, displaying Annette looking gorgeous and successful in various habitats.

There are pictures of Annette on a beach, wearing a brown bikini with shells and an enormous wide-brimmed hat. Her stomach, I can't help but notice, is as flat as the kitchen table. There are pictures of Annette at a book signing, surrounded by badly dressed overweight women clutching her book and staring at her adoringly. There are pictures of Annette hugging a thin dark-skinned child somewhere poor and hot. Pictures of Annette on the Staten Island ferry, wind blowing her blond hair off her face, Manhattan in the background. Pictures of Annette looking fabulous in a pair of jeans, holding a book, one of her own, obviously, grinning confidently at the camera. Pictures of . . . Oh no. It can't be?

I walk slowly up to the photo montage for a closer look. Yes, it is *him*. It is Tom. It is Annette and Tom and three men in suits, two of whom I recognise – Roman and Sebastian? There is a large office window in the background of the picture, framing an unmistakable New York skyline. Jesus. This must have been that American business trip he went on a few months ago, not long after he joined the agency, the one he said was a real ball ache. Yes, looks like he's working *really* hard, the bastard. Annette is wearing a slinky black dress and is all hair and lips. The men in suits flank her. Tom is right next to her. One of her hands dangles down. One of his hands dangles down. Their hands look like they are just touching. But worse than this, much worse, is the look in Tom's eyes. He is not looking at the camera. He is looking at Annette the way he used to look at me.

Twenty-two

I sit on my Annette obsession like a chicken sits on an egg, keeping it alive and warm, waiting for it to hatch. I've got another week before I go back to do her flowers. And I cannot stop dreaming about her. Or Googling her. The more I think about her the more real the prospect that *something*'s going on becomes, as if every thought, every Google, is actually a little bit of incriminating evidence itself. Obviously, I need proof. So I must restrain myself from accusations and carry on as before, on and on. Faking it. This takes some effort. In fact it takes more discipline than getting up at some ungodly hour to go to the flower market. Because part of me wants to cut holes in Tom's suits or, even more delicious, send childishly rude comments to Annette's website. But that would be Glenn Close-style weirdo wife behaviour. To keep myself occupied – away from the scissors and the keyboard – and to fake it with conviction I decide to follow Enid's advice and up my game on the domestic front. I will not only stock the fridge with costly prepackaged supermarket titbits, I will actually, ahem, cook, armed with recipes from Delia Smith and Perfect Pam.

I make two lasagnes. (Delia.) The first sets off the piercing shriek of the smoke alarm and has to be thrown into the bin, smouldering malevolently. The second lasagne, to my amazement and immense pride, is neither burned nor undercooked. In fact it bubbles happily in its pan like a normal edible foodstuff. Buoyed by such success I embark on Pam's trifle, using the recipe she furtively pushed into my palm at the nursery gate as if it were the code to a secret bank vault. It is harder than it looks. I whip the cream. Blobs fly off the electric hand whip and stick to the ceiling and walls. But eventually the cream is stiff and, as Pam advises, in mountainous peaks. I shove down the jammy sponge with my fingers. Dollop in spoonfuls of tinned yellow Devon custard. Then it's done. I stare fascinated at this strange, alien wobbly thing that I have created, its ruby red jam squidging against the side of the glass dish, and think, wow, it's kind of beautiful. And it wasn't even that hard to make. Then I collapse on to the sofa with a multi-unit glass of wine. I can barely keep my eyes open. My back aches. It is absolutely exhausting being two people, the perfect wife who makes trifles and the demented wife with the secret growing, pulsating suspicions. Perhaps my double life will do me in completely and I'll end up running naked down Tesco's vegetable aisle or something, like a totally deranged housewife.

The front door slams. Tom walks into the room, unknotting his tie. He looks bloated and hot like he's been spending too long in dark cocktail bars. 'Is Danny asleep, Sadie?'

I nod. 'Of course.' It's nine o clock. Danny goes to sleep at seven.

Tom's face falls. 'Shit. I really hoped to get back earlier tonight. I feel like I hardly see him these days.'

That's because you don't, I think. But I bite my tongue. Be nice. Fake happy. Do not, under any circumstances, mention Psyche Viagra. Or That Photograph. I look up at Tom and smile so hard the muscles in my cheeks hurt. My name is Sadie Drew and I am a happy wife.

Tom slumps on to the sofa and unties his shoes. When he bends down a little bald disc is visible on his crown. There are dark circles around his eyes. 'What a fucking day.'

'You poor thing.'

Tom looks at me for a few moments, evidently puzzled. 'Are you stoned, Sadie? Has Chloe been round?'

'No! Why do you say that?'

'There's a smell of burning.'

That would be the first lasagne.

'You're smiling in a weird way.'

That would be the second lasagne.

'And you look kind of odd. You're freaking me out.' He rubs at my chin with his thumb. 'What's that?'

'What's what?'

He looks at his thumb, the pad is red. 'You've got a smudge of something on your chin.'

I rub my chin. Lippy. I must have missed it with my cotton wool balls. How did it migrate from lips to chin? 'Lipstick.'

Tom smiles. 'Yes, I did notice.'

At last!

'Suits you.' His tummy rumbles. He slaps it and it wobbles. 'Starving.'

'There's a lasagne in the oven.'

He rubs his tired eyes. 'Pardon?'

'There's a lasagne in the oven.'

He looks puzzled. 'Really? Blimey.'

'And a trifle for pudding.'

'A trifle?' he repeats in disbelief as if I've just told him I've got a live yak in the fridge. 'Well, what can I say? Thanks.' He peels off a city-soiled sock. His feet are white and hairy. They are very male feet. I remember when we first met I used to think they were sexy – the male knobbliness, the thickness of the toe – but that was before we argued over who last did the laundry. 'Are you sure you're OK?'

'I'm feeling . . .' I hesitate, the photograph in Annette's kitchen flashing up in front of my eyes again. No, do not think of it. Do not mention it. '. . . so much better about everything.'

Tom's shoulders drop away from his ears. 'Really?' he asks, as if he can't quite believe what he's just heard. He looks more boyish all of a sudden, like a weight's been lifted off him. 'That's good, really good, to hear.'

I walk over, rub his shoulders.

Tom coughs. 'Did you get the email?'

'What email?' I immediately imagine Tom's email to me: 'Dear wife, I've decided to spring clean my heart and get rid of . . .'

'From your dad. He's set the date for the engagement party.' Tom stands up and slides his hands around my waist, a gesture that, being uninitiated and freely given, nearly floors me.

'The third of September.'

The date rattles around in my head like a dried pea. Third of September? Now that does sound familiar. A birthday? A holiday?

'Sadie!' He pulls his arms away.

I look at him desperately, searching his face for clues.

'Our wedding anniversary.'

Shit. 'Of course!' *And* my secret deadline for resurrecting our marriage. That would have been a natural day to discuss our future, our babies, pick the fruits of my wifely labours, if he hasn't run off with Psyche Viagra by then of course. Trust Dad to wade in with a hideous social clash. 'They wouldn't dare have the party then, surely?'

Tom winces. 'He said it's the only Saturday in September that the hall Loretta wants is free and it has to be September because they've got a Nile cruise in October.' Tom walks to the fridge and pulls out a beer.

'He's invited everyone. Including my folks. Dad's got a golf thing that weekend, rather conveniently. But I'm afraid Mother is *very* keen.'

I bet she is! Rona will live off it for weeks. Before my mother died Dad couldn't incriminate himself in any way. But when he met Loretta . . . When Rona met Loretta . . . It happened at Christmas. Better than any Jo Malone gift box, she could barely conceal her delight. A real life commoner from Milton Keynes! A woman who wears acrylic-wool mixes and uses sunbeds! A woman who calls magazines 'books'! Oh, the joy. Loretta reinforced Rona's own sense of social superiority so much that by Boxing Day I'd never seen her perkier. Yes, how she will revel in a tasteless engagement party in some godforsaken sports hall outside Milton Keynes.

'And . . . ' Tom looks a little unsure. Rona has been a sensitive subject ever since she lopped off Danny's hair. 'She was wondering if she could stay this weekend, I'm afraid. Dad's at a golf thing in Scotland and she's at a loose end.'

Rona the perfect wife indeed! She's the perfect wife because her husband has created the perfect opportunity to get away from her as frequently as possible. I don't say this of course. I smile. I act happy.

He hesitates. 'You don't mind if she stays, do you?'

I take a deep breath. I make myself say, 'Of course I don't.' Sparks fly from between my gritted teeth. 'She's your mother.'

Tom looks at me, puzzled, then just happily resigned

like he hasn't got the energy to think about anything too hard. 'Great.'

Later I get undressed: Tom gazes at me sleepily from our bed. I remember to look like I've got a sexy secret – so many things to remember – and lower my lids in a way I hope looks seductive rather than stoned, and think about Eddie's brown sliver of a belly, just visible beneath his T-shirt. I slip off my knickers, and, feeling a little self-conscious, leap beneath the covers. The familiar routine begins. His hand on my belly, my breast, my nipple. My hand on his tummy, through the arrow of hair, towards the leaning tower of Pisa. OK, it's marital sex, it's not wild, but it's not bad. And I use my Eddie fantasy to secretly rev myself up, feeling my body curl towards him. I try to remember where I am in my cycle: could tonight be the night? It could be! I'm almost mid-cycle. Before we can consummate there is a rumbling noise. 'Tom?' I kiss his soft familiar tummy.

Tom doesn't answer. Tom is snoring. Tom is asleep.

Twenty-three

Appearances are everything. I'm getting used to slipping on different masks. There's the good wife mask with Tom. The earnest student with Enid. The confused immature teenager trapped in a thirtysomething's body with Chloe. Of course, there's also the tragic case who sniffs Babygros and Googles Annette when no one else is looking. But no one knows about her. Certainly not fellow guests at the fundraising clothes swap party.

For the first hour I'm 'on the door'. This means sitting on the silver pouffe outside Pam's living room and asking all the nice west London ladies to part with their cash – £5, hell they can afford it – and explaining that it goes to Save the Children with Anderson matching the amount raised. Embarrassingly I recognise a couple of women as Anderson Wives from the lunch at The Ivy. A willowy blonde with a long nose dressed in a camel cashmere sweater and white jeans, that stain-free Euro-chic look. She doesn't seem to recognise me thankfully. Nor does the sharp-faced brunette with a conspicuously swishy blow-dry in the simple, cream shirt dress and tan heels. I take their money quickly, usher them in and watch them gravitate to the pile of clothes in the middle of Perfect Pam's sitting room where the early arrivals are already hungrily circulating. The willowy blonde adds a cluster of silky tops to the top of the pile. The brunette, I notice, hasn't brought anything, which goes against the spirit of the swap. Still, I'd be amazed if anyone in their right mind would want my hand-me-downs for anything but cleaning rags.

Tara appears at my side, holding up a denim skirt. Pam is beside her. 'What do you reckon? If only it wasn't too big for me. It's kind of sexy in that trucker girl way.'

Pam smiles. 'Used to be mine. Am quite sure you'll be able to squeeze into it.' Then she starts getting undressed herself, stripping off her T-shirt and Juicy maternity jeans without any self-consciousness right there in the middle of the room. I don't know where to look. Her pregnancy bump emerges. Not a stretch mark in sight, obviously.

'Kensal Rise's clipboard Nazi!' Someone taps me on the shoulder. I turn round. Chloe.

'No. Your name's not on the list, you can't come in,' I laugh.

Chloe kisses me. 'Check out my bag of booty.'

'Still five pounds please.'

She rolls her eyes, and tips her enormous plastic bag showily on to the pile. There are gasps and a wave of fidgety excitement amongst the sale-goers.

'Ooo.' Pam wiggles over in her cute polka dot bra and under-the-bump knickers ensemble. 'Wow! I knew you'd be brilliant, Chloe.'

'Sadie, go forage,' says Ruth quietly, who is not her usual self today. She looks washed out. There are rings under her eyes. 'I'll take over the door. No, seriously. I don't mind. I'm not really in the swapping mood to be honest.'

'Thanks. Are you OK?'

'Fine. Go now before it all gets gobbled up.' Ruth bites her lip and really doesn't look fine.

'Elbows at the ready!' shouts Pam and we all rush towards the replenished pile.

It's easy to know which clothes to discard quickly. Those belonging to Tara look like they might fit a ten-year-old girl. Chloe's are too snug a fit too. Pam's are all far too big on top because of her enormous bust. I stand back as Tara and another lady in a leopard print sweater both lunge at a long, grey cardigan – suspected donator, Chloe – and end up in a tug of war, clinging on to the sleeves. Tara wins. The swapping turns into a free-for-all. Pam cracks open a bottle of wine. Then another. The room splits into wifely cliques. A group of mothers from the nursery arrive and chat amiably around the coffee table about the children. The willowy Anderson blonde and the brunette hover by the window, occasionally looking over at me and speaking in hushed voices. Pam, Tara, Chloe and I cluster next to Ruth at the door. 'A good afternoon's work, ladies.' Pam raises her glass. 'To us! To poor Ruth.'

217

'Is something the matter, Ruth?' I ask.

'Alex has moved out,' says Ruth quickly. 'To his mother's.'

'Moved out?' gasps Chloe.

Ruth looks down at the floor and nods. 'It's been brewing for a while.'

'I'm so sorry,' I say, shocked.

'Don't mention it to the husbands though, will you?' asks Ruth, looking suddenly panicked. 'Or to those two.' She nods at the willowy blonde and the brunette. 'I don't want it all over Anderson. Not yet.'

'Of course not. Lips are sealed.' I wonder how many other marriages are shifting behind Anderson's public façade.

'But why?' Tara's eyes are watering. 'Alex seems so nice.'

'He *is* nice,' Ruth says quietly. 'It's just we're not very nice to each other. Things have been much harder since he started work again. I thought things would get easier, that he'd feel happier now that he had a job . . .' her voice drifts off.

'I'm sure it's unimaginably tough when you both work,' says Pam softly.

'Well, other people seem to manage it,' says Ruth.

'With difficulty,' I say.

'Something had to give,' says Ruth. 'We're fighting all the time. It's no good for the twins.'

'Oh, Ruth,' sighs Tara.

'Sorry to rain on the parade,' adds Ruth drily.

Pam shakes her head. 'We're gunning for you, Ruth. We're gunning for you.' She slings an arm around her shoulders and presses Ruth towards her giant bosoms. 'You can cry. It's OK, Ruth. Let it out.'

Poor Ruth, who probably came to the sale for a little light relief, doesn't cry. But I notice that her hands are shaking. 'Do you mind if we change the subject?' she asks, looking pained, turning her back to the room to avoid the curious stares of the other sale-goers. 'Sorry, ladies.'

We stand in silence for a few moments, trying to absorb the news. What is it that makes one couple phone the lawyer while another soldiers on in an imperfect marriage? And is soldiering on really better? Maybe there's no way of knowing if you are happier hanging in there or happier cutting your losses. Unless you're like Enid and Albert of course. Or like Mum and Dad. (Pre Loretta.)

'Lift the mood then, Tara,' says Pam suddenly, looking mischievous. 'Tara has a new, rather radical top tip for wives, Sadie.'

Tara shifts on her feet and blushes. '*Pam*. It's not appropriate.'

'God, inappropriate sounds just the ticket,' says Ruth, brightening up. 'You're blushing. Tell all, now.'

We all turn to stare at Tara who starts to giggle nervously.

'Shall I do the honours?' Pam leans forward and, not waiting for Tara's response, whispers loudly. 'She's having weekly sessions with a masseur who does "happy endings"!'

Happy endings?

Chloe's mouth drops open. 'You're not! Give me his number!'

'You don't mean? Oh. My. God.' I slowly realise what they're talking about. 'Massage with orgasm?' I look at her afresh, notice the bright eyes, the glowing cheeks. 'Is that legal?'

Ruth smiles. 'Probably not.'

'Shussh!' exclaims Tara. She covers her face with her hand. But she can't repress a smile. 'It's sure helping my marriage. I feel totally relaxed, content for the first time in months.' And she is radiating orgasm-sated happiness. I gaze at Tara with a strange, reluctant admiration. I don't approve. Well, of course I don't! But the longer I am married the harder I find it is to judge anyone else. 'How very French.'

'Well, it's only a massage,' she says. 'With fiddly bits.'

'Yuck,' sniffs Pam. 'Apart from anything else – such as those awkward little things like morals – I wouldn't dare. You might catch something.'

'It's totally hygienic,' says Tara. 'I mean it's not sex or anything. It's kind of manual. I just lie there.'

'Hell, men do it all the time, don't they?' Chloe laughs. 'Pay women to deliver and go away afterwards.'

The willowy blonde and the pointy-featured brunette sidle over, attracted by the giggling promise of gossip. But Ruth and Chloe drag Tara off into a quiet corner for interrogation and full disclosure of the juicy details.

'You remember Sadie from the lunch at The Ivy?' asks Pam chirpily.

Thanks for clarifying that, Pam.

The blonde lets out a little yelp. 'I knew it! I knew I recognised the T-shirt. Show her, Joanna!'

Laughing, her friend unfurls the T-shirt that's tucked under her arm. It's the cursed Lick Me T-shirt. 'Couldn't resist it!'

I put my hand over my mouth, horrified to see the incriminating evidence in the manicured hands of a fellow Anderson wife.

'So you're Tom Harrison's wife? I've heard so much about you,' says the blonde, a smile playing at the corners of her mouth.

'Yes, Tom's wife.' The label they understand. Who do they belong to?

'I'm Linda. Roman's wife,' she clarifies.

Shit, Roman was a witness to the gold dress incident.

'Joanna, other half of Sebastian,' smiles the swishy haired brunette.

No wonder they look like they're trying hard not to laugh.

'Doesn't Sadie scrub up well?' says Pam sweetly. 'Right, ladies, I'm going to fix some tea.' She leaves me marooned with the Anderson wives and the offending trophy T-shirt. There is a moment's awkward silence as we all smile glassily at each other and try to think of something to say.

'Tom must be very busy,' says Linda eventually, smoothing down her blond hair with one hand. She's wearing tasteful gold chains around her wrist. Everything about her is so damn tasteful.

'Ridiculously so. Do you ever see your husbands?' This is meant as a joke but falls flat.

'Well, the company is doing well at the moment,' Linda says a little defensively. 'Very busy.'

'Fantastically well,' repeats Joanna as if she's been pre-programmed in wifely support mode.

'I hear Tom's been very successful,' says Linda. 'Especially with . . . what's the name of that motivational woman, Joanna?'

'Annette Eastern.'

I splutter uncouthly into my wine glass.

Linda smiles. 'That's the reason he's never home, Sadie. Blame the luscious Miss Eastern.'

Joanna unsubtly nudges Linda sharply in the ribs. Linda's laugh stops in its tracks. Joanna coughs and studies the floor.

Not knowing what to say, just that if I say anything it'll be the wrong thing, I make my excuses. 'Great to meet you. But I must give Pam a hand with that tea.'

As I flurry off I overhear Joanna hiss to Linda, 'Shit, do you think she *knows*?'

Twenty-four

The sky is the ridiculously cheerful blue of Danny's poster paint. It transports me right back to the freezing cold days of Toronto's winter with its brilliant skies, icy pavements and air so cold it hurt to breathe in. I was just pregnant then and excited about my future as I walked cheerfully downtown, the baby making its presence felt only in the low swing of nausea, a congested nose and breasts that felt like bruises. I didn't mind any of it. I liked the reminder that there was a new life budding inside me, a sibling for Danny, someone to complete the family. I sigh and try to forget.

Angie opens the front door. 'I'm so sorry, Miss Sadie. Enid is still out at the shops. Running late. Will you wait?'

'Don't worry, Angie. That's fine. I'll just get on with it.'

'She told me she wants you to wait.' She shrugs apologetically and smiles. 'You know what Mrs Fisher is like.'

'I do. I'll just wait here in the garden, it's a lovely day.' I sit down on the low stone wall and lift my head to the sunshine, letting it smooth away last night's fractious sleep which was spent tossing and turning with Linda and Joanna's words spinning around my mind. Angie goes back inside, leaving the front door ajar. After a few moments I hear the sound of footsteps, the crushing of grass. It's a distinctive footstep. My body responds to it straight away.

'Parking up in the sunshine?' Eddie smiles. I think he's got a bit of a tan since I last saw him because his teeth look brighter. So do the whites of his eyes. Oh, he really is rather lovely.

'Yes, and admiring your planting. Angie said Enid is out shopping.'

'Again? This is the second time she's gone out to the shops this week,' he laughs. 'And there was me thinking she was becoming reclusive. Obviously there's only one old lady around here and that's me.' He squats down on the low stone beside me, scoops up a pile of earth from the bed and sieves it through his fingers, as if checking its texture.

'It's probably the sunshine, isn't it? Making her feel young again,' I say and admire Eddie's sturdy, tanned hands, think about Tara's masseur and blush.

Eddie stretches his legs out, his muddy boots falling outwards. Tom's feet would never fall outwards, not these days. He's too tense. They'd scuff the earth or tap to a fidgety internal rhythm. Eddie is a relaxed tomcat

224

in the sun. Tom is a coiled spring. 'Or it could be you. She does seem to have developed a soft spot for you, Sadie.'

'Oh, it's me tulips,' I laugh.

Eddie shakes his head. 'Paula, your predecessor, she did tulips. Tulips, every week, as requested. Enid was pretty vile to her.'

'Vile? Never! I can't imagine her being vile to anybody.'

'She doesn't tolerate fools. And woe betide . . . She can be quite a madam, let me tell you.'

'Gosh,' I say, struggling to see her in this new light. 'I hope she was nice to Chloe. A friend of mine. I sent her round.'

'Chloe!' Eddie's face lights up. 'Oh, yes! She had us both in stitches.'

'That's my Chloe,' I say but inside I feel a weird little ping of jealousy. 'Well, I hope she likes my work too.'

Eddie grins. 'Do I hear a note of self-doubt in your voice? Sadie, you are the first florist to dare to put a flower into a vase that is not one of Albert's damned black tulips in the last year. I told my mother. She was like, "I've got to meet this girl!"'

I flush. Oh, I quite like being called girl. Especially by Eddie. His mother wants to meet me? My mind races with the most ridiculous, inappropriate thoughts. I smile back at him and notice that he has the longest, thickest eyelashes I've ever seen on a man, like feathers. He catches me looking at him and smiles. I examine the backs of my nails. We sit in comfortable silence for a few moments. 'She loved Albert so much, didn't she?'

'I guess.' Eddie yawns, stretching his arms wide, opening his sinewy chest.

'What was he like?'

Eddie starts to laugh at this, as if amused at a private joke. 'Oh I couldn't possibly say. A good guy, I think. A bit of a character. Liked his clothes and his luxuries. He let Enid rule the roost. But to be honest I've only been back in Enid's life properly for the last year, since splitting up with my girlfriend Emily and moving back from Edinburgh.'

'Ah, Enid didn't sort your relationship problems out then,' I say when I probably shouldn't. It just shoots out.

Eddie looks sad. 'No. No, she didn't. Beyond anyone's abilities.'

'Why?' I ask bluntly, because there's no other way of asking it and I suddenly really want to know.

Eddie looks at me long, hard, unflinching. 'We were two very different people. That sounds like a cop-out, doesn't it? But I think that's probably the correct answer. She wanted stuff I could never give her.' He rubs the stubble on the underside of his chin. 'I just want a simple life, Sadie. I'm not materialistic, well, I don't think so. I just want a bit of peace and quiet.'

My heart thumps harder. A simple life. Not materialistic. Like me! I dig into the gravel with my foot but I want to wrap my arms around Eddie and tell him it's all going to be OK and he'll meet a lovely woman who deserves him.

'She wanted the whole package. The idea that her children – we didn't have any, thank God – but the idea that these hypothetical children might have to go to state school terrified her. She wanted prep schools. Skiing. Barbados . . .' He starts to laugh, a slightly angry laugh like a snort. 'God knows why Emily was with me in the first place.'

'Ah,' I say, staring at him, fascinated by his anger, moved by his genuine male confusion and pain. Emily is a fool. Emily has lost a good man. Emily has lost a man with distracting biceps who can plant amazing borders. 'I guess it cuts both ways. That we're all stumbling around in the dark trying to work out how to make relationships work and how to make our partners more perfect.'

'You reckon?' He searches my face. 'You know what I think? I think that we all know really in our hearts when something's right. That we know when we're lying to ourselves. I think I was lying to myself. For years. I think, deep down, I knew. I reckon she did too.'

Does he think that I am lying to myself? At what point does marital habit become a form of lying? Tom and I are both waiting for things to get better. But maybe they won't get better. Maybe this just is our marriage. A habit. Christ.

'So I gather that Enid's taken your marriage on as some kind of project?' he grins.

'Ah, yes.' I scuff the pebbles harder with my feet. How much does he know?

Eddie puts a hand out, resting it on my leg. It is big and heavy and the physical contact is a shock. 'Do you mind not ruining the drive, darling?'

'Sorry.' I quickly withdraw my foot. My calf tingles where he touched it.

Eddie leans back on his elbows, lifts his face to the sun. He has a streak of dried mud beneath his chin. I think it might be one of the sexiest things I've ever seen. 'I wouldn't listen to everything she says though, Sadie. She's a bit of a minx is old Aunty E. She loves a meddle.'

'Oh, I don't! It's only a bit of fun,' I gabble. 'You know I decided I was just the crappest wife and she thought that was very funny and decided to give me tips to make me the best wife, tips that I either ignore or get totally wrong and that backfire horribly.'

Eddie shakes his head and laughs. 'Your poor husband.'

'What he doesn't know doesn't hurt him.' For some reason these words come out hot and sticky and full of subtexts. They hang there in the sensual warm air. Eddie gives me a curious, sidelong glance.

'If you know what I mean,' I add quickly. 'I just mean it's harmless. I think sometimes it's quite helpful getting an older lady's perspective.' I pause. 'My mum died last year and I've missed an older perspective, I suppose.' OK, I really am gabbling now. I am all of a fluster. My calf is still tingling where he touched it.

'Well, marriage *is* confusing,' he says with a nonchalant shrug. 'I'm not sure I see the point in it myself.'

'Well, if you've got kids . . .'

'. . . it makes you stay in a crap relationship for longer?'

'Very cynical, Eddie,' I say, but secretly a part of me can't help but wonder if he's right.

'I don't want to pollute you with it. Ignore me. I've been burned, darlin'. Don't you worry. I'm sure you're an excellent wife. He's a very lucky man.'

The heat scorches my cheeks. I dare not look at him. We sit in easy silence for a few moments, gazing into the garden. Then Enid arrives, a vision in a turquoise skirt and jacket, the red lipstick and the wide-brimmed straw hat giving her old-school Hollywood glamour. Seeing us together, she smiles approvingly. 'Sorry I'm late. I got horribly distracted by the most divine deli. I was hoping Eddie would find you, Sadie. I knew that you two would be able to pass the time of day together terribly well.'

Eddie and I glance at each other. Something about the glance makes me feel guilty. I leap up, wiping invisible dust off my jeans. 'Right. Flowers!'

Enid sits very neatly at the kitchen table, her hands clasped in her lap, her head cocked on one side, studying me like a watchful bird. I lay out the white sweet peas over the table, admiring the fiddly prettiness of their petals, the lush spring-onion green of their stems. Not wanting to push Enid too far too quickly, I have resisted adding much foliage, just a twist of variegated ivy with their beautiful leaves like little hearts. In the reassuring solidity of her earthenware Sri Lankan vases, the effect is rustic and natural, the kind of flowers that would work well for an outdoor English summer wedding. They even make me, seasoned old florist that I am, sigh with summery nostalgia. I tuck a sprig of ivy neatly into the last vase, so that it curls around the sweet peas, appears to be growing out of them. Enid remains silent, her mouth pursing and unpursing.

'Do you like them, Enid?' I ask gently.

'Do I like them?' She looks up at the ceiling. 'Darling, Albert will be spinning in his grave.' She shakes her head. 'They are not tulips. And they are *white*, Sadie.'

I look at her blankly. Yes, white? And the problem is . . .

'White is for weddings and christenings, for new beginnings.'

Right. Oh dear. Foot in it again. 'Sorry, I thought—'

'But, my darling, I cannot help but adore them!' She grins, an almost childish grin. 'I don't want to! But I cannot help it, it's like having the Dorset countryside brought into this dusty old London house.' She reaches out and touches a flower delicately, the oldness of her hands accentuated by the succulent beauty of the sweet pea. 'Just like Dorset.'

'You know Dorset well?'

Enid looks at me surprised. 'I grew up in Arnham Hall, near Lyme Regis. It had the most exquisite gardens.' She sighs. 'I think it's a hotel now. My father had to sell it. Frightfully expensive things houses.'

Ah. She's posher than I thought.

'So I just have to make do with stuffy old St John's Wood,' she smiles.

I consider pointing out that she could sell her house in St John's Wood and buy up half of Dorset.

'Albert, he loathed the countryside, you know.'

'He did?' I say softly, intrigued by the wistful look on her face, the softness in her eyes. It's as if the flowers have transported her back decades to a world I have no hope of ever knowing or fully understanding. I suddenly feel immensely privileged to know Enid. To think that I might have passed her on the street or clicked with impatience at her slow old person's walk in a crowd. I might have helped her on to a bus but I'd have not wanted to touch her talcy old-person skin. And I'd never have guessed that beneath the calcifying bones and the cashmere lay the spirit of a young woman who once breathed in the smell of sweet peas in Dorset and fell head over heels with a man called Albert. Yes, old age is dehumanising. In a weird way I'm happy that my mother didn't have to face it. She was a woman who got happiness from small, busy capabilities, cooking the perfect roast chicken for her family, a robust walk along a canal path, a small white wine and packet of peanuts in a country pub afterwards. Yes, far better that she was healthy, and then not. It was all over so quickly. She was sixty-two.

'Albert loved the city. He loved parties and people and fun.' Enid laughs, her dry seed-pod laugh. 'Goodness, did Albert know how to have fun!' She grabs my hand. To my horror her eyes fill with tears. She speaks urgently. 'I miss people, Sadie. Old age is just . . . dull. Dull, dull, dull. I miss my friends. My girlfriends. I miss Iris and Maud and Ruby. I miss them all.'

'Oh, Enid, I'm sorry,' I say, and I feel the dynamic of our relationship shift slightly. Part of me, shamefully, is a little appalled by her vulnerability and sudden neediness and I feel myself backing away.

'Oh what a silly woman I am!' She plucks a sweet pea out of the vase, brings it to her nose and sniffs. 'Right. Let's get down to business,' she says, looking cheerier. 'I'm pleased to see the lipstick again.'

I smack my Hot Cherry Pie lips together.

'You haven't noticed mine?' she smiles.

Now I do notice that she is wearing a slightly glossier, pinker shade. 'Lovely.'

'So have you been acting . . .' she traces a line upwards around her mouth, drawing a clown's smile. '. . . happy?'

'Trying to,' I laugh. 'I deserve an Oscar.'

'Marvellous. One moment, Angie!' Enid calls, her eyes not leaving my face. 'Music! Maybe some Ella Fitzgerald or something. And lemonades please. Not too much ice.' She turns to me. 'Dispatches on this other woman, please?'

Other Woman. I swallow hard. She makes it sound so

definite. I tentatively explain about taking the job at her apartment, the photograph in her kitchen. Angie puts the cold lemonade beside us, the ice cubes crackling in the glasses.

'Excellent sleuthing I must say. Well, well. A photograph. Interesting.' She rests her drink on her palm and sits in silence for a few moments as if deep in thought. 'Men are not naturally monogamous, never were and never will be. We all knew this, me and the girls.' She smiles and her face crumples into a thousand lines. 'We accepted it, largely. As long as they were discreet.'

'Really? You didn't mind?'

'We accepted it came with the territory. You modern girls expect the impossible. Monogamy is for swans, my darling, not human beings. I was telling Chloe the very thing yesterday afternoon when she came to do all those marvellous things with my face.' Enid chinks my glass. 'Whether your husband is playing away or not – Chloe said hers did, the rogue – *especially* if he's playing away, you need to carry on as before, Sadie. Don't falter in the face of the enemy.'

'Carry on as before? If I find out he's screwing this woman I'll fry his balls! I'll kill him!'

'Now don't be hysterical. Pass me that notebook of yours.' She flexes her pen. 'A mistress means war. First rule of war: know your enemy. Second rule: up your game. When he wakes up in the morning you are the first woman he sees. Look beautiful. Smile. Make an effort . . .' She winks. 'You know where.'

I laugh at the preposterousness of it all. I'm not so bloody desperate that I will try to keep a cheating husband by performing pornoastics in the sack! I'm not an old-school Tory wife! Stand by your man! Hell, no.

Enid shoots me a sharp look, as if this is no laughing matter and I should be paying more attention. 'Make it the best he's ever had. Remind yourself of the endgame.' Enid puts her feather-light hand on my arm. 'Don't worry, men rarely leave their wives, if that's what you're thinking. There's little danger of that. Men are homebodies, little boys who won't leave their mothers. If this woman *is* dallying with your husband – and we don't know for sure yet, do we, darling? – he'll soon lose interest once he realises that he's got everything he needs at home. Besides, in my day,' she adds, 'it wasn't just the men who had affairs. My girls got their desserts on the side too. We had little ways of cheering ourselves up when the going got tough.' We glance up at the kitchen window, the flicker of movement behind its pane. Eddie saunters nonchalantly down the garden path. He doesn't seem to notice us staring at him intently from the kitchen.

Twenty-five

Tom sleeps beside me, snoring lightly, his face boyish and vulnerable in sleep. His lips compress and part, as if trying to blow invisible bubbles. There are dark rings beneath eyes that speak of air conditioned offices and not enough rest. Perhaps a better wife would feel sorry for him. But I just wonder if I am the only woman to have this intimate, aerial perspective of him on a pillow and whether he is exhausted because he's living a double life. My musings are disturbed by a loud, grunting snore. No, for once, it is not Tom. It is Rona in the spare room. I slide out of bed and sit at my dressing table, surveying my pillow-creased face, Enid's words tumbling around my head. 'It's war!' Funny to think that even a few weeks ago I didn't care what Tom saw when he woke up. But after tussling with my horrified younger self and that feminist voice in my head which shrieks 'What the hell are you doing?', I've made a decision to try it Enid's way. Why? Because I haven't got enough evidence to accuse him of an affair and right now it doesn't feel like I've got a great deal to lose. Apart from him.

I double-check that Tom is still asleep then I hit my ammunition – foundation, blush, and, of course, Hot Cherry Pie – applying it quickly, more expertly now, as Chloe taught me. I take off my old flannel pyjamas and snuggle quietly back into bed, naked but for the squirt of Chanel No. 5. Good loving . . . here it comes.

I take a deep breath and wiggle down beneath the duvet to where it's a bit stinky and foot-smelling and Tom's sleep-hard leaning tower of Pisa bends to the left against the dark hairs on his thigh. Sweating now beneath the heavy winter-down duvet, I manage to suck it into my mouth in one slurp. But I can't get a good grip so I slip my feet out of the bed and, bottom arched in the air, use the leverage of the rug to get a deeper mouthful. I imagine Tom's face as he surfaces slowly, pleasurably, the warmth and wetness of my mouth offering its wifely good morning. Tom is stirring. Tom is making soft groaning noises.

'Baby,' he mumbles, reaching for my hair.

Despite the ache in my jaw, my body softens and thrums with pleasure, pleased to actually be pleasing him for once. I suck a little harder. Deep throat. No, I haven't put so much effort into a blow job since our honeymoon.

Tom's breath is coming harder now. He flexes his toes, shoves his hips towards me. I gag. The deep throat aggravates my tonsils. Spluttering and choking I am forced to come up for air. Tom opens his eyes. Swallowing the last bit of spittle, I arch my bottom higher and lower my lids seductively. He smiles at me, then, as he usually does in such circumstances, gives a bigger, congratulatory smile to the leaning tower of Pisa. His smile disappears. He looks horrified. 'What the fuck . . .'

I glance down at the tower of Pisa too and flinch. Oh. My. God. He's had sex with a piranha. It takes a second or two for me to realise what's happened. 'Sorry, darling . . .' I say, wetting my finger, trying to rub the red lipstick away but only making it worse.

'Ow!' he says.

'It's all right, it's only . . .'

Tom winces. He is going limp. The leaning tower of Pisa has collapsed.

'. . . lipstick.' I rub and rub and it doesn't budge. Do Hollywood goddesses have this problem? There is a knocking on our bedroom door. I start.

'Just a little query,' barks Rona through the door. 'Danny says he's allowed chocolate biscuits for breakfast. Is this true? I never know in this house. May I come in?'

'*No!*' Tom and I shout in unison.

Tom dives into the shower to wash off the smears of Hot Cherry Pie. I throw on my clothes and clatter downstairs to rescue Danny from a breakfast of chocolate digestives.

From the hall I can see Rona sitting primly in a kitchen chair, hair pulled back with a towelling head band, face covered in white gunk. Teddy is sulking in the corner of the kitchen. Danny refuses to sit on her knee and cannot understand why the granny that he's not allowed to call granny has painted her face with what she describes as 'an extremely expensive bespoke face mask from Dr Prenwood'.

'It looks like bird poo,' observes Danny.

'Danny, my dear,' she says, her mouth hardly moving on account of the drying clay. 'One day you'll get married and be very grateful when your wife takes care of herself.'

'I'm going to marry Mummy,' retorts Danny, scraping the jam off his toast with his finger and licking it.

Rona plunges the cafetière down with extra force, as if the comment riles her. I walk into the room. Teddy jumps up and starts yapping.

'Down, Teddy! Hi there, Sadie, I see that you've taken my advice about sprucing yourself up. And the house is looking so much tidier, far less of a health hazard. Well done, darling.'

'Your advice?' I'll be damned if she thinks I've taken her advice on anything.

'Yes, I've noticed the lipstick and I have to say it's a vast improvement, Sadie. Although I think a slightly pinkier tone can be more flattering to mature skin. Coffee?'

Tom walks into the kitchen rubbing his wet hair with a towel. He looks at me and grins. Then he flops down in the chair, his long legs stretching out before him. Teddy jumps up and starts smelling his crotch.

'Down, Teddy!' Rona gives the dog a pat on the nose, then feeds him a piece of toast. She gazes at Tom adoringly. 'You look tired, Tom. All that hard work,' she sighs approvingly. 'It'll be worth it. I promise you. If you want to get to the top, you've got to sleep, eat and breathe your job. That's what Ted always used to say.'

'Toast, darling?' I don't wait for his answer, I slip into good wife mode, spreading the butter on two rounds of wholemeal bread. This is probably the first time I've buttered his toast in our entire marriage. Well, why would I? He's a grown man, not a toddler. (Most of the time.)

Rona eyes my wifely toast-spreading largesse suspiciously as if I'm trying to cover something up, pillaging the joint account for example, or joining a motorway dogging club. 'Too much butter, Sadie,' she says sharply. 'Are you trying to kill him off?'

'I think working such long hours will get him first. Marmalade, darling?'

'Not if he's got a supportive wife,' she says quickly. Irritation twitches at the corners of her mouth. I think she prefers my usual fragrant display of failings. It is my bad example, after all, that lets hers shine so brightly. 'Your father always liked a fried breakfast on a Monday, Tom,' she trumps. 'Set him up for a hard week at work.'

'Miracle he's still alive.' I can't resist.

Tom rolls his eyes. 'Ladies, ladies . . .'

'Apparently if a man is married he has a far smaller chance of having a heart attack.' Rona gazes at me. Pauses. 'Although I guess that depends on the marriage.'

I kick Tom with my foot under the table. Teddy growls.

'Don't kick Daddy!' shouts Danny.

'I wasn't kicking Daddy, honey.'

Rona smiles smugly just to show that she knows that I was kicking Tom under the table. Her voice rises in pitch. 'So what's the story this morning?' she asks, practically rubbing her hands with excitement. 'More executive meetings? Deals? Mergers?'

Tom gulps back some coffee. Danny clambers on to his knee. 'A late breakfast meeting at the Wolseley. So easy on the toast, Sadie. I shouldn't really eat twice. I'm turning into Billy Bunter as it is. Look at the state of my waistline. Then I'm wrapped in meetings for the rest of the day.'

'Who are you meeting for breakfast, anyone of note?' she asks.

Tom coughs and glances up at me uneasily. 'Um, Annette Eastern,' he says quietly. 'A client.'

The kitchen starts to spin. The air feels tight. It feels like I'm choking under the duvet again.

Rona looks puzzled. 'Annette Eastern. Annette . . . Now why is her name familiar?'

'Oh, she's written a couple of bestsellers,' says Tom, trying to shut the conversation down.

Rona slaps the table. Teddy growls. 'Oh yes, I know!

Spring Clean Your Heart! That's the one, isn't it?'

'Yup. Right. What are you up to today, Sadie?' he says, quickly changing the subject.

I open my mouth to speak but Rona interrupts me. 'How funny,' she says. 'I saw her on *GMTV* last week. Blonde. Absolutely gorgeous. Looked a bit like your lovely old flame, Lucinda Lawn.'

Tom's foot taps nervously under the table. He glares at Rona.

'She's a knockout, isn't she? What a figure. And she was surprisingly good on telly, I must say. Not just a pretty face. Talking about how she teaches people how to leave bad marriages.' She glances at me. 'Very interesting.'

Twenty-six

I emerge from Green Park Tube, stride hurriedly along Piccadilly, nervously glancing behind me, checking I've not been seen. I am at the grand entrance of the Wolseley. Wishing it were winter so that I could wrap a scarf around my head and assume a more convincing disguise than my baseball cap and big shades, which just makes me look like a lost tourist from the American mid-west, I walk through the gleaming doors into London's most glamorous bistro. *Know your enemy.*

'Have you booked, madam?' asks the pretty lady in black behind the desk.

'I'm just . . . just trying to see if my friend is here,' I declare in my poshest, most English voice to counteract the effects of the baseball hat. I scan the restaurant quickly, poised to spin on my heel or hide behind a menu if in imminent danger of being spotted. The tables are full of chattering glamorous women in neat jackets, crisp white shirts and high heels. A hiss of conversation hovers above them like a mushroom cloud. There are countless men who look like Tom and countless blonde women who could be Psyche Viagra. Then, in the far left-hand corner, my eye is drawn to a familiar shaped back. Yes, that's the back I married: V-shaped, muscular with a large brown mole hidden beneath the suit on the right shoulder. Opposite him is my nemesis.

Her hair is the blondest in the room, blonder than she looks on her website, the colour of condensed milk. And she is flirtatiously twisting it behind her ear with her fingers and laughing, one of those girlie – 'hey, you're so funny' – laughs. Yes, the body language expert is sending out clear signals. Very clear signals. A fierce red rage pumps through me. Psyche Viagra and my husband! I stand there impotently for a second, trying to stop myself from marching over and making a scene.

Someone shouts 'Sadie!'

I freeze.

'Over here. Behind yer.'

That voice. It can't be. I turn around. It is.

My father. He is sitting about five feet away wearing a pale pink golfing T-shirt. Next to Loretta.

'Dad! What the hell are you doing here?' I hiss, pulling the baseball cap further down so that its elasticated rim pinches my forehead.

'Manners! I could ask you the same question.' Dad turns around to another table, grabs one of their spare chairs and drags it over, getting glares from the other diners. 'And what's with the hat? Take a pew.'

Glancing nervously at Tom's table, I duck down on to a spare seat.

Dad pats his stomach. 'Great brekkie, wouldn't you say, Loretta? *Time Out* was right.'

'Lovely,' chirrups Loretta, picking a flake of croissant out of the gunk of her pink lipstick. Her blouse – very bright, very pink – matches the lipstick. As do her pink wedge heels. 'Do help yourself, Sadie. We're stuffed to the gills.'

'Thanks, I've already eaten. What are you doing in London, Dad?'

'Don't look so bloody pleased about it.'

'Sorry. It was just a shock. It's the last place I'd expect to bump into you. I didn't even know you were in town.' What I don't say and only now begin to acknowledge is that it feels a bit of a betrayal that Dad has come to London and not thought to phone me. I've always assumed that me and Danny are the reason he comes to London. Not any more.

'Ah, we've come up to see the *Grease* matinée. You know. The musical. Have you seen it?'

I shake my head. Hate musicals. All that stamping and faux-jolliness.

Loretta sighs. 'Oh, can't wait. It's going to take us right back, isn't it, John?' she says nostalgically, as if they've been together for twenty years. '*Pain au chocolat*, Sadie? Very yummy.'

'No thanks, Loretta.' Annette is laughing now, throwing her head back and really laughing. (Tom's jokes aren't that bloody funny!) Tom is looking at her, one of his sexy lazy smiles plastered across his face. Damn him. Top client. I bet she bloody well is.

'Are you all right, love?' asks Dad. 'You look troubled.'

'Yeah, yeah.' I pull my baseball cap lower, anxiously glancing over at Tom's table. They're still engrossed.

'Cool hat,' coos Loretta. 'Makes you look like you're from LA or something.'

'I've got to go.' Before I'm seen. 'Danny would love to see you, Dad.' I say this to Dad, not Loretta, who I know will come anyway. But I don't want to give her any encouragement. A part of me wishes desperately that she'd get the message and back off and leave me to continue my relationship with my father as it was after Mum died. But I can't. Where Dad goes, Loretta follows.

Dad glances at his watch. 'I'd love to see him. The only thing is—'

'We must see our little Danny!' interrupts Loretta.

Our little Danny?

'But I've booked us a little surprise.' He winks. 'Turn away now, Loretta babe.'

Babe?

Dad leans over and whispers into my ear. 'After *Grease*, Thames cruise then dinner in Soho tonight. A little Italian pizza place off Regent Street. Quite the "in" place, apparently.'

Just then a flicker of movement. Fuck. Annette is

standing up. Shit, she's tall. She's bloody Amazonian. She's got legs that go up to her ear lobes. Like Gisele. She's reaching down for her bag. I see a flash of leopard print. Tom is holding up the white tailored coat that was slung on the back of the chair. Yikes. What if he sees me? What if he sees Dad?

'Actually. Maybe I will order something.' I grab a menu off an adjacent empty table and stick it up over my face like a shield. I cannot, unfortunately, do the same thing for Dad and Loretta. I can only hope and pray that they don't draw more attention to themselves. I sit with the menu in front of my face, heart in my mouth, waiting for the sound of Tom's surprised voice, the excruciating unveiling.

'Are you ready to order?' asks a pretty, brunette waitress.

I am forced to emerge from behind my menu. I glance up nervously. No sign. Tom's table is empty. They have gone. I breathe a sigh of relief and take my cap off, shaking my hair out with my fingers. 'A cappuccino, please.'

Dad leans back on his chair and studies me. 'Did Tom tell you about our engagement party date?'

'He did.'

Loretta coughs and fiddles with the napkin in her lap. 'I know it clashes with your wedding anniversary. I hope you don't mind.'

'Hey! Of course she doesn't mind,' booms Dad. 'We can all celebrate together.'

We chat inanely about Danny for a few minutes while

I gulp my coffee as quickly as I can without burning my tongue. 'Well, it's been lovely bumping into you. But I must go,' I say, picking up my handbag and slinging it over my shoulder.

'OK,' beams Dad.

I'm a little surprised he doesn't try to make me stay as he normally would. There is nothing needy about Dad any more. He is definitely over my mother. He's kind of over me too.

'But you never did tell me what you were doing here?'

'Oh, nothing. I came to meet someone. They blew me out. Anyway, see you soon. Enjoy *Grease*.'

'Oh, we will,' Loretta says, patting the frosted glaze on her hair. 'Come and see us in Milton Keynes soon, won't you?'

I nod, knowing that I won't step foot in Milton Keynes as long as I can help it. I kiss my dad on the cheek, his familiar bristly old cheek. There is a moment of awkwardness as I bend forward to kiss Loretta – it's as if we both would rather be excused the pleasantry but know it's expected of us for Dad's sake. Loretta's cheek smells of scented make-up and feels tacky.

Dad shakes his head. 'It's so strange, meeting you here. I mean in this great big city of yours. I feel like it's one of those days. Full of strange coincidences, isn't it, Lottie?'

'Bloody hell yes!' says Loretta. 'You wouldn't believe it, Sadie. When we first arrived here we saw a dead ringer for Tom walking into the restaurant.'

I smile tightly. 'How funny.'

Dad guffaws. 'They say we each have our double.'

Loretta lays a tanned pink-nailed hand on mine. 'Don't look so worried! It wasn't him. This one was snuggled up arm in arm with some woman who looked like she'd stepped out of the pages of a magazine!' She turns to Dad. 'I tell you, you don't get women like that in Milton Keynes. Didn't she have a smashing handbag, John? All that leopard print. Bloody massive. I've never seen anything like it! I turned to your father and said, "If you are taking notes on my Christmas list . . ."'

Dad chuckles. 'Do I look like the kind of man to notice a handbag?'

Loretta winks at me. 'I'm working on him, Sadie!'

I force myself to smile. But the gleaming marble floor is rushing up to meet my head. The brass columns are falling towards me like felled trees. Snuggled arm in arm? Yes, it's war.

Twenty-seven

Pam offers a Tupperware box containing tiny, perfect homemade quiches, trailed by a buzzing wasp. 'Did Tom appreciate the trifle?'

I pick out a quiche, wave the wasp away and stretch my legs out on the picnic rug. 'Absolutely stunned.'

'I'm very impressed you attempted it. Not the easiest recipe.'

'I'm a woman reformed, Pam. But you know the weirdest thing? I almost enjoyed making that trifle. Most bizarre. Ah, blasted wasp. To wasp hell with you!'

'If only there was a recipe for a perfect marriage,' Pam sighs.

'You seem to have it down, Pam.'

We're having a picnic beside the bandstand in Queen's Park, ostensibly to discuss a possible Anderson wife charity fun run – 'Oh I'll be up for running days after the birth!' – but really because it's a glorious Friday afternoon and Pam organised it last minute with her usual efficiency. Her enormous picnic blanket is gingham and has a waterproof lining. There are plastic polka dot picnic plates in tasteful retro shades of pink and green. There are more Tupperware tubs of food than we can possibly eat, and fast emptying bladder boxes of white wine. Ruth, who has this Friday afternoon off, is crouched forward, eating a cocktail sausage, flicking anxiously between an article on divorce in the *Guardian* – Alex is still at his mother's – and her twins who are tearing round and round the bandstand making hysterical whooping noises. There is an ear-splitting yell. Ruth rolls her eyes and gets up. 'Excuse me, ladies. Disreputable progeny calls.'

Tara watches nonchalantly as Ruth breaks up a fight. Then checking out – nothing to do with her – she strips off her blouse and lies back on the grass in her white bikini top and closes her eyes. Her breasts do not slump into her armpits like saggy bags of sugar, as mine do in such a position, but remain suspiciously round and upright. Has she had a boob job?

'Hmm, amazing quiche, Pam,' I say. It really is a symphony of cheese, ham, onion and pastry. I never thought of myself as a quiche person but I do now.

She shrugs. 'I don't have such high expectations.'

'That's exactly how I'd approach a quiche. But it wouldn't turn out like this.'

'Not quiche, silly, marriage.'

'Oh right,' I laugh. 'Well, I think my bar's pretty low these days too.'

Pam doesn't smile. 'Rubbish. You expect to have a

career, your life, a man, a man like Tom. To have it all. I never expected that.' She gazes into the distance. 'I knew I had to give something up.' She sounds so uncharacteristically defeated I wonder if the fact her eyes are so pink today has nothing to do with hay fever, as she claimed, and more to do with crying. Or maybe she's just pregnant and tired. She continues to stare ahead to where the children are playing beside the bandstand. We sit in silence for a few moments.

'What do you mean by "a man like Tom"?' I ask, suddenly paranoid. Does she know something I don't? Hell, do all the Anderson wives know something I don't, not just the likes of Linda and Joanna who certainly appeared to know something dark and secretive at the clothes swap sale. The urge to ask Pam about Tom and Annette becomes almost unbearable. I bite my lip and remind myself that she's an Anderson wife and not a particularly discreet one either. If I mentioned anything it would find its way to Seth, to work, to the Anderson office . . . No, it just doesn't bear thinking about. I can't confide in her.

'I mean I bet you never feel like you've settled.'

'Settled?' This throws me. 'No. I never felt that. Tom and I were madly in love when we first met, then . . .' I hesitate. 'Oh I don't know. Marriage, kids, it's tough, well, it has been for us. It hasn't been the fairytale that I thought it would be.' I pick another quiche from the tub. They really are melt-on-tongue delicious. 'You don't think you settled with Seth, do you?'

Pam is silent for a few moments. 'Sometimes,' she says in a very quiet voice. 'Don't repeat that to anyone, will you?' She glances over at Tara anxiously.

'No. Of course not.' I'm a little stunned, and touched, that she has admitted to her life being any less than perfect. She is Perfect Pam after all.

'I mean I know I did the *right* thing.' She speaks with emphatic urgency now, as if trying to undo the earlier comment. 'By marrying Seth. The other guys brought me nothing but heartbreak, endless drama. I look at my single friends, take Chloe for example, and think, there but for the grace of God . . .' She laughs, a forced musical laugh. 'Oh, I don't know. I mean look at Tara, just look at her.'

We glance over at Tara who appears to be dozing now, her exposed, tanned belly breathing up and down lightly. Her eyes are peacefully shut, her face is untroubled – although that could be the Botox – and her mouth flickers with a secret smile as if she's reliving something delicious and filthy in the privacy of her own head.

'I can't remember the last time I felt like that. Can you?'

I laugh. 'Nope! We might have to get this masseur's number.'

'It would be nice to take a one day marriage sabbatical, you know, do what Tara's doing.' Pam shakes her head quickly, as if checking herself. 'Not that I approve, don't get me wrong.'

I think of Eddie, the way he looks at my mouth when he talks to me, his dancing leaf-green eyes. 'I know what you're saying.'

'Do you?' Pam looks relieved. 'I thought you'd get everything you need at home. Tom's a catch.'

'Have him,' I snap too quickly.

'Oh I would,' teases Pam, laughing. 'He's fun. And he's so good looking. Compared to all those stuffy fat old Anderson husbands he really stands out. In fact, he looks more like a boyfriend than a husband. Like one of those sexy bachelor types we all thought would never settle down. But they did, evidently.' She shrugs. 'Just not with me. More quiche? These little beauties are spinach and Gruyère.'

'I shouldn't,' I say, taking another quiche. 'But I will.'

'Give me your hand!' Pam suddenly grabs my hand. 'What?'

I drop the quiche on to a plastic plate. She presses my hand to her belly. 'Can you feel it? That! There it is again!'

I do feel a small movement, a pulse beneath my palm. It's an electric shock of nostalgia. I immediately think of the unused Babygros in the linen cupboard at home.

'The baby.' Her eyes start to fill with tears again. 'You know what, Sadie? When it kicks like that it makes all the other shit worthwhile.'

Twenty-eight

'So I don't need a key to get out?' I ask Annette Eastern's cleaner Louise for the second time. Getting locked in this apartment would be more than I could bear. It would be Sadie Drew's Law of Sod in action. 'Are you absolutely sure?'

'Sure,' she says a little wearily. 'See you later.'

I get to work quickly, arranging two displays of pink peonies and bear grass, using foam and wiring so that the flowers will not droop. When I'm done, I place one vase in the grand hallway, the other on a mirrored console table in the sitting room, the peonies prettily reflected in the mirror so that there is a vibrant burst of pink against the white walls of the apartment, the flowers at once humanising the space. My old Notting Hill floristry mentor once told me that rooms without flowers are like faces without smiles; never has that been more true than in Annette's clinically perfect apartment.

The job is done. It is time to leave. But I don't leave. Enid's words hit me again: *Know your enemy*. She's damn right. I stare at the photograph on the kitchen wall. There she is. There *he* is. A furious jealousy prickles beneath my skin. I can't help myself. I start to pace the joint. The first door I open leads to a bathroom, a spotless arrangement of marble and gleaming chrome. I imagine Psyche Viagra's Gisele-like slim, toned body standing beneath the shower, eyes closed, water splattering her blond hair to her sinewy shoulders. I shut the bathroom door and walk quickly down the corridor, anxiously listening for the sound of a key in the front door. My hand – now sweating – turns another brushed chrome door knob. Oh. Merely a vacuum cleaner and a collection of brushes – Louise's terrain. I creep further down the corridor. Another room. A large double bed. Perfectly laundered white linen. One flash of tasteful abstract modern art above the bed. Her bedroom? Perhaps. But it has the neatness and inertia of a guest bedroom. My heart quickening, I open the closet door. Coats. Racks and racks of coats.

I hurry out and open the door to the adjacent room. As soon as I see it I know I am at the epicentre of Psyche Viagra's flat: her bedroom. The bed is as big as a yacht, covered with layers of silk throws and so many cushions that she must spend a large part of her evening removing them from the bed before she can go to sleep. Something in my stomach twists. How many lovers have been in here? Has Tom ever lain on this bed?

Beside the bed is a thick white pile rug. A mirrored dressing table. A large bottle of Dior perfume and a ceramic jewellery hand dangling with long, sparkly necklaces.

It takes five minutes to find what I am looking for because the wardrobe is seamlessly disguised alongside the wall. There are no handles. I push a door gently. There is a soft click and it opens, displaying the most orderly wardrobe I have ever seen. There are cubby holes for shoes and socks and drawers that slide open soundlessly. There are dozens of dresses hanging up on cedar hangers. There are about thirty shoe boxes with photographs of their contents – Chanel, Jimmy Choo – stuck on the outside, along with the season of purchase. My mind computes the facts. This woman is super-organised. She is ridiculously wealthy. She is a size ten. Her feet are size seven. She particularly likes red and dove grey. She does not own any old clothes. Or anything shabby, saggy or cheap. She is in fact the exact opposite of me. Hell, why did I expect any different?

But where are the handbags? This is a woman who would not own one handbag. No, this is a woman who . . . Then I see them, on the very top shelf of the wardrobe. Black totes, red clutches, Kelly bags, endless. There seems to be a second row of handbags behind the first. I reach up but my fingers can barely touch them. I look around for a stool or chair and see none. How the hell can I reach? I get an idea. Thrilled at my brazen naughtiness I pick the highest pair of stiletto heels that I can see out of their Manolo Blahnik box, labelled 'evening spring 06': navy blue, a heel like a pencil.

Pulling my trainers off but retaining my sweaty black Primark trainer socks, I step into the heels, one foot – God, they're high – then the other. I can now just about reach the handbags. I pull each one away carefully to check out the one behind it. I am a little disgusted at myself. I am a woman obsessed. I am a woman without dignity. What is wrong with me?

Then I see it.

I grab the red clutch, toss it to the floor. And *the* bag is revealed: enormous, feline, leopard print. I stare and stare at it as if willing the print to change its spots. It doesn't. It is surely the bag that Loretta noticed at the Wolseley. Balance faltering on the blue heels, I lean forward to grab it and end up plunging, hands outstretched, into Annette's wardrobe. The dresses clatter on their hangers. There is something silky in my mouth. The smell of her perfume in my nose. A sharp pain in my left foot.

Then I hear the front door slam.

Shit. Louise is back. Shit. Shit. I scrabble to my feet and quickly shut the wardrobe door. I'm about to kick off the heels when I spot the red clutch that I've dropped on the white rug. I lurch towards it.

'Hello?' It sounds like she's standing outside the door. 'Is someone there?'

I freeze. Panic. I shove the clutch back in the wardrobe. I kick off the blue heels. One sticks to my foot. The other flies across the room.

'Who is it?'

'Only me, Louise. Sadie!' I'll tell her I was scouting for the perfect space to put the vase, scouting to see if the flowers clashed with the wallpaper. I make a lunge for the flyaway blue heel and fall forward, prostrate on the white rug.

The bedroom door opens.

Annette. We stare at each other for a few awful moments. She begins to back out of the doorway. For a fleeting second she looks scared. 'Who are you?'

'The florist,' I say eventually, wishing the earth would open and gulp me away. I can't believe this is happening. I take in her long tanned calves shod in camel slingbacks, the fitted black dress, the hair tumbling from her face. If anything she is even more beautiful in the flesh.

'The florist?' she says, staring in disbelief at the blue heel on my left foot. 'What the hell . . .'

'I can explain.' But I can't obviously.

'Get out,' she says, squaring up to me, eyes flashing angrily. 'Get out of my house or I'll call the police.'

'I . . . I . . .' Then out of nowhere tears start to flood my eyes. I bat them back furiously, not wanting the humiliation of tears to compound the humiliation of being caught. 'I just saw these shoes and thought I'd try them on.' I pull the offending shoe off, pick up the other one and pair them together at the side of the bed. 'I'm so sorry. I don't know what came over me. I'm sorry if I gave you a fright.'

She shakes her head at me incredulously.

My hands tremble as I pull on my sweaty trainers.

'I'm so sorry,' I mumble, so appalled at my own irrational behaviour that for the moment I've forgotten that this woman could be trying to steal my husband and ruin my life.

Annette carefully watches my every move to check I'm not going to make a grab for her necklaces. 'One always wonders what staff get up to when one isn't around. Now I know.'

What if she realises I am Tom's wife? What if . . . Oh God. It just doesn't bear thinking about. Still, Tom and I don't share a surname. I will never work for her again. This incident will just die a slow undignified death in her memory – the bonkers florist who had a thing about shoes. 'I know how it must look.'

'Come on. Out of my bedroom, lady.' Her fear has gone. Her voice is clear and controlled now, the kind of voice I imagine does very well in big auditoriums. 'Collect your stuff from the kitchen.'

I follow Annette down the corridor. In the kitchen she leans back on the table and observes me buffoonishly throwing my stuff together. 'I was not stealing or anything.'

'Get out!' she roars.

Twenty-nine

'It's nice to be out together for once, isn't it?' says Tom gently, resting his chin on his hands and staring at me across the snowy white expanse of linen-draped restaurant table. His eyes are soft and liquid in the flickering candlelight. 'You look very lovely tonight by the way.'

I'm wearing a red dress that matches my lipstick. My hair is pulled back into a neat chignon. I've even accessorised with three gold bracelets that chime every time I move my wrist. But inside I feel like a horrible fraud, dirty almost, mortified and tainted by my encounter with Annette Eastern. I can still feel her blue shoe on my foot, the constricting pinch of its toe, the wobble of its high heel. I can see the curl of her lip, her appalled horror. I am so terrified she'll find out I'm Tom's wife I can barely speak.

'Mum suggested it,' adds Tom. 'She said that when she and Dad went through tough times they'd always make an effort to go on a date.'

'So this is a date?' I feel a surge of compassion for Tom. He *is* trying. If he was messing around with Psyche Viagra, would he be trying? Or is this a double bluff?

'I guess it is.' He grins a sloppy schoolboy grin, which doesn't quite hide his unease.

'I've forgotten how to do it,' I say quietly.

The waiter refills our glasses with ruby red Rioja.

'It went something like dinner, taxi, sex, didn't it?'

I start, jolted by this mention of sex. He never mentions it any more, not wanting, I suspect, to invite the elephant into the room. We're turning into one of those couples that freeze when a sex scene comes on telly, every sensual slurp and grind of the actors merely highlighting our own disastrous bedroom non-antics. I pick at my sea bass politely. 'I guess things have changed.'

He smiles and I smile back and in our smiles is an agreement that we'll skip the bigger stuff for the sake of a couple of hours' harmony. Neither of us is totally relaxed, not like you would be with someone you knew less well. No, right now we're out of our comfort zone: stripped of the distractions and routines of domestic life, a little raw, like we're eating naked. It occurs to me that perhaps the Tom I now know is the Tom that only exists in the rush to get to work in the morning, or the tired TV fuzz of an evening, or our Danny-centric weekends. Where is the old Tom? The boyish, charming man who slapped my bottom and called me his 'naughty little flower girl'?

He leans back and pats his belly. 'Good steak.'

'You've got used to finding an empty fridge.'

'Not any more. We've moved on from out-of-date Petits Filous, haven't we?' he laughs.

'Just.'

'I noticed.' He reaches out and touches my hand gently. 'Thanks.'

I look down at my meal. This small, gentle acknowledgement – the one I've been waiting for – makes me feel even more hysterical and duplicitous. Because I know that while I may have whipped together a trifle I've also been whipping through the wardrobe of his client (likely mistress) trying to find evidence of an affair, and my head is simmering and spitting with angry, unwifely thoughts. We sit in silence for a few moments.

'Work want me to go to New York for a few days,' he says, nervously, waiting for my reaction. I don't give him one. He looks relieved. 'Which bodes very well for the directorship,' he adds. 'You know I can feel that I'm close, Sadie.' He indicates a tiny gap between thumb and finger. 'Damn close. I can smell it.'

'That's great.'

'I'll have to leave the Monday after the Anderson summer party. In two weeks. Is that OK?'

'Sure.' Then something else sinks in. I stop chewing my forkful of food. 'God, the Anderson summer party is in two weeks? I thought it was months off.'

'No, it's almost upon us. The invites have gone out . . .'

A horrible likelihood dawns. 'Will your clients be there, all your clients?'

'Let's hope so.' He cuts into his steak. Blood puddles out on to the plate. 'Or I'm dead meat.'

Oh God. The horror. I cough into my napkin. 'You won't want me there this time then. Not after the Ivy lunch.'

'Don't be silly. Of course I want you there. All the spouses are invited. Pam and everyone will be there. It'll be fun.'

'I'll get trapped in a flat, or a lift, or turn up with my skirt tucked into my knickers and a canapé stuck to my front tooth.' I torture the napkin in my lap. I can't go, can't possibly.

'You can invite some more friends if you like, attractive women preferably. I'm kind of worried there are going to be too many suits.' He grins. 'We need colour.'

Fragrant wives don't count as colour. Wives represent children and couples' dinner parties. Single women represent sex. Annette Eastern is single. 'I'll call Chloe. I'll tell her to show off her legs.'

The waiters clear away our plates. Our hands fold and unfold at opposite ends of the empty table. The atmosphere is still polite: this meal that shows we're capable of actually going out and consuming alcohol and not tearing at each other's throats. But there's a sense that there are Issues circling overhead like a vulture around a dying animal. Tom's mouth opens. No words come out. He is hesitating. Yet there is clearly something he wants to say. I realise that we're not just on a date. We're here for something else too. 'Sadie . . .'

Here it comes. I stare away from him into the restaurant, the other diners, the quiet couples, the chatting groups of girlfriends, all these lives and loves. It occurs to me that everyone here is either building something – a closer friendship, a more intimate relationship – or they are doing the opposite, like us, dismantling in slow motion over glasses of wine.

'I was wondering . . .'

I feel the beat of the vulture's wings against my face. 'What is it?'

Tom blinks at me. He always blinks when he's in an awkward spot, it's one of his emotional tics. Then he stares at my forehead. 'Do you remember when you got bashed on the head by that branch?'

I touch my forehead and wonder why he mentions it. Have I still got some unsightly lump that I haven't noticed?

Tom clears his throat. 'Well, don't take this the wrong way. But you've been acting kind of strange since then.'

'Strange? What do you mean?'

'You've not been acting quite like yourself,' he says softly, too softly, like he's speaking to a slightly insane person. 'This lipstick, this new housewifey thing, well, it's just not you, is it?'

I start to laugh. Oh, the irony. Then the hysteria turns

to something redder, madder. The temperature at the table changes. We are suddenly no longer on a date. We are at war again. 'I thought you might like it,' I say, voice laced with ugly sarcasm.

'It's not just that, Sadie. It's a few things. Even Mum's noticed.'

'I might have guessed she was behind this.'

'No, not at all.' Tom suddenly looks terribly tired, as if I – we – exhaust him. 'I'm not explaining this very well, sorry. Do you think it might be a good idea if you went to a doctor and got yourself checked out? Bumps on the head . . .'

I can hardly believe what I'm hearing. 'A doctor? You are fucking joking?'

Tom drags at his cheek with his fingers. He looks like he'd rather be anywhere else but here. 'Do you have to overreact to *everything*?' The table adjacent to ours swivels around to the source of the raised voice. 'I just thought it was worth getting it checked out,' he hisses, sending the voyeur diners off with one of his glares. 'I'm concerned about you.'

I drop my head into my hands. A less worse wife indeed. He thinks I'm a mad wife! The futility of it all smashes into me like a great wave. I try to stop myself from crying. But it all pours out in furious snotty gulps anyway. 'But what about *you*, Tom? Why don't you get yourself checked out? You have fucking issues too.'

Tom looks down at the table. 'Don't let's rake up the past again. Let's move on, Sadie.'

'But you work so late. I never see you! Not properly. And you have the cheek to say to me—'

'Sadie, you know I've got to work long hours at the moment.' He talks in a low angry whisper. 'If I've got any chance of that directorship I've got to do it. I've got no choice. You're just going to have to bear with me.'

'Many wives would think you were having an affair, you know that!' There, it's out. Loudly. The diners at the table next to ours sit up straight and stare disapprovingly at Tom.

'An *affair*? An affair?' hisses Tom, his face turning red as the Rioja. 'Are you completely insane?'

'I don't know what to think, Tom.'

'Don't you know how much I'd love to spend more time with Danny?'

'See more of him then! Get up in the night when he cries, like I do!'

Tom shakes his head. 'I'm shattered. I don't hear him in the night. But you shouldn't be getting up in the night anyway. He's almost three. He's not a baby. Let him grow up!'

'I will not leave my son crying alone at night. I think *you* should get up. And I work too by the way,' I hiss.

'But you don't have to,' he says with an air of desperation.

'I want to! I may not have some fancy title and a big job but I don't see why it always has to take a back seat.'

Tom blows air out of his mouth crossly. 'Back seat? Back seat? It's all about you, Sadie!' Other diners are really staring now. 'It's all about trying to make things right for you! That's all I ever try and fucking do. Can't you see that?'

My eyes are blinded by tears and fury. 'But all I want is a normal family life. I want a husband that I see. I want a future. I want a . . . a . . .' The word baby sits on the end of my tongue, refusing to leave my mouth. I daren't say it. But Tom knows. I can tell by his expression that he knows. His head is in his hands. 'There is nothing wrong with me, Tom!' I stand up from the table, the chair making a screech as it scrapes the floor. 'You really can't work it out, can you?'

'Work what out? What the fuck's going on, Sadie?' he asks desperately.

I don't answer this question because I no longer know the answer.

We don't stay for pudding. Nothing will sweeten the mood now. After a silent, moody taxi ride home we discover that Danny has wet himself. I get him out of bed and he stands there, his eyes open but blank as if he's still dreaming, while I change his sheets and pyjamas. Within seconds of lying back down in bed he is asleep. I watch the rise and fall of his chest and brush my fingers lightly over the newly grown wispy curls on his forehead. He looks tiny, so vulnerable. I stare at him, my beautiful, exquisite child, and wish I knew what to do for the best. Because I am apparently a grown-up and should therefore know what the right thing is. But I don't.

Tom softly creeps into the bedroom, bends down and kisses Danny on the cheek. He sits on the side of the bed. But our bodies don't touch. The dark bedroom is filled with our separateness.

'I hate arguing all the time. What's happened? What happened to us? I miss us. I miss how we used to be,' I whisper into the dark. 'I can't go on like this, Tom.'

'Nor can I,' he says in a voice so quiet I can barely hear it. 'Nor can I, sweetheart.'

Thirty

The smell of lavender hits me like a punch. I'm transported back to my first visit when the bruise was still tender on my forehead and I was full of secret childish hope that this elegant, odd old lady would somehow have the power to fix my marriage with a few clever household hints, as if removing a stain from a tablecloth. What on earth was I thinking? No wonder my marriage is in a bigger mess than ever. Yes, it's time to bring the whole mad charade to a halt.

Angie answers the door with a surprised smile. 'Hi, Sadie. We weren't expecting you.'

'Sorry, an impromptu visit.'

'One moment. Madam is in the sitting room, the private sitting room,' she says. 'I will fetch her.'

I stand in the hall among the photographs and the fancy brolly stands and the chessboard of black and white tiles. I wait for at least five minutes. Eventually the door to the secret sitting room opens. I manage to get a glimpse of its carpet – white – and a few photographs on the wall. It looks perfectly normal. Why on earth is it out of bounds? I wonder if it is just another bit of Enid's dramatic staging. More smoke and mirrors.

Enid walks out, noticeably doddery on her feet today. 'A surprise! Oh, I do love a surprise. What appointments add in anticipation they lose in the dullness of expectation. Angie, drinks please. We'll take tea in the garden.'

We walk into the lush, green garden. It smells of lilacs. A chatter of birdsong comes from the apple tree, whose boughs are already filled with bigger, heavier apples than last time I was here. It is a tree already preparing for autumn. Time has gone so quickly. Our deadline is almost up.

'Now, darling,' Enid says, sitting down on a garden chair and reknotting the pale blue silk scarf at her neck. 'What brings you here? Thrilling new developments I hope.'

Angie puts two Pimm's down on the table. Cubes of ice crack and hiss below leaves of mint and wafer-thin slices of cucumber.

'I wanted to see you in person, Enid,' I begin, sounding far more formal than I feel, which is weepy and hormonal. 'I wanted to say that I've appreciated all your advice about Tom, about being a wife. And I feel better, I really do, in many ways. Hell, I can make trifle! I don't look like a member of a Christian rock group, nor do I wear flannel pyjamas to bed.'

Enid looks at me, puzzled. She doesn't laugh. The

light has gone out of her eyes, as if she senses what is to come.

'And I've made some great wife friends, who I wouldn't have deigned to mix with had it not been for you,' I blurt, feeling my confidence flounder. 'I view you more as a friend than a client, I really do. But I need to do this on my own now.' I stop, waiting for her to reassure me that it's all going to be OK. Of course she understands. But she doesn't. She just looks hurt. 'I mean it's not a game,' I add a little desperately. 'It's real life. It's *my* life.'

'Right,' she says stiffly, twisting the scarf round and round one finger so that the diamond of her ring bulges out from the silk.

'What I'm trying to say is that I can't come here any more. You're such good company and such a persuasive lady but . . .' I shuffle awkwardly on my chair, feeling like I'm drowning a kitten. ' . . . I need to work out my marriage in my own way, if that is at all possible, which it may not be.'

Enid puts up her hand to stop me talking. Her painted red mouth sets in a horizontal line. 'The storm brought us together for a purpose. I was always sure of that.'

'I feel the same.' I still do not know what it was that made me not throw her card away, that made me return to this strange, beautiful house, made me believe in the unbelievable. It did feel like it was meant to happen. But I don't believe in fate, I remind myself.

'You weaned me off black tulips.'

My eyes start to water. I blink quickly. This is not the time to emote. Enough emoting.

'But if my advice is not wanted I'm certainly not going to force it upon you,' she says sharply, all nostalgic sentiment gone. 'It seems you are determined to do things your own way.' She shrugs then stands up slowly. 'If I was your age I'd probably not want to listen to some old lady witter on either.' With that she totters forlornly down the garden path, away from the lilacs and the lavender beds, reminding me – damn it – of my nan again, weaving her way through her west Oxford garden when I was a child. Nan's garden felt like the longest, lushest garden in the world, she the oldest, wrinkliest person I knew, the mother of my mother, a boggling thought in itself. As Enid disappears I get a sharp stab of homesickness, for Nan, for Mum, those kind, idiosyncratic women who coloured me in, as if somehow Enid is my last link to them. I sit very still for a moment, watching her, unsure what to do next, feeling like I've been excommunicated, and very alone.

There is a rustle behind me. I swivel around expecting to see Angie pointing me to the door. But it is Eddie. He wipes a curl off his tanned, sweaty forehead. 'Sorry, I couldn't help but overhear.'

'It's for the best, Eddie. It's got so intense.'

He pulls up a chair and sits heavily. 'Yes, I guessed that. Paula—'

'The florist before me?'

Eddie nods. 'Paula didn't like it after a while either, all the advice and inquisition about her private life. That's why she left in the end.' He shakes his head. 'But unlike Paula, you've brought her so much happiness. She looks forward to your visits so much.'

'I'm just a florist. I can't be her friend. And I can't be . . . I don't know, a project. It's silly. I don't know what I was thinking. I've been confusing things,' I add, thinking of Mum and Nan.

'Sadie,' he says, sitting down and leaning close. 'Please don't not come back.' He says this so intensely that I blush. He takes a swig from one of the untouched cocktails, winces and puts it down again quickly. 'God, that's fearsomely strong. Listen, there's something you should know . . .' he hesitates, pulling at his baggy navy T-shirt and flapping air into it to cool himself down. I notice a sexy little shadow in the dip beneath his clavicles.

'I wasn't going to tell you. But I think you'd want to know.' He pauses and runs a finger slowly round and round the rim of the glass.

I stare at the finger. My heart pumps harder. Gosh, I will miss him.

'Enid is dying, Sadie,' he says matter of factly. 'She's got cancer. Infested with it. She's refused chemo and is just taking morphine and various pills. She's not got long, not long at all.'

Thirty-one

Chloe and I weave our way through the crowds on the Portobello Road. We smell baking bread, fried onions, spliff and coffee. The sun breaks through the clouds and with it brings a new surge of people. The crowds intensify and a blanket of heads bob in front of us. Chloe shrugs off her fitted leather biker jacket but keeps her Arab check scarf on despite the heat because she's got a love bite on her neck courtesy of a young actor who once had a small part in *Hollyoaks* and now wants to play a big role in her life. She's not interested. 'I'm so sorry about Enid,' she says.

I tug Danny along the pavement, feeling the bored resistance of his little feet. 'Well, Enid's old, I guess. She's had a good innings. That's what they say, isn't it?' I try to mask my sadness with cool rationalisation. 'Still. I suppose dying is always going to be shit, no matter when it comes. The weird thing is I had no idea. Did you have any inkling?'

Chloe shakes her head. Her chandelier earrings

shimmer and tinkle lightly like wind chimes. 'No. But I don't know her. Not like you do. I'm hardly a suitable recipient for marital advice. She thinks I'm terribly cynical, and . . .' Chloe puts on Enid's posh accent. '. . . "rather spoiled". We just play with make-up and have a giggle and talk about you. She really does adore you, Sadie. She thinks you're one of her "ladies".'

To my surprise my eyes fill with tears. It feels silly being so upset. As Tom reminds me, Enid is not family. But she does now feel more like a relative I've unexpectedly inherited than a client. I also feel strangely guilty when I think about her. Like I've just used her advice – questionable though it may be – and not given anything back. 'I know. I wish there was something I could do.'

'Why don't you just let her believe that her advice has saved your marriage? That would make her up.'

I laugh. 'She's a wily old thing. She'd smell a rat.'

'OK. Let's send her out with a bang, rather than a whimper. Let's throw her a party or something.'

I smile. Chloe's answer to any of life's problems is to have a party, as if throwing a cold glass of champagne at anything nasty will rinse it away. 'She does love a party.'

'Can I have an ice cream?' interrupts Danny.

We stop and buy him a strawberry ice cream, which is a way of buying a bit more uninterrupted chat time, and sit on a wall in Elgin Crescent while Danny eats it.

'Did you ask *him*?' says Chloe trying to speak in code over Danny's head. 'About A.'

275

'No. I couldn't bring myself to after . . .' I wince. '. . . the matter in the, ahem, closet.'

Chloe puts her hand to her mouth to stifle a giggle. 'God, I'm so sorry. I know it's not funny. It's just that I have this image of you wearing one of her shoes.'

Danny looks up. 'Whose shoes, Mummy?'

'Oh nothing,' I say quickly. 'Mummy did a silly thing with a pair of shoes. She tried someone else's shoes on and they didn't fit her.'

'Like Cinderella's ugly sister?' says Danny.

Chloe and I burst into giggles.

'Ah, priceless. Yes, that's about the size of it, Danny,' I say, patting him on the knee. 'Now, Chloe, it's Tom's office party next week. What the hell am I going to do? What if Annette recognises me? I'll be flambéed. You're invited by the way.'

Chloe looks doubtful. 'I am?'

'Yes. Tom's going to send you an invite. Please come. Pam, Ruth and Tara will be there. Selfishly, I need you there, too. The last time I saw most of that Anderson lot I was wearing a T-shirt saying Lick Me and carrying a pair of murderous secateurs like something from a David Lynch movie. And I'm terrified of bumping into *her*.'

Chloe grins. 'Hold your head high.' She swings her long, tanned legs from the wall. 'You're a fierce adversary, Sadie.'

Danny licks his ice cream thoughtfully. 'What's adversary?'

276

'Someone who fights back,' says Chloe.

'Like Daddy and Mummy do?'

Chloe and I exchange glances. We don't burst into giggles this time. I try to think of something that you are meant to say to children in such circumstances – 'we're not fighting, we're discussing and resolving, darling' – but don't want to lie to Danny either. So I put an arm around his little waist and pull him close. He leans his head on my shoulder and I feel his childish confusion and I feel like the worst mother in the world now, too.

Thirty-two

First white lie. As Chloe suggested, I tell Enid that her advice is finally working and Tom and I are getting on better than ever. I don't feel too bad about this lie because it's for an ill old lady and Enid looked really, really happy and said, 'Albert would be so pleased.' Then she grabbed my notebook and scrawled: *Almost there now. It won't be long, my darling. E xx*

Second white lie. Rona asked if we needed a baby-sitter for Tom's office party on Thursday, not herself of course, because she's coming too. It's Tom's moment. She wouldn't miss it for the world. She's got a new Bulgarian dog-walker who is keen to earn a bit of money. I say, no thanks, we're covered. We are not covered. But I'm not having Rona sabotaging my excuse for getting out of the terrifying prospect of Tom's Anderson & Co summer party and the risk of running into Psyche Viagra.

Third white lie. Ruth's ex-househusband husband Alex is still sulking at his mother's. Ruth has lost half her body weight. I tell her that she's never looked better. Actually she looks terrible, big black circles under her eyes, mouth turning down like those poverty-stricken single mothers in Channel Four social documentaries. And the weight has gone from her cheeks which makes her look older. Life can be so mean.

Fourth, fifth and sixth not-so-white lies. All to Tom, of course. I can't get a babysitter for the Anderson & Co party. No, Trish can't do it. Besides, Danny has got an immunisation jab that day and I can't change the appointment and he is likely to be ill in the evening and I should be there. I'll be so gutted to miss the party. Tom just says, 'You can't possibly miss the party. Not an option, Sadie,' and storms off. Since our disastrous date we've been like ships in the night, avoiding any kind of interaction. I've even taken to going to bed early so that I don't have to face pillow-chat and the glaring absence of our love-making.

A week before the party, as I am scribbling down a list of flowers in my notebook – Dr Prenwood's order that I'll pick up at the market tomorrow morning – Tom appears in the room, smiling. 'Good news. Your dad emailed me. He's up in London with Loretta next week.'

'That's good news?'

'He's happy to babysit for the party.'

OK, I can do this. I won't get drunk and forget not to be myself. I will smile a lot. I will not make Tom look like he's in A Bad Marriage, or embarrass him. I will not talk about my dead mother or mention that I plan cunning wifely air attacks on my relationship with a terminally ill lady called Enid in St John's Wood. I will confound all expectation and do Tom proud if it's the last thing I do. The show must go on. And if I see Annette Eastern I will just have to hide behind a pillar. I take a deep breath and fix a silk flower into my hair, smooth down the blue Mary Archer tea dress that I was going to wear to the Anderson Ivy lunch and didn't. Plus the killing killer silver heels. I am not wearing a Lick Me T-shirt. Or a gold dress. I am not locked in a flat. Nor am I two hours late. So far, so good.

'Taxi's here, love!' booms Dad from downstairs.

I totter into the living room and discover Dad bouncing Danny up and down on his knee so fiercely I'd worry about shaken baby syndrome if Danny was any younger. Loretta is clutching a tube of Smarties and has evidently been feeding them to Danny, who is gazing up at her adoringly and stroking her over-dyed candyfloss hair. I grab my keys and kiss Danny, then Dad on the cheek, and give Loretta a limp wave.

'Don't worry about us. We'll have a fine old time,' says Dad. 'Won't we, Neddy boy?'

Danny grins.

Loretta pops a blue Smartie into his mouth. 'There you go, my little smasher.' She looks up at me. 'You have a good time. Let your hair down. Oo, like your dress. Very proper.'

The taxi stops outside Chloe's flat. I phone her. 'Taxi outside, ma'am.'

'Two secs,' she says.

Ten minutes later Chloe slams the front door behind her. The taxi driver's eyes pop out of his head. She looks like something from an LA pap shot, all big hair and tanned legs and shimmering gold dress. Gladiator heels climb up her calves. She looks like some kind of Roman sex warrior.

'My old friend – the gay wedding dress!' I laugh.

Chloe tries to get into the taxi without flashing her knickers and fails. 'The wedding's off, that's why. One of the two grooms has got The Fear about signing up for a lifetime of monogamy. Sensible man. So I thought I better wear the damn thing.' She tugs it down over her thighs. 'Do you think it's a bit OTT for Tom's bash?'

'No,' I laugh. 'They'll love it.'

'I like your dress too, very pretty. Very Prada.'

'Not Prada. Jigsaw.'

'Keep that quiet.' She kisses me on the cheek. 'You look quite the perfect wife.'

'I will try to take that as a compliment.'

The taxi pulls up at the hotel, a grand hotel with a large roof terrace that overlooks Trafalgar Square. There are two large charity donation collection buckets at the door to the terrace: Pam's work. The terrace itself is drenched in golden evening sunlight and has been dressed with flowers – a bit self-conscious for my liking, lots of lilies and white roses in tall white sculptural vases, showy as Russian It girls – and there are attractive model-like waiters wandering around with plates of sushi and Bellinis. Chloe isn't the only bit of 'colour' here. There are an alarming number of twentysomething girls with swishy hair and long colourful maxi-dresses who look like they might be about to set sail on a yacht in Cannes. Does he work with these women? Shit, I feel frumpy.

'Ah, lovely. Sunshine. Bellinis . . .' Chloe says, looking around her. 'Cute waiters.'

'Can you see her?' I peek out cautiously over the pithy surface of my Bellini. 'You must warn me the moment you spot Annette. I'll need to run for cover. Promise me. Don't get drunk and forget or I'll kill you.'

'Understood,' says Chloe, flicking her hair off her face and staring at a tall, dark, handsome man in a white suit wearing a Panama hat. She's already forgotten. 'Sadie, I'm desperate for the loo. I drank a litre of Evian before I even got into the cab. When I walk I sound like a shaken hot water bottle.'

'OK. See you in a minute then. I'm going to circulate to see if I can locate my husband. But I won't have gone far.'

I move between the faces and trays and handbags anxiously, searching for Tom, drinking more and more of my Bellini out of nerves until, to my surprise, my glass is suddenly empty. Occasionally I bump into one of Tom's colleagues who immediately glance down at my dress with its flowers and fabric-covered buttons and look a little disappointed, as if they'd expected me to arrive wearing nipple tassels. I grab another Bellini as it swishes past on a silver tray. The sunshine, even this late in the day, is very bright and I wish I'd brought my sunglasses like every other woman. At last I spot a confident suited man in the crowd. He is handsome and fiercely animated, a bit cocky looking. He is my husband.

'There you are!' Tom smiles, but it is a tight smile, the smile of a man who is pretending to party but is actually working very hard. 'You look—'

'Don't,' I say, immediately defensive about my dress.

'I haven't seen that dress before. It's sweet.'

Sweet? Oh. I now know for sure that I've misjudged the sartorial code terribly. I was made for flower markets not media parties. Chloe in her gold frock is more appropriately dressed than me. In my effort to look like a wife I've ended up looking like I'm running the local church fete. 'You look tense,' I say to childishly get him back for the 'sweet' comment.

'Just trying to keep everybody happy, Sadie,' he says in a hushed voice, looking around him, rictus grin in place. 'We've got some incredibly important clients here. Ah, Peter!' He turns and gives a man with a sunburned bald head a shoulder punch, which makes me cringe. 'How are you? Have you met Trevor, Trevor Headling? You must.' Another man appears at his side. Soon there's another man in a suit, then presumably a senior female colleague or client, in a sharply cut black dress and architectural spectacles, another in a glistening lime green dress, younger and less ferocious looking. Perhaps she's one of the many bombshell secretaries Ruth once mentioned. I'm introduced jovially as 'the other half' but feel like the extra half, not knowing quite what to do with myself. God, sometimes it's weird being a wife. It really is. Tom's female colleagues are polite and friendly but awkward around me, as if I am not part of the Tom they know. While most of the men politely overlook me. I am not worth flirting with, nor am I important to their careers so not worth networking either. I feel strangely invisible. And watching Tom in such a professional capacity is like watching a stranger, not one I'm sure I like very much.

I look around for other familiar faces. I spot Linda and Joanna standing on the other side of the terrace. Joanna, in a bright red dress, gives me a tight, brief smile. Linda looks even more blonde and willowy than normal in her pale green, Grecian dress, like feathery ornamental grass. They quickly go back to talking between themselves. As my sense of exclusion grows, panic rises in my throat. I don't want to look like frumpy-no-mates. Even bloody Rona, thankfully wrapped in conversation and yards of turquoise chiffon near the bar, seems to be more at home here than me. What if everyone knows that Tom is having an affair with Annette? What if they're looking at me with pity? Oh God. Where is Chloe? Or Ruth? Or Pam? I spot Tara, who looks like Eva Longoria, all killer curves and heels, then she's whisked back into the crowds by her fat, ageing husband who seems intent on parading her about like a prize pony. I think of her masseur and smile. Perhaps there's a warped kind of justice in it somewhere.

After a while the men in suits turn their backs to me and in desperation not to look like a social leper I siphon off to the sub-group, the Anderson & Co wives, which looks like the court of Linda and Joanna, both of whom greet me with fake enthusiasm. I sink my insecurities into another Bellini as we chat about children and schools. Then, to my huge relief, I finally spot Chloe, sauntering through the crowds in her gold dress, a sea of heads turning in her wake.

'This is my dear friend, Chloe,' I say.

The Anderson wives glare at her as if she were about to spear their husbands with her stiletto heels and start humping them on the terrace there and then.

'Chloe. Linda. Joanna. Um, sorry, I've forgotten your name. Yes, of course, Sally. Er, it's Emma, isn't it? Sophie. Wives of Tom's colleagues.'

'Great to meet you,' smiles Chloe.

The wives murmur in unconvincing agreement and throw disapproving glances at Chloe's impeccable legs.

'Look, there's Pam,' exclaims Chloe, pointing into the crowd. 'With Ruth. And, wow, is that Alex? It is Alex.'

Ruth and Alex are standing beside one another stiffly. Spotting us Ruth scoots over. The Anderson wives politely disperse and stand next to women who probably don't make them feel as fat and unfashionable as Chloe does.

Ruth shakes her head. 'This is totally, totally out of body weird,' she whispers. 'I feel like I don't know anyone, apart from us lot. Like the new girl. And about twenty years too old to be here.'

'Rubbish!' I say. 'You look great. I wasn't sure you'd come.' I lower my voice. 'Has Alex moved back in?'

'No! He bloody well hasn't. But he wanted me to come anyway. He still hasn't told anyone at work about, well, us. He's neurotic about being the subject of gossip. He wants to keep up appearances.'

'Very big hearted of you.'

'Yes, it's a fucking cheek. I know that. And I wasn't going to come. But I changed my mind at the last minute. You inspired me actually.'

'*Me?*'

'I thought of all the effort you've been going to for your marriage,' she says softly. 'And although I think it's a bit freaky and it kind of appals me as a feminist, I kind of admire it too. I want to look back and know I did everything I could.'

I squeeze her hand.

She looks at me appreciatively and smiles. And I suddenly know for sure that we're going to be friends for a very long time. It's a nice feeling.

Pam swishes over. 'Look at you, Chloe! Wow!' she says, running her hands down Chloe's gold dress. 'I love the fact that you still wear the kind of dresses we wore when we were twenty-five.'

Chloe and I exchange amused glances. Pam is expert

at the slightly worrisome back-handed compliment, especially in situations where she feels her beauty queen crown is threatened. It's not of course. As the evening sunlight falls on her hair and skin, she glows rudely with health, as opposed to just large pores and sweat, as it does with lesser pregnant mortals. Still, she doesn't have Chloe's sex appeal. It occurs to me that Pam is the kind of woman men like to marry and Chloe is the kind of woman they like to shag in lifts. Or perhaps it's just that men know that Pam is the kind of woman who wants to get hitched and Chloe is the kind of woman who'd rather have a good shag in a lift.

Chloe elbows me in the ribs. 'Annette alert,' she whispers. 'She's over there. No, not there. To your left.'

I freeze and stare through the crowds. Not her. Not her. And then, there she is. The whole party seems to rearrange itself and blur at the edges, like I'm looking through a camera lens slicked with Vaseline. Only Annette is in focus. Big hair, a tight cocktail frock covered in poppies, those legs of hers in . . . No. Shit. *The* shoes. The blue shoes I tried on. 'Oh. My. God.' I grab Chloe's arm. 'She's wearing the goddamn shoes.'

Chloe puts her hand over her mouth. 'She's not? Bloody hell. She is.' She looks at me and winks. 'Fierce shoes though.'

'What?' says Pam, sniffing gossip. 'Who are you looking at? Have you spotted Tara?'

'Oh it's nothing,' I say quickly. But it's too late.

Pam has followed my frozen sightline. She grabs my

elbow. 'It's not Tara. It's Annette Eastern! Oh. Wow. It is, isn't it? Seth said she might be here.'

I want to shake Pam. Do not stare. Do not turn into a goggle-eyed fan. Do not attract attention! 'Is it?' My voice comes out in a high squeak in my attempts to sound as casual as possible.

Pam flushes right down to her cleavage. 'Isn't she gorgeous? I've got a serious girl crush!'

A wave of panic sweeps over me.

Ruth eyes me curiously. 'Are you OK, Sadie? Is anything the matter? You've gone white as a sheet.'

I drain my drink and grab another from a passing silver tray. Is it my third? My fourth? No. I've not managed to not get drunk.

Chloe whispers into my ear. 'Calm down for God's sake. You look like you're about to have a seizure. Turn your back to her. That's right. Turn. Turn.'

I am reluctant to lose Annette from my field of vision but do as I'm told. 'OK, but tell me if she's coming too close. Sound the warning.'

'Have you read Annette's amazing self-help book *Spring Clean Your Heart!*, Ruth?' asks Pam. 'You might find it really helpful.'

Ruth rolls her eyes. 'Not my kind of thing. I'm afraid I'm not a big fan of self-help books. And any marriage that can be fixed by reading one was not broken in the first place. Believe me, I know.'

'I couldn't disagree more.' Pam's voice gets louder as she warms to her theme. 'After reading her book – I so love her shoes, don't you? – I left the boyfriend I had . . .'

Oh God. They're going to row about Psyche Viagra. This is all so wrong. I begin to get the strange sensation of being back in the storm again, the whirling, the hiss of the wind inside my head. I shut my eyes and have to open them immediately because I feel like I'm on a boat. Maybe I'm drunk.

Tom comes up behind me and slings an arm around my waist. His breath has that sour champagne pong to it. 'Excuse me, ladies. There's someone I really want my wife to meet.'

It irritates me that he calls me 'my wife' when he normally calls me Sadie. But I smile – pick your battles – and try to look normal.

'You're not drunk, are you?' whispers Tom as we move away. 'You're wobbling.'

'The shoes.' I summon every cell in my body to act sober. I concentrate on not wobbling or tripping up, which means looking at the terrace paving and carefully judging the strangely shifting distances between people's feet. A flicker of disapproval passes over Tom's face. But he doesn't say anything, not now, not here.

'OK. Background,' he whispers. 'She's just landed an enormous publishing contract. I went and brokered it. I tell you, sweetheart, she'll win me the directorship.'

I stop and look up, head fuzzy with Bellinis. 'Sorry. Who, Tom?'

'Annette Eastern,' he hisses, pushing me forward, his

hand on the small of my back. 'She's desperate to meet you.'

I freeze. 'Please, no,' I mutter under my breath and it really feels like the floor beneath my feet is shattering and splitting. I have to struggle to keep my balance. And it's not the Bellinis.

'Aha! Here she is,' booms Tom. 'Annette! Our gorgeous star client. Exactly the woman I'm looking for.'

Annette, who has her back to us, swivels round, all blinding white teeth and rolling eyes, like a frisky, beautiful horse. 'Tom, my darling Tom. Quite my favourite Anderson man.' She laughs like how I imagine Jerry Hall might laugh, flips her hair flirtatiously off her face then wraps Tom in a luxuriant, unnecessary luvvie hug.

'I want to introduce you to my wife,' says Tom, quickly unpeeling himself from her arms.

Annette extends a muscular, tanned hand. Her handshake is so firm it travels all the way up to my armpit. 'Great to meet you, er . . .'

'Sadie.' I feel myself folding into myself, shrinking into my Mary Archer dress.

Tom looks at me a little strangely. If I can only get through the next five minutes of inane small talk then I can make an excuse to go to the loo, pretend Chloe's calling me over . . .

'So what do you do, Sadie?' asks Annette breezily in her transatlantic drawl. She glances over my head as she speaks, as if a little bored by my presence already and scouting for more fabulous people to talk to.

'Um. Not much. I'm a mum and . . .' I let a lock of hair fall in front of my face. I don't brush it away. It's camouflage.

'She's being modest,' says Tom chirpily. 'Sadie is a brilliant florist.'

'A florist?' says Annette slowly, stepping back a little and staring at me more intently. '*Really?*'

I stare at the buttons on my dress. 'Yes. Um, just . . .'

Annette looks at me, then at Tom. Her nostrils start to flare. 'It's weird, I swear I recognise you. Have we met before?'

'Oh, no. I'd remember. I'd remember definitely.' The words rush out in an unconvincing jumble.

'Maybe you did her flowers in another life,' laughs Tom a little uneasily, sensing the awkwardness.

I see something shift in Annette's face as the puzzlement changes to appalled recognition. 'You . . . you're not . . .' Her nostrils flare faster now as if she's sucking up great quantities of oxygen. 'You didn't do my flowers a couple of weeks ago? You look just like this girl that . . .' I watch as a stern certainty rearranges her features. And I can see that she *knows*. Yes, shit, she knows. I brace myself. 'You're not Sadie Drew, are you?'

'Yesh.' My voice comes out a little slurred. I feel very, very drunk, disorientated, as if the Bellinis have just hit my bloodstream, at the same time, all at once.

'I'm sorry, Tom.' Annette's voice lowers to a growl.

She puts a hand on Tom's arm. Her nails are maroon and glossy. 'I'm afraid that your wife and I have met before, haven't we, Sadie? I never forget a face.'

'Have you?' says Tom. 'How strange. Where?'

I swallow hard, my eyes pleading. She wouldn't do it, would she? She's not going to cause a scene, not now, not here?

Annette sticks out a foot. The blue shoe. 'Do these shoes mean anything to you, Sadie?' She's playing with me.

I say nothing, scared my voice will break. I shake my head and try to look puzzled and smile.

Tom looks at me, fighting to keep his smile. 'Sadie, what's going on here?'

'I employed your wife to do my flowers, Tom.'

Tom looks at me in astonishment. 'You never told me!'

Annette nods to Chloe, who is standing a few feet away, staring at us all, aghast. '*That* make-up artist put us in touch. The one in the gold dress. Chloe, isn't it?'

'Gosh! What a coincidence,' says Tom. But he doesn't sound too cheerful any more. The muscle on the side of his neck is beginning to twitch violently. He is wondering why the hell I never told him. He knows something's up.

'She did my flowers. Very nice,' says Annette drily. But there is anger, real anger in her eyes. 'A nice way with peonies.' She pauses. There is a smashing, horrible silence. And I know it's coming. And it comes. 'Then I found her rifling through my wardrobe.'

At first I feel humiliation. But it changes into something else. It's as if a switch flicks on. The cowering goes. The fear goes. I just feel rage. Possessive, boiling rage. I find my voice. 'Get your hand off my husband's arm.'

'Sadie!' Tom puts a hand over his mouth. He looks around to see if any of his colleagues are nearby. 'Please.'

Annette removes her hand and clutches her red handbag in front of her. 'You must have known we worked together, Sadie. Is that what this is all about?'

'What?' Tom looks from me to Annette and back again. His face has drained of all colour. 'What's going on here?'

The blood is still pumping. I feel fire beneath my skin. I cannot pretend any more. I cannot do the act any more. I don't feel like a good wife. I feel like a bad, pissed off, cheated on wife. 'I saw you arm in arm at the Wolseley! I saw the dedication in the book! And what is it I'm not meant to know, eh?'

'What on earth are you talking about?' she scowls.

'Why don't you write a guide to stealing other men's husbands?'

'Oh my God, Sadie.' Tom grabs me by the arm roughly. 'I'm so sorry, Annette. She's drunk.'

I flick Tom off me. 'Get off me!'

'She needs help, Tom,' says Annette.

Help? The patronising bitch, how dare she! I step towards her, head steaming with white rage, and before I realise what I've done my half glass of Bellini is splattered down her cocktail dress. I stare at it in disbelief, sobering up fast.

Thirty-three

Tears are splashing down my face faster than I can wipe them away. It's hard to breathe properly, or see. London whooshes past outside the cab's bleary window as we career down the Strand, through Euston, Marylebone. Tom looked at me with such anger, such disappointment, like I've ruined his career, and his life. He'll never ever forgive me. Perhaps even worse than the expression on Tom's face was the sight of Rona, her champagne glass frozen in mid-air, a look that I've never seen before in her eyes, a triumphant fire, as she watched me run from that party, leaving my jacket and the smouldering shards of my marriage behind. I cannot believe what I just did. I've never thrown a drink over another woman in all my life. In trying to be the perfect wife I've become so much worse than I ever imagined, resentful, paranoid, and angry. What the hell has happened to me? Who the hell have I turned into? My mother would be appalled.

I pay the cabbie and get out of the taxi. There was

only one place I felt it was safe to come. I throw myself against the iron gates. I ring Enid's doorbell.

Angie opens the door. 'Sadie? Are you OK?'

'Can I come in?' I sniff.

'One minute.' She disappears for a few seconds, leaving me standing in the hall. 'Do go through. Madam is in the sitting room.'

'Thanks, Angie.' I walk over to the sitting room and turn the cut glass door knob. It feels cool as crystal in my hot hand.

'Oh, no, not that one, madam,' smiles Angie. 'The one on the other side of the stairs. She told me to send you through there.'

The *other*, forbidden sitting room? Really? I walk over to it and push the door open tentatively. 'Enid? May I come in?'

'You may.' Enid is sitting very upright on a pristine white sofa with gold claw feet, beaming. 'A most delightful surprise. I'm glad I haven't been entirely ditched.'

I look around the secret sitting room. Nothing in it looks particularly secret. In fact it is not so different from the other sitting room, identical in shape and proportion, although it is notably more glamorously furnished, more theatrical, with red velvet curtains, a deep white carpet, leopard print cushions, large Chinese vases and lots and lots of photographs – parties, boats, people – on the walls and horizontal surfaces.

'Do sit down.' She notes my tears with her usual

unflappability, pulls a tissue from its white ceramic holder and hands it to me.

I arrange my drunken, wretched self on the small French-style sofa opposite hers. 'Sorry to descend on you like this. I . . . I didn't know where to go.'

'You can always come here.' She smiles. 'I always used to say that my girls could drop in on me any time. And I do get restless in the evening.' She stops and squints. 'Your mascara is smudged. On your cheekbone, darling. No, the left one. Oh dear, have you been weeping terribly?'

I dab at my cheekbones, sniff back the tears. 'I'm sorry. God, what a mess.'

'I'll ask Angie to fix some medicinal cocktails and then . . .' Enid looks at me, her blue eyes sparkling, practically rubbing her hands in glee with the drama of it all. '. . . tell me *absolutely* everything.'

So I do. I tell her every grisly, toe-curling, humiliating detail. She nods but says little. Occasionally she laughs. (Am not seeing the joke.) Finally, when I'm spent, she sits, hands clasped neatly on her lap, studying me. She sits like that for what feels like an age. Eventually she speaks. 'Sadie, my darling. This does not *quite* make sense. The jigsaw pieces are a little out I fear. Have you told me everything, absolutely everything?'

'Yes.'

Enid winks. She doesn't believe me. 'This Annette. She sounds plausible. Annoying but plausible. She probably does flirt with your husband but, the more I think about it, the more I've come to the conclusion that if your husband was having an affair, he'd be nicer to you. I think, perversely, you'd both be getting on much better by now.'

'But you told me . . .' Hell, she encouraged me to think Tom was having an affair. She can't change her mind now. Too late!

'I've been trying to puzzle it all out.' She sits forward, fixes me with a very direct stare. 'What I am wondering is, darling, and have been wondering all week, has this Tom chap had an affair *before*?'

My mouth goes dry. I'm back in the storm, the whirling blackness, the wind hissing around me. I feel a rushing sound in my head. A whistling inside. I can't speak.

Enid shakes her head, her diamond earrings sparkle. 'OK. Who was she?'

Rumbled. The only other person who used to rumble me every time was Mum. She'd always know if there was a bit of the story missing. She'd know if something cost £150 when I said it cost £50. I've blocked this out for so long. I'm not sure I can talk about it even now, not even to Enid. It's a secret, a secret between Tom and me and, when she was alive, Mum; a collusion of silence. We buried it, deep, deep beneath the domestic strata of our relationship, like an old broken cup buried beneath layers of soil.

'Go on.'

'It was not long after we'd married. I was pregnant.

He . . .' I stop. The words feel like they're burning my tongue. 'He went to Toronto on his own to do a recce, while I tied everything up back here.'

Enid shakes her head sagely. 'Ah, men abroad on their own. Disastrous. Why do you think we diplomat wives trailed around after our men?' She sighs. 'Was it a long-standing paramour?'

'A one-night stand.'

'He told you?'

'He phoned me the next morning in tears, the morning after he'd done it. He said he'd got drunk, very drunk, at a party and he'd been alone.' I stop. Not wanting to bring up the image of Tom and this woman together. 'He couldn't remember her name.'

Enid shakes her head. 'Tears. Confessions. Goodness. He wasn't very accomplished at infidelity, was he? You took him back, evidently.'

'I almost didn't. I almost didn't go to Toronto after that. Everything fell apart.' I wipe tears away. 'The trust never comes back, does it?'

'Not always but it can. I promise you it can. It's a conscious decision. You have to actively decide to trust. It won't just happen.' Enid sips her drink. 'And you didn't leave so part of you must have believed that too.'

'My head was spinning. I didn't know what to do. But my mum thought I should stick with it. She knew Tom . . .' I stop, a clear image of Mum hits me, like a video film unrolling. She has rushed over to my flat and she is a bit puffed from the rushing and she is sitting on the side of my bed – it is midday, I can't get out of bed and I can't eat or sleep – and she's handing me tissues, one after another, pink tissues from a floral box. She holds me tight and tells me that I'll be miserable if I take him back but I'll probably be more miserable if I lose him. And I owe it to the unborn child to forgive him. 'It felt like a choice between two imperfect scenarios. And Tom was desperate for me to take him back. He said it was his self-destructive streak, the last bit of Jack the Lad, his fear of commitment. And he'd never made a bigger mistake in his life. He said he wanted a family more than anything in the world. He promised me that.'

I remember it so clearly, the teary wetness of the telephone receiver pressed against my ear, the sounds of Toronto taxis honking in the background, the feeling that my future was hanging in the balance and could go one way or another, like a car that had come off a cliff road and was rocking on the crash barrier, its front bumper tipping up then perilously down. I have often wished that he hadn't told me, that he hadn't used that phone call to expunge his guilt. If it had happened and that had been it – a drunken, aborted one-off – I think I'd rather be ignorant. 'It must sound like the oldest line in the book.'

'It is the oldest line because it's true, I think. You were brave, Sadie, taking him back. And wise,' she adds kindly.

'I'm not so sure. It messed everything up. The dynamic changed after that. He was so nice, so nice it hurt when we were in Toronto. He felt so bloody guilty. I could do anything.' I smile at the memory: Tom trying to repay me in flowers, steaming hot chocolates from Starbucks and foot massages. 'And I actually thought that we'd patched it up, that we were happy. And we were kind of happy in Toronto. It was all strangely unreal. But that all changed when we got back to London and I lost the baby,' I blurt, the words tumbling out of me like hot, red things. I feel the tears well up again. Not wanting to sit and weep on her pristine white sofa any longer, I stand up and walk around the room, anything to contain the sadness and fear which are spinning off me like sparks from a Catherine wheel. I peer at the photos on the wall, happy faces from a simpler, chicer past, good looking people on boats, in open-top cars, on elephants. There is one face that pops up again and again, alongside pictures of Enid and Albert. He is blond and handsome and wears a Panama hat. 'Who's that?'

Enid smiles and stands up, a little falteringly, holding the sofa arm for support. 'That, my dear, is Archie. Isn't he dashing?'

'Very. He's in lots of pictures. Is he a relation?'

'No.' Enid taps the glass with her crooked old person's finger, the enormous bulb-sized diamonds glinting. 'Albert was very fond of him.'

'Ah.' I sit back on the sofa, tears, for the moment, contained. 'Do you mind if I ask why you keep this sitting room closed, Enid? I've always wondered.'

Enid leans against a console table, sits down, puffing at the exertion. 'So many questions, Sadie.' She looks up wryly. 'I'm meant to be asking you the questions.'

'Sorry. Just curious.'

'I don't let many people in here as you know.'

'I know.'

'I like to keep it as Albert kept it, which was private. He liked these photographs to be private.' She smiles and raises an eyebrow wryly. 'He didn't want all the questions either.' Enid doesn't speak for a few moments. 'But I think I can tell you, dear Sadie.' She pauses. 'Archie. Archibald Crane his name was. He . . . he . . .' She clears her throat. 'Our marriage was crowded.'

'You were lovers?' I venture, trying not to sound too bourgeois and shocked.

Enid laughs and shakes her head. 'Dear me, no.'

I stare at the photographs again. I notice that in a lot of them Archie and Albert have arms slung around each other's shoulders. When Enid's in the picture too she's often slightly further from the lens, standing behind the men. 'They were lovers?' I joke.

Enid nods, a resigned nod. 'They were.'

'Oh my God. But . . . but . . .' None of it makes sense. *Albert* had a male lover? 'But you always say you had a perfect marriage!'

Enid laughs. 'I've never said perfect, my darling. I said we were married for fifty-eight years. We had an excellent marriage, in many ways. I loved him very much, very much indeed. He was my soulmate.' She stares at a photograph of the three of them laughing, huddled against the wind on a shingle beach. 'Dear Albert.'

'I don't understand.'

She sighs a long lungful of air. 'He was split in half, but as he grew older he was less torn. We all grew to accept it, I suppose. He couldn't fight it. Nor could I. He met Archie the year after he met me and they'd play chess in here you know, in this living room, right up to the day before he died. We'd joke that it was the boys' sitting room. It was their domain.'

'Where's Archie now?'

'He died a few months after Albert. The doctors said a heart attack. A broken heart, I believe.'

'But how could you have stood it for all those years, Enid?' I can't even bear the idea of Tom having breakfast with Annette, how could she have shared Albert with another *man*? The mind boggles. 'How did you . . .'

'A little piece of him wasn't mine, darling. I knew that there was a bit of him I couldn't reach. It was heartbreaking at first, I was so young, naïve, silly and romantic when we first got married.' She pauses. 'The children never arrived.'

I don't want to pry any further. But I can see pain pass fleetingly over her face, like a small twitch, and my heart goes out to her.

'I wanted children, Sadie. But the urge gradually faded. It doesn't for everyone but it did for me. And as time went on I began to enjoy my freedom, the travel, the time and space to read and write, my life with Albert.' She sighs. 'It sounds strange but he was a marvellous husband in so many ways, such good company, loyal as anything and he gave me a wonderful life.' She smiles gently. 'That counts for a lot. And you never own a person. It's a mistake, a delusion, to think you can ever own their private thoughts and desires. If you think that you only get lies.'

'I couldn't accept that.'

She shrugs. 'I had my girlfriends. And I had my fun too, my darling.' She walks unsteadily over to the far corner of the room, picks a photograph off the mantelpiece and holds it up. 'This is Stanley.' Stanley is a fair man with a round, handsome, rather jolly face and bright, twinkly eyes.

'Another of Albert's . . .'

Enid laughs. 'Oh no! He was *my* friend was Stanley, for many years.' She winks at me.

'Oh, I see. Gosh. Your . . .'

She nods. 'Exactly.'

'What happened to Stanley?'

'Stroke,' she says matter of factly. 'You know, Albert was far more jealous of Stanley than I ever was of Archie! Funny, isn't it? Men are such possessive creatures.'

'God, Enid. I'm amazed. I don't know what to say.' The shock has dried up my tears.

'I bet you're wondering why I think I'm in the least

bit qualified to advise you or anyone on their marriage, don't you?'

'Well, yes.' How on earth do I square it all? Advice from the wife of a homosexual diplomat? Bloody hell, I'd have been better off listening to Chloe.

'I'm not qualified at all, of course. All I do know, my darling, is that there's no right way. And there's no such thing as a perfect marriage. We all have our secrets. We all make sacrifices. But a few principles remain, whatever your circumstances. I do believe that.'

I laugh. 'Like wearing lipstick?'

'Yes! Both Stanley and Albert *adored* my lipstick!' says Enid, as if to think otherwise would be to misunderstand her whole life. 'Albert in particular loved to see me dressed up. It was a mutual pleasure. He hated the thought of me being some boring old wife.'

It makes a muted queeny kind of sense. 'He'd rather you faked happiness?'

'I didn't have to fake it in the end. In the early days, when I first found out, yes, I was devastated. But I decided that I still loved him – divorce didn't really seem much of an option then, not for a girl like me – and I quickly realised that a moaning, weeping wife brought out the very worst in him. I think we both faked happiness for a while, until it eventually became real.'

Suddenly there is a commotion outside the window. The sound of chatter, excitable voices. There's a loud, extended ringing on the doorbell.

'Goodness, who on earth can that be?' wonders Enid.

'One unexpected visitor is rare. Two unheard of.'

The bell rings again. Then there's the sound of a woman laughing. Angie knocks on the sitting room door. 'Sadie, some people are here for you.'

'Me?' Blood whooshes from my head to my feet. Could it be Tom? Annette? Have I been tailed?

'Don't worry! Only me!' Chloe's voice booms from the other side of the door.

'Is that Chloe Mansfield? It is, isn't it? Show yourself, girl. How delightful!' Enid's face lights up. 'Oh what the hell, Angie, let them in here! Let's bring Albert some proper company at last.'

The door opens and Chloe falls forwards through it, incongruous and gleaming in her gold dress, then Pam, Tara and Ruth, who hovers apologetically by the door and looks around the room wide-eyed as if she's never seen anything like it.

Enid claps her hands. 'Girls! Goodness, look at you all. What marvellous frocks! Do come in, make yourselves at home.'

'Oh my God, what are you all doing *here*?' I ask dumbstruck. 'How on earth did you know where to find me?'

'Just a hunch. You weren't at home.' Chloe air-kisses Enid on both cheeks. 'Hi, babe.'

Babe? She calls Enid *babe*?

'My darling Chloe, do sit down next to me. And you too, girls.' Enid is fluttering and animated, newly alive in all the company. 'Oh I do love that gold dress, Chloe.

Ravishing. Now, Angie, drinks all round please. Make them strong.'

It's all too much to take in. I feel unsteady, disorientated, my two worlds clashing like this. 'These are the wives I was telling you about, Pam, Tara, Ruth . . .'

'Charmed,' says Enid, giving them her most dazzling smile. She suddenly doesn't look in the least ill. 'Now rest your dancing feet, girls.'

Pam and her enormous bump, Tara and Ruth sit primly on the opposite sofa, like three girls in the presence of a rather glamorous and formidable headmistress, their heels lined up – one gold pair, one blue, one tan – on the carpet. They smile a little shyly.

'We were all so worried about you, Sadie. Glad to see you're still in one piece,' says Chloe. 'Oh here's your jacket by the way.' She tosses it over.

I catch the jacket and cover my mouth with it. 'I rather wish I weren't in one piece actually. Was I very dreadful?'

Pam, Tara and Ruth stare at their shoes. Chloe smiles gently. 'Yes, you were perfectly dreadful, Sadie. It was a revert to your fiery old form. I was rather impressed.'

'Good aim,' grins Ruth cheekily.

'Why didn't you tell us about your Annette suspicions?' says Pam, looking a little hurt. 'We could have done some digging, found out it was rubbish! Why were you so secretive? Didn't you trust us?'

'I know, I know. Because I felt humiliated. Because I didn't want it getting back to Tom via your husbands. I know, it sounds so stupid now. I should have confided in you. Before it was too late.' I wince. 'What did Annette do after I left?'

'I helped her clean herself up. Nothing that a squirt of Vanish won't get rid of,' says Pam. 'She behaved very gracefully, I must say. Considering.'

'She didn't stay?'

'No. She left.' Chloe picks a bit of fluff off Enid's shoulder and smiles. 'With her girlfriend, Sarah.'

'What?' I stare at Chloe. 'Who's Sarah? Oh no. You don't mean . . .'

Enid claps her hands together. 'Nothing changes!'

Chloe smooths down her gold dress. 'Yes, I do mean, Sadie. She has a rather fearsome girlfriend – you're lucky you didn't get her left hook quite frankly – called Sarah, tall, dark, a bit Angelina Jolie.'

'Oh no.' I put my head in my hands. World swallow me up. 'Why didn't Tom tell me? Shit.'

Chloe shrugs. 'Maybe he didn't know.'

Pam starts to giggle. 'Gosh, had I known I might have had a flirt myself. Annette's enough to make one bat for the other side.'

'Well,' says Enid, who is almost purring with pleasure now. Either the gin and tonic or the company has had a funny effect on her; she seems to have dropped ten years in five minutes. 'Well, well. Life is many things but it's never boring, is it?'

The drinks arrive. My Bellini-throwing antics are forgotten. Enid takes centre stage. At Tara's breathless request Enid shows them all round the ground floor, explaining curios and photographs as everyone oos and ahs and Pam declares something 'quite the loveliest example of needlepoint I've ever seen'. We drift into the garden. It's a warm, clear night and the stars glitter like jewels. Angie lights up the garden with lanterns and candles. The sound of everyone's excited drunken chatter seems to catch in the honeysuckle and the lavender, confidences are exchanged, rude asides cracked and more cocktails are brought out on a silver tray by Angie. Frank Sinatra booms loudly. Enid winks at me. 'Sorry. But I do love Frank. Now turn it up, Angie! Can't hear a darned thing.' She pulls a cashmere shawl over her shoulders. 'This is more fun than I've had in months! Just like old times.'

I watch Tara and Ruth kick back on the swing chair at the bottom of the garden, giggling. It seems I'm the only one here who remembers that I am a disgraced wife and that I have a husband who must hate me and to whom I must return. I can't sit here for any longer pretending that everything is fine, that this is real life. 'Girls, I think I better get home and face the music.'

'Oh, I won't let anyone else leave!' laughs Enid. 'Consider yourselves prisoners. You must all stay exactly where you are.'

Chloe gives me a hug. 'It's still quite early. I'll hang out for a bit here.'

'I'm going to have one for the road,' slurs Ruth, leaning back on her garden chair.

'You know what? So might I,' says Pam. And we all turn and look at her. No one's seen her drink throughout her whole pregnancy. 'Stop staring, you lot. A glass of wine is not going to maim my unborn child is it, not at this stage? Anyway, I'm bored to tears of being sensible.' Pam whoops and does a shimmy on the grass. We all stare at her in disbelief. 'Let's get the party started!'

'Told you she was a hedonistic beast really,' laughs Chloe.

'Well, have a fab time.' I walk down the garden path sombrely, away from the colour and noise and laughter into the darkness.

'Sadie!' shouts Pam.

I turn round.

She is holding her wine glass in the air. 'Good luck! Remember, the wives are with you!'

They all laugh and raise their glasses in the air. 'The wives are with you!'

Thirty-four

The sitting room lights are on. But there is no sound of chatter as I unlock the front door. The silence feels temporary, like an intake of breath before a loud shriek. I hear my father's voice coming from behind the closed living room door.

'My Sadie would never do that,' he booms. 'That's a bloody outrageous suggestion.'

'Yeah!' says Loretta's unmistakable voice-over voice. 'Yeah.'

Then there is a yawning silence. A cough. I recognise it as Rona's. The front door clicks shut.

'Is that you, Sadie?' calls Dad.

I walk into the living room. It is like a courtroom. They are all there. Rona, Tom and my father, pacing anxiously around. They turn and stare. I can't meet Tom's eyes. 'Where have you been, love?' Dad asks gently.

'At Enid's, my friend in St John's Wood.' They all look at me like I've really lost it. 'I . . . I couldn't think where else to go. Everyone else was at the party.'

'Funny that!' Rona snorts. For some reason I'm surprised to see her still in her turquoise party ensemble. She's no longer wearing her party face of course. Her face is puckered with fury like a blister.

I glance at Tom. He looks away, just stares silently out of the window, one hand pressed against the glass.

'Tom, I'm sorry,' I say in a voice so low it's a whisper.

'Sound like you mean it!' snaps Rona before he has a chance to respond.

Dad turns to her. 'Rona, ease off!' He looks at me and speaks in a gentler voice. 'Are you all right, love?'

I nod, my throat locking. Don't cry. I don't want Tom to think that I think I'm the victim. I touch him lightly on the arm. 'Tom . . .'

He shrugs me off like I've burned him. 'Don't.'

'I'm sorry,' I repeat. 'I know there's no excuse. I don't know what happened.'

'You knew how close he was to that directorship,' snarls Rona. 'Why did you have to sabotage it, Sadie? You! You who should be supporting him?'

'Mum, stop it,' says Tom quickly. 'Leave her alone.'

I hover near Tom, wanting to touch him again, knowing he'll shrug me off if I try. I want to tell him that I can't repress myself any longer and I realise I've been angry about so many things and it's all been bottled up and I've tried to hide it but it came out sideways, well, more precisely, it spurted out of a glass.

'I won't shut up,' says Rona. 'What are you going to do, Tom? Try to pretend it hasn't happened?'

'No one's ignoring it, Rona,' says Dad. 'Now calm down, Rona. Please. For everyone's sake.'

Rona's eyes flash. She swoops down to pick something off the coffee table. 'Throwing a drink at your husband's most prized client is one thing. *This* is another.' She grabs the pink notebook lying on the coffee table. 'How do you explain it, Sadie?'

My eyes fall from her angry blister face to her hand. 'What on earth's my notebook got to do with it?'

Dad slings a protective arm around my shoulder. 'Exactly what I said, love.'

The air in the room gets tighter and tighter and for a moment I feel like I can't breathe. Tom is still looking out of the window. He has detached himself from me. I am on my own now.

'I happened to pick it up,' says Rona slowly, relishing every moment. 'And I couldn't help but read—'

'You've been reading my notebook?' I gasp in disbelief.

'Rona, let's leave this for tonight. We've had enough upset,' says Dad quickly.

'Yeah,' says Loretta, giving my arm a nervous little stroke. 'Are you all right, Sades?'

I become aware of a new mood in this room, something awful, a breathing, prowling misunderstanding. I can feel it waiting to pounce.

Rona opens the notebook. 'No, John, I will not leave this. Not when it's *my* son involved.'

Tom shoots her a desperate look. 'Mum. Actually this is between me and Sadie.'

What's going on? Why does everyone look so worried? 'It's a bloody notebook for God's sake.'

Rona steps closer to me. 'Is there a man in this house you work at in St John's Wood? This old lady's house?' She spits the words out.

'No, her husband's dead. No men. Apart from her nephew Eddie, the gardener.'

'Eddie!' Rona grins triumphantly and looks at Tom who looks away. 'Eddie,' she repeats like a barrister who has successfully set a trap for the accused. She looks down at the book again. 'That *does* explain things.'

'Would someone please tell me what else I've done apart from ruin everyone's evening, or life, or whatever it is I did when I threw that drink over a woman I thought was sleeping with my husband!'

There is a shocked silence.

'Oh for fuck's sake.' Tom slams his hand hard against the wall.

Rona laughs, a high, sarcastic laugh. '*You* have the cheek to accuse my Tom of infidelity. My God, you don't know how lucky you are! You . . . you . . .' She is pointing at me, her finger waggling.

Dad steps forward. 'Watch your tongue, Rona. Don't you dare slate my daughter.'

'Yeah,' says Loretta, putting her hand on her hip like a schoolgirl in a playground gearing up for a cat fight.

'Your daughter is a trollop!' spits Rona.

'How dare you!' growls Dad, a deep, baritone growl that comes from the pit of his stomach and makes everyone step back. I haven't heard it since I was a teenager.

'Please, everyone,' pleads Tom. 'Stop it. Just *stop* it.'

'Will someone tell me what on earth is going on?' I shout, desperate now.

Rona opens the notebook and starts to read in a sarcastic mocking voice. ' "Hold a secret close to your heart. Never tell your husband! E kiss." Or how about? "If you're not happy pretend you are, darling. Fake it until it becomes real. E kiss kiss".' She stops, looks up for my reaction.

My mouth opens then closes. No words come out. Tom presses his head against the wall.

' "Good loving. E kiss kiss",' continues Rona, her voice heavy with sarcasm. ' "Almost there now. It won't be long, my darling. E kiss kiss".'

'Enough!' roars Dad. 'Enough, Rona!'

'It's all right, Dad. For God's sake, Rona, those messages are from Enid, the old lady, not the bloody gardener!'

'You see,' says Dad quickly. 'I told you there'd be an innocent explanation.'

Rona and Tom exchange glances, then Tom looks quickly away, refusing to meet my eye.

'And you expect us to believe *that*?' snorts Rona. 'Come on, Sadie. We weren't born yesterday. You suddenly start doing yourself up! You get a smile on your face for the first time in months, well, huh,' she snorts. 'I'm not surprised. All this fussing around, pretending to be house proud, I should have known you'd have another agenda.'

'Don't be ridiculous. The messages, they're from Enid. She was . . .' My mouth goes dry and there is a sudden disconnection in my head, like my brain's crashed, as I struggle to find the words to describe the project with Enid. '. . . giving me advice about being a less worse wife.'

I look at Tom. Does he see the funny side? He doesn't.

Rona slaps the notebook shut. 'Come on, you can do better than that, can't you, Sadie? I thought you were meant to be a creative type after all.'

'No seriously . . .' I stop and look at Loretta, then Dad, then Tom and it hits me. Nobody believes me! Not even Dad.

Beep! Beep! There is the sound of a hooting horn outside the living room window.

Rona slings her handbag over her shoulder. 'Right, that's my taxi.' She looks at Tom. 'You coming to the station then? You better pack quickly. Teddy will be missing me like mad, poor little thing, stuck in Hampshire without me.'

'He should stay here and sort things out with his wife,' growls Dad.

Tom hesitates then stomps upstairs. We all stand in stony silence waiting for him. He reappears with an over-stuffed gym bag.

I grab his arm. 'Where are you going? Not Hampshire? Don't be stupid.'

'I need some space,' he says. He doesn't even sound angry now, just exhausted. 'I don't know what to think any more.'

'Please. Please don't go. You're going to New York in a couple of days. Don't leave like this.'

Tom hesitates. Rona holds open the sitting room door, willing him through it, as if it were a primal battle between me and her.

'I need a break, Sadie.' And with that he walks away. When I hear the front door slam a sense of betrayal stabs me like a knife. There is a deathly hush in the room.

'You OK, love?' asks Loretta eventually, patting my arm.

'No!' I say, shrugging her off.

'Hey, watch it, Sadie,' says Dad.

Loretta's eyes start to water. 'Why do you hate me, Sadie?'

My whole body rushes with hurt and anger and a million emotions I don't understand. It feels like everything is silently exploding. I turn on her because I need to turn on someone. 'When did you and Dad start dating, really?'

'What are you implying, Sadie?' Dad says.

'It was very sudden, wasn't it, you two meeting? Mum was ill for a while. It would have been easy to have an affair.' I hate myself for saying this and actually can't believe the words are dropping from my mouth. As soon as I say them I know I can't take them back.

Dad looks hurt rather than angry. 'You are wrong,' he says very quietly. 'So wrong. I loved your mother till the very end. I still love her. She made me promise . . .' his voice breaks.

'Promise what?'

'Tell her, John,' says Loretta. 'Tell her.'

'That I'd get out and meet other women. Marry again if I could. Don't look at me like that, Sadie. It's true. You know what your mother was like, thought I was incapable of looking after myself. She worried that I wouldn't be able to cope without her. Maybe she was right.'

Suddenly it all makes sense. Yes, of course, that's exactly what Mum would think.

'The classified ad thing was her idea,' Dad adds.

'Jesus.'

'Sadie, love,' Loretta says. 'I know I am not your mother. And you don't think I'm good enough for your dad, and maybe I'm not. But I love him very much.' She looks up at him and smiles. 'And I try to make him happy.'

Her evident vulnerability fills me with guilty self-loathing. It's like a dam breaking. The sobs come out heavy and hard. I can't breathe and my whole body starts to shake. For the first time in years I fall into Dad's arms and sob into his chest like a little girl. He hugs me tight and strokes my hair. 'It's all right, love. It'll be all right.'

Thirty-five

It's not all right, well, of course it's not. Tom doesn't come back the next night. He doesn't answer his mobile phone. I leave him lots of gabbled messages which start off reasonably conciliatory – 'Let's talk' – and gradually get more desperate and less reasonable – 'For fuck's sake, call me' – and then finally, after breaking the 'never drink and text' rule, resort to childish black-mail, 'expect locks changed!' He eventually texts back: 'We'll talk later.' His measured, mature-sounding response is infuriating, and makes me feel even worse about my behaviour at the party. I start to get visceral flashbacks to the exact moment I threw the Bellini at Annette, the sling of the liquid across the air, the new weightlessness of my glass, the horror on everyone's faces. And I'm relieved when the time comes to do Dr Prenwood's flowers. On the way home I take a small detour and drop in on Enid, telling myself I should check that she's OK but really I just want an excuse to see her.

'She's not in,' Angie says, opening the front door. 'She's out with the girls.'

'The girls?'

'A nice lady called Pam has invited her to lunch. She said you would be there.'

Shit. It dawns. I have a stack of messages from Pam on my mobile but I've been in such a state I haven't answered them, assuming that they are just enquiries into the state of my marriage and a request for details. I say goodbye to Angie and walk slowly back down the drive. It starts to rain, a fine lace of drizzle. The sky feels heavy, white and low. I close my eyes. And for a moment I'm back in the storm again, that wind, the flowers at my feet. I put a hand on the iron gate to steady myself and wonder if I'm going to faint.

'Sadie, are you all right?' The voice sounds like it's at the end of a tunnel.

There is a large warm hand on the small of my back. I open my eyes.

'Oh, hi, Eddie. Sorry, I was miles away. Yes, fine. I'm fine.'

'You don't look fine.'

'I thought I'd drop by. I was working up the road.'

Eddie looks at me intently as if he's trying to work something out. The rain leaves a sheen over his handsome weathered face. 'Would you like to see the garden before you go? I've just planted loads of new things.' He looks up. 'Look, I can see the sun. It's only a bit of drizzle.'

'I should get back.'

He smiles and puts an arm over my shoulder. 'Oh, come on. You're here now. Might cheer you up.'

We tour the garden slowly, my arm tucked in his. The rain stops and the sun comes out. He points to the new camellias beneath the lilacs that droop seductively from the trellis, the rare species of French lavender with flower heads thick as toothbrushes. Ten minutes later we are sitting together on the old swing at the bottom of the garden, Eddie's large booted foot tipping us gently back and forth. The rocking motion and the sun give me my first sense of calm since the Anderson party. I take a deep breath.

'She finally told you about Archie then?' laughs Eddie, kicking the swing away from the ground.

'I can't believe you never told me.'

'It wasn't for me to tell you.'

'No. I guess not.' I think of all the times he could have told me. All the times I would have blabbed had I known and I'm impressed by his discretion and loyalty. I suddenly become very aware of his thigh – its warmth, its taut muscularity – wedged next to mine on the swing. A very bad thought trips across my mind. 'It makes you think, doesn't it? People's marriages are just the strangest things.'

Eddie sighs. 'Aren't they?'

We sit in comfortable silence for a few moments, swinging gently, the scent of lilacs heavy in the air.

'Enid seems to be coping very well,' I say. 'On fire the other night.'

He laughs. 'Yes, I heard about that. "The girls are back!" she told me. God, she was beside herself.' He puts a hand on my arm. My whole body stills. I daren't move. I fear that if I do move I'll jerk wildly or start trembling or do something embarrassing. I only breathe when he takes his hand from my arm.

'You've been amazing with her. I know you didn't set out to be, that it's a happy by-product of your flowers, but you've made her much more cheerful than anyone else has for a long time. You've given her a project, a reason to get up in the morning.'

My eyes fill. 'That's good. I seem to make everyone else miserable.'

Eddie pushes us off harder with the tip of his boot and we swing higher, and higher. The chains of the swing begin to squeak. I feel the air rush against my face. Is it my imagination or is he edging closer? He shrugs his arm over my shoulder.

'Wahay!' he shouts, pulling me tight towards him.

I feel something hum between my legs, a warm, pleasant sensation, like a flower opening. Goodness. The swing goes faster. The chains squeak some more. I feel dizzy, which could be because I haven't slept properly since the party, or because of the swing, or because of the disconcerting sexiness of the hands that grip the swing. A midge flies straight into my eye. My heart begins to thump. I'm hit by how much more alive I feel here next to him. How much more connected to both my body and the world around me,

322

how free and light. It's the opposite of marriage.

'Sadie,' Eddie says, dragging his foot along the ground to slow the swing. 'There's something . . .' He sounds embarrassed. 'There's something I want to ask you.' He uses his foot as a brake and the swing judders to a halt. 'I hope you don't think I'm speaking out of turn . . .' He is blushing! Eddie, unflappable, sexy Eddie is blushing! I suddenly know what is coming. My mind begins to race and somersault. Will I be able to turn him away? I'm not at all sure I will. I'm sick of being a good wife. I'm damned as a bad wife, why not behave like one?

'I'm no good at this . . .' he starts to laugh nervously. 'I feel like a teenager.'

Oh. My. God.

'I dig you, Sadie, I really do.'

My whole body starts to sing, a sweet harmony in my veins, in my chest, beneath my skin.

'And you've got your head screwed on.'

'Others would disagree,' I squeak.

Eddie skewers me to the seat with an intense stare. 'If I ask you something do you promise to give me an honest answer? Don't try and protect my feelings.'

I swallow hard. My heart is thumping so hard I can't believe he won't hear it. I feel about fifteen years old too. 'Yes?'

He clears his throat.

I close my eyes, waiting for it, waiting to be hit by the most tormenting and delicious moral decision. This has never happened to me before. I never thought it would. But I was right all those weeks ago, strange things do indeed happen to a woman alone in a park. The storm. Enid. That's why I'm here after all.

'Do you think Chloe likes me?'

'*Chloe?*' I sit upright, eyes startled open.

'Shit, you sound shocked. Is it so unimaginable?'

'No, no, not at all,' I stutter. Oh so immensely stupid. Why on earth? Oh God. 'I just never imagined that . . .'

'Yes, I know we would be a bit of an odd couple. But I really like her, Sadie. Really like her. She's the first woman I've met for ages who . . . well, I think she's just great. And I'm sure she must be inundated by adoring men and I don't want to flatter myself by thinking . . .' He hesitates. 'But do you think she'd mind if I asked her out?' He coughs. 'I suppose what I'm buffoonishly struggling to ask is, is she single?'

As I drive home, I feel like someone who has walked in front of a train, only to find it was a ghost train that has charged right through me and come out the other side, leaving me untouched. What on earth was I thinking? Who is ever going to fancy *me* in that way? Old, sad, eccentric Sadie Drew. Nice as a friend, disaster as a wife, absurd as a lover. Eddie. Eddie. Those ivy-green eyes. I squirm inside, reliving again and again the cringe of my own misplaced arrogance. Before I turn off the street, I look back over my shoulder at Enid's house, the grand, Regency house that impressed me so much. It looks plainer now, strangely ordinary, the same as the other houses on the street but scruffier with better flower beds. It doesn't feel magic to me any more. Inside that house, I realise with a cold deadening certainty as I drive away, there is no marriage guru, only a terminally ill rich lady who was in love with a gay husband and likes to meddle in other people's affairs. And there is no back-up position, no sexy young gardener to scoop me up if my marriage doesn't work out. The Wizard of Oz was, after all, just a loudspeaker behind a curtain.

Thirty-six

Danny is clingy and insists on following me to the bathroom when I have a pee. I worry he'll recall this as an adult, in therapy. He also cries during *Thomas the Tank Engine*, the bit where Percy gets stuck in the flood. Is Daddy stuck in a flood? he asks. No. I explain as breezily as I can. Daddy is visiting Grandpa and Granny – 'she doesn't like being called Granny, Mummy' – in Hampshire and then he's got to go to New York for a few days. He'll be back soon. That night Danny sleeps in my bed, which is probably more of a comfort to me than him. He wets the bed and I wake up after a fractious night's sleep smelling of pee.

The front door slams early Monday morning. I recognise Tom's tread. I rush downstairs in my T-shirt and knickers half expecting him to be there with his arms open. But his arms are pressed tight to his sides. He looks like he's aged twenty years over the weekend. He doesn't look like his heart is thumping at the sight of me, no, not at all. He looks like his heart is hidden in a panic room with a triple locked door.

'We need to talk,' says Tom in his blankest, most distant voice. 'But I've also got to get to work, if I've still got a job. So let's talk later.'

'You fly to New York today.'

'Not until this afternoon. Need to run into the office first.' He walks heavily – thump, thump – up the stairs. As he passes I get a whiff of him. He smells different. He smells of Rona's Hampshire house, all pot pourri and over-perfumed room sprays. I hear him in the bedroom rifling through his suits.

'How can you not believe me?' I say quietly, following him. I notice that our bedroom still smells of Danny's wee.

'I don't know any more,' says Tom, kicking a leg into the trouser of a dark blue suit. 'I don't know what to think.'

'Come on, Tom, you *know* I wouldn't have a bloody affair.' I'm suddenly seized by the injustice of it all.

The muscle in his temple pulses. His hands are shaking.

'I'm not like you.'

'Are you ever going to let it go?' he hisses.

'No! I'm not. It's here.' I tap my head. 'All the time. And you wonder why I get fucking paranoid?'

He knots his tie roughly. 'Paranoid? Psychotic! I can't believe you went through Annette's wardrobe. That you even went to her house! Jesus.' He turns to look at me. His eyes are wide and bloodshot, like he's been up all night drinking whiskies.

'Is what your bloody mother did – spying on my private things – any worse than what I did at Annette's flat?'

Tom stares at me for a moment. And I can see thoughts whizzing through his head, thoughts like flickers of light in his eyes. 'The way you behaved with Annette. Hell, the way you've been behaving with me, it's just so bizarre. I . . . I don't know what's happened to you.' His voice breaks. 'To us.'

'I've been trying to save our marriage, Tom. Can't you see that?' As I say this I realise how ridiculous it sounds. Save our marriage? Who do I think I am, Superman?

Tom looks at me like I'm stark raving bonkers. 'Sadie . . .' he hesitates and starts to speak very slowly. 'I think we should consider therapy or . . .'

'What? A separation?'

He doesn't correct me. I sit down on the edge of the bed, head in my hands, feeling like I've been kicked in the stomach. A separation. Shit. The horrible coldness of the word fills me with dread. How did we sink this low? How did we get here?

'I just . . .' Tom's voice falters. 'I feel like I'm not helping you. I don't make you feel secure. I can't give you what you want.' He sits on the bed next to me. 'I feel totally fucking useless.'

Tom feels useless? Competent, successful Tom? This shocks me. I'm the useless one around here. That's my line.

'I'm trying to do the right thing,' he whispers. 'I don't know, Sadie. I don't know how to do this, how to make us better.' He stops and looks at me searchingly. 'I'm not sure you'll ever forgive me. All this talk of marriage advice from Enid, if that's what it was. It makes me feel like you've been conning me, that I'm part of some weird contrived plan, that the last few weeks have been kind of staged.'

My mouth opens then shuts. No words. I see how it might – hell, does – look and I desperately want to explain myself but there's so much to say that I don't know where to start.

Tom blows out air from his mouth like he's trying to exhale the universe. 'Did you really think a trifle would fix things, Sadie?'

Thirty-seven

All pretence is pointless now. Every mask has slipped.
The house, even by my old standards, is disgusting,
properly disgusting. Like a travellers' site after the
travellers have left, or the wreckage left in the wake of
a teenager's Facebook party. I'm not in a dissimilar
state. I don't bother showering before breakfast. My
hair has reverted to its natural state of Christian rock
group frizz, with extra greasy bits at the roots. My
make-up bag is back in its rightful place, forgotten at
the bottom of the bathroom cupboard, leaking gunk
and covered in exploded loose face powder. The lipstick
itself – Hot Cherry Pie, pah! – has proved very popular
with Danny as a craft implement and is now smeared
over an A3 piece of green sugar paper, alongside glued-
on macaroni and dried lentils. At best I'm back in my
dirty kidult outfits. At worst, it's those increasingly
whiffy flannel pyjamas. Even Danny is dressed in
yesterday's jeans and a pyjama top because there are no
clean clothes and I can't, well, be bothered to put the

washing machine on: I need to buy some washing powder and I can't be bothered to do that either. It just doesn't seem important somehow. Instead I make myself a coffee with milk that is three days out of date and feed my darling child stale toast and Hobnobs for breakfast in front of *GMTV*.

Afterwards he curls his small, plump body into my arms. 'Don't feel well. Want Daddy.'

I consider whether this has something to do with the stale toast or the mainlining of Hobnobs and press my hand to his forehead. He is hot. But he can't be ill today. I've got two jobs on. I spoon him the maximum dose of Calpol, willing his temperature to drop. As soon as it does I take him to nursery like a proper selfish mum. When Scary Hanna grabs his hand and leads him away Danny looks over his shoulder with a mournful accusatory stare that doesn't leave me. It isn't until I get back home later that I notice that I've got a message on my mobile phone. A text: fat Pat the cleaner's resignation. Who cares! I didn't like her fussing around the house anyway, I think, deleting her text. There is also a voice message: the nursery. Danny is ill. Can I come and get him? The message was left two hours ago. My heart lurches.

I drive too fast to the nursery, my mind leaping with potential catastrophes and fatal childhood illnesses. When I arrive I am directed to the sick room, a claustrophobic, boxy green cupboard. Danny is whimpering on the sick bed. He has a raging temperature and a streaming nose.

'We're not insured to give Calpol,' Scary Hanna says briskly. 'Has he had chicken pox yet? There's a lot of it around.'

'Um, I don't think so.'

'You'd know surely.' She shakes her head at my ineptitude. 'Well, that could be it. Keep an eye on him.'

I scoop up my poor, darling latchkey child, left to fever and cry on a pink nylon sheet beside Scary Hanna while I blithely arrange sweet peas and white roses. When I get home I realise that the bottle of Calpol is empty – I gave him the last drop this morning – so I phone Pam because she's the person who lives nearest and is most likely to have it. Danny is beginning to look really ill now. I'm starting to get really paranoid. Is it something worse than chicken pox? How bad *is* chicken pox? Suddenly I need my mother. She'd know what to do.

Mum doesn't arrive, obviously, but Pam – bless her – does. She is out of breath, the most pregnant you can be without popping and her complexion glows like a bulb. She charges into the house. 'Where's the patient?' Armed with a full-blown medical kit more suited to an Afghan field she rushes straight upstairs to Danny's room, leaving me gaspingly grateful for her extraordinary competence.

There is another light knock on the front door, which is still ajar. Ruth, then Tara, appear in the hall. 'We were at Pam's when you called, discussing a masochistic charity fun run,' says Ruth, who is staring at me with a slightly odd expression like I'm wearing a mask or have an enormous spot at the tip of my nose, which I quite possibly do, having not checked in the mirror this morning. 'We called you too but you weren't answering. Will we get under your feet, Sadie?'

'No, not at all. Come in.' I rush upstairs to Pam and Danny.

Pam is sucking up Calpol in a syringe with the efficiency of a junkie. 'Don't be alarmed. It's the easiest way to get it in,' she says. Then she gives me a stern look. 'Calm down, Sadie. Stop hopping from foot to foot. You look in a right state. He's going to be just fine.'

I have to trust her. She's got two children. She's a natural. She knows more than me. She shoots the Calpol down the back of poor Danny's gagging throat, stripping off his clothes until he is stark naked. 'We've got to get his temperature down or he could have convulsions.'

'Convulsions? Christ. Should I take him to St Mary's?'

'I'm sure he'll be fine. Wait for the medicine to kick in,' whispers Pam, smoothing back Danny's hair. 'Where were you, Sadie? I phoned and phoned. Enid invited us over to lunch the other day. We wanted you to join us. It felt weird being there without you.'

'Didn't pick up my phone, sorry.' I brush the hair off Danny's red face. 'Bad day. Bad week.'

Pam puts a warm, fleshy arm around my shoulders, her long dark hair tickles my throat. 'I know, I know.'

'Spots! Look, Pam, weird spots!' I point to them, two, no, three, four little raised bumps on Danny's torso beneath his armpits. 'Lift your arm, Danny.'

Pam peers closer and smiles. 'Ah, there's your chicken pox. I'll leave you the calamine lotion.' She points at a bottle of bubblegum-pink liquid. 'Just dab it on the spots before he goes to bed to help with the itching.' Pam waddles downstairs. I'm unexpectedly touched. Maybe being in a wifely coven isn't such a bad thing after all. I feel bad for all the times I've thought spiky, unkind thoughts about Pam, tinged with jealousy about her pregnancy. When it came to an emergency, well, she was there, wasn't she? I hug Danny tighter, my body rushing with relief that it's not something else like meningitis or an invasion of one of the flesh-eating viruses that Rona says live in children's playgrounds. 'It's only chicken pox. It's good to get chicken pox,' I whisper into his hot, pink ear.

'Doesn't feel good, Mummy,' whimpers Danny.

I lay him on his bed and open his window. I try to phone Tom. It goes through to voicemail. I don't leave a message. I don't want him to think that I'm trying to blackmail him home. I stay until Danny's dozed off then I go downstairs.

The others are waiting, sitting around the kitchen table, chatting animatedly, as if energised by the drama. In the time that it's taken to put Danny to bed they have made tea and laid out homemade chocolate chip biscuits – nothing to do with me, Pam must have brought them

– on the house's last clean white plate. I sink into a chair. 'Thanks. You didn't need to do that. It's a mess, I know.'

'What's happened?' asks Ruth.

'I happened,' I say. 'And my cleaner resigned.'

'She was rubbish anyway,' says Pam.

'In case you were wondering, I have also well and truly screwed up my marriage,' I add for clarification. 'I'm pretending I'm single again. I've reverted to my true, squalid nature. I've given up being a wife.'

There is a silence. Tara breaks it. 'I've got into the most dreadful mess too,' she says breathlessly, her large, blue eyes blinking. 'I was just telling Ruth that I've been spoiled by having amazing orgasms with Mr Happy Endings and now sex with Nick feels wrong, almost like a violation. I know, I know, it's entirely my own fault but it's frying my head.'

Pam looks at her sharply. 'Tara, please. This isn't about you.' Her majestic bump has lent her a certain matriarchal authority.

Tara looks down sheepishly. 'No, of course not, sorry.'

'Please, I'd much rather talk about Tara's sex life. Sounds rather more fun than my own,' I say.

'Don't be silly.' Pam wants more dirt. She wants the meat and bones of my marriage's rotting carcass. 'Let it all out, Sadie. And don't forget, you'll get through this. What you did wasn't *that* bad. It was only a Bellini. It could have been worse.'

'It could have been a Bloody Mary,' winks Ruth.

'Tom is talking about separation,' I say, amazed at my candidness. A few weeks ago I would never have confided in this lot.

'*No!*' chime Tara and Ruth in unison.

'Oh, Sadie, oh, darling.' Pam leaps up and hugs me into her enormous bosom. Her skin smells faintly of peaches and is butter soft. Its maternal softness is strangely reassuring.

I break out of her grasp, steamrollered, by her breasts, by her sympathy, by everything. 'I don't think he can stand it any more. And who can blame him?'

'*I* can blame him. Where is he?' snorts Ruth crossly. 'I'll bust his bloody balls.'

'On the other side of the Atlantic. Rona, mother-in-law, will be working on him the moment he gets back, and probably via Skype as we speak. She's never liked me. And I've proved all her worst fears. We haven't got a chance.'

My phone rings. Tom? My heart starts to beat faster. I dive towards it.

It's Chloe. 'Just checking in to see that you haven't stuck your head in the oven.'

'The oven would spit me out and tell me to have a shower first. No, I'm sitting here with Pam, Tara and Ruth. Danny's got chicken pox . . . oh, it's a long story. Why don't you come over? The house hasn't got a red cross on the door or anything, promise.'

Chloe laughs. 'I've just finished work. Usual. You know. Mad model with a rabid pit bull called Pussy.

Bloody Pussy chewed up my best powder compact. Don't get me started. Anyway, I've got some gossip for you. I'm down the road. Be with you in ten,' she says and hangs up.

Leaving the others debating Tara's sex crisis, I go upstairs to check Danny, sit on the edge of his bed watching him, loving him so much I feel like my heart will burst. After a few minutes I hear Chloe at the door, chatter and laughter as she walks into the kitchen. I think about Eddie and his declaration on the swing. When I go downstairs Chloe is leaning against the kitchen units, wearing skinny jeans and Converse trainers and a boating blazer. She looks gorgeous and perky and full of life. Of course Eddie fancies her! What red-blooded male wouldn't?

'Right,' she says, hugging me tight. 'Tell me everything.'

'You've got an admirer,' I say quickly.

'Oo!' squeals Tara.

Chloe looks puzzled. 'What? Who?' she asks warily.

'Eddie.'

Chloe's face doesn't register any emotion at all. I wonder if she even remembers who he is. Poor Eddie.

'Enid's sexy gardener, he's got the hots for you, Chloe. He asked me if you were single.'

Ruth gives Chloe a nudge. 'Ooo. A gardener. Very *Desperate Housewives*.'

'How exciting!' sighs Tara.

'Good marriage material?' demands Pam.

'Definitely,' I say.

Chloe looks terrified. 'He told you?'

'He asked me if you were single,' I say.

'I like him. But not my type,' says Chloe quickly, as if trying to close the matter.

'Oooh,' giggles Tara. 'Defensive.'

'He sounds lovely!' coos Pam.

'Stop trying to marry me off, for fuck's sake, you lot. I don't want to join the wife club. Anyway, can we talk about something else?'

We all start a little at Chloe's reaction.

'What was the gossip you had to tell me?' I ask, changing the subject, feeling bad for making Chloe uncomfortable.

Chloe winces. 'Ah, yes, gossip. I'm afraid I heard some you probably would want me to tell you. But don't want to hear.' She sighs. 'The shoot I've just been on. The hairdresser, Sam, had heard all about the Anderson party . . .'

I put my hand across my mouth. 'Great. News travels fast.'

'Well, he's got a few clients there. They are all talking about it. But it's not that. It's just that he mentioned that Annette was leaving the agency. Sorry, babes, but I thought you'd want to know.'

Thirty-eight

Guts. That's what I need. Not lipstick. Not trifles. Guts. The next morning I know exactly what I must do. I phone Trish and arrange some childcare. Then I perch on the edge of Danny's bed, dab his spots with the pink calamine lotion. He now looks like he's been lashed by the suckers of an octopus then dunked in strawberry milkshake. 'I'll bring you some breakfast in bed then I'm going to shut your curtains again, sweetie,' I whisper into his ear. 'You sleep. Trish is coming round. She's going to come and look after you for a little while. I've got to go out. I won't be long.'

Danny starts to cry. 'Miss Daddy.'

'Oh, baby, Daddy will be home in a few days,' I say, lump rising in my throat. I suddenly miss him too, little things that I never thought I'd miss in a million years like his grouchiness in the mornings, the way he shakes out a newspaper, makes tea way too strong and leaves the tea bag steaming on the sink. I miss the way he rolls over and takes up the whole bed. The way he snores. To my surprise I miss our whole stupid, dysfunctional marriage. And I realise that for all his late nights in the office, just knowing that he, another adult, is coming home at the end of the day is not to be underestimated.

The other strange thing about his absence? I'm increasingly blown sideways by powerful gusts of nostalgia, details from the past and our courtship that I'd long forgotten. Is this what people mean by 'my life flashed before me' but in the last gasps of a relationship, rather than a life? I remember funny, incidental things such as the colour of his socks on our first date – hideous lime green and grey stripes – and what we drank – dry Martinis before lunch – and the way a sliver of olive stuck to my front tooth. I was embarrassed. But he picked it off gently with his fingers and ate it himself, an act of such sexy sweetness, I think, perhaps, I fell in love with him at that moment. I also remember other, more poignant things that have been lost in the minutiae of resentment in the last few months, like when Tom surprised me last year by flying Mum over first class to Toronto – he could ill afford it – for my birthday weekend. She appeared at the front door, beaming and looking, despite her thinness and scarf-covered baldness, ridiculously happy. It was the best birthday present ever. It was also the last time I saw her alive.

I wipe a tear from my eye. Right! This is no time for sentiment. I need to at least try and right a few wrongs. I dig around for clothes that aren't crumpled or on a flight path to the laundry basket. This leaves one pair of black trousers and a white shirt, a combo that makes me look like a waitress but will have to do. I stand in front of the mirror and do as Enid once suggested – try to pretend that I am playing a role, that I am an actress slipping on to stage for an important part.

Outside the air is thick with seeds or pollen of some kind and I can feel my eyes water behind my darkest, fuck-off-world sunglasses. I take a bendy bus to Belsize Park. An old woman smelling faintly of wee sits down beside me and starts to eat smoky bacon crisps. An anxious-looking guy in a baseball cap talks aggressively to one of the yellow support poles. I stay on the bus and disembark just as the weird guy gets really aggressive with the pole. Walking slowly towards Annette's apartment I'm flooded with wince-inducing memories of the last time I was here. I stand outside the apartment building, pacing, back and forth, back and forth. The doorman starts to eye me suspiciously, as if I might be a crazed fan. I take a deep breath and walk in.

'What can I do for you, madam?' he asks politely.

'I'm here for . . .' The shining marble floor feels like it's coming up to me. The pot plants become a lurid fluoro green. I feel sick and disorientated all of a sudden. 'Miss Eastern.'

The doorman phones a number. There is no answer. 'Not answering, I'm afraid.'

Deflated, I walk out of the building and wonder what on earth to do now. Then I hear a noise. Footsteps. Voices.

'Ah, you are here? A lady called for you a few moments ago.' The doorman's cockney voice. 'No, she didn't leave a name. Have a nice day, Miss Eastern.' Heels clip clop across the marble floor. Oh shit. Feeling wholly unprepared, I scuttle away from the doorway, back to the wall, head turned sideways to watch her exit without being seen myself.

A foot appears first, then a snakeskin stiletto, a tanned ankle. A swish of blue: wide-legged trousers, a nautical style jacket. A glossy curtain of hair. It's *her*. I press myself against the wall, shoulders back, as if I might be able to disappear completely. She strides down the street. I watch helplessly. Do something, Sadie, I tell myself. Follow her! My toes wiggle inside their trainers, like bait hooked to a line. Then, finding the courage from somewhere, I start to run. 'Annette,' I yell. 'Annette.'

She stops, mid-step, turns around slowly and flicks a mane of blond hair off her face. 'Hello? Do I know you?'

I take off my sunglasses. 'It's me, Tom Harrison's wife, Sadie. The florist.'

Her face changes. Her eyes flash. Her lips curl back to a snarl. '*You!*'

'I wonder if you have a minute. I wanted to apologise . . .'

Annette snorts and starts walking away. 'Thank you. I've sent Tom the dry cleaning bill.'

I have to run faster to catch up with her large,

Amazonian strides. 'Annette. Could I take up five minutes of your time?'

'I have better ways to waste five minutes, thanks.'

'Please.'

She stops and stares at me. Maybe she sees my desperation because something softer flickers beneath her haughty racehorse eyes. 'Five minutes then.'

There is a coffee shop right next to us, a small, cheerful-looking neighbourhood coffee shop with small Formica tables and ferns in terracotta pots. I nod to it. 'May I buy you coffee?'

Annette doesn't answer but when I hold open the door of the café she walks in. We sit down at a small rectangular table with a yolk-yellow top. She orders an espresso. I copy her, even though I never order espressos, much preferring the foam teaspoon-licking event of a cappuccino. It's just that an espresso feels more appropriate somehow: short, and strong.

'I haven't got long,' she says. For a fleeting moment I feel like I get a glimpse of the engaging woman behind the successful speaker. She's got charisma, even a warmth, albeit a reluctant one.

I swallow hard. 'I'm so sorry, Annette. There is no excuse for the way I behaved, either at your flat or at the party, well, certainly not at the party.'

Annette sips her coffee casually. 'No, there wasn't.'

'I thought you were having an . . .' I can't bear to say the word 'affair'. It suddenly sounds completely ludicrous.

I don't need to say it. Annette looks at me and she begins to laugh, not a fake, brittle laugh, but with genuine pent-up mirth.

I shift self-consciously on my seat. I can't help but smile too. 'I've since learned you've got a girlfriend.'

She stops laughing, sighs and looks at me wearily like I'm a persistently annoying child. 'I wouldn't have an affair with a married man anyway, thank you very much, Sadie. And certainly not Tom.'

'Right. Of course. Annette, I feel terrible about what happened at the party.'

She looks distinctly unmoved.

'But leaving Anderson will punish Tom, not me. It's not his fault. He was so proud of having you as a client.'

She puts her coffee cup down and looks at me sternly. 'Sadie, I want a strictly professional relationship with my agent. The moment personal stuff starts intruding . . .'

'Annette, I beg you to reconsider. Please.'

'Impossible. I've made up my mind.' Her jaw sets at a firm angle. It strikes me that there is something about her that is appealing, a confidence, a lack of female silliness or apology.

'He'll be gutted. And he'll blame me.'

Annette smiles. 'As he should.'

'As he should.'

She drains her coffee quickly, leaving red lipstick marks on the white china cup. 'Now I hope you feel suitably atoned and sleep better at night. But I must go now.' She picks up a large shiny black bag festooned with serious silver hardware and slings it over her shoulder.

'Can I ask you one more question?' I dare, sensing that the atmosphere between us has shifted into something a little more companionable.

She glances at her watch. 'Quickly.'

'Did you encourage him to . . .' I start to smile, because it sounds even more ridiculous saying it in front of her. 'Spring clean his heart or whatever? Encourage him to get rid of old baggage, people who held him back?' I grip the salt cellar for comfort, rotate it in my fingers.

'I should have!' She bends forward on her elbows. Up close her mouth seems bigger than ever, her lips absurdly motile, twitching like two small animals in red rubber socks. 'Sadie, listen to me. I will do you one favour, and one favour only. For Tom's sake I will be honest with you. Yes, Tom harangued me for opinions all the time. It was actually quite annoying, fond of him though I am. I told him to go read my books.'

My heart sinks.

'If you want my opinion. He is struggling.'

My heart sinks further.

'He is also that rare thing, a man who is actually still in love with his wife. He wants you to be happy.'

I look at her blankly. What did she just say?

'Do I really have to spell it out? I should be charging for this.'

'I don't understand,' I say quietly.

'He needs time to get over losing that baby. He's scared of it happening again. Your grief scared him. And he needs to know he won't lose you too.' She adds more softly now: 'I think I've said enough. Now if you excuse me, I must go.' She throws a generous handful of pound coins into the saucer as a tip and strides out of the café, Gisele hair swishing from shoulder to shoulder.

Thirty-nine

I open the nursery door gently, a little nervously. I haven't been here for a few days. While the rest of the house has reverted to its messy original state, in here it is as pristine as always. There's no mess, no clutter, nothing to untidy itself. I check the flower in the jam jar on the mantelpiece. A dandelion. I double take. A dandelion? Am I going mad? It was a rose. Yes, a new, partly budded white rose which should have lasted at least a week. I touch the frill of the dandelion's small stiff yellow petals lightly with my fingertips. Nobody could have been in here. Apart from Tom.

I feel strange. Everything I know to be true starts to tremble and rearrange, like shimmering, shifting pixels on a flickering old television screen that is struggling to form a picture. I think back to the Monday morning before he left for New York. After our row in the bedroom, I sat crying in the living room on our lime green sofa. I heard Tom walk outside to the garden. I heard him stomping around upstairs. I presumed he was packing. Yes, it must have been Tom. My mind races. This dandelion undoes everything I held to be true. Perhaps I haven't been mourning the baby alone. I stare and stare at the dandelion until my eyes fuzz and it becomes a small bright yellow sun.

I walk over to the airing cupboard, reach for its door. But something stops me opening it, there's a disconnection between my brain and my hand. My fingers hover mid-air then I withdraw, back away and walk slowly out of the room. I go downstairs, head spinning, overwhelmed by the fact that I no longer feel that I am leaving part of myself in the airing cupboard. There is a lightening inside that I didn't anticipate, a whooshing feeling, as if I am surfacing, shooting up, up, up towards the light. I tiptoe into Danny's bedroom and kiss his spotty forehead. Then I realise. And it's like a torch flicking on inside the darkness of my head. Danny is enough. He is my son and he is here and he is wonderful. All the energy I've spent trying to get another baby! My energies should be with Danny. No more hungering for a replacement. I kiss him again and again. He doesn't wake but a little smile curls the corners of his mouth for a fleeting second then it is gone.

My phone beeps in my hand and makes me jump. I look down, hoping it will be a message from Tom. It is not. It is a text from Pam: 'boy, 7lb, born 4.15 am, 2 hr labour, no drugs! LOL Pam & Seth x'.

I read the message again and again. A baby boy. To

my surprise, and enormous relief, I do not feel envy or bitterness, as I feared I would, but a spark of joy that Pam has had a healthy baby. I pull back Danny's curtains, washing the room in bright, seaside-clear light.

Danny wakes and smiles for the first time since he got ill. His temperature has gone. The maddening itching has gone. His energy is back. He eats four pieces of toast. 'Want to go out,' he says.

'Oh, baby, I'm not sure. It's a bit soon.'

He looks at me indignantly. 'Not a baby. Am big boy now.'

'You know what? You are right.' And he is, I realise proudly. He really is. It's time to let him grow up. 'Come on buster, let's hit the road.'

We set off in the car. Danny checks the wing mirror to warn me about buses. We put on the radio and sing along to The Rolling Stones' 'Start Me Up' and stop at a smart, overpriced florist in Little Venice and buy an armful of wisteria, iris and jasmine, and a bag of jelly babies from the newsagent next door. A few minutes later we pull up in Enid's drive, gravel crunching under our wheels.

'Big house,' he says, biting the head off a green jelly baby.

'This is where my friend Enid lives. You remember I told you about her.'

'She's old. Older than Grandma in heaven.'

I smile. 'Yep, that's the one.'

There is a strong smell of honeysuckle around the

front door. Danny stands on his tippy toes and rings the bell.

'Oh, look! Your little boy!' exclaims a delighted Angie when she opens the door. 'What's happened to your face?' She runs a finger over his cheek.

'Pox,' says Danny.

'Chicken pox. He's not infectious any more,' I say quickly. 'Enid said it was OK to bring him. I hope you don't mind.'

Angie pinches his cheek. 'Of course not! Come in. Enid's in the garden. She's expecting you.' She hesitates. 'She's not too good today, Sadie. Very tired.'

'We won't stay long,' I say, wondering whether I really should have brought an energetic pox-marked boy to visit a terminally ill woman. Enid might think she likes children, but like so many older childless people she might well find them tiresome after thirty seconds. It takes ages to get through the house because Danny stops every few steps and discovers a new curiosity, the elephant foot waste bin, a sword on the wall, photographs of tigers, things that I've rushed past all too quickly. For a moment I see it all through his eyes and once again I marvel, not only at Enid's house, but at Enid herself, this extraordinary old lady in her beautiful, fading old house, with all its hidden loves and secrets.

I see Enid before she sees me, sitting on a wrought iron chair beneath a gnarled branch of her old apple tree. She looks thinner than I've ever seen her – too thin – and is sitting typically upright wearing the blue silk housecoat embroidered with cockatoos. Her silver hair is swept neatly off her face and her eyes are shut. She is pale but smiling and tapping her fingers on her lap as if listening to a pleasant, interior music. Again, she reminds me so much of my nan, who used to do exactly the same thing – eyes shut, fingers tapping, sitting on her favourite sage green wingback chair in the sitting room of her canal-side house. If me and Mum ever walked in on her doing it, Mum would roll her eyes, like daughters do, and whisper, 'Mother's at the disco again.' This would always give me the giggles and then Nan would open her eyes immediately and look at us like we were two naughty schoolgirls.

'Enid,' I say, touching her lightly on the shoulder. 'It's Sadie.'

Her face furrows. Because she's lost weight her lines are deeper. Then her eyes open slowly, gracefully, like the wise, wrinkled, ancient eyes of an elephant. A smile spreads across her face when she sees Danny. 'Oh, your darling little boy.' She beckons him over with curled bejewelled fingers.

Danny hovers, unsure and unwilling to leave me. I take his hand and bring him to Enid. He stares at her like she's some strange exhibit in a museum. 'I have pox,' he says with great seriousness, as if to pre-empt any enquiries.

'But you are still devilishly handsome,' smiles Enid. 'Drag up a chair and tell me all about yourself. Ah, look, here is Angie with the supplies.'

Angie walks down the garden path carrying a tray full of cakes, pink fondant fancies, long buns oozing cream. Danny loosens his grip on my hand, torn between diving towards the cakes and hanging on to me.

'Angie, can you dig out some of those old toys?' she asks.

'I have already, madam,' says Angie. 'I'll bring them out.' A few seconds later she re-emerges with an old stickered tea chest full of ancient paint-chipped tin cars, misshapen balls and hand-painted bricks.

Danny's face lights up. He grins at Enid, lets go of my hand and sits on the grass at Enid's feet, rifling through the toy box.

'Ah, you've won him over,' I say.

'Toys and cakes. Boys are simple.' Enid sighs. 'It's so nice to see a child enjoying them. They used to be my toys, you know. Eddie used to play with them too when he was little.'

I start a bit at this mention of Eddie. Part of me is dreading seeing him in case he asks me again about Chloe and I'll have to sugar the truth.

Enid gazes at Danny. She is quieter than I've seen her. It's as if her thoughts have turned inwards and she's conserving energy. I recognise the contented placidity. That's what happened to Mum in her last days, too.

'We've brought you iris, wisteria and jasmine. I'll vase it up.'

'Lovely,' she says, not taking her eyes off Danny.

'You OK here, Danny?' I ask.

Danny nods, preoccupied with a carved wooden dinosaur. I set out the flowers in the Sri Lankan earthenware vases in the kitchen, letting the flowers fall out loosely, as if they've just been picked from a field. Then I watch Enid and Danny from the window. I can't hear what she's saying but I can see Danny smile, then hold up the dinosaur for her examination. They have an intense discussion about the dinosaur, then both start laughing. It's a strange sight, the elegant old lady and the boy with chicken pox.

'Sweet,' says a voice behind me. Eddie. He is standing there, tanned from the garden, a streak of mud up his cheek, his T-shirt stripped off revealing his Action Man chest.

I brace myself for the blush. But it doesn't happen. Nor, to my enormous relief, does my heart lurch. 'Isn't it?'

Eddie washes his muddy hands in the sink. 'How's things, Sadie?'

'Good,' I say. 'Nice to be out of the house. Tom's in New York. Danny's had chicken pox.'

'Enid's not got long, you know,' he says quietly. 'My mum was here this morning. She spoke with her doctor.'

'Oh no.' I put my hand to my mouth. 'But she is still so . . . so vivid.'

'She's a tough old cookie, of course. She's not one for lying in bed, but she probably should be.'

My mobile starts to ring and vibrate on the kitchen table. 'One sec.' I pick it up. 'Hello?'

'Disaster!' Dad shouts. 'Bloody unmitigated disaster.'

'Excuse me, Eddie.' I hold the phone away from my ear to save my eardrum, walk outside and sit on a small bench beside Danny and Enid. 'One minute. Calm down, Dad, for God's sake. What's the matter?'

'The flaming hall we've hired on Saturday. It's only gone and burned down. Burned to a bleeding. pork scratching!'

'Shit.'

'Arson, they reckon. I tell you, the world has gone mad,' fumes Dad. 'Loretta's having kittens, kittens, I tell you. She's in a right state. I'm worried sick about her.'

'There must be somewhere else you can have your party, Dad. It's only what, thirty people? No, no, sorry, I can't think of anywhere off the top of my head.'

Dad mutters a stream of expletives. 'Gotta go, girl. I'll phone you later. Loretta's off again. Loretta, baby, it's gonna be . . .'

I hang up.

Danny looks up. 'Who was that, Mummy?'

'Grandpa. He's upset. The hall he booked for his engagement party on Saturday has burned down.'

Enid's face furrows. 'Dear me, that's horribly bad luck, isn't it? Your poor father.'

'Poor Loretta,' says Danny.

'You know what you must tell him, don't you, darling?' Enid lifts her head into the sunshine and closes her eyes. 'He must have it here of course. We've got an enormous garden. Angie's got friends who'll pour drinks and be happy for a bit of extra work. We did it for Eddie's thirtieth. It was a hoot.'

'Here?' I laugh. 'Gosh. Thank you so much. It's such a sweet offer. But I couldn't possibly, Enid. I'm afraid you've got no idea what they're all like. Loretta is just . . .' I bite my tongue. But the idea of Enid meeting my father, let alone Loretta, is unspeakably awful. They are the ultimate embarrassing relatives. My worlds cannot collide like this. No good will come of it.

'Don't tell me you haven't got over that yet?' she laughs. 'Have I taught you nothing? My darling, men will *always* love the Lorettas of this world. God made them for a reason.'

'It'll be too noisy and far too much for you, Enid.'

'I'm not six feet under yet, darling.'

'But . . . it's on Saturday. There's no time to organise anything.'

'All you need is some champagne, strawberries and cream. Why fuss so?'

'And cakes,' adds Danny, leaning against Enid's knee.

She tunnels an arthritic finger into his curls. 'And cakes. Very good point, Danny.'

'But . . .'

'I do so adore a garden party, darling,' she sighs. Then she looks at me slightly mischievously. 'It might be my last.'

Forty

There is an empty Tom-shaped void in the house. If this is a taste of a new single life, I don't like it, don't like it one bit. The only way I can cope is by keeping busy. So I pack up my bits of florist trickery – foam and wires – and get ready for Dr Prenwood's. Because I have to wait for Trish and Trish has to wait for a plumber I'm a few hours late. But it shouldn't matter because Dr Prenwood is out all day at work. Anyway, considering everything that's happened it's a small miracle I'm dressed, let alone here at all.

I use the key I've had since the locked-in debacle to let myself in. I slip off my shoes and tread over the acres of spongy white carpet towards the crystal vases. I am finishing the second vase when I hear a noise, the hum of whispery chatter, a low hiss of laughter. I freeze. Shit. Is he in? The noise seems to be coming from behind the closed bedroom door. There is a giggle of laughter and the crystal glass handle of the bedroom door turns. The door opens. I cannot believe my eyes. Rona!

She stares back at me in a white towelling dressing gown, her hair dishevelled, her feet bare. Her mouth opens and closes silently and a violent blush flares over her throat. We stand there staring at each other for a few moments in utter disbelief.

'Sadie,' she says eventually, covering her mouth with her hand. 'I . . . I . . .'

Dr Prenwood pops his head out of the door. His receding hair is standing up at strange angles and he is covered in a thin layer of waxy sweat. 'Ah, Sadie, flowers, lovely.' Then he looks from my face to Rona's and the penny drops. 'Ah, yes, um . . . we were . . .'

I untie my apron. 'I was just finishing up, Dr Prenwood. I'm sorry to disturb you. I thought you'd be at work this afternoon.'

'Not this afternoon,' he says, hastily retreating back into the bedroom.

Rona pulls her towelling gown tight. She can no longer meet my eye. Her flush is so red it looks like a burn.

I fluster around, picking up my sundry bag, clearing up the mess as fast as I can, despite a part of me wanting to draw out the process to make it as excruciating as possible for Rona.

'Sadie, please . . .' Rona looks at me, begs with her eyes. 'I can explain.'

'Save it for Tom,' I say, shoving the last bits into my bag.

'No, Sadie, please. You don't understand.'

'I think I understand perfectly.' I shut my bag with a click.

'Wait, please. Ted and I . . .' Her face is bright red now. It seems to be folding into itself as she speaks, like a deflating balloon. 'Nothing's been right in *that* way for years, not since his blood pressure . . .'

'More information than is strictly necessary, thanks.'

'This,' she says pointing at the shut bedroom door with a trembling finger. 'It means nothing, nothing at all. Ted and I have a good marriage. We really have. Nothing's changed.' She pauses and takes a deep intake of breath. 'Tom doesn't need to know, Sadie. You won't tell him? Please.'

I don't say anything. My silence kills her. I want her to sweat. In her white towelling dressing gown, she looks hunched, shrivelled, pathetic. It's like seeing the Wicked Witch of the West dissolving. I sling my bag over my shoulder.

'Sadie, I'm sorry. I'm truly sorry for the other night, all those things I said.' There is a new desperation in her voice. She is powerless now and she knows it.

I shrug. 'Well, no one can accuse you of not speaking your mind.' I walk to the front door, flick the latch. 'You've never liked me, Rona. Not since I lured Tom away from Lucinda Lawn. I'm not stupid.'

She takes a few steps towards me on her bare feet, which, I notice for the first time, are swollen and misshapen with bunions, like the gnarled feet of an old goat. 'I thought Lucinda would have made Tom the perfect wife. But Tom loved you, loves you. I accept that. Look, let's call a truce.' She puts a hand on my arm. 'We've all done things we're not proud of, haven't we?'

I look at her square in the eye. 'Not like this. No, I haven't actually.' I close the door and leave the building. There was a part of me that believed that Rona was the wifely yardstick against which I should measure myself. That part of me has just died. Her power has gone. A spell has been lifted.

Forty-one

'Tom!' I feel my hands tremble as I grip the phone. I'm so relieved to hear his voice. 'Hi.' I look down at Danny. 'Daddy!'

Danny grins ear to ear. 'Hi Daddy!' he shouts.

'How is he?' There is the sound of a loud speakerphone in the distance. It sounds like he is somewhere busy, a New York street perhaps.

'He's much better, aren't you, Danny? He's been helping me with my flowers. Do you want a word?'

Danny hops from foot to foot in excitement. 'Hello Daddy!' he shouts, tugging the phone from my hand. 'I ate jelly babies. And I went to Enid's house – she's very, very old – and played dinosaurs!'

They chat for a few more moments until Danny loses interest, drops the phone at his feet and goes off to push a train along the floor. I take the phone. 'My dad's engagement party barn has burned down. To a cinder. And, you won't believe this, Enid said we can have the party in her garden.' I'm struck by how normal I sound when inside I'm churning. Shit, I don't even know if I'll be married this time next year.

Tom laughs. 'No way?'

'I've spoken to Dad and Loretta, who are now both beside themselves with excitement, as you can imagine, and it looks like the whole of Milton Keynes is going to descend on St John's Wood. Yes, there goes the neighbourhood. And I've invited Ruth and Pam – she's had her baby by the way, a little boy, so I doubt she'll come – and Tara and whoever else—'

'I think that you're doing the right thing, Sadie, helping out your dad and Loretta.'

'You do?' I thought he'd be anti-Enid, anti the party.

'Far better that your dad is happy with someone else than alone and miserable,' he says, his voice faltering slightly. 'Or even like Mum.'

'What do you mean?' I say quickly, tensing up.

'Oh, seeing Mum and Dad together in Hampshire last week, well it just hit me how they kind of live separate lives now. Dad's in his own world, switched off really. It must be lonely for Mum. I felt sorry for her. Anyway, have you two spoken since . . . since . . . that night?'

I hesitate. One day I will tell him about Dr Prenwood, maybe. He'd probably understand. Or maybe he suspects anyway. But no, I'm not going to tell him now. There's enough hurt and recrimination circulating as it is. I bite my tongue for Tom's sake. Not hers. 'No. No, I haven't.'

'It would be good if she came to your dad's do,' he says tentatively. 'Good for everyone.'

I swallow hard. 'OK. I'll call her.'

'Thanks, Sadie. I know she's been . . .' he stops, loyal to the last. 'Well, thanks, that's all.'

'Don't worry about it.'

'There's one other thing.'

'What?'

'I've been offered the directorship.'

'*What?* Oh. My. God. I can't believe it! That's fantastic!'

'We'll talk about it later. Listen, I've got to run. Another thing, quickly—'

'But Tom—' I'm about to ask him about Annette and whether she is staying with Anderson. But he interrupts me.

'I'm at JFK as we speak. I'll be back this evening.'

Eight hours! He'll be back in eight hours! I am supercharged. I am super-me. I throw myself at the mess, sweeping crumbs off the table on to the floor, picking up all the stray clothes and boots in the hallway – which has reverted back to its natural state, The Corridor of Chaos – and shoving them in a chaotic bundle in the under-stairs cupboard. I toss anything vaguely kitchen related into the dishwasher. I consider cooking some food. Then I think better of it. No, accept it Sadie, you are busy. You are working and you are mostly a lousy cook and when you're not a lousy cook you make more mess than food. Stop beating yourself up! Buy the goddamn food! So Danny and I run to the deli and buy delicious boxes of squid and Greek salad and posh cuts of pink ham. And I don't feel in the least bit guilty for not making it myself. Or not attempting a trifle. Nor do I feel guilty for digging a pillow slip out of the laundry basket and putting it on the bed. Or for knocking Danny's toys under the sofa where they can't be seen.

We race to the airport. We are still late, of course, but saved by the fact that Tom's plane is late too. I begin to feel nervous. He won't be expecting me as I've never met him at the airport after a business trip before. I have no idea whether I'm going to be greeted with a divorce or a kiss. Danny is beside himself with excitement, unable to stand still. A trickle of people begin to emerge from customs: two expensive looking women with over-dyed blond hair, a businessman, a family arguing . . . My heart starts to beat. Why have I never fetched Tom from the airport after a business trip before? It is not difficult and it feels romantic. I think of all the times I've let him come home to a sleeping house and snapped at him for waking me up as he's staggered to the bedroom, tired and jet lagged.

'There he is!' Danny starts to hop from foot to foot. 'There's Daddy!'

Tom is wheeling his small carry-on suitcase round the corner, out of customs. He hasn't seen us yet. To any other person waiting at Arrivals, he looks like another businessman in his late thirties, a bit too many expensed dinners around the middle, a little bald on top, jowly. But to me and Danny? He is the centre of our universe. Just the sight of him makes me feel immediately calmer, like part of the jigsaw, the dysfunctional family jigsaw, can now be completed. This tubby, cantankerous man with all his faults is *my* husband, I think with an unexpected swell of pride. He put a dandelion in the nursery. He is in love with his wife, that's me that is. And I realise that that deep angry place inside me isn't angry with him any more.

'Daddy!' shouts Danny.

Tom looks up, astonished. 'Danny! Sadie! What are you doing here?' He rushes towards us and Danny leaps up at him like a puppy.

'I thought I'd pick you up from the airport.' I'm aware of my hands sweating profusely. I wipe them on my jeans.

Tom looks at me and his whole face softens. 'You've never picked me up from the airport before.'

'I know,' I say quietly, not daring to hope for a kiss. It doesn't come.

'I love airports!' squeals Danny. 'Can we stay at the airport all day?'

'You know what, Danny?' Tom looks at me with a soft, resigned smile. 'I really, really want to go home now.'

We walk side by side, not hand in hand, towards the car. Part of me is a little deflated that we didn't get the Hollywood airport happy ending, when the two thwarted lovers rush into each other's arms, the music rises and the titles roll. But then I remember that this is real life and actually, considering everything, I should be grateful that he hasn't just taken one look at me and run screaming for the nearest taxi rank. I drive everyone home, quiet and contained, leaving the conversation to him and Danny.

Later, after Danny is sleeping peacefully, Tom sits next to me on the sofa, his thigh resting against mine, sipping beer from a tin. The news is on but neither of us is watching it.

'Tom,' I say softly. 'You do believe me about the notebook, that it was Enid's writing, not Eddie's?'

'That gardener tosser.'

'Nothing happened.'

'I know.' Tom grins. 'I checked your phone.'

'You didn't!' I gasp. A little part of me is almost titillated by his jealousy. 'When?'

'The night of the party. When I was packing my bags for New York. You left your phone in the bathroom, on the soap dish.' He smiles. 'I did find one text from him. Asking for Chloe's number. And I phoned Enid from New York.'

'No!'

'She hasn't mentioned it?'

'She hasn't.' Crafty old thing. I bet she lapped it up. More meddling.

'And Sadie . . .' He turns the TV down with the remote control. 'I also know that you had a chat with Annette.'

'I wanted to apologise, that's all. God, I didn't make things worse, did I?'

'No. Not at all. She's not leaving Anderson now.' He puts his hand on mine and stares at me for a long time, his eyes, soft and tender, criss-crossing my face as if absorbing all its details afresh. 'If it hadn't been for her, and you, I'd never have been offered the directorship.'

A large lump sticks in my throat. Hearing his praise is harder than hearing his criticism. I can't deflect it with sarcasm or a fast retort. It makes something inside me break a little. I think of all the times we've gone so mercilessly for each other and all the things we've said, and how few of the things we've said we've truly meant, and all the wasted opportunities to just be, well, half decent to one another.

He sips his beer. 'I am going to turn it down.'

I sit up straight. 'What? You can't!'

'I can.'

'Tom, don't *not* take the directorship. Please.'

'I've been offered another job,' he says, a big broad grin spreading across his face. 'Headhunted actually. I've been able to negotiate pretty hard. It'll be as much money but not so manic. I'll be able to work one day from home. The company's a lot more laid back, it's more me.' He smiles apologetically. 'More us.'

'Really?' I say doubtfully. 'But you wanted to be a director of Anderson more than anything. You would have sold your mother to be a director of Anderson.'

'And that's the problem.' He stares at the sofa arm. 'Sadie, I've had time to think in New York, so many horrible long dark nights of the soul. I've been waking up with this cold dread in my stomach, terrified, more terrified than I've ever been in my life, that I've lost everything I ever cared about.' He looks up and strokes my cheek lightly with the tips of his fingers. 'I'm ashamed, so fucking ashamed, of the way I've behaved. I haven't been there for you since your mum died. Since . . . the baby and everything.' He stops. His eyes look very blue, appealing as a child's: Danny's eyes. 'All I could think about was that directorship, like a man possessed. I wanted to prove to you, to Mum and Dad, Mum especially, that I could make something of myself, that I could be this successful man, this alpha husband . . .' To my horror a tear falls down the side of his nose. He wipes it away briskly with the pad of his thumb. It is the first time I've ever seen him cry.

'Alpha husband?' I repeat, disbelieving. 'But I never wanted—'

'I know, I know.' He shakes his head. 'It's all so fucked up. I was like a square peg in a round hole, a walking fraud, a person I didn't even like,' he blurts. 'And, oh God, I'm sorry, Sadie. For everything. For what happened in Toronto all those years ago. For making you feel like you weren't a good enough wife. You *have* to know that I never wanted anyone else but you. Not then. Not now.'

'It's OK.' And it is OK. It's strange hearing him say

these words, the words I've been dying to hear for months. I should feel vindicated, triumphant. I was right all along, nah, nah, na-nah, nah. But it's a hollow victory, and a false one. Because I realise that it was both of us. Both of us posturing, fixed on our own selfish aims, he on the Anderson job, me on replacing the baby we lost. And it was *us* who lost that baby. Not just me. I realise that now.

'I just want us back, the old us. I don't want a wife-bot, I really don't.'

'Shush,' I say, pressing my fingers to his lips. 'You'll be pining for the return of The Corridor of Chaos next.'

'Give it a few hours, sweetheart,' he says, kissing my fingers. 'I'm sure the hallway will organically return to its former state.'

'I missed you, Tom.' It strikes me that this is the most honest thing I've said for weeks. Just the raw, unembellished truth.

'I thought you hated me,' he says quietly.

'Well, I do too, of course.'

'Likewise.' He bites the tips of my fingers lightly.

'Ow! Do you think we'll always be like this? Two completely immature adults playing at being grown-up?'

'Probably,' says Tom. 'But you know what I love about you?'

'You love me?' Say it again, say it again, I want to scream.

He rolls his eyes. 'Do you think I'd put up with you otherwise?'

I laugh. 'Well, I've become a less worse wife. You should do.'

'Have you indeed?' he laughs and beams with such a shiny contagious happiness it lights the whole room.

'I have, Tom,' I say, lowering my eyelids coquettishly. 'I've found my inner domestic goddess. Look around you. This house is untouched by a cleaner.'

He grins, a boyish, carefree grin. 'I know that. A cleaner wouldn't shove all the toys under the sofa, would she? Nor would she leave a bag of rotting cherry tomatoes behind my tinnies.' He laughs and pulls me on to his knee. 'Grrr. Come here.' He nuzzles his face into my hair, dips his hand into the back of my jeans and into my knickers. 'God. It's good to have the old Sadie back. My naughty, chaotic little flower girl, how I've missed you.'

Forty-two

The day is as peaceful as it was wild the first time I met Enid. The sky is still, white feathery clouds suspended in powder blue. There is a slight breeze which buffets the folds of my dress against my bare calves. It is the dress from the honeymoon picture, green and silver, forgivingly smocked at the back. It doesn't make me feel in the least like a wife, or someone who buys kitchen roll. It makes me feel free and happy, like I could dance barefoot on a beach.

Frank Sinatra is booming out of the kitchen window, making the huge vases of pink and orange tulips tremble. Loretta's friends from Milton Keynes are stumbling around Enid's garden, already steaming – Angie and a friend are refilling champagne glasses as fast as the guests can gulp – and making frequent trips to the toilet so that they can get a good nose inside the house. At one point Loretta's sister, Donna, dances out into the garden flapping Enid's enormous antique peacock feather fan, then trips on her heels and falls into a lavender bush.

Loretta has not disappointed either. She is wearing a white bridal dress, encrusted with plastic pearls, which drags along the ground and makes a noise like a collapsing concertina blind. Dad has gone all man from Del Monte in a cream linen suit and Panama hat that he bought in South America and is subjecting Ruth to long-winded cautionary travel tales: 'I tell you, Ruth, be wary of ice cubes. I got terrible runs in Mexico. Flaming they were, flaming.' Ruth's husband Alex stands beside her and squeezes her hand. He is back from his mother's. They are giving it another go. 'We couldn't afford to split up,' Ruth whispered to me earlier with her usual deceptive coolness. 'We're stuck with each other. Which is just as well because we're not very good apart,' she adds, the light back in her eyes too.

Tara is laughing at her husband Nick's joke while glancing over her shoulder and eyeing up Eddie. But Eddie only has eyes for one woman: Chloe, who is sitting next to him on a bench in a silk lime green dress and gold platforms which she kicks up from time to time as she swings one long brown leg over the other. She is giving Eddie a wry, sideways look. Then she laughs and shuffles a bit closer to him on the bench.

Enid is in her element too. Unable to stand now, she is enthroned on a wheelchair on the lawn, propped up by pink silk cushions and wearing her finest turquoise turban. She holds court with a crowd of admirers, defiant cigarette in one hand, champagne in the other. Rona eyes her a little warily, unsure which pigeon hole

371

she can slot her into. Unsurprisingly Rona is not her usual self. Dressed in sombre pale grey – high atoning neckline, low heels – she is on her best behaviour towards me – 'Oh, Sadie, you do look beautiful when you make an effort!' – and is standing very close to Ted, Tom's dad, who has made a rare, grudging appearance in London.

Rocking on the swing beneath the apple tree at the end of the garden, Pam cradles her new baby boy in the pale blue crochet blanket that she knitted herself last month. Seth stands proudly behind her like a centurion, hands in their usual Prince Charles clasp behind his back. OK, she might have settled. But, right now, she looks terribly, terribly happy. I've been avoiding her for most of the party, terrified that she'll make me hold the baby. Or I'll say the wrong thing, or start crying, or everyone will be watching my reaction too closely.

'Sadie, darling!' Enid waves from her wheelchair throne.

Tom and I walk over. Enid offers her hand for Tom to kiss.

'Nice turban,' says Tom cheekily.

'Thank you. I believe I should offer you an apology, my dear fellow.'

Tom grins. 'Oh no, quite the opposite.'

'I'm afraid I did try to tutor Sadie, as I explained on the phone when you so sweetly called me from New York. But I confess she has been one of my biggest challenges.'

I giggle. 'Enid, I always told you I was unteachable.'

'I got breakfast in bed once,' says Tom. 'And a fantastic trifle. I'm sure I have you to thank for that. Still . . .' He slings an arm around my shoulders. 'I'll take her as she is, thanks.'

Enid nods approvingly and smiles. 'You see, Sadie, do you understand now?'

'Understand what, Enid?' What's she looking so damn pleased about? It strikes me that this is what Enid wants, has always wanted more than anything: attention. She's seventy-seven going on nine.

'I always knew you'd fail, my darling,' she declares imperiously, blowing out a scarf of cigarette smoke.

'Thanks!'

'I set you up to fail, darling! Don't you see? I knew you couldn't possibly become the perfect wife. The raw materials were never there. All I ever wanted to do was to prove that you can be the worst wife in the world and *still* be loved.' She adjusts her turban, tucking a stray strand of silver hair beneath it, and gives me a wry smile. 'Goodness. You think you were a bad wife? I was simply dreadful! Now go and see the baby, darling. They're so much more interesting than us tiresome oldies.'

I hesitate.

Enid lays her cool, dry hand on my forearm and whispers firmly, 'You must go.'

I take a large fortifying gulp of champagne and Tom and I walk over to the bucolic scene beneath the apple tree.

'He's very lovely,' I say, peering into the bundle in Pam's arms.

'Isn't he?' she says, pulling back the blanket so I can get a good look at his face. 'Do you want to hold him?'

I swallow hard. The baby is tiny, far tinier than I ever remember Danny being. He has a crop of dark curls stuck close to his scalp, strange blue-black unfocused eyes, little hands that furl and unfurl like leaves. His face is red, kind of raw-looking, and when he yawns there's a little white line of scurf inside his mouth. His fragility is terrifying. 'Oh, I don't know. I'm not very good with other people's babies.'

'He won't bite,' winks Seth.

I look at Tom, feeling helpless, wanting him to rescue me. Make the newborn baby go away! 'Go on, Sadie,' he says softly.

Pam, not waiting for my response, lifts her brand-new, precious little son into my arms. The baby stirs. I panic that he will cry. But he doesn't. He yawns again, shuts his eyes and falls asleep, a smile – or wind – moving across his face like a cloud.

Tom peers down at the little bundle. 'He's beautiful.'

'He is,' I say, tears welling up. But they are not tears of self-pity. It's just that he is *so* beautiful. Not wanting to embarrass anyone and make a scene, I quickly hand the sleeping baby back to Pam. Tom laces his fingers through mine and whispers in my ear. 'Shall we go for seconds, too?'

I look at him in disbelief, not sure how to reply, scared in case I've misinterpreted him.

He kisses me on the tip of my nose. 'Happy anniversary, Sadie.'

'Ladies and gentlemen!' booms a voice. It is my father, precariously balanced on one of Enid's delicate garden chairs. Loretta stands beside him, frantically brushing a smear of yolky pollen off her white dress. 'Speech!'

The guests stagger drunkenly towards my father until they're packed into a tight, swaying huddle. I grip Tom's hand. Dad thanks Enid for her hospitality then starts to talk about Loretta. There are jeers and whoops from the crowd. Loretta cries and dabs furiously at her mascara. They clutch each other's hands and stare intently into one another's eyes like love-struck teenagers. Despite trying not to, I can't stop thinking about Mum. And I'm back in the storm again, trying to stay upright. My hair prickles on my scalp. I am suddenly hit by the overwhelming sensation that Mum is standing next to me, right here, on the grass. I can feel the softness of her freckled forearm against mine, the warmth of her breath. I can even smell her clean, doughy smell. It's not frightening, nor, strangely, even that strange. The air crackles with energy. It is a good, happy energy. Is this why I am here? Did you lead me to Enid all those weeks ago? I murmur under my breath.

'Hi, Mummy.' Danny curls his small, hot hand into mine and gazes up, smiling.

'Hi, Danny.' I squeeze his hand and smile back. Mummy, yes, I'm *his* mummy. The baton has been passed. When I look up again everything feels different. There's just summer air around me, scented with lilacs, only the soft evening sun on my arm. Something tight inside of me releases like a knot. Mum has gone.

'I'd like everyone to raise their glass,' booms Dad, taking off his hat and holding it to his chest. 'To the woman who made life worth living again, who picked me up and dusted me down and saved me from the bleeding knacker's yard! To my future wife! To marriage! To Lorettttta!'

Tom slips his arm around my waist. I raise my glass.